WAITING ON A PART

A Series of Novellas

WAITING ON A PART
A Series of Novellas

BAHAMA GEM
THE GEORGIAN AFFAIR
ALMOST, IN ALTAMONT

by

Diane E. Grabo

A little something to read while you are waiting on a part, or the weather, or a bridge, or a lock, or the tide, or whatever.

CONTENTS

Bahama Gem

Waiting on a Part

DIANE E. GRABO

DISCLAIMER

This is a work of fiction. Although the bars, Nippers and Grabbers, are actual bars, and the locations of Lake Worth, Florida, Marsh Harbour on Great Abaco Island in the Bahamas, as well as the surrounding Abaco islands, are real places, they are used in a fictional manner. Pine Ridge, Tennessee, along with the marinas, resorts, other businesses and movie titles mentioned in this novel are products of the author's imagination. All characters have been fabricated. Any resemblance to actual persons or businesses is completely coincidental.

ACKNOWLEDGEMENTS

This work of fiction was first hatched while in the laundry room of a marina where my husband and I kept our 42-foot trawler. Various plot ideas were batted around with our daughter, Steph, when she and her family visited for a week. After her departure, the book continued to evolve over the course of many cocktail hour discussions (aka docktails), with our various dock friends. (Special thanks to the human and canine crews of *Southern Heat* and *Destiny*.) Then eventually, while awaiting an engine part to arrive, the story took shape and was completed. I am very grateful for all the friends and family members who encouraged me, offered ideas and proof read the initial copies. You know who you are and thank you.

Cover design: S. M. Savoy

Written in 2018. Revised in 2019.

*To Bob: My love, my friend, my mentor
and sometimes, my tormentor.*

Prologue

The man from Tennessee started the twin Detroit diesels promptly at 6 a.m. The water and fuel tanks had been topped off the night before, and he had enough provisions to get by. A last look at the weather confirmed he should have a comfortable crossing of the Gulf Stream from Florida over to the Bahamas. The next cold front of any significance looked to be about five days out. No sense in looking at weather forecasts beyond five days. Mother Nature was not meant to be predictable.

With a pod driven yacht, maneuvering out of his slip at the Billfish Marina was a breeze, and he quickly wound his way to the nearby Lake Worth Inlet. Once out of the no wake zone, which he often ignored, he revved up the engines to a cruising speed of 30 mph. He adjusted the autopilot and went below to get yet another cup of coffee. He had chartered the 50 foot Viking Sport Fisher for two weeks. Plenty of time to get the job done. He mused at the boat's name: *Reel Relief.* He planned to achieve just that.

The southwest winds piped up to 15 mph with wave heights of two to three feet at nine second intervals. No issue for him. At 10 a.m. he went by what looked like an armada of catamarans and mono hulled sailboats. He waked the whole fleet unmercifully, but he didn't care. Stupid blow boats, he said to himself. He couldn't wrap his head around owning a boat that only traveled a maximum of seven miles an hour, if that. What was the point? Half the time they motored anyway. Protests about his wake over the VHF radio fell on deaf ears. He had reservations at Spanish Cay Marina in the Abacos for later that afternoon, and he had no intention of slowing down. He planned to stay just one night. Once he cleared customs in the morning, he would head over to Harbourside Marina in Marsh Harbour. There he had reserved a slip for one week. Marsh Harbour was essentially the hub of the Abacos and further provisioning could be easily accomplished. He would set up a routine of daily fishing trips. No one would suspect his true agenda.

Reel Relief hummed along nicely as the vessel approached the northern Abaco islands. Pristine beaches came into view. The turquoise sea across the Little Bahama Bank along with frolicking dolphins brought joy, peace and serenity to the many boaters traveling through the Sea of Abaco. But not him. He was on a mission to make fish food.

"Bitch," he said out loud. "I'll have her begging for her life."

Chapter 1

The communal laundry room at the Harbourside Marina was pretty nondescript. Four washing machines, four dryers and a folding table in between. There were a few pictures on the walls and two chairs. Could have used a book share shelf. Cara idly skimmed through Facebook as she waited for the wash cycle to end so as to throw the clothes into the dryer before anyone else did. On busy days in the marina it was a science to get your laundry done in a timely manner. Cara was particularly annoyed when two loads of wash became an all day event.

Catherine from the boat *Dalliance* walked in with her laundry bag. Behind her was her ever present large black lab Jabber. Like the nursery rhyme of *Mary Had A Little Lamb*, everywhere that Catherine went, Jabber went. "Hey, Cara, how's it going?"

"Just fine," Cara replied. She gave Jabber a pat on his head. He nuzzled his snout into her hip so she would keep petting him. For whatever reason, that dog was very fond of her, almost to the point of being protective.

Cara had grown to become quite fond of Catherine over the past few years even though Catherine was perhaps 40 years her senior. She could be my grandmother, Cara often thought. But she's so easy to talk to. Maybe the lack of a blood-line relationship automatically launched them into being friends without any emotional baggage. Cara quietly reprimanded herself for initially dismissing Catherine as a frumpy old snow bird not worthy of her time. So wrong! She wondered how many other people she had so quickly dismissed because they didn't fit her mindset of "someone I can hang out with." Such a snob I am, Cara thought.

"Hey, Cara, did anyone ever tell you you look like Milla Memphis?"

"Milla Memphis? Milla Memphis as in *Calypso Girl* or as in *The Long Walk Home*?"

"Yeah, that Milla Memphis. You both have those dark brown eyes, you're the same height, build, and current hair color. And then there's your jaw line, same squareness to it."

"Humph, never thought that at all."

"Well, I was thinking about your resemblance today because rumor has it she'll be walking down the dock sometime soon, maybe even today."

"Really? That's cool. Haven't seen a celebrity in a while. Who told you that?"

"Gerald did. I don't know how he gets his information, but he's usually right."

Harbourside Marina in Marsh Harbour on Great Abaco Island in the Bahamas was the landing point for taking celebrities to and from their private homes in the exclusive Sea Star Resort. It was almost a weekly event to see a dignitary, football player or movie star being hustled to one of the over the top mini mega yachts to travel the 45 minutes across the Sea of

Abaco to Great Guana Cay, location of Sea Star Resort. Mini mega yachts was what Cara called the 45 foot cabin cruisers that were ridiculously well appointed. There were also two 30-foot center console runabouts with 900 horse power each. Those boats were in and out of the marina so often that the docking lines were precut to stay on the dock and the keys were always in the ignition. She had gotten to know several of the crew men, but they never divulged who their guests would be. Sworn to secrecy she supposed. But Gerald, on the other hand, who didn't work for Sea Star and who didn't say much at his nearby conch salad stand, seemed to have ears that could hear whispers a mile away. If you tipped him well, he occasionally let it slip that "so and so" was headed to Sea Star.

The washer stopped spinning and Cara quickly threw her wash into the dryer. Catherine put her wash in and set her timer. They had determined many washes ago that it took 25 minutes to complete the wash/rinse/spin cycle. The yacht Cara attended to did have a washer and dryer, but she rarely used them. She hated dumping all that gray soapy water into the innards of the harbor. The water around the marina was gross enough.

"Well, see ya in about a half hour. Going to Martin's any time today?"

"No, all set in that department. Boss isn't coming until next week so I'll wait to re-provision until Thursday."

The one and only grocery store, Martin's, relied upon container ships to bring in fresh food. Typically they arrived on Tuesday which meant the shelves weren't fully restocked until Thursday. However, if you didn't get there by Thursday afternoon, your chances of finding fresh fruits and vegetables were severely limited.

"Well, see you later Catherine, I'm headed back to the boat too."

Cara lived on the 80 foot, 1988 Cheoy Lee Motor Yacht, as its main caretaker. Steward was her official title. Benton Foster, the owner, rarely set foot on the boat as of late, but when he did, he expected it to shine. Cara's life had become a tedious task of cleaning an already clean boat. At first, the job seemed so glamorous, living on a beautiful yacht in the Bahamas surrounded by turquoise water and waving palm trees. When Mr. Foster was on board, he was accompanied by a professional captain and two crewmen to attend to the steering, lines and engines. The crew changed frequently because Benton was so demanding. Somehow Cara had gained Benton's admiration, and she had been working for him for nearly five years. Every time she mentioned she needed to move on, he upped her salary making it difficult for her to leave. But it was an unsettled life of living someone else's dream on someone else's boat. Her duties of keeping the boat clean and well stocked quickly became monotonous. To keep herself from becoming brain dead, she pursued getting her captain's license and learning as much as she could about all the systems on the boat including engine maintenance and repair. Over the years she assisted the mechanics in keeping the engines "humming." Benton insisted she live on the boat full time so that "his baby" wouldn't be lonely and would be ready at his beck and call. Funny, she thought, not OK for the boat to be lonely, but what about me? Ever since her fiancé decided her bridesmaid-to-be was more desirable than she was, her love life had taken a turn down a series of dead end roads. Hiding away on a yacht far far away from her hometown in upstate New York seemed to be her only recourse.

Cara walked up the gang plank to the main salon door. Tide was unusually high today due to the upcoming Super Moon. Good thing it would return to its normal swing of two feet next week. She noticed Benton was becoming increasingly more frail and even walking up four steps seemed to leave him winded. Next week it would only be a two-step climb for him. Emphysema? Cara had never seen Benton smoke, but apparently back in the day he was known to be quite the chain smoker. She also noticed she was fielding more and more of Benton's long laments about losing his wife to cancer three years ago and having been a nearly absent father to his son. He was essentially estranged from his offspring. Too busy with making money, he said. Such a cliché she often thought. "Don't know what you've got 'til it's gone." She wondered about his grandson. There were a few pictures of him on the boat, but they were so old. Maybe Benton preferred him to be frozen in time as a ten-year-old. It was odd to her that he had never visited Benton. She didn't ask and he didn't offer. She guessed he must be in his thirties by now.

"Damn!" Cara said out loud to no one. She had forgotten the bag of towels that needed to be washed. Not that they were dirty, but after hanging up in the various heads for over a month, they smelled stale. It was a particular quirk of Mrs. Foster's that the towels had to smell fresh. In her honor, Benton continued the quirky notion. "This is stupid," again to no one. Cara often tortured herself with the ridiculousness of her life and job. Thoughts of washing clean towels, such a waste of time, water, electricity and soap when half the world doesn't even have a pot to piss in! swirled around in her brain. And this boat is just a waste of space! All this beauty for nothing! That's it, she continued the torture, next week I'm just going to tell Benton he and I are done. He doesn't need this boat and I need a new life.

Just then Catherine called up to her. "Hey, Cara, do you mind switching my load into the dryer? I have a ride to the post office that I'd like to take advantage of."

Cara appreciated taking advantage of rides; cab fares were ridiculously expensive on the island. She immediately answered "Sure, no problem. Who's your ride?"

"George, the mechanic. He just finished up a big job on *Happy Hearts*, and now he has to run around town to get more parts for *Island Girl*."

"Seriously? Hasn't he fixed just about everything on that boat?"

"Yeah, you should hear him talk about the boat and the owners. He likes Bob well enough but Deanna drives him crazy. This morning when she found another leak for him to fix he told her he was going to rename the boat *Job Security*."

"That's funny, but I do like Deanna, crazy as she is."

"Me too. Well, gotta run. Thanks so much, I owe you!" And with that, Catherine hurried down the dock.

No big deal, I'm going to spend the day in the laundry room anyway, Cara thought to herself. She gathered up a few more towels and stashed them into the canvas bag. For a fleeting moment Cara laughed. Her canvas bag collection had grown to perhaps 20 bags of various sizes, shapes and colors. Her sister, Dana, found the perfect perpetual present for her. Every birthday and Christmas Dana gave her a new bag with her initials "C. A. M." embellished on them in the form of code flags representing the letters. Sometimes she switched it up for her monogram of CMA. For whatever reason Cara had loved code flags as a kid and had memorized the entire flag alphabet by the time she was ten. Dana, always wanting to please her, thought she'd enjoy her initials in code flags. Now, after five years, it had become an inside joke between the two of them. And then Cara went from a warm fuzzy feeling to annoyance. Jesus Christ, she thought. Could my name be any plainer? Cara Ann Moore. Boring! Her parents were minimalists, Cara, not Karen, Kayla, Kayleigh, Clara or Carla, and no unnecessary "e" at the end of Ann. It was a wonder they didn't reduce Moore to Mor. Her mother rationalized the name completely: "Well dear, no one will mispronounce it, and you'll always find your name on souvenirs."

Cara trudged down the dock putting on her happy face to the various boaters along the way. The marina had such a mix of people keeping their boats there: snow birds who arrived after Christmas and stayed until April first, boaters who kept their boats there and only used them for three weeks a year, transients, the boaters going from here to there and only staying a few days, sport fishermen who came over from Florida in the spring and summer, and charterers: in on Friday night and gone by the following Saturday. Her least favorite were the sport fishermen; they simply rubbed her the wrong way. Her favorites were the snow birds, like Catherine. She had gotten to know many of the snow birds, and they often included her in their "docktails" and dinners. Awkward at first but then, as with Catherine, she grew to appreciate their genuine concern for her. Mabel, in particular, was always on the prowl to find her a suitable mate. "You know, Cara, that biological clock is ticking, it would be a shame not to pass on your genes," Mabel would often advise.

Thanks, Mabel, Cara thought, you know I do have a mother who pretty much packages that same message to me on a weekly basis. Never mind Dana with her three kids. Or her cousins with kids…

As Cara approached the laundry room she was met with an onslaught of Sea Star crew men off-loading baggage from the parade of high end SUVs. Soon to follow would be the owners of the baggage, either ultra rich corporate types, sports figures or celebrities. She knew the drill well. With an air of disdain, she turned toward the laundry room as if she were entering a palace and she was the queen.

Nice try she thought to herself, absolutely no one, I repeat, no one even noticed you. She set her canvas bag down and transferred Catherine's laundry into the dryer. She loaded the towels into the washer and then remembered she was out of laundry tokens. "Damn it!" She had forgotten to get more laundry tokens which meant a trip to the office. Before leaving she took her dryer load out and jammed her personal clothing into her blue canvas bag which had large code flags nearly covering one full side of the bag. She decided to haul it to the office and leave it outside while getting more tokens. At least that bag would be part way down the dock.

Cara got into conversation with the office manager Kaitlin. Kaitlin was bemoaning the lack of babysitters for her kids. Plans to go out for dinner for her anniversary were quickly dashed when Kwashina suddenly came down with yet another mysterious cold and was unavailable that night. Oddly enough or actually not odd at all, Kwashina's cold would disappear by the next morning. Cara resisted taking the bait. She had babysat for Kaitlin before, and it was just shy of a disaster. Whatever maternal instinct she may have had was squelched by her inability to discipline the twin two-year-old boys, much less get them into bed in a timely manner. I'm 32 years old, how can I be completely undone by two kids 30 years younger than I am?

"Oh, I'm so sorry, Kaitlin, can you reschedule for when Kwashina is feeling better?"

"I don't know…. John will be out at Sea Star for the next two weeks on the night shift, so it's single parent me until he moves back to the day shift." Again Cara resisted the temptation to help her out. Selfish, she thought, but also self-preservation.

"Well, again sorry…. oh, by the way, I need about six more laundry tokens." During that short conversation and token transaction, numerous bags and suitcases piled up just outside the office door, completely engulfing Cara's meager canvas bag. Several of the suitcases were embellished with gold threaded initials or code flags, all announcing C.A.M. The mountain of luggage was transferred to about five dock carts and swiftly loaded on to *Adventure I*. The entourage of celebrities followed immediately behind and three seconds after the passengers set foot on the boat, the lines were tossed and *Adventure I* quickly headed out to Sea Star Resort. Cara took the time to use the ladies room in the office and peruse the latest *Abaco Life* Magazine. When she exited, her canvas bag was nowhere to be seen.

"What the hell? Nobody steals anything around here, am I losing my mind?" she burst out half to herself and half to the not listening Kaitlin. Cara nosed around and then noticed a blue canvas bag tucked behind a potted plant. Upon picking it up she immediately noticed that the code flags dutifully displaying C.A.M. were even larger than hers. Quite simply, it was not her bag. Again she blurted out, "What the hell?" She peaked inside and noted the beach towels were richly embroidered with MM instead of CAM. But the high end jeweled beach wear really caught her eye. Well, that's nice, thought Cara. I wonder if the bikinis fit? Maybe there is a Santa Claus after all.

"Hey, Kaitlin, someone mixed up the luggage transfer. They've taken my laundry bag and left me with this gem."

The girls oohed and ahed at the jewel speckled bikinis and had a good laugh at the thought of wearing them.

"No doubt there'll be hell to pay aboard *Adventure I* once they realize they have my sorry assed clothes. Better give the crew a call and forewarn them," Cara said.

And just like that, as Kaitlin picked up the phone, the electricity went out. Which meant the phone was dead. Cell service had gone down earlier that day and her VHF hadn't been charged up.

"Oops, guess we'll have to wait until the generators do their magic. I'll let you know when I get through to them."

"How cool that my initials are plastered all over this stuff. Guess I'll just pretend to be Queen for a Day for the next few hours. I'll keep the bag on *Bahama Gem* until you get through to them."

"What are you talking about? You don't have the corner on the market for those initials. Camilla A. Memphis, aka C.A.M., aka MIlla Memphis, just walked down the dock a few minutes ago, didn't you see her?"

"Holy shit! I heard she might be coming here. Wow!" Thinking about Milla's facial expression when she opened her bag up to reveal very boring tan underwear put a smile on Cara's face. "This should be fun."

"Hey you know what, Cara—you kinda look like her."

"Yeah, so I hear......"

Chapter 2

Milla was pissed and that was PISSED written in font 900, bolded, italicized, underscored, capitalized, followed by 20 exclamation points. That stupid pissant Trenton Smithson. How dare he? Sue her? Seriously? She snubbed him at their high school reunion last year and now he was suing her for harassment and assault. Harassment? Assault? He stalked her for an hour to get her autograph, then literally stumbled into her, pushing his yearbook in her face and demanded her signature on his picture. She shoved him aside, told him to go fuck himself and left the reunion that she didn't want to go to in the first place. Her agent had convinced her it was good for her publicity to attend the affair and somehow managed to make her appearance into a charity event for literacy programs. But as far as she was concerned, it was just a ploy to boost attendance. As for Trent, she felt he harassed her with his stalking and assaulted her with his yearbook. Well, good thing for lawyers on retainer. She knew she'd be spending thousands of dollars just to make this annoyance go away. In his formal letter to her he said he would consider settling out of court for a mere million dollars. What an asshole. She hated him in elementary school, only to have him follow her in middle school and then high school. He was a sniveling mama's boy whose mama happened to be her mother's best friend. For years the two mothers tried over and over again to fix them up together.

She was an up and coming movie star with two successful lead roles under her belt and more movie offers on tap. At 5 foot 4 inches, with intense brown eyes, square jaw, slight build, it was easy for directors to have her shaped into a multitude of characters. Her latest film, *The Georgian Affair*, required her to have blond hair and a slight anorexic look to her. The movie was set to start production and all she wanted to do was enjoy the next few days doing nothing but wandering the beach near her vacation home in Sea Star Resort. One of the scenes of the movie was to be filmed nearby the resort on a spoil island before relocating to Savannah, Georgia. But no, she'd have this stupid law suit hanging over her taking away what little enjoyment she could have. What the world didn't know and what she masterfully covered up was that she worried about everything. Her mind never seemed to relax. Insomnia plagued her. Her current boyfriend was too egocentric and was probably cheating on her, her first assistant was sick with all day morning sickness, her lawyers demanded more money to deal with all the frivolous lawsuits against her and her director didn't like her attitude. The list went on and on. Basically Milla couldn't remember the last time she was just simply happy and unbothered. Stupid life she thought to herself, I'm getting paid millions of dollars and I'm miserable.

Milla looked over the turquoise waters of the Sea of Abaco. For about five full seconds she allowed herself to enjoy the view. *Adventure I* was only ten minutes away from entering the channel leading into Sea Star's marina. A golf cart would zip her off to her house followed by a small pick-up truck with all her luggage. Thirteen bags in all. Yes 13. Can't have too many shoes she thought to herself. She changed her outfits no less than three times a day. And everything had to coordinate from earrings down to the flip flops or high heels. Richard, her boyfriend, would be flying in tomorrow and they planned to dine out almost every night. So of course that demanded lots of clothing options.

Milla had counted her bags when she went through customs, had counted them at Harbourside and planned to do the same at Sea Star. Cara's blue bag had already been loaded into the pick-up truck and was only partially showing when the other 12 bags were loaded on top. Satisfied all 13 bags made it to Sea Star, she told the cart driver to go ahead to her house. Her first assistant, Brenda, helped her unpack but had already set the blue bathing suit bag in the closet to be dealt with later. First up was getting Milla dressed for dinner. Bikinis could wait. Besides, Brenda needed to throw up again. Fourth time today.

Milla heard the buzz of the generators as she walked across the beautifully landscaped pathway to the exclusive Blue Paradise Restaurant. In this gated community of million dollar vacation homes, celebrities and dignitaries could dine without fear of being hounded by the paparazzi. The restaurant had a breath taking view of the Atlantic which Milla never tired of. Brenda opted not to join her since the look of even a saltine cracker made her nauseous. Brenda was going to finish out the month and then take an early maternity leave. Her replacement, her cousin Susan, would start shadowing Brenda next week. It was agreed that Susan and Brenda would basically job share as the two of them birthed and raised children. Milla agreed to this arrangement with a bit of skepticism. Children simply didn't fit into her world or theirs for that matter. Sooner or later Brenda and Susan would be too overwhelmed with child rearing to continue this life of travel and long hours on the set.

Milla didn't like dining alone, but that all would change tomorrow with Richard's arrival. After dinner she ambled back to her house and decided a night dip in her pool would be nice. Maybe it would help her calm down from all the demons swirling around in her head.

"Hey, Brenda, did you get a chance to organize my swim wear?"

"So sorry, Milla, I'll do that right now." Brenda grabbed the blue canvas bag and was immediately surprised by the contents. "Oh dear, this isn't your stuff!"

"What are you talking about? Let me see."

"Well unless you've had a personality change and lowered your standards to beige underwear, this simply isn't your stuff."

Milla ran off a string of obscenities that would make a sailor cringe. "Is this some sort of cruel joke?"

"I'm sure it's just a strange mix-up. Weird that someone else has your same initials and likes code flags. I'll check with the *Adventure I* crew. Probably by now Miss Tan Bra CAM has notified them her bag was taken by mistake," Brenda offered.

"Or not, let's see—boring brown underwear or diamond studded bikinis? Who would ever let on she just hit the jackpot of beach wear?" Milla whined.

"Well, in Miss Tan Bra CAM's defense she does have a nice line up of crew wear. Looks like she's aboard a boat named *Bahama Gem*. So typical—white polos embroidered with the boat name and khaki shorts."

"Wait… I think I noticed that boat in the marina. Her boss will certainly like her wearing jeweled bikinis rather than those dreadful uniforms. What size is she?" Milla asked.

"Looks like she's your long lost twin, same size as you."

The lights flickered and the hum of generators ceased. Milla and Brenda waited for the electricity to turn on. Electrical outages were so common in the Abacos they hardly commented when they occurred. But the lights didn't turn back on, and the generators didn't restart. Both women groped for their cell phones. Brenda found hers first and turned on the flashlight. Then she located Milla's.

"Wait here, I'll go to the service desk and find out what's going on." No electricity meant no land phones and for whatever reason cell phone service had been down all day.

"Thanks, Brenda." Milla went into the bathroom to relieve herself. She flushed the toilet and it immediately backed up on her. Milla was horrified to see fecal material and toilet paper spilling over the seat. "Oh come on!" she yelled out loud. She tried to wash her hands but no water came on. "Well this just caps off the fucking evening!"

CHAPTER 3

RICHARD WILLIAM WINTHROPE III led a charmed life. At six foot five, 195 pounds, broad shoulders, six pack abs, long brown hair and killer blue eyes, he knew he was handsome. The only son of a wealthy hedge fund CEO and school teacher, he was doted on by his parents along with two maiden aunts. His mother stopped working after he was born, never to return to the classroom. She tended to his every need whether needed or not. He was highly encouraged to play sports especially by his father whose college football career came to an abrupt end when his knee was shattered by a linebacker. Essentially Richard William Winthrope II lived vicariously through his son's victories on the playing field. "Number III," as his father often referred to him, didn't seem to mind that his father was the loudest parent on the side lines either cheering him on or chewing out the referees for a bad call.

Four years of private high school quickly rolled by as he transitioned from football to swimming to lacrosse and then summers at some exotic vacation resort. Number III was readily accepted at four Ivy League Colleges with scholarships for lacrosse. He chose Dartmouth and initially did quite well.

He fully planned to continue on to earn his MBA to follow in his father's footsteps, climbing the ladder of the corporate world. But during his sophomore year, an unexpected event occurred. Richard spent hours in the gym, many times with a personal trainer, sculpting his body to perfection. He loved looking at himself in the numerous mirrors surrounding the equipment, and one day he happened to notice a suited man looking at him taking notes. Richard set down the dumb bells and looked over at the gentleman. "Hey, what's up, pal?" he called over.

"Sorry to intrude, my name is Frank Winston and I'm on a scouting mission for *Nordic Conquest.*"

"*Nordic Conquest?* The TV series?"

"Yes indeed…"

Richard could hardly believe it; he loved that series. Basically the series was just a showcase for men to show off their muscles and for women to bare their breasts. In almost every other episode some poor village was taken over by the brutal Vikings and of course, the local women had to succumb to the marauders.

"Yes indeed," Mr. Winston continued, "we need some extras who not only have the right build but are adept at handling ancient weapons, you know, spears and maces and such. Your lacrosse coach told me I'd likely find you in the gym. He said you're pretty good with the lacrosse stick and can play right and left handed."

It was true about Richard being ambidextrous and that skill was what most likely got him the scholarships.

"We're filming a few scenes at Brenback Mountain next month. Do you think you could be available for a few weeks?"

"Well I uh… I uh…" Richard couldn't believe he was stammering. Get a grip he said to himself. "Uh, I… Yes…. I'll make it work."

"Very good, here's my card. I'm staying at the Radisson Inn. My staff and I will be meeting with all the extra candidates in Conference Room One at 10 A.M. tomorrow. We'll have paperwork for you to review and sign. See you then, Mr. Winthrope." And with that he shook his hand and departed.

Once Mr. Winston was out of the room, Richard literally jumped with joy. "Holy Shit! Holy Shit!" he exclaimed out loud. First he called his then girlfriend Mina, then his coach, then his parents.

"Whoa son, take a breath! Next month? What about finals? You can't just walk out two weeks shy of the end of the semester!" argued his father.

"Dad listen, Coach Harley thinks I can talk to my professors and either take the exams two weeks early or take a leave of absence and take the exams this summer. Our lacrosse season wraps up in three weeks so I won't be letting my team down." Richard was arrogant, conceited, full of himself but miraculously, he did have loyalty and he was a team player.

"Son, don't get me wrong, this is very exciting, but being an extra in a two bit series is not exactly going to put bread on your table and we're certainly not going to throw away $50,000 for you to leave school two weeks early. If you can work it out with your professors and not lose the semester, then OK. Otherwise, sorry, I can't sanction it."

Dorrine, his mother, was shocked. This was possibly the first time Number II had essentially said no to Number III.

In the end, it did work out, but Richard never returned to Dartmouth. Richard took on the role of an extra as if he was a team captain. He organized the extras' stunts and taught many of them how to handle all the Viking weapons, not unlike organizing a game of lacrosse with a bunch of rookies. The Director loved Richard and quickly advanced him from an extra to a minor speaking part to a main character. Within a year Richard William Winthrope III was transformed into Einar Aronsson. His parents were devastated and embarrassed at first that their son was a college drop-out, but his new salary of $500,000.00 per episode quickly erased any regrets they may have had. Mina was a casualty of his new persona and a long series of love interests soon followed.

Now, four years later, he just completed Season Six and had a few weeks of vacation before returning to the set to start filming Season Seven. He often pondered how a nearly plotless series could continue, given how many characters were killed off and how many unresolved situations continued unresolved with added layers of new unresolved issues. But for now, life was good and it seemed Einar Aronsson was going to live forever. Richard stepped off his Gulf Stream Jet into the hot humid Marsh Harbour Private Airport and was quickly escorted to an awaiting Sea Star Resort Suburban. Soon he would travel the 45 minutes across the Sea of Abaco to his awaiting current girlfriend Milla. They had met two years ago at the Marina Pool while Milla was also vacationing between sets. Her then boyfriend, Charles, was quickly brushed aside when the ultra handsome Richard picked up her beach towel that had blown off her chaise lounge and handed it to her. The rest was history.

Walking down the dock with a Sea Star crew man hauling his luggage behind him, he thought he saw Milla ahead of him. "Hey, Milla, what are you doing here? I thought you were at the resort already."

Cara Moore turned around, her facial expression quickly changed from annoyance to surprise and back to annoyance.

"Oh sorry, miss... I uh... thought you were someone else."

"No worries," she lied.

Damn, she said to herself, Holy shit, that's Einar Aronsson, or whatever his real name is. "Happens all the time..." she continued, and she walked on as if he were the most insignificant person on the planet.

CHAPTER 4

ORION MATTHEWS WAS TROUBLED. Six years after the fact, he was still stewing over his ex-girlfriend Rebecca. She had harshly ended their four-year relationship of which two of those years involved living together. He replayed their last argument over and over again wondering where he could have stepped in to make things better. They met in college through a mutual friend and simply hit it off immediately. They liked the same sports, the same movies and books, had similar political views and had a terrific sex life. As soon as they graduated they moved in together, both having landed jobs in the same company. She was a sales rep for Dustin Pharmaceuticals and he worked in product development. Her job entailed travel four to five days each week, but the two to three days at home were always full of fun and good sex. Rebecca just assumed the next step would be marriage followed by starting a family a few years later. They had broached the subject of marriage several times, but Orion just couldn't come around to fully committing himself to her.

"Things are so great right now, can't we just go along as we are?"

"Orion, how much more time do you need to get to know me? You know everything about me. You've seen me at my worst and you've seen me at my best. I thought you wanted a family. I thought you wanted to be with me for the rest of our lives. We have such energy between us. Were all those I-love-yous just empty phrases?"

"I do love you, Rebecca, it's just that I don't see why we have to get married. What's the rush anyway?"

Unbeknownst to Orion he had pushed the wrong button. The words of Rebecca's very ethnic grandmother came back to her all too loudly and clearly. Bubbeh had warned her not to move in with Orion until there was that proverbial ring on her finger. Rebecca could hear Bubbeh saying in her over the top ethnic accent: "Why buy the cow when the milk is free?"

Rebecca was beet red and on the verge of tears. "You're right, Orion, there is no rush because there won't be a marriage. If you don't want to marry me today then what will make you want to marry me tomorrow or next year or ten years from now? Nothing! That's it, I've had it. This is all about your parents' divorce isn't it? Well, I've listened to you whine about their divorce for too long now. That divorce was them, not us. No more free milk!"

And with that she stomped out of the room. She stayed the night with a friend of hers and over the weekend her belongings were moved out of their apartment. All the pleading and bouquets of flowers did nothing to change her mind. Orion puzzled over the "free milk" phrase but came up empty. And empty became his new adjective for everything: an empty apartment, empty job, empty relationships, empty life. Since Rebecca left he wandered in and out of short lived liaisons.

Did every woman on the planet just want to get married and have children? But it wasn't just the marriage-have-children thing he eschewed; he had to admit it was the whole concept of commitment. And what he craved the most was the very thing he threw away when he let the best friend and lover he had ever had, just walk right out the door.

The phone rang and jarred him out of his thoughts. Seeing the name on the caller ID primed him on his tone of voice. "Hi, Dad" he said cautiously, never knowing if his father was calling with good news or bad news.

"Hello, son.... I'm afraid I have some bad news… your grandfather has had a bad stroke and is not expected to live long. Can you get home as soon as possible? We'll take the company jet down to New York City."

"Of course Dad," Orion replied almost robotically. "I'll gather up some clothes and drive right down."

It was only 90 minutes to his Dad's place. Enough time to call up the jet and have it ready for take off as soon as he arrived at the private airport. There were many plusses and minuses to being related to James Benton Foster; the jet was one of the plusses. When he was younger, he would be flown to the Bahamas to spend his winter vacations with his grandparents on their yacht. When he was eight he was convinced the boat was as large as the *Queen Mary*. In reality it was 80 feet long. His grandfather never tired of his unending questions about the running of the boat. In fact, his grandfather seemed to thrive on teaching him about all the various systems. Nanny simply smiled and nodded, content that Benton found a way to fully turn off his business brain and attend to their grandson. Every now and then Grampa Ben would even let him steer. What Orion didn't know to this day was that the boat had been on autopilot when he was at the helm. Everything changed when he turned 11. He knew his parents didn't always get along but of course he wasn't privy to the source of his mother's discontent. Turned out to be the same old same old. James simply couldn't be monogamous. His mother Elizabeth tired of being in second place and being humiliated. She divorced him and basically his whole family. She felt his parents were unsupportive of her even though she pleaded with them to talk some sense into James. Then not only did she drop the hyphenated Foster from her maiden name of Matthews, she also paid the high court fees to have Orion's name changed as well. And thus he was simply Orion Allen Matthews.

The animosity between Elizabeth and James grew to epic proportions. She fought a hard battle to get 90% custody and nearly bankrupted James before the divorce was completed. She wouldn't allow Orion to visit his grandparents anymore on their boat, only allowing occasional visits at their home for holidays. Grampa Ben was furious with his son and ex-daughter-in-law. Furious at James for being unfaithful and furious at Elizabeth for taking away his only grandson along with his name. And for all that fury and anger so loudly displayed among his parents and grandparents, the psychological scars grew deeper and deeper under Orion's silent demeanor.

James paced nervously until Orion arrived at the airport. James was afraid his father would die or worse—live as a vegetable for years, without having had the conversation he had wanted to have for twenty years now. He knew he had disappointed his father but over time he had done everything he could to rectify the situation. He eventually remarried a wonderful woman, Joella, and was ever faithful to her. He ran his father's Syracuse Division very successfully, turning profits every year. But he failed in the grandchild department and that seemed to be all that mattered to Benton. Joella's two daughters from her previous marriage were well into their teens when she married James. They never thought of Benton Foster as being their grandfather; besides they had two sets of loving grandparents of their own. James desperately wanted to have it out with his father and have his father finally say he accepted his apology. He needed redemption.

James and Orion spoke little on the jet. Orion was at a crossroads with his father. Certainly James was a loving, supportive father but Orion resented him for being unfaithful to his mother yet so cloying of his step-mother. Why didn't he just do that in the first place? He also resented playing second fiddle to Joella's annoying daughters. But above all, he was particularly troubled with his father's failure to step up to the plate and demand that he be allowed to visit his grandparents on their boat. As the years went by, instead of the boat memories fading, they warped into "the best times ever" which his father then denied him. Interesting that he never blamed his mother for that crime. Orion hadn't seen his grandfather since his grandmother died three years ago. It seemed as if the world stopped turning for Benton. The yearly birthday and Christmas cards filled with checks came to an abrupt halt when Nanny died. It never occurred to Orion to reach out to his grandfather, and now it was probably too late.

Just before landing Orion went to the small bathroom to relieve himself. He glanced in the mirror as he washed his hands. At five foot ten, light reddish brown hair, green eyes, he was somewhat good looking but certainly not a standout. His best assets were being medium weight and having high cheek bones. Otherwise he had long ago succumbed to being mediocre in looks and personality.

A limo was called upon touchdown and before long they entered the New York University Hospital's Intensive Care Unit. The look on the nurse's face told them all they needed to know. Benton had died. James and Orion simultaneously shouted out the F word. A flurry of emotions passed between them, from hate to blame to hate to love. The English language sorely lacked a word for intense love and hate at the same time. In the end they comforted themselves with shoulder hugs, wiped away the tears and got down to the practical matters of morgue, funeral home and memorial service arrangements.

Two weeks later James called Orion to tell him there would be a reading of the will and they needed to meet with the lawyers in New York City. Once again the corporate jet was summoned and off they went. Orion knew his grandparents were rich, but how rich, he had no idea. He figured his father would be the sole recipient of the spoils anyway, and thus he only expected a nominal inheritance.

The handing over of Benton's business, assets, house and personal affects to James was a long, tedious process which would take months. James kindly spared Orion of those details since Orion had made it quite clear to his father that he was happy with his job in which there was room for "upward mobility" and that he had no interest in moving into the family business. Idiot, James thought to himself but he wasn't going to go down that rabbit hole of making the son follow the father's footsteps. The meeting therefore continued with what Orion would be inheriting. In just two simple words Orion's whole life was about to change: *Bahama Gem*. Orion and James were equally stunned. "Dad! I love that boat! But I can't run it much less afford its upkeep."

"Oh not to worry, Orion," Chloe Featherstonaugh, the lead attorney interjected, "your grandfather set up a fund for that purpose and there is a crew on retainer: a captain, two deck hands and a steward. It seems the steward lives on the boat and Mr. Foster was emphatic that she stay on board and remain employed as long as she wants to be employed, no questions asked. Basically the yacht is at your service."

"She? Not the boat, I mean the steward. The steward is female?" Orion immediately felt like a chauvinistic jerk, especially when Chloe looked up from her reading glasses with a look that could cut through steel. "Sorry, Ms. Featherstonaugh, I didn't mean to imply…"

Chloe stopped him by icily interrupting with, "no offense taken, Orion. But I would suggest you keep that opinion to yourself. Ms. Cara Moore is a very capable woman and has done a superb job of minding your grandfather's boat for over five years. I've taken the liberty of informing her that you'll be meeting with her after the memorial service next week. My secretary has an itinerary for you."

Screw that Orion thought to himself. I'm taking some much needed vacation time and flying down immediately to the Bahamas.

"Thank you," was what he said out loud, but in his head he was already envisioning setting foot once again on the *Bahama Gem*.

CHAPTER 5

CARA CHUCKLED TO HERSELF. Wow, can't believe Einar Aronsson thought I looked like Milla Memphis. Cara didn't keep up with the tabloids and didn't know that Einar and Milla were an item. Then she chided herself for not knowing what Einar's real name was. How pathetic was that? she thought, I'm sure that guy has a real name.

An "ism" of her mother's popped into her brain: "You know, Cara, no matter how rich or poor you are, at least once a day everyone has to sit down, expose his ass and take a crap."

Thanks for that image mom… but it was true, why did she and the rest of the population think actors and actresses were so almighty? Aren't they just pretending to be someone else? If I did that, they'd lock me up or accuse me of fraud. Whoever "they" were.

She set her blue canvas bag down on the transom of *Bahama Gem*. She had just returned from greeting the crew of *Adventure I* who had brought back her bag from Milla Memphis. Earlier she had given them Milla's bag. What a pity, Cara lamented, such great stuff in that bag. Oh well, back to work… let's see what part of this clean boat needs cleaning?

Kaitlin from the office knocked on the side of the boat, "Hey, Cara, there's a letter here for you that requires your signature."

"Really? Humph, what could that possibly be?" As soon as she saw the return address she blanched. "Oh no, this can't be good news." She signed the receipt and handed it back to Kaitlin. "This may require a shot of rum to digest..." she said to Kaitlin, but Kaitlin was already headed back to the office.

She went into the galley and took out the bottle of Mount Gay. She poured herself a shot and then opened the letter. She was geared up for being let go or that Benton was simply too old and frail and the boat was being sold. She wasn't geared up for learning he had passed away. There would be a memorial service next week and she was expected to attend. Plane tickets with an itinerary were included along with an itinerary for meeting Benton's grandson who had inherited the boat. She looked at the ten-year-old's picture. Really? That little pipsqueak? Apparently the grandson had also been frozen into her mind as a ten-year-old. And what the hell kind of name was Orion Matthews? Shouldn't his name be Ryan Foster? Who names their son after a constellation? But actually she was intrigued; kind of cool to be named after a constellation. She herself had wanted to change her name from Cara to Cassiopeia on many occasions. She drank two shots and decided she needed the wisdom of one of the dock moms. Either Mabel or Catherine would do.

Mabel was painting some sea biscuits on her back deck. This was Mabel's passion now. She always had some sort of project going. Now in their late 70s, Mabel and her husband Jake were content not to move much. It was only the lack of pump out services in the Abacos that forced them to go out once a week into deep water to unload the contents of their holding tanks. A gross topic that almost all boaters avoided, but what could they do? If they were stateside they would simply go to the nearest marina for that ugly service. Or better yet, many Florida marinas offered "dock-side" service similar to RV parks which had hook ups for water and sewage. Mabel read Cara's non-poker face and quickly said, "Oh dear, Cara, what happened?" Cara didn't shed a tear when she read the letter but now the flood gates opened up. Mabel swept her up in her permanently bronzed arms and held her for what seemed like a lifetime. Finally Cara came up for air, stopped sobbing and announced "Benton's dead!"

"That's awful, what happened?"

"He had a massive stroke a few weeks ago and died two days later. I knew he was getting frail but I guess I expected a slower passing."

"But isn't it better this way, Cara? He really hasn't been the same since his wife died, and to have him linger in a nursing home would have been horrible. He went out at the top of his game. I'd like to do that."

"Mabel! Stop that! Don't even think about dying, what would I do without you?" blurted Cara.

"Well, God willing I do hope to celebrate my 60th wedding anniversary. Isn't that the Diamond Jubilee Anniversary? I've always wanted to add to my diamond collection," Mabel said facetiously in an attempt to cheer up Cara.

"Oh Mabel… this is awful. The Corporation is paying me to fly up to the Memorial Service next week, and I guess I have to meet the new owner. They actually want to keep me employed, but I'm sure his grandson is a jerk, so what's going to become of me?" Cara caved in to another round of crying. Mabel, bless her soul, as they say in the South, mercifully held her until the tears stopped.

"Cara, what makes you think he's a jerk? You're basing your opinion on one school photo of him as a ten year old? What's his name anyway?" Mabel was well acquainted with the school photo; it was the topic of many of the docktails after two or three drinks had been consumed.

"It's Orion Matthews... I know, I know... who names their son after a constellation?"

"Well, it's unique, I'll give him that." Mabel invited Cara for supper as she correctly ascertained Cara needed some company that evening. Mabel's husband was not the warmest individual on the dock but with Mabel kicking his leg under the table, he kept his opinions in check and dutifully remained pleasant during the meal.

Later that evening Cara returned to *Bahama Gem*. She pulled her black "all purpose" dress out of her wardrobe. It was the perfect funeral dress. Then she looked through her jewelry case for something appropriate to wear. She pulled out her suitcase and noticed a small purse on the floor. "What's that?" It was in the vicinity where she had pawed through Milla Memphis's bag. She wasn't proud of the fact that she had looked at all the bikinis and lusted after them and even tried one on. But she thought she had returned all items to the blue canvas bag.

"Shit!" she said out loud. "Milla probably thinks I stole her belongings."

She picked up the purse and opened it. Inside were ten crisp 100 dollar bills along with diamond earrings, diamond bracelet and diamond necklace. Then there were two pill bottles, one filled with unidentified small pills and one filled with a white powder. One little swipe of the white powder confirmed it was cocaine. Zing! Jesus Christ! What the hell? How did she get that through customs? Oh man, I'm in trouble now! It was 11 P.M. She had to call Milla, but how? Well, I'll just get up at 7 A.M. and send it over with the first run to Sea Star Resort. For some reason she looked at the diamond set again. Why did that look familiar? Humph… She returned to the bottle of Mount Gay and drank two more shots. Combined with the entire bottle of red wine she consumed with Mabel and Jake, it didn't take much for her to fall asleep.

Chapter 6

Richard could see Milla on the dock waiting for him. The *Adventure I* Captain expertly backed the boat into its slip and moments later when the lines were secured, Richard hopped off the boat. Milla had already texted him telling him what an awful night she had had. She spared him the full details so as to tell him in person. Milla loved drama, and Richard often thought if there wasn't some sort of drama going on in her life, she'd merely make some up. Being an actress came rather naturally to her.

After a hug and a kiss, Milla quickly launched into the details. "First my beach ware bag got mixed up with some stupid deck hand, then the cell service went down, then the electricity went out, then the generator ran out of diesel so there was no back up which meant no water or toilets. My toilet overflowed and made a horrible mess which couldn't be cleaned up until the water came back on. It was hours of being in the dark, being so hot I almost melted and then the smell of the toilet mess, oh the smell! It was awful! And poor Brenda, I don't know if she'll ever recover. I think she's going to have to leave her position earlier than planned. Then what'll I do? No assistant for weeks?"

Cara and Milla's bags had been returned to each other earlier in the day by one of the runs *Adventure I* made back and forth to Marsh Harbour. But the worst problem was something Milla had to keep to herself. Her purse containing her extra cash, her mother's diamond jewelry set, her amphetamines and her cocaine, was missing. That little bitch, Milla said to herself. Somehow she would need to find out the deck hand's identity and confront her directly but discreetly.

"There, there, Milla," Richard said in an almost patronizing voice, "it seems things are resetting back to normal, what do you say we grab some drinks at the pool side bar and just relax a bit?"

Basically all Richard really wanted to do was to get Milla in bed, but he knew her well enough to know she'd need to calm down from 10 on the Richter Scale to about a 1 and then be pretty oiled up with a few cocktails before any action would be happening in the bedroom department. He knew he would have to hear her restate the complaints several times more before the alcohol worked its magic.

"Well, all right," she said reluctantly. All she wanted to do was chop some heads off, but a drink or two wouldn't hurt.

The pool area was luxurious with tasteful groupings of comfortable patio furniture for two, four, six or eight people. The nooks for two dominated the area and they choose one nearest to the bar. After repeating herself several times in a high pitched hysterical voice, the pina coladas were mercifully taking affect. Even Richard, deemed the world's most self-centered male, was embarrassed to have the wait staff hear her complaints. He was well aware that most of the wait staff lived without air conditioning, endured long hours of power outages and couldn't even afford to buy one of the many drinks they were being served.

"So Milla, what would you think about taking one of the sailboats out tomorrow?" he offered, trying to distract her from her self-exaggerated trauma.

"Well actually, I wanted to go back to Marsh Harbour to check out an art show," she lied, "I think the villa needs a few more paintings and I heard Teri Rodan's oil paintings were going to be featured." Teri Rodan was a local artist famous for her oils and water colors of Bahamian scenes as well as a whole series of whimsical mermaids.

"Oh, well…. I…." Richard stumbled for an excuse not to go….

"Don't worry, I know that's not your thing… how about going sailing later in the week?"

Maybe there was a God. Richard was relieved not to have to go art-work shopping. He couldn't think of anything more dreadful. Plus going into "public" meant risking the ever present paparazzi. He was hard not to notice. When he was off the set he really just wanted to be Richard and not Einar. For Milla, being in "public" was easier. She could just pull up her hair, put on a big floppy hat with large sun glasses and blend in. Strange though, he thought, that she so easily let him off the hook. Usually she was hell bent on making him endure everything she was interested in and not doing anything he really wanted to do. He often wondered what exactly did hold them together. For the most part their crazy life of being on filming sets for long stretches at a time worked well. It could sometimes be months before they saw each other. The Villa at Sea Star was a perfect solution for them. Whenever they had time off, they flew down to the Bahamas and for the most part just hung out. The only thing nagging at him in the back of his brain was what would happen if she ever found out about his many on-set affairs. He loved Milla, but there was no way he could go without sex for weeks at a time. Maybe she was also having affairs on the side.... that would be OK with him.... or so he convinced himself.

The next morning Milla told Brenda just to lay low for the day while she went into Marsh Harbour. She had arranged to take the 9 A.M. run on *Adventure II*. Meanwhile Cara had arranged to take the workers' ferry over to Sea Star to personally return the purse. It would be a hassle to dock *Bahama Gem's* tender in the Resort Marina and she didn't trust anyone to hand the purse over to Milla. Although Cara had fallen asleep easily she woke up at 3 A.M. in a pool of sweat conjuring up the worst case scenario. She excelled at that. What if Milla accused her of purposely holding on to the purse and not returning all of the money, jewelry or drugs? It would be a shit storm of "she said—she said." No way to prove what was originally there. She also feared being caught with cocaine and being thrown into jail. Milla could simply deny she had any drugs and Cara was just trying to taint her reputation. And on and on it went until finally at 6 A.M. Cara got out of bed and made some coffee.

"Ugh... my head," Cara groaned out loud. Thoughts of her younger but older acting sister, Dana, saying, "You know Cara, shots are always a bad idea," floated up to the surface. "Yeah, yeah, yeah, Dana, you're always right..."

Cara downed three cups of coffee along with a bottle of water, an English muffin and three aspirins. The throbbing of her headache came down to a tolerable level and she jumped into the shower. Feeling much better after a prolonged rinse, she donned one of her sun dresses, not wearing her uniform today. Her big floppy hat had a ribbon around it that matched the pink in her sundress and her sandals coordinated well with the outfit. For a moment, Cara actually thought she looked pretty good. Her plan was to go straight to the security office at Sea Star and ask an officer to accompany her to Milla's home. Security was tight there so there was no way she could just waltz over to the Villa unescorted. Cara quickly walked down the dock and was momentarily shocked with the smell of cigar smoke coming from a sport fishing yacht. Really? How could anyone smoke a cigar this early in the morning? She exchanged a quick glance of mutual distain with a tall, beer bellied, balding man. And of course his boat was named *Reel Relief.* It seemed that almost all sport fishers contained the word "reel" in some form: *Reel Therapy, Reel Time, Reel Life, Reel Intentions, Reel Fun, Reel Havoc, Reel This* and *Reel That. Reel Assholes*, she thought to herself.

On the ride over to Marsh Harbour, Milla pondered her attack plan. It would be easy enough to find *Bahama Gem* and the deck hand. She would simply have Gary, the crew man for *Adventure I,* who knew who the "deck hand" was, summon Cara. Then Milla would dismiss Gary until she cell phoned him to be returned to Sea Star. Simple. But what if any of the items were missing? To accuse her of theft would bring to "public" the jewelry and drugs. The drugs were an obvious problem, but the jewelry was also problematic. She didn't exactly have her mother's permission to take that diamond set. And for that matter, her mother didn't exactly have permission from her mother either. Damn… maybe not so simple.

Brenda not only "laid low" for the day; she holed herself up in one of the guest suites and put a "Do Not Disturb" sign on the outside of the door. Richard could fend for himself; he was a big boy, she laughed to herself.

Cara sucked up every bit of pride she had and walked over to the security office. "Hi, um, I'm Cara Moore, I had a personal bag of Ms. Memphis' returned to her yesterday and she had a bag returned to me?" She paused hoping the very stern humorless officer would recall the mix-up. Nothing. "Well, it turns out there was a small purse that must have fallen out of her bag during the exchange. I'd like to return it to her personally, can you escort me?"

Long pause. Finally he asked, "Is she expecting you?"

"No, but once she realizes her purse is missing, she'll be pretty upset and most likely she'll be calling you to call me. Just saving you a step."

"All right miss, stay here, I'll be right back in my jeep." Ten minutes later they drove down the beautifully land-scaped road to Milla's Villa. Cara got to peek at some of the other homes. Per her internet research the homes here cost anywhere between 1. 5 million and 12 million. At four million, Milla's Villa was considered modest. The officer rang the doorbell and waited a good five minutes before ringing it again. It seemed like an eternity. A disheveled Richard answered the door. Where the hell is Brenda? Why am I answering the door? Who is this anyway? Richard angrily questioned himself as he opened the door. To his delight a beautiful blonde said a cheery but reserved "hello."

The officer quickly took charge. "Is Ms. Memphis here?"

"No, sir, she left this morning, just about a half hour ago."

"Well, this woman has a personal belonging of hers and would like to return it. Hand it over, Miss."

"Pardon me, sir, uh… I really wanted to give it to her personally, is there anywhere I could wait?

Simultaneously the officer said no and Richard said yes.

"Really, Officer, she looks harmless enough," Richard said as he flexed his muscles turning into Einar, "I think I can handle her."

Silence. The officer finally responded. "Well, this isn't routine but if you insist… call this number when your visit is completed and I'll escort her off the property." He handed Richard his card and stomped down the pathway to the driveway.

Cara wanted to crawl into the nearest wall socket. Could this be more humiliating? I'm not really a criminal, just trying to do the right thing. Out loud she said "Thank you. Where can I wait?"

"We'll find a place. Just come in." And to the officer who was still in ear shot: "Thank you, Officer, I'll be sure to give you a call."

The officer got into his vehicle. His groan of disgust could be heard over the engine noise.

"Well, well, Miss?…"

"Cara, Cara Moore. Yesterday you thought I was Milla."

"Yes, yes, that's it! I thought you looked familiar. Can I get you something to drink or eat?"

"Oh no, don't go to any trouble. Any idea how long Milla will be gone?"

"No idea, could be two hours, could be all day. She went to some art show in Marsh Harbour."

"Really?" There weren't a lot of events going on in Marsh Harbour. Usually the art shows were held in Hope Town or Treasure Cay. There was a big show at Treasure Cay coming up next week but she didn't recall anything going on today. Hmmm.... going right to thinking the worst of Milla, Cara suspected Milla had lied to Richard. On the outside she continued, "Well, she could be hours, any chance you could call her? I could simply return the purse to her in Marsh Harbour."

She looked up at Richard and he seemed to be looking at her rather amorously. What's going on? she asked herself.

Richard and Milla had had a nice round of sex last night and he was fully expecting more this morning. But Milla was on a mission. She got up early, fussed with her make-up and outfit and was out the door before he even awake. To find the bed empty put him in a sour mood; he had had other plans… then conveniently this pretty blonde showed up which renewed his desires. Typically, once he gave a woman his "look," the clothes peeled off rapidly and joyous recreational sex followed. Cara, on the other hand, looked at him quizzically.

"Einar, I mean Richard, can we just call Milla?"

"What?" Obviously he never processed her original question. "Call Milla, why?"

"To set up someplace for me to meet up with her… I have a job and although it would be nice to spend time with you," trying to sound as polite as possible when she was really revving up to be angry, "I really need to move this transaction along."

Cara and Richard were at an awkward crossroads. Cara was not a star seeker and was only minimally excited to be in the presence of a screen idol. And that minimal excitement was being reduced by the minute once she realized he only wanted to get into her pants. Richard, on the other hand, was in disbelief that any woman would deny herself the opportunity to jump into bed with him.

"I should go. This was a stupid idea."

"Don't be in such a rush I'd love to hear all about your job."

"Bullshit, it's quite obvious what your intentions are."

"What makes you so sure?"

Cara was about to blurt out a string of obscenities and unload all of her anger concerning the male gender, but Richard reached over to her, swept her up in his massive arms and kissed her. She pushed him away but not before allowing herself to enjoy a nanosecond of the most passionate kiss she had ever been given. Once disentangled from him she was about to slap him, but he gently fended off her wrist and held her hand.

"Sorry, couldn't help myself. Did anyone ever tell you how beautiful you are when you're angry?"

"Really? That cliché? You know what, you're just one gigantic cliché yourself! Call that officer, I need to leave!"

"So what's in that purse anyway? Richard completely caught her off guard with the subject change.

"What? None of your business! And I'm not leaving it with you." Cara didn't know Milla even though she suspected Milla was a bitch and had her dark side, but she wasn't going to throw her under the bus.

"Hey, hey… let's calm it down… I'll give Milla a call and we'll get that purse back to her."

CHAPTER 7

MILLA WALKED DOWN THE dock with Gary. *Bahama Gem* was only a few slips down from where *Adventure I* landed. The couple on the Jeanneau 42 across from *Adventure I* looked up. Milla could tell the woman knew who she was but the woman respectfully looked back down at her cell phone, whereas the husband was clueless as to her identity. She was grateful that the many boaters on the dock never did the paparazzi thing. Maybe it was in the docking agreement, "thou shalt not be a jerk when you see a celebrity," she mused. But then as she passed by a sport fisher named *Reel Relief* the man on the boat gave her the most frightening glare. He looked familiar but with his baseball cap and aviator sunglasses she couldn't be sure… it was an unnerving moment.

Gary preceded her and knocked on *Bahama Gem*'s main companion way door. "Excuse me, Cara? There's someone here to meet with you.… Cara?" No answer. He knocked again and this time a young man, Orion Matthews, came to the doorway.

"Excuse me sir," said Gary, "is Cara here?"

"That's a good question, I'm looking for her too. Can I help you?" asked Orion.

"What do you mean she's not here? Did she leave a note or anything?" Milla piped up in her annoying voice that wreaked of "how dare she?"

"Actually, ma'am, I don't even know what Cara looks like, she um… wasn't expecting me. But I'm guessing she won't be gone long, the boat was wide open. Would you like to leave a note?" Orion asked a bit too sarcastically.

She was about to let out an F bomb but her phone rang. Richard's face came up and she immediately sent him a "can't talk right now" text. And that was almost instantly followed up by a text from Richard stating that a Miss Cara Moore was at the Villa with her purse. They were headed to Marsh Harbour and wanted to know where to meet her. "Shit!" she blurted out loud.

"Is something wrong?" Orion asked.

"Yes… No, it's nothing. Gary, we need to return immediately. Get on the radio and tell Sea Star not to transport Richard." She rudely turned her back to Orion and rushed down the dock. He guessed she was a somebody, and she certainly looked familiar. Yeah, I know I've seen her somewhere… he thought, it'll come to me. And he gave her no further thought. Back to nosing around the boat looking for what? He didn't know.

Once Milla was back on the boat and out of Gary's ear shot she called Richard. Good thing she was an actress. She turned on her lying, sickeningly sweet voice and said "Sorry, Richard, the engines were just starting up when you called and I knew I wouldn't be able to hear you. Stay put, sweetie, I'm on my way back. Silly me, I got the date of the art show wrong. How nice of Cara to return my purse."

Chapter 8

Orion walked through the main salon and immediately noticed his framed fourth grade picture near a book shelf. He knew for a fact that his father dutifully sent his grandfather annual school pictures. Clearly his grandfather was making a statement. After fourth grade he never set foot on the boat again... until today. He looked around some more and the boat was pretty much how he remembered it with the exception of different upholstery in the main salon. And it no longer seemed enormous. In fact, at the marina it was in, it was actually dwarfed by a few boats 120 feet long. As he descended to the staterooms he went straight to "his" room. The stateroom had bunk beds, a small desk and bureau. No change there. He looked at the other two staterooms and decided to take one that had a full sized bed in it. The stateroom his grandparents stayed in was large and luxurious, but Orion felt it was permanently off limits to him. Silly he thought, but still off limits. So where did Cara sleep? He found the quarters for the captain and crew immediately behind the pilot house on the top deck when he first boarded the boat. He descended further to the level of the engine room and sure enough, toward the bow were two small cabins. Cara seemed to have occupied both of them. One for sleeping and one for her possessions. Who could blame her? They were so small and claustrophobic. Only one small round port hole per room. He only looked around for a few seconds. How embarrassing would it be if she happened to return right now, only to find him in her private quarters? He headed up to the main deck and prowled through the galley for something to eat. He had absolutely no idea what was next on his agenda. He made himself a sandwich and started prowling through the log books.

Cara and Richard decided to wait for Milla to return at the pool side cafe. A few guests passed by them with looks of suppressed surprise. Milla and Richard were a well-known couple at the resort. Their faces seemed to be asking: "Who was this new woman and where was Milla?" Cara could feel the stares and felt increasingly uncomfortable. This was shaping up to be the longest 45 minutes she would ever have to endure. Meanwhile, Richard ordered a light breakfast along with two Bloody Marys. Apparently, "No thank you" meant, "Yes please, I'll have one," to Richard. Oh what the hell, she succumbed, maybe a Bloody Mary was just what she needed.

"So I actually am interested, what is this job you have all about?"

Wow, thought Cara, this is a departure from his normal script of "it's all about me." "I'm a steward on an 80 foot yacht named *Bahama Gem*. In a nut shell I have to make sure the yacht is ready to go at any time the owner wants to be on board."

"Do you like it?"

"Yes and no," she answered honestly. "It has its challenges and I certainly get to see interesting, exotic places, but then there are long periods of monotony."

"Not unlike being on the set for weeks at a time."

"Really? I guess I've stereotyped your life into one of constant excitement."

"Au contraire, mon amie," he warped into a lovely French accent that actually made her giggle. Oh good grief, she scolded herself immediately, can two sips of a Bloody Mary make me giddy already?

"Ah ha! Score!" he said triumphantly. "I finally made you laugh! Yeah," he continued, "I'd like to say life as an actor is one big ball of fun, but sometimes it can be quite tedious."

"You know, I'd love to know how you can bludgeon so many people and have it look so real. Actually, sometimes I can't even look."

"I'd need the better part of the day to tell you all our little secrets. Think about this, for every minute of bludgeoning you see, it takes about two hours of set up time... Boring!"

"Humph.... never thought about that."

Their conversation continued in a very safe zone of complaining about the downsides of their jobs. Cara found it amazing that she was having a regular conversation with perhaps one of the world's most well-known actor. Richard found it amazing that she hadn't asked for his autograph by now. Then suddenly they were jolted by Milla's abrupt appearance.

"I see you two are enjoying yourselves," she said in a way that lobbed criminal charges against them.

Richard stood up and, ever the gentleman, pleasantly said "Milla, hello, this is Cara. Cara, this is Milla." With that he pulled over a chair for Milla and they sat down. He nodded to the bartender and almost instantly a waitress appeared to take Milla's order.

"Just water with lemon, I'm parched," Milla stated.

Cara immediately dove in with, "I'm so sorry about all of this, here's your purse."

"Well, good, at last, that was a lot of worry you put me through," Milla said in a most ungrateful manner.

Cara couldn't help herself. "Hey, it wasn't my fault your crew took my bag and left me yours."

"What I'm referring to, Miss Cara, is that you obviously went through my bag."

"Obviously, I looked in your bag, I needed to find out who it belonged to… and obviously you went through mine. Look, no harm no foul, our bags have been returned, no one died here. But could you please look through your purse? I want to be sure you're satisfied that all your belongings are there."

Milla was actually quite eager to look inside and turned to the side so as to use her body to block Cara and Richard from seeing the contents. "Seems everything is here."

"Great!" Cara said with just a bit too much relief showing, "and without further ado, I'll exit stage left and let you two get on with your vacation." Cara's attempt to be humorous put a smile on Richard's face but a frown on Milla's.

Richard could tell Milla was gearing up to say something negative so he quickly intervened with "I'll call the Security Office and someone will escort you to the ferry. Good day, Cara Moore, it was a pleasure."

With that he started to escort Milla back to their Villa. Milla paused and turned around. "Oh by the way, Cara, there's a man on your boat who says he doesn't know what you look like."

Why Milla offered that information she didn't know, especially since it pretty much confirmed she had another agenda other than the art show, but there was something about Milla that nagged at Cara. Somehow, somewhere she knew she had seen Milla before. Or maybe she saw her on the dock on a previous trip to the Resort... but no, it was longer ago than that.

CHAPTER 9

ON THE FERRY RIDE BACK to Marsh Harbour Cara pondered Milla's last statement. A man on the boat? Who would that be? One of Benton's lawyers? Can't believe I left the boat wide open; what an idiot. And why would that Bitch offer any information at all? It was odd that in that final sentence, Milla wasn't a Bitch. She just seemed to be giving her information as one friend would to another. Humph.

When Cara entered the Harbourside Marina gate, Catherine was there, obviously waiting for her return. "Cara, Cara! The new owner is on *Bahama Gem!* Well that answers one question, Cara thought to herself. Then out loud, "How did you find that out?"

"I just asked him!" Both Cara and Catherine burst out laughing. "Of course you did, Catherine, got to love your direct approach."

"What did you expect? I saw a stranger on your boat so I asked him to identify himself. Simple!"

"Yes, yes, simple."

"And, Cara, I've told you a million times to lock up!"

"Yes, mom, next time, mom...."

Cara could see a young man in the pilot house. He

appeared to be reading. Well at least he's good looking and not fat and ugly. For some reason she had imagined him to have a beer belly and already balding.

"And I expect a full report as to why Milla Memphis went over to your boat and where you were this morning."

"Of course, over a bottle of wine... but later, Catherine. Guess I need to meet the new boss..."

"Yes you do, any time, Cara... you know where I live!"

Cara admonished herself with a silent "duh." Now it makes sense about the art show sham, Milla was just as anxious to get her purse back as Cara was to return it. She walked up to *Bahama Gem* and was about to call out "hello" when Orion appeared at the companion way.

"Hello! I assume you're Cara Moore? Please forgive me for boarding without permission, but I guess after all, it is my ship."

"Yes, it is." For once, Cara was at a loss for words.

An awkward silence continued until Orion collected himself and cheerfully stated, "Welcome aboard!"

"Yeah, here's to that." Cara mustered up a smile and entered the main salon. "So let's just cut to the chase. Are you going to sell the boat?"

"No!" Orion reacted with surprise. "No, I want to figure out a way to live on the boat."

"Really?"

"Really. I was an idiot not to stand up to my parents and demand to visit my grandparents. And when I was 18 I could have just flown down myself. And why I just abandoned my grandfather after Nanny died.... I just don't know.... and now of course... it's just too late...."

Orion looked as if he was going to cry. For a moment a thread of maternal instinct in Cara wanted to comfort him, but that was quickly squelched with her need to punish him for being so absent. He mirrored what she had thought for years. She let him drown in his self pity. Finally, she broke the silence with a barely sympathetic "Sorry."

"Anyway," he continued as if none of the above had just occurred, "I'm pretty much the head of my Division at Dustin Pharmaceuticals and there's no reason I couldn't set up a remote office here. Gotta love the internet."

"Ha! The internet? In the Bahamas? Well, it has gotten better lately. But you are aware the power goes out frequently here."

"Don't we have a generator?"

"Yes we do," Cara replied with a bit too much emphasis on the pronoun "we." She liked that: "We."

"Hey, are you hungry? I could make you some lunch."

Orion blushed a bit. "I... uh... already helped myself."

"Yes of course, after all it is your boat." Cara turned sour again.

"Sorry," they both said simultaneously, followed by a laugh when they saw each other blush a bit.

"No really, Cara, I'm sorry. It seems you really liked my grandfather. It must have been a shock to you too that he passed so quickly."

"Yes it was. He was gruff but always nice to me. I miss him...."

"Well, let's turn this around. What do you think about me living on the boat?"

"Well… I… guess it could work." In her mind she thought quite the opposite. *God damn it. Sharing my boat with him? He seems like such a wimp. We're about the same age, eventually hormones are going to win out and then we'll have that awkward sex scene in the forward state room… ugh…* Her mind wandered.

"I can see you're reluctant… say, is the tender ready to go?"

"What?" Cara was once again surprised with a change in subject.

"Yeah, *Diamond Girl?* Pops used to take me to Shell Island when I was a kid. How about we go out there for the afternoon?"

"Pops?"

"That's what I used to call my grandfather."

"Well, I…" Cara stalled looking for an excuse not to go, but then she thought, what the hell? In fact she loved going out to Shell Island. In her long list of "things to do" one was making sure the tender was always in working order. She warped that into a weekly trip to Shell Island, an uninhabited spoil island just off the freighter channel for Great Guana Cay. "I would love to," she finally said out loud.

"Great, let's pack up some beverages and towels and get going."

They went to their respective staterooms, changed into beach clothes, filled a cooler with water and beer, packed a bag with towels and some chips, then cast off the painter to the tender.

The man on *Reel Relief* stared at them as they undid the lines to the tender. *Assholes*, he thought to himself. And then he untied his lines and headed out as well.

CHAPTER 10

C ARA LOVED BEING BEHIND the helm. She loved the salt air on her face and she loved being in charge. It would take just under an hour to get to Shell Island. Weird that for different reasons Shell Island was special to her and Orion. As they approached the island Cara could see that there was a landing craft on the island. What? She'd been living in the Bahamas for five years and every time she went to this island she was usually the sole inhabitant. What the hell was all of this? As they got closer, it was evident the landing craft had off loaded a crap load of equipment. They beached the tender after having thrown out an anchor in anticipation of the tide going down. Cara and Orion walked up to the worker-bees off-loading more equipment from the landing craft.

"What's going on?" demanded Cara having no authority whatsoever. "Who the hell are you?"

The first man they approached seemed to be in charge. "Hey just doing my job, mon…" adopting the local accent.

"And what job would that be?" asked an unrelenting Cara.

"Setting up for a film scene. Gotta get in a scene before the weather changes."

"What movie?" demanded Cara.

"Not allowed to say, Ma'am."

"Fucking A," Cara blurted out. "You don't own this island, no one does. So I'm just going to walk around and you can't stop me!"

"Actually, Ma'am, that's no problem. We just need this small segment of the island. The rest is yours to enjoy."

Off the island on the lee shore, so as to be wind protected, there were a few catamarans and one sport fisher. The man on the sport fisher briefly followed Cara and Orion with his binoculars as they traipsed across the sand beach. Pockets of couples from the other boats were also milling about. He didn't care about them. He was most interested in the landing craft. He stared at the activity surrounding the craft for a good long time, then up-anchored and returned to slip 23.

Cara and Orion thoroughly enjoyed the outing. Cara collected a handful of shells even though she already had plenty and had no idea what she would do with the new ones. Maybe I'll give them to Mabel to paint, she thought. Orion seemed intent on finding sand dollars. Several broken pieces were easily found but not intact ones.

"When I was a kid here there were literally dozens... what happened to them?"

"Uh 20 years went by and about a million people have combed the beach clear of them?"

"Guess you're right.... How does 20 years just go by? Doesn't that make us old when we can talk about things in terms of decades?"

Again, there's that "we" thing. I like it, Cara smiled to herself. "You know, I really don't think of myself as old. Your

63

'Pops' was old. And if you're my mother, you personally will never be old. In her world 'old' is ten years older than your current age."

"Well, I'm feeling old…"

"Tide's really going down. Perhaps we should head back." The tide status didn't really matter; Cara just wanted to change the subject.

"Sure."

They walked back to the tender in silence, but it was a good silence. Nice that they had quickly gotten to that point in which you didn't feel obligated to fill up every second with verbiage. Sometimes it was nice just to walk along lost in your own thoughts.

Orion untied the painter from a tree branch while Cara readied the engine. Just as Orion was about to step into the boat, he noticed the rim of a sand dollar sticking up in the sand in about a foot of water. He pulled it up and miraculously it was intact. "Wow!" he burst out loud. And for ten seconds he was 11 years old again. Felt great.

Chapter 11

Milla's film crew captain knocked on the Villa's Door. Brenda answered the knock and let Jermaine enter. "Hey, Brenda, feeling any better?"

"I wish."

"Sorry. Hey, I hate to bother you, but we've got a bit of a weather situation developing. I'm afraid we're going to have to move up the filming date to tomorrow."

"What? Milla will flip, she's barely been here 48 hours. I thought she was guaranteed at least a week of R and R?"

"We need the water to be flat, meaning no wind, no waves. If there are any waves, we won't be able to shoot the scene. There's a cold front coming in faster than expected and the next calm day is at least a week away. Meanwhile, we're due to start filming in Savannah next Tuesday. Everything's set up. Look, it's just a short scene. We could get it all done in just one day and then Milla can get back to her little vacation."

"Fine, but you tell her. I'm tired of being the bad guy. Besides, I think I need to throw up now."

Jermaine simply couldn't relate to Brenda's plight. But he knew he'd have to be the bearer of bad news. "So where is she?"

"She and Richard took out one of the sailboats. I expect she'll be back in time for dinner."

"Will you at least call me when she's back?"

"Yes, and never mind, I'll tell her. What time does she need to be ready tomorrow?"

"Seven A.M. Lighting will be best in the morning. I've got the catering crew lined up to provide breakfast and lunch on the beach. If everything goes well, we can wrap it up by 4 or 5 P.M."

"OK, I'll have her on the dock by 7 A.M. You owe me."

Jermaine thanked her and quickly headed back to his headquarters. Brenda rehearsed in her head how best to break the news to Milla. Christ, she said to herself. If I had known I needed to be a psychologist to have this job, I wouldn't have signed up.

Milla and Richard returned to the Villa around 4 P.M. Milla's usual routine to "get ready" for dinner was basically a two-hour process. She wanted to be eating by 6 P.M. so as to enjoy the sunset at 7 P.M.

Brenda let her pour herself a drink before breaking the bad news to her. Although really, was this bad news? Bad news was a tornado wiping out a town or a fire destroying a hotel full of people. So she had to work a day early. So what? Brenda took a deep breath to calm herself down and very pleasantly informed Milla that the scene filming was moved to tomorrow morning.

"What the fuck? Can't I have one week off? Jesus Christ! Well, you know what? No! I'm not doing it. Screw them!"

Brenda and Richard knew better than to interrupt her tirade. Child psychology once again flashed through Brenda's brain. Richard simply made himself another drink and waited for her rant to fizzle out. Finally, she ran out of steam.

"Jesus H. Christ! What time do I have to be ready?" Milla relented.

"Seven A.M., but don't worry, Jermaine will have breakfast for you on the island, lunch too for that matter. And, if all goes well, you'll be done by 4:30 P.M. and then you can have the weekend off."

Milla took her usual two hours to get ready for dinner. Richard got in a three-mile jog, lifted a few weights, showered, napped and took about five minutes to get dressed. Milla ordered steamed clams for dinner which tasted a bit funky. The sun disappeared behind a bank of ugly gray clouds and set without any discernible colors. Milla continued to be in a piss poor mood and huffed off to their bedroom leaving Richard to fend for himself for the evening.

At four A.M. Milla woke up vomiting. Richard quickly surmised it must have been the clams she complained about. Not good. If it was food poisoning, he'd have to watch her vomit for the next 12 hours or even 24. Not good, he repeated to himself. And Brenda, the vomit queen, would have to be notified.

"Brenda, I'm so sorry to wake you up, but Milla is throwing her guts up. I think she ate some bad clams."

"Shit…. let me think. I'll call the Resort doctor and get him over here. But what are we going to do about the filming?" she pondered out loud.

"Call the Doc, then we'll figure out what to do about the filming."

Dr. Michaels returned Brenda's call about 20 minutes later. It seemed pretty straight forward. She was fine before dinner and then about eight hours later she was vomiting. She had had clams which tasted "funky." No mystery there or need for a medical degree. Just keep her hydrated as much as possible and call him back at 9 A.M. with a status update.

Brenda knocked on their bedroom door. Richard answered after a minute. "Brenda, can you put her hair up? It's in her way. She wants me to shoot her to put her out of her misery. Do you have a gun?"

"Stop it, Richard, that's not funny."

"No shit Sherlock. None of this is fun."

Brenda returned a few minutes later. She had swept Milla's hair back into a pony tail, forced her to drink some water, returned her to bed and put a bowl by her bedside for the next round of vomiting.

"Can't we just have Jermaine postpone the filming? They can film this shot sometime later after Savannah. What's the scene all about anyway?"

"It's the beginning scene. Milla's character, Marsha, has just found out her husband George has had an affair and wants a divorce. She's distraught. She hops on her paddle board and paddles over to this uninhabited island where she wanders about collecting shells and then starts throwing them back into the sea. It's to symbolize how unimportant she must have been to George to have him just throw her away after 15 years of marriage."

"Jesus Christ, another chick flick. Let me guess… prince charming comes around the corner and rescues her from being despondent."

"Yeah… pretty much."

"Well, you know what? Can't most of that be done with a stunt double? The paddle board scenes could be shot from afar, she can be filmed walking away from the camera on the beach. Any head shots can be redone in the studio later on."

"I think you're on to something. I'll call Jermaine, gotta let him know the situation in any event."

It took Jermaine a few minutes to comprehend what Brenda was trying to tell him.

"You mean she keeps throwing up and can't stop? And this could last all day? Shit!"

"Yeah, Dr. Michaels predicted she'd be incapacitated for at least 12 hours, maybe 24. Here, talk to Richard, he actually has some good ideas."

They discussed the scene particulars and Jermaine agreed a stunt double could work. But it was now five A.M. and they would need to start filming by eight A.M. at the latest.

"So where are we getting a stunt double in the next three hours?"

"Don't you have doubles already lined up?" queried Richard.

"Yes in Savannah, but not for here. Really this was just supposed to be a quick, simple scene."

"And Milla was going to actually paddle board?"

"Yes, she goes out all the time on her paddle board, but only if it's not rough. It's going to be dead calm this morning and not at all for the next week."

"Shit…. hey I have an idea."

"Shoot partner, I'm all ears."

"There's this deck hand, I mean steward in Marsh Harbour, I honestly thought she was Milla. She looks athletic enough, I'm sure she can handle a paddle board. She won't have any speaking parts, maybe you can just coach her through this."

"What?" interrupted Brenda. "We're going to call what's her name.... Cara? Hey, Cara, it's five A.M. could you just hop in your boat and meet us at Shell Island? We need you to walk down the beach and look despondent. Right! I'm sure she'll be thrilled."

"Hey, she'll get paid, and what a thrill it might be for her. Doesn't hurt to call."

"You're crazy, Richard!"

Jermaine interrupted. "At this point I'm with Richard, doesn't hurt to call. Does anyone know her number?"

"As a matter of fact I do," Richard smirked. "Let me do the honors."

"Be my guest," Jermaine stated.

Chapter 12

Reel Relief left the dock at 5:30 a.m. The man from Tennessee was intent on firmly establishing his pattern of going fishing every day starting before sunrise and returning by sunset. As he pulled out of the slip, he noticed some lights turning on on *Bahama Gem*. Odd, he thought at first, but maybe not. Early risers weren't all that unusual in the boating world.

He actually did like to fish, something he starting doing as a kid with his Dad. What he really loved about fishing was that it didn't require a lot of talking. He'd had a bad stutter as a child and his father chose to keep the conversation minimal rather than listen to him struggle through a sentence. They quickly became quite content to fish in silence. He actually relished not having to perform for a few hours. The kids at school teased him unmercifully, especially Cammie. She'd be so sweet to him when she and her mother came to visit, but then at school she seemed to be the leader of the pack for teasing him. "T-T-T-Trent darling, c-c-c-can you c-c-c-come here? I have s-s-something to t-t-tell you," mimicking his mother's southern accent with an added stutter. And still he had a crush on her. His mother arranged for her mother to talk her into going to the Senior Prom with him. She was gorgeous! She was his Cammie. But at the end of the prom, as most of the students headed for the after prom parties, she dumped him for Sean Memphis, the football team captain and quarterback. Sean's date was dumped just about as fast as he was. It was a horrible night and the emotional nightmare was imprinted in his brain in indelible ink. Her eventual marriage to Sean lasted about a year. He swore she only married him for his good looks and last name after she dropped Cammie and became Milla.

When he found out Cammie would be filming in the Bahamas, he left his fishing charter business in Fort Myers and chartered a boat from a reciprocating marina in Lake Worth. Given a bit more lead time he would simply have brought his own boat over from Fort Myers. The passage through the north end of Great Guana Cay, known locally as "The Whale," was dead calm that morning. He would be able to land a few fish before heading back to Shell Island to keep an eye on Cammie's whereabouts.

Cara groped for the light and then her phone. 5:30? Really? Who could possibly be calling her this early? She broke her rule of not answering the phone if she didn't recognize the number figuring it must be important. She didn't anticipate hearing Richard at the other end.

"Cara, it's Richard, I'm so sorry to wake you, but we have a situation."

I must be dreaming, Cara thought to herself. Even though Orion was a perfect gentleman, he was like milk toast and simply didn't do anything for her—on a sexual level that was. But Richard, that complete asshole, somehow turned her on. Like half a billion other women, you jerk, Cara, she exclaimed to herself and she snapped back to the conversation at hand. "What… what is it?"

"Milla ate some bad clams last night and now she's throwing up every 15 minutes. Doctor says she'll be down for the count for 12 to 24 hours."

"I'm sorry, but why is this my problem?"

"Let me finish. She has to shoot a scene today, it's a short one but apparently there's some stupid weather situation coming up and it has to be filmed starting at 8 A.M. It's not a speaking part, but it involves paddling on a paddle board and then walking along a beach. Can you handle that?"

"Wait… you want me to be her stunt double? Why me? Doesn't she have a whole team of stunt doubles?"

"Well from afar you look just like her and her 'team' isn't available. By the time they could be flown in, it will be too late."

"So let me get this straight, you want me to come over to Sea Star Resort right now and pretend to be Milla."

"Basically, yes. We'll send *Adventure I* or *II* over to get you."

"Don't bother, I'm awake now. I can drive myself over, but you're paying for the gas."

"That won't be a problem. Actually, just go directly to Shell Island. Jermaine, the film crew captain will meet you there. I'm going to stay with Milla."

Well shit, thought Cara, if I'd known Richard wasn't going to be there I'd have said no. But what the hell, it's not every day you get recruited to be in a movie. So do I wake up Orion?

Cara threw on some clothes. She figured it didn't matter what she wore. No doubt a costume person would be out-fitting her. She headed to the galley to make herself a cup of coffee and a bagel. The lights in the galley were already on, and Orion was next to the coffee machine.

"Couldn't sleep any longer and then I heard you talking to someone."

"Yeah, you'll never believe this but I've just been asked to be a stunt double for Milla Memphis."

"That's who she was!"

"What? Who?"

"That woman the other day. She came on board and asked for you, got a phone call and stomped off. I knew she seemed familiar but couldn't place her. You know you look like her."

"Yeah so I've heard… and now I'm hired because of that. I have to be at Shell Island by 7 A.M."

"Can I come… um… sorry, didn't mean to glom in on your debut… but… well… would you mind?"

"Oh what the hell, sure, come on."

Chapter 13

When Bob Packard, the Director of *The Georgian Affair*, learned of all the abrupt changes from Jermaine, he simply muttered "shit" under his breath. Bob had learned long ago from thousands of dollars of psychotherapy to skip the blame game stage and move right on to problem solving. If he had been female and had a close girlfriend, this advice would only have cost him a bottle of wine consumed over the course of an evening. Returning his mind to the present, he was proud of himself for becoming one of the most renown directors in the industry. It boiled down to not having a fit every time something went wrong on the set. He remained calm and got the job done.

"All right, get a contract from my secretary, Eloise, for Cara to sign ASAP. God forbid she cut herself on a shell and sue the bejesus out of us. And does she have any acting experience at all?"

"Don't think so, but she can manage a paddle board, and I don't think it takes much talent to pick up shells."

"Oh shut up, you asshole," Bob laughed kiddingly, "let's get this circus going."

There was no wind that morning as Cara and Orion sped off to Shell Island. When they approached the beach, there were two landing crafts and three center console runabouts already on the shore. Tents littered the beach and a few generators could be heard in the distance. A classic director's chair was on the beach. "No shit," Cara exclaimed out loud, "they really do use directors' chairs. Guess this is real after all."

"Yeah, pretty cool, and hey, look at all those cameras and sound booms!"

In a way Cara found Orion's childlike enthusiasm pretty endearing.

They beached the tender next to the nearly identical other tenders and were immediately greeted by a swarm of people. Cara readily recognized Bob Packard.

"Good morning, Cara, thank you for assisting us. This is my assistant, Eloise. She has some papers for you to look over and sign, and then Felicia will assist you with make-up and costuming. There's a tent over there for you to change. And this is Jermaine, the film crew captain." Bob then looked up at Orion. "And you are…?"

"He's my assistant," Cara interrupted. "Orion Matthews."

Orion was embarrassed but didn't let on. The men shook hands. No formal introduction was needed for Bob Packard.

"Nice to meet you Bob", said Orion, "I'm a definite fan of yours."

"Thanks, Orion, like your name by the way. OK, crew, let's get going."

Quietly to Cara, Orion said, "Assistant? Really?"

"Sorry, Orion, couldn't help myself. Just let me enjoy my 15 minutes of fame. Well, looks like I gotta go."

Orion wandered over to the tables set up for a buffet breakfast. No one paid him much attention and he simply put together a nice plate of eggs and toast. Amazing, he thought to himself, all this effort for what would probably whittle down to about five minutes of film time.

After Cara signed a contract to be a one day stand-in and basically gave up all rights of fame, she was handed a cup of coffee and a bagel. She declined the bagel but kept the coffee. Bob and Jermaine outlined the scene to her and the sequence of events to accomplish the scene. Felicia then accompanied her into the tent.

"OK, first up I'm going to have to trim your hair a bit to style it like Milla's. We won't really need to do much more than that because in the very first scene you'll have wet hair. And actually, your hair color is close enough to hers. Then we'll try out a few bikinis and then we'll do make up." Felicia rattled off the sequence of events almost robotically. Cara mused. Obviously not her first rodeo.

Milla's bikinis fit her perfectly, but Cara already knew they would. She exited the tent with a robe on and took in the goings-on ahead of her. Several crew men had waded out in thigh high water lugging cameras and what not on their shoulders, and one man was holding a paddle board in place.

Bob had a mega phone in hand. Once again Cara silently mused, a mega phone! So cool.

"All right, Cara, I'll need you to swim out so you're soaking wet when you paddle onto the beach. We'll be taking shots of the front of you and then from behind."

It only took about six or seven, attempts to get the angles Bob wanted. Next up was having Cara actually land on the beach, step off and start looking at the shells. And right there was the whole reason for that location and weather circumstances. The cameramen expertly filmed the crystal clear water under the paddle board showing sand ripples and shells. Shell Island was literally carpeted with millions of shells, something that would be hard to duplicate anywhere else.

Bob was meticulous and a bit of a perfectionist. Filming her walking down the beach, bending over to examine the shells, then cast them into the water took hours. He wanted every possible angle filmed, especially since later the editors would have to insert face shots of Milla.

They did take a break for lunch and Orion finally got a chance to talk to Cara privately. He could hardly contain himself. Seeing her in a wet bikini put a whole new spin on how he looked at her. It was now too hot to put on a robe; in fact most of the crew had stripped down to the barest minimum.

"Cara, this is amazing. I can't believe how they can simultaneously inhabit this island with a city of people and gear and yet keep the island looking so remote."

"Yeah, pretty amazing, but man, so tedious! How many freaking angles do they need of my feet digging into the sand?"

"Guess Bob wants to get it right. Word on the set is that the weather is going to turn sour tonight into tomorrow so they won't have another chance to re-film for quite some time."

"Word on the set? Oh come on!" Cara laughed.

Off in the distance dozens of small runabouts and a few larger boats were milling around with obvious curiosity. A handful were actually anchored. One of the crewmen's job was to guard the filming area in his runabout. About every

5 minutes one could hear "Please keep your distance, we are actively filming here" from his bull horn.

One of the larger boats was *Reel Relief.* Trenton had gone out into the Atlantic around 6:15, caught a few fish, stashed them into an enormous ice filled cooler and then returned to Shell Island. He had planned to anchor in the bay closer to the resort hoping to catch Cammie on the beach, but when he saw the landing crafts on Shell Island along with other runabouts, it was obvious that this would be her location for the day.

Through his powerful binoculars he saw Cammie emerge from a tent. Watching her take off her robe and swim out to the awaiting crew was almost more than he could handle. He owned that body. Patience, he said to himself, patience....

By about 4 P.M. in the afternoon Cara and the crew were visibly worn down. Sweat rolled off everyone and the collective morning pleasantness and enthusiasm had deteriorated to group crankiness. At first Bob was quite happy with Cara. She was so much easier to work with than Milla. She listened, did what he said and didn't argue. But that was before lunch. After lunch as the tedious filming continued and the temperature increased, Cara's true colors came out.

"Jesus Christ Bob, Cara lashed out, "all these shells look alike, why do you need eight million shots of them?"

Yup, Bob said to himself, I've turned Cara into Milla in more ways than one.

Bob looked over the filmed sequences in the editor's tent. The generators pumping electricity into the computers and monitors seemed to be louder than ever adding to everyone's irritation. "OK, he finally said. I think we're good here. Let's break it down and get back to the resort."

Eloise handed Cara yet another bottle of water which was problematic because that meant she'd have to use the porta-john once again. She hated the stench and longed for different anatomy so she could just pee behind a tree. "Guess it's a wrap Cara."

"Oh thank God!"

"Bob wants to have you and Orion over for dinner tonight, he's so appreciative that you literally saved the day."

"Can I take a rain check? I'm exhausted. I want to take a shower in my own shower and collapse on my own bed."

"I'm sure that can be arranged. He doesn't fly out to Savannah until Sunday.

Bob came over to Cara and Orion as they headed over to *Diamond Girl*. "Are you sure you can't join us tonight?"

"Thanks Bob, but no, I've had it. Perhaps tomorrow night?"

"Actually, that's fine, just fine. Let me have one of our tenders pick you up, say around 6 P.M.? That way you can really relax and not have to worry about driving back."

"Sounds good, Bob, and sorry I was such a bitch this afternoon, I'm…"

Bob quickly interrupted, "Say no more, Cara, it comes with the territory. You did a fantastic job, and I'm in your debt. I'm looking forward to seeing you and Orion tomorrow."

He kissed Cara on the cheek and shook Orion's hand. Then he turned back to the flurry of activity on the beach to help dismantle the entire set.

Through his binoculars Trent could see the obvious end of the filming operation. He followed Cammie and her companion as they stepped into their runabout. The angle of the sun obscured the boat's name. He assumed they would be headed back to the resort. He would have to make a move immediately since it was such a short distance over to the resort marina. But wait, where were they going? What's going on? They weren't headed back to the resort, looked like they were headed to Marsh Harbour. Even better. There was a ten-mile stretch of open water with no nearby boats. He sprang into action.

Orion pulled up the anchor, letting Cara just sit and decompress on the back deck. Most of the on-lookers had dispersed and only a few larger boats remained. Sometimes boats anchored off the island for the whole night when seas were calm. He didn't pay much attention to the sport fisher boat captain who was also pulling up his anchor. Once he went by the remaining boats he revved up the outboards.

Cara let the wind flow through her hair that was now impossibly knotted. She'd probably go through an entire bottle of conditioner just trying to untangle her hair. Well it's shorter now, that should help. It was nice having Orion drive the boat and after a few minutes the knots in her muscles started to relax. She thought back on her conversation with Richard about how he found most of his job to be boring. Tedium on the set he had said. I now know that varnishing isn't the most boring job on the planet, she mused.

Five miles out Cara heard a loud engine from behind her. She and Orion turned in unison as the engine noise grew in intensity. To their horror a large fishing boat was about to ram them. Cara screamed and Orion uselessly yelled out to the boat's captain. He had to take immediate evasive action, but as an inexperienced boater, he turned the boat too fast and too sharply. Between that dangerous combination and the enormous wake of the fishing boat, *Diamond Girl* was nearly capsized throwing Cara off the boat.

Cara surfaced after what seemed like minutes but in actuality was probably only a few seconds. She immediately yelled out for Orion. She assumed he had been thrown off the boat too. Where was he? She started to dive down to look for him around the flotsam from *Diamond Girl* which was now drifting away from her. Before she could yell out again the fishing boat circled around to her. A large man threw a life ring toward her. He yelled over. "Grab the ring!" She was so dazed she assumed this was yet another boater coming to rescue her, not the man who just tried to kill her. She swam to the ring and allowed the man to pull her into his boat.

"Cammie… Cammie? Wait, you're not Cammie!" Who the hell are you? Where's Cammie?"

Cara started to blurt out "Cammie? Who the hell is Cammie and who the hell are…?"

But she didn't get to finish. The man slapped her across the face sending her reeling across the back deck and into the fighting chair. Her head slammed against the arm rest and she fell to the sole of the boat.

CHAPTER 14

RICHARD GLADLY LET BRENDA attend to Milla. Maybe they could just take turns throwing up. He would appear from time to time to check up on her, making himself appear to be the ever doting boyfriend. The doctor confirmed at the follow-up phone call that it must be food poisoning from the clams. Brenda dutifully called the restaurant to complain about the clams. At the end of the day, after all the fuss, the chef was fired. Such a shame Richard thought to himself. My meal was excellent. For most of the day, however, his mind wandered over to thoughts of Cara. Something about her was attractive. Could she really pull off being a stunt double with no previous experience? Actually, he knew she could, she seemed capable of doing anything. On the surface he continued to be gallantly attentive to Milla, but on the inside he was lusting after Cara. Finally, at about the same time the film crew was filtering back to the resort compound, Milla stopped vomiting and was actually able to keep down water and saltine crackers. Even her mood improved a bit. There appeared to be light at the end of the Milla tunnel.

Between trips to the bathroom Milla did a bit of soul searching. At first she truly did want someone to put her out of her misery. Then the demons from her past started bubbling up from the tar pits. She went all the way back to her father, an alcoholic who essentially bankrupted her family and emotionally deserted her and her mother. Her parents divorced when she was about eight and her mother moved to Tennessee at the encouragement of her best friend Mary. Her mother never remarried, but she did have a string of "man" friends who soon tired of her heart being somewhere else. Then there was Mary's creepy son, Trenton. Only now did she feel a bit guilty for teasing him so much. Her first husband Sean crept up in her thoughts too. She loved him so much in high school and on into college, and then it all fell apart. The two of them were such great co-conspirators; their biggest crime being breaking away from their dates for the Senior Prom, she from Trent and he from Jayne. Neither one of them felt guilty for their crime at that time, but now the guilt was growing exponentially. Could vomiting up half your body weight make you want to seek redemption she wondered? A small segment of her didn't blame Trent for wanting to get back at her with frivolous law suits. And then her mind drifted to the theft of the jewelry.

The diamond set, yes that. Like most heirloom jewelry it wasn't the actual cost but the sentimental attachment that made it so valuable. Milla's grandmother was a social queen and proudly wore her diamond anniversary set at every possible appropriate occasion. It seemed to identify her. She was poor as shit growing up, only to be rescued by a physician who landed her in high society world. Lilian thrived there. Sadly, Lilian's mind turned to mush in her eighties after her husband passed away and her daughters reluctantly placed her in a nursing home. And once Lilian passed away the two sisters had the painful task of dividing up all her belongings, the nursing home having swept away what little finances she had left after six years in the home. They were civil for the most part until it came to the diamond set. One would have thought the diamonds were made of the glue that held the earth together. Finally, after a screaming match in which the sisters dredged up every detail of why they ultimately hated each other, they decided to "share" the set. In reality, neither one of them was in a social position in which there would ever be an occasion where the diamond set could be worn.

Aunt Linda took them first in the hopes of wearing them to a gala that never materialized. After a few years, at her mother Joanne's insistence on the pretense of an upcoming event, Linda returned them to her. Once Milla and her mother moved to Tennessee the diamonds were placed in a home safe only to collect dust for years. After that move the sisters drifted apart. There wasn't a falling out, per se, just a series of life events: distance, no extra cash or desire to travel that distance, occupations that occupied them, kids, husbands and man friends to attend to, and the underlying wedge of who should rightfully own the jewelry. When Milla returned home for her high school reunion, Joanne insisted she wear them even though it was a bit over the top to do so. Joanne just assumed Milla had put them back in the safe afterwards, as requested; in fact she had heard the click of the safe door, but instead, Milla had quietly placed them in her suitcase. She just figured she would be inheriting them anyway, disregarding her cousins altogether as possible heirs. Milla couldn't remember the last time she saw her cousins. It had to be all of 20 years or more. Hmmmm… what would her cousins look like now? That thought brought Milla back to the present and her anger that some stupid deck hand was being her stunt double. Could anger cure food poisoning? Seemed to be working.

"Brenda, I think I could handle some gingerale. Do we have any?"

"Actually, we do. Do you want to try something else to eat besides saltines? You must be starved."

"No, I'll stick with the crackers for now, thanks."

"Milla, you're off duty until Monday. You should try to at least sit out and soak up some sun. Do you want me to let Richard know you're feeling a bit better?"

"Yes… no, he said he'd be back in about an hour anyway, so let's just leave it at that. I should be back to myself by then."

And which self would that be, Brenda wondered to herself. Gentle, Kind Milla or Angry Bitch Milla?

CHAPTER 15

WHEN RICHARD WASN'T ATTENDING to Milla he was splitting his time between the gym and the pool bar. Keeping up his physique went from being a necessity to his vanity to job preservation. Basically his acting sucked; his looks and his muscles were what carried him through the scenes of Einar bludgeoning the other Vikings and having his way with the women. There were several scenes in which he merely grunted, no speaking talent needed. Perfect! He was going to carry on with this existence as long as he could.

On the pool bar front he was actively pursuing the waitress Delilah. Delectable Delilah. He knew it would be days before Milla would grant him permission to enter her nether area, and he simply couldn't wait that long. Besides, half the allure with Delilah was the conquest. Sometimes the lines between Einar and Richard were a bit fuzzy. Adding to the challenge, however, was how and where to score with Delilah without getting her fired. Fraternizing with guests called for immediate termination of employment. And the resort did not provide housing for their staff, so at the end of their shifts a fleet of ferries carried them across the Sea of Abaco to the main island. There they dispersed to the nearby slum like communities, well hidden from the many tourists. But there were no rules about him fraternizing with staff... so where could they go? Idiot, he almost said out loud. I'll just rent one of the small condominiums. Milla will find it perfectly believable that I want to set up a small office and gym room. In fact, she'll probably encourage it. She often lamented she needed her own "space."

Richard sauntered over to the housing office. Several beautiful homes were smartly displayed on the "Readily Available" board.

"Pardon me, ma'am, I'd like to talk to you about renting one of the smaller, furnished condominiums. Do you have anything available?"

"Oh my! Einar! I mean Richard... oh my!" gasped Helen. She couldn't believe she was actually talking to Richard Winthorpe. Lucky her. "Let me see, the new wing of condos on the ocean side were just completed and were to go onto the market next month.... but maybe we could move that date up a bit..."

"I only need the condo for a week, price isn't really an issue..." he trailed off looking at her with his most engaging eyes.

Helen blushed to the point that her cheeks matched her fuchsia blouse. In her head he had already stripped her and was making mad passionate love to her.

"Um, Miss...?"

"I'm sorry, it's Helen, Helen Summers." Helen was able to recompose and redress herself and resume the search for an available condo. "Actually, if you don't mind facing the Sea of Abaco, we have three right near the marina that are available. Would you like to take a look at them?"

"Can you just show me where they are on the resort map?"

"Certainly."

He didn't really care what they looked like, as long as there was a bit of a distance from Milla's. He chose the one farthest away and paid upfront for the one-week rental. He paid an extra fee to have some provisions brought in and to be able to move in later that evening.

For a day that literally started out in the toilet, things were nicely shaping up. "Love my life," he said smugly to himself. Next on the list, how to get Delilah into the bedroom and then off the island without raising suspicions.

CHAPTER 16

"SHIT-SHIT-SHIT," Trent exclaimed out loud. This was not in his plan. His plan was so simple: he would send a message to Cammie apologizing profusely about his behavior at the reunion, the law suit and the settlement request. He would let her know he was in the area and wouldn't she just love to join him on his boat for a day of fishing so he could make it up to her? Please, for their mothers? Please, for old time's sake? Of course she would say yes. And then once they were out in the ocean where depths readily exceeded a thousand feet, he would grab her, kiss her, fondle her and rape her. Then he would tie her up, slash her face and hands with his fillet knife, stab her in the heart, literally tear it out and push in a chunk of tuna. After chumming the water with other chunks of tuna he would throw her overboard. It gave him a hard on just thinking about the sharks finishing her off, tearing her apart bit by bit just as she had done to him for all those years. His plan was so flawed on so many levels, but in his mind, after he had replayed it dozens of times, it had become a seamless reality.

And now this. Did the driver survive? If so, he'd have to deal with him too. "Fuck!" he yelled out loud. It was getting on toward sunset. His routine was to be back at the dock before then. Not enough time to run out to the ocean and dump this girl overboard.

Think-think-think he demanded of himself. One thing he knew for sure was that he would need to contain this imposter. He zipped tied her wrists and ankles and placed duct tape over her mouth. She wasn't unconscious but in some sort of daze. When she came fully around, she was like a wild cat intent on freeing herself. She yelled as loudly as the duct tape would permit, but to no avail. Trent was immune to her pleading.

In the corner of his eye he noticed one of the inter-island ferries headed his way. No doubt heading back to Marsh Harbour. He didn't need a boat load of passengers to witness this wild woman struggling with him. He swept her up in his arms in a manner that looked very romantic from a distance and brought her into the main salon. Out of sight of the passing boat he gripped her neck in a choke hold. She stopped screaming and went limp. That's better, he thought to himself giving himself credit for subduing her. He threw her into the guest cabin and locked the door from the outside. He hesitated for a minute to make sure she was still lifeless. He grabbed a beer from the galley and returned to the helm. With the engine noise, wind and distance from the cabin to the tuna tower helm, there was no hint of her screams. He popped open his beer and headed back to his slip. Tomorrow was another day, easy enough to dispose of her then.

Chapter 17

It had been over an hour and Milla was beginning to wonder where Richard was. No doubt working on that body of his. He was known to get lost with himself—or so she thought—for hours just toning and re-toning his many magnificent muscles. She was feeling so much better that she ventured into the kitchen and made herself a peanut butter and jelly sandwich. So many forbidden calories, but then she figured she was down a bit in the weight department and she really didn't have any weight to lose.

Just then Richard came in. "Wow sweetheart, you look so much better! I trust you're feeling OK now?" He wrapped his arms around her and attempted a kiss. As predicted she gently pushed him away.

"I'm better, but not that kind of better. Sorry hon, give me a day or two, okay?" her voice transitioned into a saccharinely sweet high pitched squeak. He got the message.

"No problem, honey. As a matter of fact I figured you might need some recovery time. I've got a lot of calls to make and things to set up for the next season, so I just rented one of those small condos. There's just enough room for an office and some gym equipment. I really like my privacy for working out."

"There's not enough room here?" she queried but then, since she really liked the idea of him having his own place to retreat to but didn't want to admit it to him, she quickly countered with "Well, I guess you're right. Sometimes listening to you drop those weights does get a bit annoying."

"Oh sorry… that probably really is annoying. So okay then, you need a little more recovery time and I have some setting up to do. See you later?"

They kissed superficially on the cheeks and Richard was off, perhaps with a little too much spring in his feet.

CHAPTER 18

TRENT BACKED THE BOAT into his slip and noticed that the busybody lady on the boat next to him was standing on the dock with her dog. He could remember the dog's name, Jabber, short for Jabberwocky, but he never even attempted to remember her name. In fact he tried to avoid her as much as possible. He did not want to establish a relationship with anybody.

Unbeknownst to him Catherine was basically the mayor of the marina. She made it her business to greet all new boaters and extract as much information about their backgrounds as possible. Cara often wondered what she did with all that information. But she was so darn pleasant, most boaters gladly supplied her with all the information she wanted.

When he first arrived at the marina, Trent had to feed her a line of bullshit to cut his conversation with her as short as possible. He told her his brother was supposed to spend the week with him but had a work emergency. He was hoping "Patrick" would be able to join him by the end of the week.

Catherine stood pleasantly by. She used some gestures to indicate she would be happy to receive his docking lines. He hated that. He had a system and didn't need anyone to screw it up. But he mustered up a smile, came down from the tuna tower with his remote fob for controlling the engines and essentially docked the boat without her help.

"Hi, Trenton, how was your fishing outing? Get anything good?"

"Just a few mahi. I'll fillet them later."

"Well since you're still alone, I was wondering if you'd like to join us for cocktail hour."

"Oh thanks, ma'am, but I'm pretty tuckered out, I think I'll just stay in for the evening."

"Well, if you change your mind, we're just next door."

Catherine started to lead Jabber towards their boat as Trenton stepped onto the dock to adjust some of the lines. Jabber growled at him.

"Jabber! Stop that! Oh dear, sorry, Trenton, I'm so embarrassed," exclaimed Catherine. Trent simply glared back and returned to his boat.

So odd, Catherine thought to herself. Jabber never growls…

CHAPTER 19

Once Cara realized this mad man was intent on kill-ing her, she tried to enact an escape plan. She had read somewhere that in a hostage situation it was best not to let the kidnapper know how strong or determined you were to escape. Best to acquiesce and fool the opponent. Of course she fought tooth and nail not to be tied up, but once she was, she played possum.

She also stopped screaming. She knew her cries would be futile on a moving boat. No one would hear her. She thought it was best to rest up on the bunk and reserve her energy. This guest cabin had bunk beds and she had been thrown onto the lower bunk, at least he didn't throw her in the bilge. She had already hopped over to the door and turned around so her hands could grope for the door knob to try to open it. Nope, but she pretty much knew he would find a way to lock the door from the outside. Has he done this before? Why would there be a lock on the outside of the door?

The doorway to the head was locked as well. Terrific, I'll eventually have to pee my pants.

Oddly there were no ports for her to look out or use to attract attention. There was an overhead hatch, but the blackout curtain was pulled across. Didn't all cabins on luxury yachts have at least one port? Damn, it was going to get pretty dark in here soon.

She heard the pitch of the engines change and felt the boat slowing down. Then she could tell the boat was being put into reverse. Good. He's docking. As soon as the engines get turned off, I'll start screaming again. She had already tried to inch her wrists down around her butt and shimmy her legs through but to no avail. She returned to plan A. Scream as loud and long as possible. Someone has got to hear her.

Chapter 20

Richard found out who Delilah's immediate boss was and smooth talked him into allowing Delilah to be a waitress for him at his condo later that evening for a private party he was having. A few twenties in his palm when they shook hands helped seal the arrangement. The boss need not know that the party was a party of one.

Delilah readily accepted the extra employment opportunity. Didn't matter that she had already put in a ten-hour day. She cell phoned her boyfriend, Quentin, and told him to pick her up at the 10:30 ferry instead of the 8 p.m. ferry.

Delilah saw right through Richard's "private party for a few friends" ploy. Over the past six years or so she had been asked so many times to be a private waitress that she actually packed her ultra sexy French Maid's outfit in her overly large day bag. Her boyfriend had no problem with her extracurricular activities. Paid the rent.

The charade was played nicely. In ear shot of her boss, Richard told her to start setting up for his guests around 8 p.m. and he would be along shortly. He handed her the condo keys and disappeared.

There were essentially no personal affects in the condo.

A dozen miscellaneous bottles of booze were on the kitchen's small island and a few bags of snacks were on the counter-top near the refrigerator. She opened the refrigerator and saw some bottled water, soda, mixers, lemons, limes and bricks of cheese. Then she headed for the master bedroom where the actual party would take place. As with all the homes and condos in the resort, it was nicely appointed.

She made herself at home in the ensuite bathroom and started applying her make-up. As a day time waitress the dress code demanded minimal make up and a very conservative uniform. She gladly changed into her French Maid's outfit. She loved how her ample breasts were barely contained and how the thong under her mini skirt showed off her volup-tuous ass. It turned her on so much that she took the time to pleasure herself while waiting for Richard to arrive.

Lost in her reverie Delilah didn't hear the door open. Richard stood quietly for a moment to observe this most pleasant sight. She's a goddess, he thought to himself. He was quickly turned on by watching her trace her beautiful mound with her right index and middle fingers. He started to undress which caught her attention.

"Oh sorry, sir... she said as she sat up, I uh was just get-ting ready for your guests..."

"No worries, Delilah, the guests are all here. In fact why don't you just lie back down and keep doing what you were doing?"

As she laid back she watched Richard finish undressing. Even Delilah was impressed with his manhood. The thought of this month's rent and probably next month's rent being paid pleasured her even more.

CHAPTER 21

BEFORE TRENT TURNED OFF the engines, he turned on the television. He anticipated the captive would start her screaming again and he needed a sound buffer. Fortunately, the guest cabin was in the forward, starboard section of the boat and the slip on his starboard side was empty. Right on cue her muffled screaming started when he turned off the engines. He turned the TV's volume up even more and soon a continuous news feed was blasting through the main salon. Let her scream to exhaustion, he said to himself, she'll give up soon. He went up on deck and pulled some sunning mats over the hatch to her cabin. The more sight and sound protection the better.

Catherine had changed her mind about returning to her boat. Instead, she led Jabber down the dock. Surely Cara should be back by now. She was so curious as to why Milla Memphis had stopped by her boat. Cara never did get back to her on that.

Bahama Gem was dark. Not even one light on. The tender wasn't there, which was very odd. There were so little navigational lights out in the Sea of Abaco that most people avoided traveling at night. With the advent of chart plotters night time navigation was more possible, but overall, most boaters, except for the ferries, were at their docks by nightfall. Well maybe she and her new boss decided to stay late at Nippers or Grabbers, the local bars on Great Guana Cay. That would be nice. Catherine already had them married off with children on the way.

After Jabber finished his business, she returned to the dock. As she approached her slip she could hear Trenton's TV even though he had the doors shut. Good God, I can't listen to that all night. Bad enough that on weekends she had to listen to loud music from Sammy's, the restaurant next to the marina. But at least that was music, not never ending, over dramatized bad news. She'd have her husband Fred ask him to turn it down if he didn't do so by 10 p.m.

CHAPTER 22

DELECTABLE DELILAH TURNED OUT to be a magnificent lover. Richard was already looking forward to their next liaison.

"So I'm having another party Tuesday night. The boys really enjoyed you," he said looking down at his massive anatomy.... Can you be available?"

"Of course, sir, just work it out with the management."

"Call me Einar. Well, I better be going, can you let yourself out?"

"Certainly sir, no problem, Einar."

Richard took a quick rinse off shower, dressed in a hurry, combed his hair, and was out the door in a matter of minutes. Delilah lingered a bit. She had just enough time to clean herself, change back into her stiff uniform and be at the ferry dock by 10 P.M. She tucked her cell phone back into her bag.

"Perfect," she said out loud. Richard, in his egomaniac love making, in which he actually took time out to pose in front of the full length mirror, didn't notice she had snapped a few pictures of him with her cell phone. These might become very handy... she mused to herself.

CHAPTER 23

DIAMOND GIRL HAD STALLED in the near capsize and for hours was drifting slowly towards Minos Rock. Soon the boat would run aground. Orion came to, but he didn't know how long he had been unconscious. It was night, so a couple of hours for sure. His head felt ten times larger than it normally did. What had he hit? Didn't matter, he was now awake. Where am I? he pondered. He was definitely confused. Then his mind jerked back to reality. Where was Cara? "Cara!" he screamed over and over. "Shit!"

He fumbled around for a flashlight and found one in a small compartment. Searching the water around him he saw nothing other than waves lapping against the boat. I need help, he said to himself. He kept shouting for Cara as he located the VHF. He called out May Day but there was no response. In his panicked state he didn't notice the VHF had not been turned on. God damn it! OK, slow down, think.... He looked at the chart plotter and saw some coordinates. He fumbled around some more, found his cell phone and took a picture of the screen. OK, I know where I am and where Cara should be. Now why won't this stupid radio work? Fuck! Idiot! It's not even on! What the hell? He turned it on and reattempted the May Day call. Finally, a man named Dave responded and said he would call BASRA, the Bahamian equivalent of the Coast Guard, albeit a volunteer operation. The man heard the panic in Orion's voice and explained as gently as he could that it would probably be hours before there was a response from BASRA. Dave was actually at his seaside cottage. He often had his portable VHF on in the off chance one of his buddies wanted to call him. It was cheaper than having a land line. He offered to get in his boat and come out to assist him.

"Yes please! Actually, I need to go back toward Shell Island, that's where we were nearly rammed. She may still be floating there, what if I run over her looking for her, what if…?"

Dave, a retired police officer with EMT training, knew Orion was spiraling out of control with his panic. He kissed his wife goodbye. "Don't stay up, honey, this could be a long night." After he called the police, he got back to Orion on the VHF.

"Orion, this is Dave again, throw out your anchor, I'm going to raft up to you. It'll take me about 20 minutes to get to you. We'll look at the chart and figure out a plan. I've called the police as well. This sounds like a criminal matter."

Orion was happy to have Dave take charge. He was now in about 6 feet of water and could essentially walk to shore if he had to. As predicted, about 20 minutes later, Dave maneuvered his boat alongside *Diamond Girl* and threw over the docking lines. Once on board Orion provided more details and was starting to calm down. Dave mercifully kept it to himself that the chances of finding Cara alive after all these hours were slim to none.

And then, without warning, Orion fainted.

CHAPTER 24

MILLA GOT OFF THE PHONE with Jermaine. Even though she had cocaine and amphetamines, what she really wanted tonight was a joint. That would help her feel better, she convinced herself. Jermaine was happy to oblige.

About 30 minutes later Jermaine was at her door. "Where's Richard?"

"Oh he's off working out, making calls, the usual. He set himself up at one of the condos, supposedly to give me more privacy. Right. But he should be back soon. So how much do I owe you?"

Suppressing what he really wanted for payment he said, "Oh just the usual, price hasn't changed much lately. Do you think you'll be okay to travel on Tuesday?"

"Sure, I'm already feeling much better. So how did it go today?"

He wanted to say better than he could have imagined. Cara was so much easier to manage than Milla. She was in great shape and didn't complain at all about having to keep re-filming the swimming and paddle boarding scenes. It wasn't until the end of the afternoon that she fell apart. But so did everyone. What he said out loud was, "Well it was tough at first, but we managed. Now the challenge will be to edit in the face shots, do you think you'd be up for some close-ups tomorrow?"

"Tomorrow? Are you kidding? If you want me to fully recover, I'll need another day. So no. Absolutely not, I...."

Jermaine knew her well enough not to let her escalate. "Hey my bad, of course you need more time. Take the weekend. I'll catch up with you later." He quickly exited as if he were dodging a bullet.

Milla lit the joint and walked out to her verandah. She could see Richard heading her way. Good. His account of his "work out" for the night ought to be Academy Award winning.

Chapter 25

Cara needed a new plan. Between her muffled screams she could hear the loud TV. The mad man must have docked at the Boat Works Marina across from Marsh Harbour where most of the sport fishers docked. In a grouping of these boats it would not be unusual to have several TVs blaring. At her marina for sure one of the snow birds would complain. Shit… was it Friday night? At both marinas there was likely to be loud music playing from the local restaurants.

OK, I need a new plan… but in her exhaustion she fell asleep.

After a six pack of beer and a few slugs of whiskey, Trent had nodded off too. He was abruptly awakened by someone knocking on the side of his boat.

"What the hell?"

"Sorry, Trenton, it's Fred…. on the boat next to you?"

"Yeah, yeah… coming," he said as he walked to the doorway. "What's up?"

"I'm sorry to bother you, but your TV is so loud and it's after 10 p.m. Would you mind turning it down a bit?"

"Yeah sure, sorry." He didn't linger or make small talk. As he shut the door, Jabber started barking. Now who's being loud Trent thought to himself.

"Shush Jabber!" Fred pleaded, but Jabber kept at it. Fred led the dog away but not before Jabber got a few more barks out.

Just as Trenton turned the TV down ever so slightly, Cara woke up with a start. Jabber? Was that Jabber barking? Oh my God, the boat is next to *Dalliance?* Yes! Cara sprang up. She used her forehead to flip on the light switch and looked around for something she could make more noise with. She laid down on her back and put her feet up on the door. In unison with her screams she banged her feet against the door. In the distance she could hear Jabber resume his barking. Then Trenton was at the door.

"Shut it up! I've got a fillet knife in my hand and if you don't quiet down, I'll start hacking you up!"

What? Cara screamed in her head. Hack me up? What the hell was wrong with him and why her? Wait, was this that new guy on the dock who smoked cigars first thing in the morning? She stopped banging her feet against the door and lay still for awhile. Then she heard other voices.

Fred and Catherine were trying to understand why Jabber kept barking, and then they heard some very strange noises from *Reel Relief.* Catherine went back over with Fred and Jabber behind her.

Catherine called out to the closed door "Trenton, Trent? Are you okay? Did you hurt yourself? Can we help you?"

A few moments later Trent was at the doorway again but only opened it a sliver. As he was about to tell them to mind their own goddam business, Jabber literally nosed his way through the doors and ran forward.

"Jabber!" Catherine and Fred cried simultaneously.

"Jabber, come here! Oh dear, I'll go get him, so sorry!" continued Catherine.

"Stop right there! I'll get your goddam dog and then please, leave me alone!"

Trent ran after Jabber who by now was outside of Cara's cabin and was pawing at the door. As articulate as she could be with duct tape over her mouth, Cara called out "Jabber, help, Jabber, help!"

Catherine and Fred could hear that someone was behind the door Jabber was pawing at and looked rather surprised.

"What's going on?" Fred asked in a very demanding tone.

"Nothing! You're just hearing my other TV, now please take your dog and get out of here!"

Cara yelled out "help" in an SOS pattern of three short helps, three prolonged helps and then three short helps.

Catherine and Fred froze. Were they really hearing a distress call?

Fred spoke up: "Our dog doesn't normally growl or bark like that and that sound is not a TV!" Then Fred turned and yelled toward the cabin: "Person behind the door—do you need help?"

A muffled series of "yesses" were heard. As Fred approached the door Trenton raised his arm in an obvious move to slash Fred with his fillet knife. Wrong move in front of a protective dog.

Jabber leapt up and bit into Trenton's arm. "Jesus Christ! Call that dog off!" Trent screamed.

Catherine took the opportunity to get past Trent and reached for the cabin door. It only took her a few moments to unlock it.

And there was Cara.

CHAPTER 26

ORION CAME TO A FEW moments later with Dave standing over him calling out his name.

"Wow, don't know what happened."

"Here, drink some water, you're probably dehydrated."

Orion was happy to oblige. Then he asked, "So what's the plan?"

"I think we'll use your boat since it's faster than mine and your track is still evident on the chart plotter. We should be able to tell where it was that you were nearly hit. We'll tow mine so when we do get close to where Cara fell over, I can search in my boat too. Unfortunately, the police aren't going to be too helpful. Your description of a 'large white boat' fits about 90% of the boats down here. I'm still waiting for BASRA to get back to me. They have a boat with searchlights."

The two men worked together to get Dave's boat on a tow line behind *Diamond Girl*. Dave took over the helm and sped off toward Shell Island. The winds were picking up and the choppy seas added an element of unwelcome discomfort. The chart plotter showed a rather zig-zagged line at first, indicative of the drifting course, but eventually it returned to a straight line leading back to Shell Island. At that point, Dave stopped the boat.

"I'll circle to the south and east, you circle to the north and west," Dave shouted as he separated from *Diamond Girl.* The increased wind and waves made the search essentially futile. The flashlight's beam was no match against the intense darkness and the shouts out to Cara were quickly swallowed up by the howling wind. Orion's fears of running over her before seeing her were not unfounded, except of course if there was even a body to run over.

CHAPTER 27

RICHARD WAS SURPRISED TO FIND Milla out on the verandah. He figured she'd be in bed by now.

"How was your workout?"

"Great, just great, got a lot of lifting in."

"I'll bet," Milla said sarcastically.

Richard heard her tone of voice but ignored it. She'd probably been on to his many affairs for quite some time now.

"Hey got any more of that?" he asked pointing to the roach in the ashtray.

"No… but Jermaine can probably get more tomorrow," she responded icily.

"Okay, but in the meantime I'm going to make myself a drink. Want anything?"

"Yeah, how about you stop cheating on me? It's one thing to have your affairs on the set, but here? Really? You have to get your dick wet every night? It's embarrassing."

"I don't know what you're talking about," he lied. "I thought you were glad I'd be working out somewhere else. And you find all my phone calls boring, I was just thinking of you!"

"And when exactly were you thinking of me, in between blowjobs? You asshole. Why don't you just pack up the rest of your things and get back to your little love nest?"

"Milla, Milla sweetheart, calm down. You know I love you. Let's just settle it down for tonight. I think you're just over-whelmed with all that's been going on. Come on, baby, show me your smile." He looked at her with his "I'm-a-lost-pup-py-please-help-me-look."

Yup, Milla said to herself. Award winning.

113

CHAPTER 28

DELILAH COUNTED UP HER EARNINGS for the night. Not bad, and he wants me back on Tuesday. Wonderful! There were only a few other workers on the ferry, so she had the bench seat in the back all to herself. She looked at the pictures of Richard on her cell phone. The first two were pretty fuzzy, but the next three were clear and framed his manhood quite nicely. There was one she particularly enjoyed. He had griped his enormous erect cock at its base which accentuated the ample glistening inches left to spare. Now how best to use these? Blackmail? Sell them to a tabloid? Truly that one picture had the makings for a centerfold. Her name couldn't be associated with the pictures lest she be fired. But if the pictures made her enough money, maybe she wouldn't need her job.

Off in the distance she could see two faint lights seemingly going around in circles. Odd, she thought but then returned her mind to Tuesday. A few video clips would be good to add to her arsenal.

Chapter 29

Once Catherine and Frank saw Cara, they rushed to engulf her. Jabber released his bite and joined them. Trent didn't hesitate, in their frenzy to attend to Cara he slipped out the salon doors. With his knife tucked under his bleeding arm he rushed down the dock. He knew it would only be a matter of minutes before the police were called. He had to escape. A plan immediately popped into his brain. Those transport runabouts! He had noticed them earlier in the week, not so much because of their excessive horse power but that the keys were in the ignition. He hopped into the first one he came to, *Endeavor II*, turned on the engines, slipped off the docking lines and headed out into the harbor. Soon he was revving up with no concern for the anchored boats in the mooring field.

He knew the passage way out of the harbor by heart. His sole aim was to go right to Sea Star Resort, find Cammie, and stab her to death before the authorities caught up with him. Never mind that he had no idea where she actually lived in the Resort compound. And so what if he spent the last days of his life in prison. It would be satisfying.

At 45 mph the boat easily sliced through the building seas. With each descent off the crest of the waves, a wall of spray hit the hull and spilled over the bow. The wind carried the salt water in continual slaps against Trent's brow. Trent wiped his eyes to remove the layers of salt and didn't notice how close he was getting to the reef off the Fish Cays. He had been in such a hurry to leave he didn't have time to set a course and the boat didn't have auto pilot anyway. Each time he looked away to wipe off more of the salt water he inadvertently edged closer.

The three bladed, stainless steel props of the outboard engines were very powerful, but they were no match for the coral head just below the surface. In a matter of moments the sudden impact lurched Trent over the dashboard. His groin jammed into the control throttles and his head snapped down on the edge of the plexiglas windshield cutting his neck to near decapitation. The boat continued to pound against the waves and the coral jarring every part of him. Flashes of Cammie rushed through his brain as the blood poured out of his head. He lingered just long enough to feel intense pain and then his world went blank.

CHAPTER 30

CATHERINE GENTLY PULLED THE duct tape away from Cara's mouth. Fred cut the zip ties with his rigging knife and then called 911. Cara nearly collapsed in Catherine's arms. She could hardly talk.

Catherine calmed her and said "Just cry it out, Cara. There's plenty of time to sort this out, that man has left but I'm sure the police will apprehend him shortly."

"No, no, there isn't…" she finally blurted out between sobs. "Where's Orion. Did that mad man kill him?"

"Oh, dear, no I don't think he's on this boat," Catherine answered, realizing a bit too late that that was not received how she meant it.

"You think he threw Orion overboard?" Cara shrieked. "We've got to find him!"

Fred finished up with his phone call to the police. An agent would be down as soon as possible to take her story and begin the search for Trent. Hearing the tale end of what Cara had just said, he realized that more to the point, the search should focus on Orion. With the winds howling at this point and the darkness of the night, everything seemed bleak.

Rather than have Cara explain the circumstances twice, they waited for the authorities to arrive. Two officers walked down the dock; they had already been alerted to the theft of the Sea Star Resort runabout *Endeavor ll*. A third officer was attending to that problem along with fielding a phone call from someone named Dave.

Catherine and Fred had relocated Cara to their boat. She had been given water and was suddenly ravenous. Catherine encouraged her to eat. Finally the officers stepped on board.

"Start from the beginning," the taller of two officers said to Cara. She started from the point of leaving Shell Island. Could that really have only been seven hours ago? Seems like days ago now. In her rendition she vacillated from rational to hysterical. Catherine did her best to keep Cara on track. The officers showed little emotion which oddly made things worse.

Meanwhile the dock was abuzz with the theft of the *Endeavor ll,* the capture and rescue of Cara and now the search for Orion. Fred and fellow boaters were organizing a search with their various tenders, and crew from Sea Star were already headed out on *Endeavor l.*

One of the officers approached Fred and asked "Sir, did you just say you're looking for a man in a tender named *Diamond Girl?*"

"Yes, yes I did.... do you..."

The officer cut him off and informed Fred they had received a call from a Mr. David Hartwell detailing a boating accident with a missing woman. It didn't take long to connect the dots to realize Orion was alive and looking for Cara.

Fred thanked his fellow boaters but gladly informed them a search party wouldn't be needed. The police officer was in the process of calling Mr. Hartwell while Fred hurried back to *Dalliance* to give Cara the good news.

Jasper greeted Fred in his usual manner of a head nuzzle. He had been sleeping at Cara's feet.

"Cara, Cara! Orion is on *Diamond Girl* looking for you! The police are contacting him, it shouldn't be long before he's back on the dock!"

Cara almost collapsed with the good news. "Oh thank God!" she exclaimed as she leapt up and hugged Fred.

Catherine joined the hug and said, "Let's get you back to your boat to freshen you up a bit. We'll stay with you until Orion gets back. Come on, Jabber, up we go."

Chapter 31

DAVE WAS TRYING TO FIGURE out a way to propose to Orion that the search be stopped for the night. It was useless to continue, especially with the building wind and seas. He knew, however, if it was his wife out there he would never give up. Not being emotionally attached to Cara made him able to react logically and not from the heart.

Between trying to maneuver his boat in the howling seas and being lost in his thoughts, Dave didn't hear his cell phone going off at first. It was on the fourth ring that he finally felt the vibration and heard the faint jingle of his cell phone ring.

"Hello, Dave Hartwell here."

"Mr. Hartwell, are you still with Mr. Matthews?"

"He is in his boat still looking for Cara, but I can call him on my VHF. Do you have news?"

"Yes, sir, we have Miss Cara here in Marsh Harbour. Can you please relay that message to Mr. Matthews?"

"Absolutely, as fast as I possibly can."

Saved by the bell Dave thought as he ended the call.

Dave and Orion had left their radios on channel 17 so they wouldn't have to go through the normal formalities of hailing, answering and then switching frequencies. He simply picked up the microphone and blurted out "Orion! Cara is safe!! She's back at the marina!"

Dave could barely make out what Orion said in reply. Suffice it to say it was some sort of jubilation.

"It's too rough to tow my boat Orion. You just follow me, I'll lead you back to the marina." Dave phoned his wife. She suggested Dave leave the boat at the marina, she would happily pick him up in their car.

Chapter 32

Cara took a shower. It took a while to work off all the residual glue from the duct tape. Her lips were sore from working against the tape in her many shouting attempts. Her throat was sore from being parched and also from the screaming. The zip ties had cut into her wrists and ankles, but not enough to warrant bandaids. The hot water felt good as she washed away the salt and grime. She nearly emptied the bottle of conditioner to work through all the knots in her hair. She felt as if she were washing away the madness from that mad man. She learned his name was Trent, or Trenton. Trenton Smithson.

Half of her wanted to put on a sexy dress for greeting Orion and the other half of her wanted to put on fuzzy flannel pajamas and go to bed. Thoughts of seeing Orion alive again won out, but she settled for a tank top and shorts.

Mabel and Jake were now visiting with Catherine and Fred. Their conversation abruptly ended when she entered the salon.

"Oh, Cara! What an ordeal for you! Any idea why Trent wanted you dead?" Mabel asked.

"No, that's such a mystery. I mean I kind of glared at him once when he was smoking his cigar so early in the morning... but I don't think that's a capital offense."

"He was so short with me," Catherine piped in. "He made it rather clear he just wanted to be by himself. I bet his brother just made up that excuse that he had a work emergency."

"Well, *Endeavor II* is a pretty high profile boat. I don't think it'll be too long before they find him. Maybe then we'll get some answers," Jake offered.

The trip back to the marina seemed like an eternity. With the wave height and direction Dave and Orion had to plod along. Finally the harbor lights came in to view. They slowly meandered around the anchored boats and tied their boats up in *Diamond Girl's* slip. Orion practically ran into *Bahama Gem* not waiting for Dave to catch up to him.

Orion burst into the salon; he looked terrible. Didn't matter. Cara ran up to him, hugged and kissed him.

"You're okay!" They both said simultaneously and laughed out loud as a result.

Cara's two sets of adopted parents exchanged pleasantries and then politely excused themselves. They ran into Dave as they exited. Dave introduced himself and offered an abbreviated account of his role for the past few hours. Fred appreciatively invited him over to *Dalliance* where he could wait for his wife and have a drink.

CHAPTER 33

SATURDAY PROVED TO BE an unsettled day in terms of weather. Rain clouds abounded and short lived squalls dotted the morning. Milla awakened to find Richard next to her. They had argued some more late last night but in the end Milla caved in. Oh what the hell, she said to herself. If it's not Richard cheating on me, it'll be someone else. She held no hope of ever finding a monogamous lover. Hadn't happened yet and probably never would. And besides, she wasn't completely innocent in the monogamy department. At least Richard had several good ingredients: rich, famous and good looking. And not too bad in the bedroom department either.

Brenda called and asked her how she was feeling.

"Much better thanks. I think I can even handle a small breakfast."

"That's great. Say, Bob is hosting Cara and Orion for dinner. He wanted to know if you'd like to join them?"

"Who? Orion? What are you talking about?"

"Orion is Cara's companion. Don't know if they're romantically linked or not. She introduced him as her assistant." Brenda laughed.

"Why would I want to join them? Pisses me off that Cara filled in for me. And who names their kid Orion?"

"Don't know… I'll tell Bob you're still under the weather. But if you change your mind, I don't think it would be a problem. They'll be eating at the Blue Paradise Restaurant as usual."

A sleepy Richard rolled over, "Who was that?"

"Just Brenda. Bob wanted us to join him for dinner with Cara and her assistant Orion."

"Assistant? That's funny. So, let's go. Could be pretty entertaining."

"What? No! I'm so not interested!"

"Aw come on! I heard she worked hard. She definitely saved the day. At least you can thank her."

"Hmmm… well, all right. Let me call Brenda back."

CHAPTER 34

CARA WOKE UP IN THE COMFORT of Orion's arms. Felt good. And it wasn't an awkward scene after all. After the parents left, Cara and Orion broke down in a cascade of tears of relief. Cara suggested he take a shower and she would fix him something to eat. He emerged from the shower looking so refreshed. A new man. He had three bites of the sandwich, looked up, took her hand and led her to the stateroom. His grandparents' stateroom. It was no longer off limits.

Love making came surprisingly easy.

Cara looked out the port. Lousy day outside, beautiful day inside. Orion soon awoke and looked proudly over at Cara.

"Good morning, gorgeous. How is it that I feel like we've known each other for years, not just two days."

"Well, each day has been about a decade long. Wonder what today will bring?"

"Hopefully nothing… let's just stay in bed all day."

After another few hours in which more love making occurred, Cara stepped out of bed. No more thoughts of milk toast; hearty rye came to mind. It was nearly 11 A.M. She had heard her phone go off a few times and now she felt compelled to see who was trying to reach her.

"Wow! Lots of missed calls and a bunch of texts."

The first text was from Catherine. "Good news, they found Trent, call me when you get up."

Two calls were from the Police Department stating they had some information for her and to please call back. Two were from Bob Packard's secretary. The first one was very cheerful about picking her and Orion up at 6 P.M., then a second distressed one stating Bob was so sorry, he had just learned of her ordeal. He would totally understand if she wanted to cancel the dinner.

Then a funny text from her sister Dana who, of course, had no idea what had transpired from the night before and the last one from Mabel also wanting to tell her about Trent.

"OK, popular girl," she said out loud. She made some coffee for herself and Orion and popped a bagel into the toaster oven. "Let's get the police calls out of the way first."

The police officer informed her that *Endeavor ll* had been found severely damaged on a reef near Fish Cays. Basically it had broken up in the crash and the man on board was presumed dead. Again for their records was there any reason at all that this Trenton Smithson wanted to kill her? A review of his background found no criminal history. He had a fishing boat charter company in Fort Myers but was originally from Pine Ridge, Tennessee. Anything? Anything come to mind?

"Pine Ridge, Tennessee?"

"Yes, ma'am."

For some reason that sounded familiar. She had never been to Tennessee but she had an aunt and a cousin there.... Did they live in Pine Ridge?

"Sorry officer, I'm coming up empty. But if I think of anything, I'll get back to you."

She answered his other follow-up questions and assured him neither she nor Orion needed any medical follow-up. "We're fine, just fine now, thank you."

Next up Dana. Rather than text she called her. What time was it? Would Dana be at home or work? Didn't matter, she was always crazy busy.

Dana actually answered the phone. "Hey what's up, Sis? Haven't heard from you in awhile…"

"I have so much to tell you, you're just not going to believe what's gone on for the past two days… in fact can you just fly down here?"

"Oh yeah, no problem. Roger will take care of the kids and my boss won't mind a bit. Seriously, Cara?"

"I know, I know… it would just be so much nicer to tell you all this over a bottle of wine. Actually… I will be flying up to New York City next Friday. I'll rent a car and come visit."

"Wow! that would be great!" The sisters mulled over some details for Cara's visit and then Cara gave her a brief overview of what had happened to her.

"So the mad man is dead? Cara this sounds like a movie! How awful for you!"

The magnitude of Trenton's death was just sinking in, somehow she had managed to gloss over that information earlier, but now it was becoming reality.

"Say, Dana, he was originally from Pine Ridge, Tennessee. Does that town name sound familiar? Where did Aunt Joanne and Cammie actually live when they moved to Tennessee?"

"Jeez, Cara, I haven't thought about Cammie in years, can't even remember that last time we saw them... but yes, that sounds familiar. Do you want me to call Mom and ask her?"

"Yeah would you? I don't want to get involved with telling her all this stuff just yet. I will though. Let me know via text and tell her I'll be in touch later today or tomorrow. Love you!"

"Love you too!"

Cara was handing Orion his coffee when she noticed Dana's text. Yup, Aunt Joanne and Cammie moved to Pine Ridge some 20 years ago. Cammie.... weird that Trent had called out for a Cammie. Couldn't be... Cammie her cousin? Did they even look alike? Cara put those thoughts back into the "couldn't be" category and moved on with her day.

Orion was pulling Cara back to bed, but Cara's mind was too busy with figuring things out.

"There'll be more of that, don't worry." Cara responded tenderly. "I really should answer the other calls."

"Other calls?"

"Yeah... oh... you should know that the mad man Trenton was found. The boat he stole was all broken up on a reef and he's presumed dead."

"Dead? Wow! Dead? Well that's exactly what that bastard deserved. Sicko bastard. I was terrified and distraught but that must pale in comparison to the horror you went through."

"Yeah, it was probably the worst thing I've ever gone through." She was silent for a few moments, then "You know... we're still invited to have dinner with Bob Packard. I think Milla and Richard are going to be there too. Maybe we should go. Could be a nice distraction for us."

Cara called Bob Packard's number and the same polite female answered the phone. Cara couldn't remember her name so she just skipped over to having the secretary tell Bob they were still on for the evening. Cara was relieved to hear that *Adventure 1* would be picking them up. That boat was totally enclosed, no salt water to splash on them and ruin her outfit. And she was pretty sure Orion had had his fill of salt water too.

Chapter 35

Mabel and Catherine could hardly contain themselves. The dock folk were still abuzz with the police investigation and now the reporter, Madeline Aubrey, was on the dock. There was only a weekly newspaper on the island, and this was most definitely a newsworthy event. The lovely Ms. Aubrey wanted to report the story with a picture of Cara, Orion, Catherine, Fred and, of course, the real hero, Jabber. Later she would interview Dave Hartwell.

Instead of calling Catherine, Cara walked over to her boat shortly after noon. She wanted to thank Catherine, Fred and Jabber again for rescuing her. She recognized Madeline Aubrey on the back deck of *Dalliance*.

"Here's Cara now," Catherine gleamed.

Jabber greeted her in his usual manner. Cara then turned her attention to the waiting crowd as Mabel and Jake also appeared on the boat.

"Cara, Madeline would like to do a story on the events and take some pictures. Is that okay?"

Cara didn't hesitate. "Of course… do you want me to get Orion?"

"Yes, please," stated Madeline.

"Jabber, why don't you come with me? I'd like you to meet someone."

Jabber bounded up the gang plank and readily went over to a surprised Orion. "So this is our hero, great dog! Shall we serve him steak for the rest of his days?"

"Sounds like a plan." Cara explained what was going on and Orion readily followed her to the *Dalliance*. The sport fisher next door actually had yellow "Do Not Enter—Police Investigation in Progress" tape across the salon doors and a lone officer was still trying to gather information from the inside of the boat.

Madeline was pleasant and efficient. She took her notes and pictures and wrapped up the intake in about 45 minutes. At that point Cara and Orion were starved for more substantial food. They opted to eat on board. They were soon tired of being in the limelight and answering the same questions over and over again. Eating in privacy was their best bet.

Catherine talked her into just a few more photos for Jabber's Facebook page. Facebook page? Oh yes, of course, Cara quickly remembered Catherine had set that up. Cara obliged. After all, she was in Jabber's debt.

Chapter 36

News traveled fast in the islands. It wasn't long before Jermaine called Milla with the news of Cara's abduction and rescue.

"Are you serious? And the guy who abducted her is dead?"

"Yeah, some guy named Trent something."

Milla blanched and nearly dropped the phone.

"Milla… Milla? You still there?"

"Yes," she whispered, "Jermaine, can you get me more information? Find out his last name."

"Sure thing, Milla."

Richard looked at Milla quizzically. "What was that all about?"

"Cara… Cara… she uh… she was abducted last night. She's okay now and the guy… the guy who captured her stole one of Sea Star's boats and ran it up on a reef. Seemed he was headed this way. He's… he's dead." She started to cry… could it really have been Trent from her past? The look on that fisherman's face back at Harbourside Marina was still haunting her. Had to be.

Richard held her in his arms dumbfounded that she would be so upset. Of course anyone would be upset with this news, but her reaction seemed to encompass something more. Maybe she didn't hate Cara after all.

A short while later Jermaine called back, and this time Richard answered the phone.

"OK Jermaine, thanks, I'll tell her." He hung up and turned to Milla. "The only extra information he could find out was that the guy had a fishing charter business in Fort Myers and his last name was Smithson."

With that Milla collapsed into his arms and sobbed louder than Richard thought was humanly possible.

CHAPTER 37

HEY, MOM, IT'S CARA."
"Oh Cara, I'm so relieved to hear from you. Dana filled me in a bit, but tell me everything."

Cara rattled off a now almost robotic version of her ordeal following the day on the set. She then segued in to the topic of Aunt Joanne and cousin Cammie.

"This whole thing about Trenton Smithson being from Pine Ridge, Tennessee and lusting after some woman named Cammie and taking me hostage is just weird. Do you think it's just a coincidence? And whatever happened to Aunt Joanne and Cousin Cammie?" Cara knew it was a sore subject but she had to ask.

"Well, dear, it's complicated. Joanne and I, well, we just drifted apart once she moved and we just got busy with our own little lives. I found out after the fact that Cammie got married. She didn't even have the courtesy of inviting us to the wedding." Her mother's voice was now showing hurt and anger bundled up together. "She said she didn't bother letting us know because she knew I couldn't afford to attend, much less buy her a present. Screw her! I definitely would have gone to the wedding." Her mother sighed and then continued.

"So it turns out her marriage to Sean Memphis didn't last long anyway. Last I knew she went on to some sort of acting career. Sadly, honey, I haven't talked to Joanne in almost ten years. We don't even exchange Christmas cards anymore and when we did there was only a signature, no newsy note."

"Wait a minute Mom," Cara burst in. "Did you say Sean Memphis as in Cammie's last name would be Memphis?"

"Well it was then. Who knows if she went back to Addison or not or if she got married again and took on a new name.... I just don't know."

"Mom, have you ever heard of the actress Milla Memphis?"

"Can't say I have, but that doesn't mean much. You know I can't keep actors and actresses straight."

"She was the lead in *Calypso Girl* and in *The Long Walk Home*."

"Oh yes, I know who you're talking about now..."

"Well she's filming a new movie, that's who I was the stunt double for.... do you see where I'm going with this? Maybe Cammie, Camilla Jane Addison, dropped the Jane when she got married and took on the nick name of Milla. Milla Memphis!"

It took a moment for her mother to process the information and then respond. "But Milla Memphis is a blond and Cammie was brunette."

"Really Mom? Hello—hair dye? Not exactly a new concept," Cara responded with a bit too much sarcasm. "Sorry, Mom, I didn't mean to be rude."

"No, no, that's OK. Stupid comment... It's just this whole schism between Joanne and I, well, it keeps me up at night… it's so stupid and it has gone on too long. Neither one of us sucking it up and apologizing…."

"Apologizing for what?" Cara interrupted.

"Apologizing for being terrible sisters, for not keeping connected, for keeping you girls apart, for the god damn diamonds, for not……"

"Wait, wait, wait!" Cara interrupted again. "What diamonds?"

"Huh? um… Grandma Lilly's diamond set. There was a necklace, a bracelet and earrings…. we let a silly set of diamonds tear us apart… although we were headed that way anyway…."

"Where are they now?"

"I had them shipped back to Joanne and basically I never heard from her again."

"Well, Mom, I think she gave them to Cammie, I mean Milla."

"What makes you say that?"

"I saw them…"

CHAPTER 38

RICHARD, STILL TRYING TO BE a good sport and make sense of Milla's over reaction, gently led her to the couch and sat her down.

"Milla, Trent was the bad guy... why are you so upset he died?"

Between sobs she exclaimed, "It's all my fault... I was so mean to him.... he probably thought Cara was me.... Oh my God, Oh my God... Can I go to jail for this?"

Richard finally lost his patience. "Milla, snap out of it... you're not on a set. Just tell me what you're talking about!"

Milla was startled, but she composed herself and then explained. "There was this kid in my school, Trent. Trenton Smithson...

"You went to school with him?"

"Yes, anyway I hated him. Everyone did. It wasn't just that he stuttered; it was everything about him... I can't explain it... But anyway his mother and my mother were best friends... so one year they talked me into going to the Senior Prom with him. But I was in love with my ex Sean. Sean's mother had forced him to invite this very unpopular girl... Jayne... plain Jayne. We came up with this plan to make our moms happy, go to the prom with our creepy dates and then dump them for the after parties."

"Of course, the after parties, where the real fun is…."

"Trent never forgave me, but he kept pursuing me, almost stalking me… actually he was stalking me…. leading right up to that stupid incident at the high school reunion…"

"The guy who's suing you? That guy?"

"Yes, that guy…. and now he's dead…. do you think he was coming after me?"

"Could be… but now we'll never know. I think you need to put this behind you…"

"How can I? Once my mother and Trent's mother learn of his death they'll be sure to put it all together. It's amazing my mother hasn't called me yet… Oh God, what if there's a funeral?… Will I have to go to it?"

And in the cosmic connection between some mothers and their daughters, right on cue the caller ID stated "Mom."

Chapter 39

"W^ELL THAT WAS A LONG conversation, you look worn out." Orion remarked.

"I am, Orion. This whole thing is just too weird.... I think Milla is my first cousin."

"What? What are you talking about? Why wouldn't you just know that?"

"It's a long story…"

"I think I've got all day."

"First let me call Bob Packard's secretary. Milla and I can't have our reunion be in such a public place… Actually I need to meet with her right away… by now she's put this all together too. I knew I knew her from the past, and I knew those diamonds looked familiar…"

Orion waited patiently for her to call the secretary and arrange an earlier pick up time. She had a call put through to Milla's assistant to alert Milla. She would meet her at her villa, hopefully sometime around 4 p.m.

Then he listened intently to Cara explain the whole cousin connection, or was it a disconnection?

Chapter 40

Milla took the phone and went into her bedroom, shutting the door behind her.

Thank you God, Richard said to himself... this girl is getting to be way too much drama.

He started to pour himself a drink when Brenda knocked at the door.

"Oh God, Richard, what a string of events... poor Cara and Orion, how awful for them... but turns out Cara has made quite a discovery and needs to meet with Milla this afternoon. She's being picked up by *Adventure I* and they, Cara and Orion, will be here around 4."

"I don't know, Brenda... she's pretty upset at finding out the identity of the dead guy..."

"Why? He was evil..."

"Oh man Brenda, it's so complicated but it turns out this Trent guy was someone she teased in school, seems he was out to get her."

Brenda gasped. "What! That's crazy... but yet it's now making sense why he went after Cara... Turns out Cara and Milla are cousins!"

"Holy shit! Does Milla know that?"

"No, I don't think so anyway, but, that's why Cara is insisting they meet before dinner."

In the background Richard and Brenda could hear bits and pieces of Milla's conversation along with sobs, apologies and expletives.

Brenda looked up at Richard. "Who is she talking to?"

"Her mother... they have this weird thing going... Milla doesn't talk about her mother very often, but when she does, her mother calls. Anyway, my guess is that you or Cara won't be the ones to inform her of her relationship. She's probably getting an earful from her mother right now."

Milla emerged from the bedroom about ten minutes later. She looked ashen but then turned her attention to Brenda.

"Brenda!" she barked, "Get a message out to Cara, get her over here right now!"

"Already taken care of, Milla, already taken care of..."

Brenda left, leaving Richard to fill in the blanks.

"Cara is my cousin! Now it all makes sense! I knew I knew her."

"Well, sweetie, showtime is 4 P.M. You better start getting yourself ready."

Chapter 41

Bob Packard could hardly believe all the details of the past 24 hours. "Truth is stranger than fiction," he said out loud to no one in particular. Thoughts of a movie script flashed through his mind.

He made it his business to greet Cara and Orion at the dock and to accompany them to Milla's home. He had already arranged to have Richard then join him and Orion at the Pool Bar so Milla and Cara could meet privately.

Cara looked stunning. Her V-necked sundress showed a tasteful hint of cleavage and the teal color complimented her brown eyes. Wow, she cleans up nicely Bob thought to himself. He greeted her with a hug and expressed how sorry he was about her ordeal. He also hugged Orion and essentially said the same to him.

"Should be quite a reunion, Cara… perhaps a silver lining in all of this?"

"I guess… I'm so overwhelmed… I really don't know what to expect."

"I'd love to help you out, dear… but I think you've seen that Milla can be a bit… well, a bit dramatic sometimes…"

"Don't I know…"

They rode the rest of the way in the golf cart in silence. Richard was on the front porch. He shook Orion's hand and then swept Cara up in his arms. Jesus, why does he have to be so tall Orion thought to himself.

"Cara, I can't believe what you've gone through! Are you okay?" Cara simply nodded yes as he continued. "Look, I know this may be a difficult confrontation but the best way to play Milla is to let her lead… her tirades can be tedious, but then she calms down and she can actually be quite reasonable…"

"Thanks, Richard, appreciate that." Somehow Richard went from some guy she'd like to have sex with to an older brother she'd like to call from time to time for advice.

Cara knocked lightly on the door and then let herself in. Bob, Orion and Richard headed to the bar, happy not to be part of any more drama.

Milla was sitting on a barstool at the kitchen's peninsula. She looked up at Cara, and they blurted out in almost identical statements of how much they actually did look like each other. Cara's hair style matched Milla's, thanks to Felicia, their heights were nearly identical and their jawlines were eerily similar. Milla's eyes were as deep brown as Cara's. And it didn't hurt that Milla's yellow sundress had the same neck line as Cara's, showing off a similar chest area.

"Wasn't there some silly old TV show about identical cousins?" Cara asked.

"Oh yeah… now I'll be singing that stupid theme song!"

They hummed a few lines and had a good laugh. A big hug and a few tears followed.

"This is crazy! So I'm assuming you got an earful from your mother?" Cara quizzed.

"Oh yeah. Same from yours?"

"Yup."

Milla then asked "How's Dana? I don't even remember what she looks like."

"There's a sibling resemblance, but she's much cuter in a pixie like manner. And somehow she continues to be this annoying younger sister who always does the right thing: finish college, marry well, have three kids, work full time, blah blah blah. But I absolutely love her. You would too. She keeps me sane."

"I'm glad, glad to know someone out there leads a normal life."

There was an awkward pause and then Cara noticed the two bowls, the diamond set and two pairs of scissors on the kitchen peninsula. "So what's up with the infamous diamonds?"

Milla looked at Cara with an aura of relief and then a look of purpose. She handed her one of the scissors.

"Here, cousin Cara.... start cutting up these strands of diamonds. We're sending half to my mother and half to yours. No more stupid gems to keep them or us apart."

"Let's do it, Cammie, let's do it."

EPILOGUE

DELILAH UNLOCKED THE DOOR to her new home and walked into a sunlit foyer. An exquisite arrangement of bougainvillea, roses and bird of paradise adorned the dining room table. There was a short note adjacent to the vase:

Dear Delilah,

Trust you will find these accommodations and your monthly salary more than satisfactory.

Best regards,
Einar

The
Georgian
Affair

Waiting on a Part
DIANE E. GRABO

DISCLAIMER

This book is a work of fiction. Although the lakes, rivers, canals, islands, towns and cities are real locations, they are used in a fictional manner. The organization of the America's Great Loop Cruisers' Association is a real association but it is also used in a fictional manner. The characters and businesses are products of the author's imagination. Any resemblance to actual people or businesses is completely coincidental.

ACKNOWLEDGEMENTS

The nautical references in this story evolved over a lifetime of boating with Bob Grabo, first as a childhood friend on family owned sailboats, and then eventually as my husband on a trawler. Together, we embarked upon an incredible journey: completing the "Great Loop" in December, 2017. Along the way we encountered numerous boating challenges, some of which have been fictionalized in this novella. We met so many good people in our journey, it renewed my faith in humankind and also fueled my desire to write nautically based fiction. Too many to list, I'd like to at least acknowledge the crews (and canine companions) of *C'est le Bon, Vahevala, Mother Ocean, Easy Waters, Eleanor, Observer, II@Sea, Barefoot Shoes, Hush A Bye, Happy Ours, Pharm Life,* and *Happy Heart,* for providing me with inspiration. Thank you also to the many friends and family members who encouraged me to write. A big thank you to my cousin, Jean Zachos, for painstakingly proof reading the text, and to my cousin, Anne Stott, for helping me with the logistics of page set-up. Special thanks to the St. Lawrence Six (you know who you are!), for their input into the more intimate portions of the story. After all, the story is about an affair. And thanks to Andy Wight for fixing our boat many times over, and providing endless, entertaining conversation while doing so.

BACKGROUND COVER PHOTO: Screen shot of a course plotter, taken by Diane E. Grabo
COVER DESIGN: S. M. Savoy

Written in 2018. Revised in 2019.

To Alison: I know you went through painful times. You deserve more.

Prologue
July

THE PERSON LOOKED AT THE LID in a quizzical manner. "That's odd, seems thicker than it needs to be. Is there something in there?" With that, the person reached for a small screwdriver.

CHAPTER 1
Five months earlier...

MARSHA PADDLED TOWARD THE BEACH. It was a glorious day, full of sunshine above her, crystal clear water below her, and behind her, the sailboat she had chartered for the week. Two sleeping girls occupied the forward cabin. Marsha loved getting out on the paddle board early in the morning before the winds came up. She promised herself that today was going to be the day. This day she was not going to think about George or her ruined life. She was going to stay positive, no more crying, move forward, get on with it. She tried to come up with a few more platitudes, but lost her balance and fell off the board.

"God damn it!" she exclaimed out loud. She recovered the paddle, threw it up on the board and, after a few attempts, shimmied herself back up on the board. Actually, that rinse off felt good, she convinced herself.

As she neared the edge of the beach, she began to notice the untouched sand two feet below her which was soon dotted with sea stars. Off to her left a turtle darted by. So cool! The tip of the board ran up on the beach with an extra shove from her paddle. She stepped off and was treated to a shoreline carpeted with tiny shells. The girls are going to love this beach! She pulled the board up on to the beach and decided to walk around a bit before returning to the sailboat.

She reached down to examine a purple and white striped shell that looked like someone had coated it with polyurethane. So glossy, she smiled. "You're so pretty," she said out loud. Then the same phrase in George's voice passed through her brain. It was one of the first things he had said to her when they first met.

"Damn you, George!" she yelled as she threw the shell into the water. "Was I just a shell to you? A pretty thing you could just toss away?" Marsha looked around, hoping no one else was on the beach listening to her rant. No one. Okay, good, now get a grip, deep breath, count to ten, let it out…. Marsha went through her growing list of things to say or do when her divorce from George got to be all consuming. At the insistence of her girlfriends, siblings, co-workers and daughters, for that matter, she had hired a Wellness Coach, Savannah Martin. Apparently, she had worn out her friends and family members with her despondency.

What a godsend Savannah had been. She was brilliant, focused and organized. And, she had a wonderful way of being nurturing and strict at the same time. She had allowed Marsha to vent her frustrations, but only to a point; then she would step in with action plans. Savannah had outlined the eight areas of wellness to her in alphabetical order: emotional, environmental, financial, intellectual, occupational, physical, social and spiritual. Marsha reveled in this type of listing. The eight areas became a mantra to her. They had picked apart where Marsha was at within each area, prioritized the areas most in need of mending, and batted about ways to repair them.

The sunlight felt so good on Marsha's face. She dug her toes into the warm sand and decided to continue walking all the way around the island to get in some much needed exercise. As she walked, her thoughts went immediately back to her mantra, starting with emotions. She felt her emotions were still in the toilet. She really thought this distraction of chartering a sailboat in the Bahamas would keep George at bay and ebb the flow of tears. She could hear Savannah countering with: "At least give yourself credit for doing something so far out of your comfort zone. How many women do you know who can essentially go solo on a boat?" Well maybe she should give herself some credit, but it would be nice to get through at least one day without crying.

Marsha picked up a few shells and examined them while moving on to the other areas. Let's see, my environment. Well, this place is pretty good! Palm trees were rapidly becoming her favorite tree. But she truly loved her home in Altamont, New York, a bedroom community for the state capitol. Her kids, now in middle school, had walked to elementary school along with oodles of friends. She loved the sidewalks, the small shops, the library, really everything. But Savannah was quick to point out how much Marsha was actually tormented by the daily reminders of George in the house, from pictures on the wall to all the improvements he had made throughout the house. Their outdoor fire pit was particularly painful… so many wonderful nights spent around it with the kids and family and friends… Shit, okay, that was in the toilet too. She and Savannah actually talked about relocating to a new home. But she wouldn't move out of her cute little town, which she affectionately referred to as her *Mayberry*.

Her finances were not really an issue, and she loved her job, so those two areas were rarely discussed. Both she and George were medical professionals. George was a general surgeon at St. James Hospital, a Level 1 Trauma Center. She worked part time as an anesthetist in the local surgicenter. Ideal really, but eventually college tuition times two would be an issue. The girls were only 11 months apart, Irish twins, so a big cash cow would soon be needed. And now that George had a new baby to support... well that was his problem. If she herself ever needed more money, she could simply work full time. Her boss would be thrilled.

Intellectually, she felt good too. No need or desire for further education other than keeping up with her continuing education units to maintain her license. She belonged to a book club she loved, which was theoretically intellectually stimulating, although, of course, after a quick round of book review discussion, the topic always turned to how to survive your teenaged kids. But for someone as smart and perceptive as she was, why didn't she see the multiple signs of affairs? She later learned from her co-workers that George was the Don Juan of the operating room. Why was she the last one to find out? His particular favorites were the new nursing students. Of course they were his favorites. He wowed them with his grand knowledge of all things medical and wooed them right into the call room when working his 24-hour shift. Christ! She had been one of them! His affairs might have gone on forever had he not gotten the latest student, Gina, pregnant. Marsha wondered how long it would be before he wandered away from her. Three more diaper changes? Action plan? Shoot George in the balls. Okay, okay, not an action plan, she acquiesced through mental telepathy to Savannah. Maybe try to be wiser and more observant if she ever dated again.

Physically she was literally in good shape, although at 140 pounds and five foot eight, she was a bit on the thin side. She cycled through the various area gyms and the exercise routines du jour. Currently, she was into yoga. And it didn't hurt that she inherited terrific metabolism genes. Both parents were tall and lanky. At 75, her parents were physically active in their hobbies of skiing, hiking and boating. Her father still played on a local retired men's hockey team, and her mother walked three miles a day.

Marsha paused again along a part of the island that had a massive amount of drift wood piled up right to the edge of the shore. The entire root structures of trees from long ago made circumventing the beach area a bit tricky. Finally, she walked out a bit into the shallows and swam a portion of the way, parallel to the shoreline.

The quagmire of branches eventually receded and another stretch of pristine beach awaited her. Back on land, she continued her mantra. Socially she had a close relationship with her parents, sister, brother and two cousins. She had lots of friends, mainly from work, a few from high school, and some from college. But things were becoming awkward among friends who were couples, especially at work. Sooner or later the couples would assign allegiance to either George or her. She could tell a few couples had already drifted away from her. This realignment of friends bothered her greatly. Savannah's suggestion to make new friends seemed all too trite.

A large conch, partially buried in the sand, caught her eye. She picked it up and marveled at the swirls of brilliant pink in the inner folds of the shell. She momentarily thought about keeping it, but then remembered the strict Bahamian laws about taking conch shells out of the country. She set it back down and just enjoyed its beauty, which brought her to the final area of spirituality. This was usually a no go zone for Marsha. She was raised Protestant and struggled with her parents' desire for her to keep going to church, especially after the kids were born. George basically put his foot down on that, however. "Why do we need a formal religion? Can't we just embrace the wonders of the world and be good people? Do we really need to go to church for that message?" He could rattle on and on about that topic and actually Marsha agreed with him. However, his definition of "be good people" didn't quite match up to his indiscretions. Marsha felt her anger welling up. She took a deep breath and threw another shell out into the waters.

"Well, all right, enough of that," she said out loud to the sandy beach. To herself she acknowledged it was time to get back to the boat and see if the girls were up.

Chapter 2

The girls were up. In fact they were already in their bathing suits.

"What do you want for breakfast?" Marsha asked.

"Just toast," from Kimmy.

"Me, too," echoed Lindsay.

"Well, that's pretty simple. By the way, I can't wait for you girls to go to the beach. You won't believe how many shells there are. We'll take the dinghy over after breakfast."

It was day five of a seven day charter. When they first arrived, it rained all day and into the next. Not a great start to the vacation. They provisioned the boat and stayed dockside for the first night. Their initial disappointment was redeemed by engaging in conversation with other well-traveled boaters who offered much advice as where to go for the week. Fortunately, on day two the rain subsided and they ventured out. They only traveled into a bay a short distance from the dock since more rain was forecast. On day three they were able to sail over to Hope Town and pick up a mooring in the inner harbor. The girls adored the quaint houses and loved climbing up the famous Elbow Cay Lighthouse. The view from the top was spectacular. On day four they sailed over to an uninhabited island off Great Guana Cay. It was a bit too windy to take the dinghy ashore, but day five looked very promising. And so here they were, day five, a picture perfect day. Later they would sail over to Treasure Cay and then day six, late in the afternoon they would return the boat to its dock, in time for an early departure on Day seven.

Lindsay, the 13-year-old, asked her mother how she was doing today.

Marsha refrained from telling her she wanted to slit her wrists, and said with a smile, "Better. Really better. It was a wonderful paddle over to the beach, I even saw a turtle."

"You did?" piped up Kimmy, the 12-year-old. "I want to see a turtle!"

"You will, you will, don't worry."

The girls did love the beach. They collected a ton of shells and did in fact see turtles when heading back to the boat. Treasure Cay was even more fun for them with the sugary soft white sand, a steady roll of surf crashing along the beach, and other kids on the beach their ages to hang out with. On their final night at Treasure Cay the girls were invited over to another chartered boat to play cards with three siblings they had met earlier. Marsha politely visited with their parents but could feel the awkwardness of being a singleton creeping through the pleasantries of the conversation. Too many "we" references between the parents irked her, and eventually she feigned a slight headache and returned to her boat. The kids stayed to finish their card game. Back on the boat, Marsha checked her email. There was a message from George.

Would this be the email she longed for? The one in which George told her this was all a bad mistake, that he missed her horribly and wanted her back. He was sorry for putting her through hell, he must have lost his mind, would she please come back to him? He'd find a way to make it up to her, and they would live happily ever after.

The last time she actually spoke to George was when he came home that dreadful night almost a year and a half ago now and announced with as little compassion as possible that their relationship was over. Over? He stated he had felt empty for quite some time, and she just didn't have anything to offer him. He simply didn't love her anymore; there was nothing left. Nothing? Nothing? Was he just the world's best actor? Was he just pretending to have a good time with her? Building their careers, building a family, going on adventuresome vacations, socializing with their many friends, nothing? She even thought their sex life was wonderful. What about that? Nope, nothing. Of course he neglected to state at the time that his current girl on the side, Gina, was pregnant. It was almost too comical that Gina's full name was Georgina.

Since then they communicated through their lawyers and then eventually email. When they exchanged children for their every other weekends and vacation weeks with him, they both stayed in their respective cars.

There was no subject matter in the email notification so she really didn't know what to expect. Marsha took a deep breath and pressed the open button.

One lousy question: I know it's not my weekend with the girls, but could they babysit for Joey on Sunday?

Bastard! Did he not remember they were in the Bahamas? Technically, they would be home late Saturday night, but did he have such little regard for his girls to think they would be up for babysitting right after their trip was over?

Damn, probably they would be. Despite everything, once Joey was born, they immediately forgave their father for abandoning her and them. Over the years they often pleaded with their parents for a little brother and then, voila, wish granted. Didn't seem to matter that Marsha wasn't the mother.

Marsha picked apart the one-question email. "I" was of course the lead off, no apology, no "hope you had a nice vacation," no "proud of you for taking out a sailboat without a man on board." In fact, no mention of "you" at all. Marsha wasn't in the equation. Probably never had been.

And that was it in a nutshell. She simply wasn't in his equation. He had moved on. She was just a convenient source of babysitters.

She responded with one word: "No." Let him beg for an explanation; let him beg for her to reconsider.

Chapter 3

A FEW WEEKS LATER, WHEN Marsha was back at home and prepping for dinner, she called her mother. Marsha had had a lively session with Savannah earlier that day, and was excited to tell her parents about her newest idea.

"Hey Mom, do you remember telling me about that Loop thing?" Marsha asked.

"Loop thing? Oh, you mean the Great Loop?"

"Yeah, basically taking a boat in a great circle through some of the Great Lakes, down the rivers in the middle of America, out to the Gulf of Mexico, and then back up the Atlantic coast?"

"Yes, of course, Dad has always wanted to do that."

"Well now I do too. I met some "Loopers" on our charter and the idea of it has me quite intrigued."

"Really? That's great. I know you really enjoyed your sailing vacation. By the way honey, once again, I'm so proud of you for doing that. What did George think about that?"

"Mom, forget about George. I could save the world from Armageddon and he wouldn't give it or me a passing thought. All I am to him now, is a source of babysitters."

"Sorry, hon… but how would you do it? What about your job? What about school for the girls?… You don't even own a boat…"

"Mom! Stop with the roadblocks," Marsha snapped, using terminology directly from Savannah.

"Sorry, sorry… so I'm all ears…"

"So most "Loopers" are part of this group, the AGLCA, which stands for America's Great Loop Cruisers' Association."

"Yes, I recall that…"

Marsha quickly interrupted with, "It's crazy how many different ways people have done the Loop. Some by kayaks and canoes and one guy by a jet ski!"

"Really? Seems a bit extreme…"

"Well, of course, most people go by boats in the 30 to 40 foot range, usually trawlers. But some people have 50 foot luxury motor yachts, and then there are sailboats too."

Marsha took a breath and continued, "What I found the most interesting was that there's no time frame to cross your wake."

"Cross your wake?" questioned her mother.

"Oh, sorry. That means you get back to your starting point, and figuratively you meet the wake you created when you started out. So anyway, some people cross their wake in six months, but most finish up in a year. Some people do it over and over again, and some people do it in segments taking years, if ever, to complete. And, some people home school their kids. Those families even have their own sub-group forum to discuss all the challenges of raising children on boats. Wouldn't it be so cool for the kids to experience the United States and Canada on a boat? It would be like living

165

history and geography all at once. Think of all the things they could learn!"

Her mother thought of a million more roadblocks but kept her mouth shut. It was wonderful to hear her daughter so excited about something. She couldn't even imagine her granddaughters leaving all their friends… but for now, she'd leave that alone.

"Of course dear, so what do the girls think about all of this?"

"Um… well, I haven't told them yet… this is just in the larva stage… just wanted to run it by you and Dad. One of my thoughts is to have you and Dad join us on and off along the way. Is Dad home?"

"No. He just went out to the hardware store. He'll be home soon. But that's an interesting idea. I'll have him call you."

Okay, thanks mom, I'll talk to you later."

Marsha had first run the idea by Savannah. As soon as Savannah was made aware of key phrases associated with doing the Loop such as "it's a journey, not a destination," and "it's not so much the places you travel to, but the people you meet along the way" she was literally "on board" with the idea. A journey with a purpose and new people to meet. Perfect! Finally, a better suggestion than just "make new friends."

It didn't take long for Marsha to become obsessed with the idea. She loved boating, having spent most of her summers aboard the family sailboat on the St. Lawrence River. Although her parents were still physically active, the ongoing repair and maintenance of their boat had become too much for them and so, by mutual agreement, her brother Craig, who lived in Chicago, took over the 38 foot ketch. He kept it in a marina just north of his home. Marsha and her sister Heather weren't in a position to take over the boat at the time, and they were happy that the boat would stay in the family. Besides, they all had open invitations to come sail on Lake Michigan whenever they could.

Marsha joined ALGLA and read the group's forum on her email every day before heading out to work. It was an interesting forum, usually filled with incredibly practical information with only occasional snarky responses to some of the questions. Some of the threads got tedious or simply didn't apply to her, but she could quickly skim over those topics not of interest to her. Overall, she was amazed with how each one of her questions was answered immediately with several points of view regardless of the topic. One couple, Ben and Lindy, in response to her question "Has anyone done the Loop in segments over their summer vacations?" stated yes, they did. They were school teachers in California and were completing year three of the Loop. They started in Kentucky and went as far as Pensacola, Florida for their first year. The next year they went to Key West. Then the third summer they headed north, and were putting their boat up in a marina, just outside of Charleston.

In reviewing the practicalities with Savannah, Marsha agreed that her best bet was to do the Loop in segments. Just broaching the subject of being home schooled with the girls was met with immediate resistance. Marsha didn't push it. The finances and getting time off from work would have been too tricky and, besides, she really wasn't cut out to be their teacher. The other plus of doing it during the summer was that various family members and friends, especially those with school aged children, could join them from time to time. It would be a logistical puzzle getting people from here to there, especially when you had to work around weather and boat breakdowns, but it could be done.

At the conclusion of their next session, Savannah proposed to Marsha that their sessions be reduced to once a month. All Marsha talked about was the logistics of buying a boat, getting more boating education, and a million other details for actually beginning the voyage. Savannah had to practically yell at her. "Marsha! Do you realize you haven't mentioned George in the past three sessions? I think you've achieved your goal! You've found a way to move on with your life! George is now behind you!"

"Wow! You're right. It's like I don't even care anymore... how did that happen?"

Savannah wanted to say "How about hours and hours of me listening to you complain?" but said out loud, "You've found a new direction in your life, you found wellness in just about all of the major components we've been working on. The ironic thing about my job is that the ultimate goal is to get you in a place where you don't need me. I really think we've achieved that."

"Thank you, Savannah, I really don't know how I would have come out of my funk without you. But even though I'm in a better place, I still need you for a sounding board. So... monthly visits?"

"Sure, Marsha, that's good... we... can do that," Savannah replied.

CHAPTER 4

OVER THE COURSE OF THE next few months Marsha and her father traipsed across Long Island Sound and New England following up on leads for possible boats. She loved how the search had rejuvenated her Dad. Retirement had been less than exciting for him, and it seemed that he still had quite a bit of adventure left in him. She was amazed that he actually recommended going over to the "dark side" and consider a power boat instead of a sail boat. That was like changing religions. He was quick to point out that the reason he had never done the Loop was that most of it involved not having a mast. It just made more sense to him to have a low profile motor yacht—one that could get under the many fixed bridges along the way. She had never considered buying a "stink pot," but he did make a good point.

Finally, after looking at over 20 boats in person and hundreds on line, they settled on a used 43 foot Marine Trader. It was in pretty good shape for its age of 30 years. The previous one-time-only-owner had passed away suddenly, and his widow was anxious to sell it. The boat was located in Milford, Connecticut. To her horror, it was named *Sea Mistress*. Somewhere in her brain she was convinced it was bad luck to change the name of a boat. She was soon persuaded to give up that notion. Once the papers were signed and ownership passed to her, with the help of her parents loaning her some money, she started the quest of renaming the boat. "*Fuck You George*" was the first name she thought of. Not a Coast Guard approved name. She then moved on to *Reboot, Restart, Resolve, Start Over, Second Wind, Get Over Yourself....* *Carpe Diem, Wanderlust, Wonder Lost, Wander Away....* It drove her crazy...

"Kimmy, Lindsay... what do you thing would be a good name?

"*Boldly Go*" said Lindsay.

"What?"

"You know, in the Star Trek series, to 'boldly go' where no one has ever gone before? *Boldly go!*"

"Lindsay, I love it. Good, that's settled!"

Next up was bringing the boat to Shady Harbor Marina just south of Albany, New York. The widow, feeling very nostalgic, asked to be involved. It represented a form of closure for her. Marsha's parents gladly volunteered to help with the process. In a matter of minutes the widow, Susan McGovern, bonded immediately with her mother, Doreen. It was as if they had gone to college together and had been roommates for four years. Her father Jon, loved being at the helm. Between Susan's and her father's guidance Marsha learned to maneuver the boat in and out of docking slips. The landings weren't always pretty, but departures went pretty smoothly. The use of retrofitted bow and stern thrusters helped in the learning process. Going by the Statue of Liberty was an incredible thrill. Marsha had initially thought that Albany would be her beginning and end point of the Loop, but technically she would go by the Statue on her return trip. It was decided with a glass of champagne that the Statue was much more of a landmark and thus, this is where she would officially "cross her wake." Two long days later, a very friendly marina owner greeted the foursome at Shady Harbor Marina.

It was now May 10th, and the Erie Canal System was set to open on May 20th. Spring flooding had set the original date back a few weeks. Marsha didn't mind. It gave her more time to plan out the routes and get the boat properly provisioned. Some of the electronics needed upgrading, and the interior needed a new look in terms of decor. Lindsay and Kimmy were happy to help in the latter.

It took an incredible amount of organization to line up all the segments and crew for the next three months. Her boss agreed to give her a three month sabbatical as long as she agreed to work full time come September. If all went well, she would put the boat up for the season at the same marina as her brother's. Although no one in boating world would ever use the word "guarantee," it looked feasible to travel from Albany to Chicago by Labor Day. The girls would join their mother for the initial weekends to advance the boat through the canal system. Then once school was finished for the year they would join her in the Trent Severn Canal System in Canada. Thank goodness for friends and family willing to travel with her and to transport the girls back and forth. Then, after the obligatory two weeks with their father, the girls would rejoin her somewhere in Georgian Bay. At no point would she travel solo. She had no desire to do so. There seemed to be only two weeks in early August that she'd stay put in a marina awaiting the next shift in crew. Not a problem, no doubt something would need fixing by then anyway.

She got as far as Rome, New York, at about 6 o'clock in the evening, a little over a hundred miles from Albany, before the port engine starting acting up. She was able to limp it along until she reached Oswego. There she found a good mechanic, who determined she needed a new raw water pump. After installation and waiting out a weather window to cross Lake Ontario, she was back in business.

Her sister Heather, and brother-in-law, Michael, crossed the lake with her. Funny, the sisters mused, we used to hate no wind days on the sailboat, now even a ripple seemed inconvenient. Fortunately, for most of the 50 mile crossing the winds were light and variable. Checking into Canadian customs proved uneventful. Turned out they worried unnecessarily about what foods would be considered unacceptable. In Trenton, they were met by their parents and the girls. It was a pretty crowded night with her parents in the main stateroom, Heather and Michael squished on the dinette, the girls in the forward bunk bed cabin and Marsha on the settee in the main salon. Good ole times, thought Marsha to herself. Heather and Michael drove their parents' car back to their home the next day. In two weeks her friends, Donna and Mitchell, would meet them somewhere on the eastern coast of Lake Huron.

The Trent Severn, a unique waterway through the province of Ontario consisted of over 40 locks, two of which were lift locks, and one was actually a marine railroad that carried boats up and over a rocky barrier. All five crew members of the *Boldly Go* were in awe of the beauty surrounding them, the challenge of getting through some of the locks, the narrow passageways and the camaraderie of the boaters, especially the "Loopers." For the final 10 locks Marsha had grouped up with four other boats doing the Loop. All four couples were retirees, but one couple had their grandsons on board. God send! The typical bickering between sisters came down to a minimum with the girls vying for the attention of the brothers. After passing through the last lock, tears were quietly shed when the four boats went in different directions. There was hope the girls would see the boys again, as they all would eventually travel through Georgian Bay, the North Channel and into Lake Michigan.

Finding a meeting point for Donna and Mitchell turned out to be a bit tricky. Convenient ports were farther apart, and the weather was unpredictable. Jon and Doreen graciously offered to drive Donna and Mitchell's car from Midland, Ontario to a marina in the Byng Inlet. They would stay in a nearby bed and breakfast while awaiting the *Boldly Go*'s arrival in approximately five days. There Marsha would stay put for two weeks before the girls could return again.

Back in Oswego the mechanic predicted Marsha would need to replace the exhaust elbows for both engines. It was a big job and one that would necessitate having parts made. Fortunately, the mechanic knew of a marine supply company that could custom make them, but they would take three to four weeks to manufacture. Donna and Mitchell had been mailed the parts and had them in hand when they joined the *Boldly Go*. Marsha had called ahead to the marina in the Byng Inlet to arrange to have them installed while she waited for the next crew.

"You're in luck, ma'am," Gerry, the marina owner had stated. "We just happen to have a fantastic mechanic here for the next two weeks or so. He should be able to install the elbows in an afternoon. Here's his name and number and you can contact him directly."

George Wainwright. "Jesus Christ!" Marsha muttered out loud. Then to herself: George in Georgian Bay. Way too many Georges. Why does his name have to be George?

CHAPTER 5

IT WAS A BIT OF A LET DOWN when her parents, daughters and friends left. The go-go-go of the past weeks had been so much fun. Everyday a new place to go, a new place to explore, new people to meet. Being dock bound was too quiet and too boring. She spent the better part of the second day in the laundry room. All sheets, towels and personal items were overdue for a washing. One of the only things Marsha was not looking forward to on this trip was having to do her laundry in public places. However, after just a few trips to the various marina laundry rooms along the way, she now welcomed them. Without fail she would meet an interesting boater and glean from him or her vast amounts of local knowledge. Today was no different as she sat chatting with her new friend, Terri.

"Oh yeah, you absolutely must check out the ice cream store up the road, hand-made and the best I've ever had."

"Thanks, Terri. And was that your husband playing the guitar last night?"

"Yes, it's his passion, actually our passion. We have so many song books, you should join us tonight."

"Really?"

"Yes and, of course, your husband is welcome too."

"No husband… just me."

Now it was Terri's turn for "Really? You're traveling alone?"

"Well yes and no. I'm not married any more and so far my knight in shining armor hasn't shown up. So I travel with my family, my daughters and my friends. They all had to depart earlier yesterday, so I'm staying put for two weeks until my cousin and husband return with my girls."

"Two weeks… here? Sorry to tell you, but other than the ice cream store, there really isn't much to do."

"Well I've got some engine work that needs to be done, a ton of books that I haven't even opened, and you know… I live on a boat, there's always something I should be fixing or painting."

"True, true… well, do join us for dinner, we'd love your company."

"Thanks, that'll be great actually."

Marsha had called the mechanic who had an unexpected lovely English accent. He was finishing up one job and could fit her in tomorrow before he started on another.

Later Marsha did join Terri and Henry for dinner. It didn't take much encouragement for Henry to break out his guitar after dessert. Marsha actually had a fairly decent singing voice, and the three of them enjoyed a medley of Gordon Lightfoot, Simon and Garfunkel, Jimmy Buffet, among others, and a few folk songs new to her.

The next day, as promised, there was a quiet tap on her companion way door. "Hello? Permission to come aboard?"

"Yes, yes, of course." Marsha was pleasantly surprised to see that this mechanic was rather good looking and seemed to be only about five years older than her. He was about five foot ten and rather lean. He did have some gray in his short cropped brown hair, but his muscular shoulders and arms nicely showing through his too tight tee shirt were quite attractive. His cut off cammos were a bit scruffy, but maybe he needed all those pockets to house his tools. To date, most of the mechanics she had met were gnarly older men with quirky personalities. His personality was yet to be discovered, but he certainly wasn't gnarly.

"Well, let's take a look at the parts…"

Marsha handed the elbows over to him, and he looked at them as if he was eyeing a piece of art.

"These are beautiful… just like you."

Well, that comment was unexpected: not sure if it was a compliment or not to be compared to a stainless steel engine part. But now, almost two years celibate, she decided it was quite welcome.

"Uh… thank you?"

"Oh sorry, miss, couldn't help myself. Apologies to your husband, he around by the way? I'd like to talk to him about the repair."

"No and no. I don't have a husband."

"Boyfriend then?"

"Nope, just me."

"Have to say that's a bit unusual… but good on you driving this boat all by yourself. Don't see many women doing that solo."

"Tell me about it… you don't mind me watching you put in the parts, do you? I'm really trying to learn these engines."

"Don't mind you watching but if you try to help, that'll cost you double."

She couldn't tell if he was kidding or not until he looked up with a smile in his eyes. "Well, let's get to it then, don't got all day."

Replacing the port side elbow took about 20 minutes with minimal swearing. The starboard side was a different story all together. One of the retaining bolts was so corroded he needed to grind it out. At one point it looked like it was there to stay. Several swear words later he went back to the project with abandon and, after cutting his knuckles, nearly throwing the tools across the engine room, the bolt finally came out. "Jesus! About time!" he shouted. "Sorry miss, forgot you were there."

"No apologies needed, reminded me of watching some of the orthopedic surgeons."

"You're a doctor?"

"An anesthetist, almost a doctor but not quite."

"So... an anesthetist" which he pronounced as "a-neese-the-tist." "Can't say I've ever met an anesthetist."

"Not surprised, Canada doesn't recognize our profession, only anesthesiologists. Same goes for Britain."

"And the Bahamas where I live."

"You're from the Bahamas? What are you doing way up here?"

"Well, I'm a bit from all over, but, most lately, for like 12 years, I've been living in the Abacos. Marsh Harbour to be exact. Sort of a long story, but the owner of that boat over there," he said pointing to a 52 foot Hinckley, "flew me up last week."

"OK, go on, I like long stories, especially ones about the Abacos. I was just there about six months ago."

"Vacation?"

"Yes, I charted a Beneteau at Harbourside Marina with my two daughters."

"Oh yes, Harbourside, know it well... I've fixed a lot of boats there."

"Really? Small world! I found the boaters there to be really friendly. Gave me lots of good advice. But how weird, do you suppose we were on the dock at the same time?"

"I think if I'd seen you on the dock and knew you were single, I would have asked you out for a date."

"Stop it!" Marsha blushed and didn't know where to go with the conversation.

After an awkward pause, George asked, "Two daughters, huh? I have a son in the Bahamas and well... another in Germany."

"A girl in every port?"

"You could say that." George said with a glint in his eye.

"So go on, tell me about the boat next door."

"OK, so the owner, Dennis, nice guy, his wife too, although she's a bit forgetful, they had their boat in the Bahamas last January, Harbourside Marina to be exact. Did a lot of work for them. Gave them my card and Dennis said that if he ever ran into a big job, and didn't have a good mechanic available, he'd fly me to wherever he was. Took a bit of doing to get from the Bahamas to Toronto to here, but here I am."

"What kind of problem does the boat have?"

"Transmission. The whole bloody transmission needed to be replaced. Took days. Now I just have some minor problems to finish up. I fly back next week. Thought I'd take a few days off to check out this wilderness before heading back. Let's start up these boys and see how they run."

"Boys? Aren't all boats "she"?"

"Not in my world…"

"Interesting." Marsha started the engines, and George checked for exhaust leaks. Satisfied that there were none, he signaled her to stop the engines.

"So are you done for the day?"

"I could be…"

"Want a beer, maybe some lunch?"

"Never said no to that…"

CHAPTER 6

MARSHA TYPICALLY DIDN'T DRINK before 5:00. Once in a while she'd have a beer if she went out to lunch. So after three beers she started to giggle and challenge George on some of the things he said. He seemed to be weaving fact and fiction so tightly together the resulting fabric was a colorful mix.

"George, you are so full of bullshit!" she said teasingly after he told her about his escapades in Europe.

"You don't believe me? You've hurt my feelings! Now you're going to have to make it up to me..."

"And how do you propose I do that?" Marsha asked with a bit too much flirtation.

"Oh boy... perhaps, Miss Marsha, we should call it a day... I don't usually solicit my bosses."

Marsha was a bit deflated and little embarrassed. Her cheeks flushed and she turned away.

"Hey, hey there... how about we go out to dinner tomorrow? You won't be my boss then. There's really no restaurants nearby, closest one is about an hour away... pick you up around 6:00?"

"Sounds good... see you then." She handed him the agreed upon cash for the job, and he went on his way.

Marsha went down to her state room, sat on the edge of the bed and then let herself flop down. Wow! she said to herself. What was that all about? Am I really that desperate, coming on to the mechanic? She fell asleep in about three minutes.

An hour later she woke up with a start. Did I just take a nap? Pass out? Man, I'm not a good drinker. Her embarrassment quickly turned to excitement, however, when she fully processed she actually had a date for tomorrow night. A date! First one in about 17 years.

She and ex-George met when she was in nurse anesthesia school and he was a resident. Both had to take call at least once, if not twice, a week. He was so full of himself, but at the same time he had so much charisma. She just melted in his arms. It wasn't long before they plotted to be on call at the same time. Trying to keep their little liaison secret didn't last long, and soon they just openly dated one another. Marriage followed a few years later. She was 27, he was 32. Both of them wanted children, no issue there, and they both wanted to have two children as close in age as possible. Lindsay was born when she was 29 and Kimmy when she was 30. A life-long goal—two kids by the age of 30. When Kimmy was three Marsha went back to work twice a week. Then, when the girls were both in elementary school, she upped that to three days a week. It was a perfect life. A nice blend of being a professional and yet home in time to receive the kids from the school bus and have two days a week to do errands and laundry. George's schedule was all over the place since he had to take call once a week. "Had to" translated to "wanted to," so he could get in his weekly nursing student fix. What an idiot not to have been on to him sooner, she admonished herself. Now look at me, coming on to mechanics! And once again she ransacked her brain for anything, anything at all that drove George away. Wasn't she pleasant? a good sport? adventuresome? good at her job? a good mother? a good lover? Her list of accolades went on and on. She didn't realize that being predictable, dependable and totally captured translated to being boring and in need of replacement.

She looked in the mirror; 42 years old and still looking quite young. She had long, thick, blonde hair with hazel eyes and a mildly freckled face. She used to hate those freckles, but now she thought they kept her looking younger than her age. She had a lanky appearance being somewhat tall and thin. No chest to speak of, but George never complained, in fact he liked her small breasts, telling her they'd stay perky a lot longer than if she were more endowed. Asshole, she thought, he'd say anything to get me in bed.

She thought about calling her sister Heather and then Savannah to tell them the good news that she had a date, but then thought the better of it. What if it's a disaster? I could just have a private disaster and no one would be the wiser. Better to wait and hope to have something positive to report. It was odd being so far away from home where she knew absolutely no one. Her new friend Terri and her husband sailed away this morning, and no new boaters had come into the marina. Even the owner of the marina was away for the day.

Marsha mused to herself, Okay, I need a distraction. How about that ice cream store? I could use a walk and at least walking to and from the store would justify the calories.

The mile long walk was refreshing. Along the way was an entire embankment of milkweed in full bloom. The smell of milkweed flowers was one of her favorites, almost like honeysuckle. A zillion butterflies, mainly monarchs, were flitting about. Her girls came to her mind. Every summer they searched out milkweed leaves for monarch butterfly eggs. They were generally successful and enjoyed watching the eggs hatch, the caterpillars grow, the chrysalises turn from emerald green to clear and then the butterflies emerge. A wonderful cycle of life that always brought her joy. She made a note to look for some eggs on her way back. It would be a nice surprise for the girls if they had caterpillars to raise on their return trip.

The hand packed chocolate ice cream was indeed to die for. She enjoyed every morsel. On the way back she found two milkweed leaves with eggs on them, picked them and brought them back to the boat. Just as she was stepping onto the boat she heard a feminine "hello?"

"Hi! my name is Virginia, Ginny for short, I'm on that Hinckley over there… I just noticed your AGLCA burgee… my husband and I are Loopers, too."

Marsha had earlier deemed the AGLCA burgee the fast friend flag after being on the Loop for only two days. She found out that anybody flying the flag had an open invitation to say hello and be your new best friend within minutes. It was great! She now had so many "boat cards" that she started a notebook to keep them in. She also made it a habit to carry plenty of her own in her wallet to hand out. No one was shy about how difficult it was to remember new names, so they gladly referred to their boat cards for assistance.

"Hi, nice to meet you," Marsha answered back. "I'm Marsha McKenzie."

"My husband Dennis and I usually have cocktails around 5:30. Would you and your husband like to join us?"

"I'd love to, but it'll just be me, no husband."

"Oh? When will he be back?"

Now wasn't that a question she had asked herself about a million times.... "Uh... he won't be, I'm not married anymore." It was still too harsh for her to state she was divorced.

"Oh, I'm so sorry... you know what they say about that word 'assume'...."

Yes...., yes she did. Out loud she responded, "Don't be, I know it's unusual for a woman to be doing this without a husband or partner. I'm getting quite used to the reaction by now. I do have two daughters if that helps," she said, hoping to cheer up the conversation.

"Well that's nice.... are they here or..."

Marsha interrupted. "They're with their dad for two weeks. My cousin, her husband and kids will be driving them up and somehow the seven of us will be squeezing into this boat for two weeks while we explore the rest of Georgian Bay and the Northern Channel."

The look on Ginny's face belayed "how dreadful, four kids and three adults on that boat?" but outwardly she politely said, "How nice! You must be looking forward to seeing them."

"I am... can I bring anything over?"

"Oh no dear... just yourself. See you in a bit."

Marsha actually got a laugh out of the conversation. Ginny reminded her of Mrs. Howell from *Gilligan's Island*,

and she was pretty sure Dennis would remind her of Mr. Howell. Ginny looked to be 80 with overly dyed blonde hair, unnecessary gaudy jewelry and an outfit that was too dressy for a small marina in the middle of nowhere. She was better suited for a cruise ship. But good for Ginny. She was on her own boat and who was Marsha to criticize anyway?

The cocktail hour proved to be enjoyable. Per unwritten Looper Law, you always provided your own cocktail. In this case, a bottle of white wine. Ginny had a nice array of hors d'oeuvres which for Marsha would turn into "Looper's Dinner." Dennis was just how she imagined: Mr. Howell to the nth degree. It was all she could do to keep from calling them Thurston and Luvvy. She learned they were on their second Loop and then noticed the background color of their burgee was gold. Another tradition. A white background burgee denoted one was in progress of doing the Loop, gold background meant the Loop had been completed and a platinum background meant a second Loop had been completed. Marsha gleaned invaluable information about which islands to visit, where to anchor and places of caution in terms of navigation. She was surprised to learn how much they anchored out. There's that "assume" again, she said to herself. She also learned what a wonderful mechanic George was. Apparently it was of no consequence how expensive it was to fly him up, get him a rental car and a motel for the week and then fly him home. He had done a masterful job and was worth every penny. They even allowed him to have a local high school dropout hired to help him with lifting the 200 pound plus transmission and transferring it down into the engine room. What was his name? Oh yes, Lenny, recommended by the marina owner Gerry. Lenny was constantly in trouble with the law, and Gerry was trying to help him out by arranging honest employment for him. Dennis gathered Lenny must somehow be related to Gerry, hence the vested interest in redeeming him.

"Guess I'm lucky I stumbled upon George."

"Oh yes, Gerry does great work, but he's so busy you'd be waiting weeks for him to have time to devote to your boat, and who knows how long those exhaust elbows would have lasted." Dennis replied.

After she finished her bottle of wine, she dismissed herself lest she get giddy or worse yet, fall asleep on their back deck.

"Well, I'm so glad to have met you. We're leaving tomorrow after George finishes up in the morning. But keep an eye out for us as you travel, sometimes we just pick a harbor and stay there for a week. Who knows, you may catch up to us in your travels."

"I hope so." And she meant it.

CHAPTER 7

T
HE NEXT MORNING WAS MISERABLE with a cold rain
reminding Marsha just how far north she was. "Winter
is coming," she laughed to herself. She looked over at the
Hinckley with *Happy Hearts* embossed in a very large font
on the stern and a cute logo of two overlapping hearts with
a connecting smiley mouth. She wondered if George was
already on board. A scan of the parking lot revealed his rental
car. Around 10:00 he emerged and helped the Howells, or
whatever their last name was, undo their power cords, water
hose and docking lines. Dennis easily maneuvered out of the
slip and soon disappeared down the channel way. George
then knocked on her companion way door.

"Hello?"

"Hi, George, all set with Thurston and Luvvy?"

"What?"

"Thurston Howell the Third and his wife Luvvy? Oh
sorry, you probably didn't ever see the reruns of *Gilligan's
Island*. Pretty stupid yet hilarious sitcom from the 60s."

"Nope, not familiar with that show. But yes, all set. I'm
doing an oil change on another boat today, and once I get a
chance to clean up, I'll be back to pick you up. Is 5:30 still OK?

"You said 6:00, but 5:30 is even better given we have to drive an hour."

"Right, cheerio, 5:30 it is."

Marsha had packed exactly one dress. It didn't seem necessary to pack anything but tee shirts, shorts and bathing suits. At the last minute she added one long sleeved shirt, one pair of jeans, a vest and a light weight jacket in case of cold temperatures. She slipped on the dress with a V neck and empire waist. What little cleavage she had was accentuated. She chose not to wear a bra, let her little tits do their magic if her nipples became hard and pointed while out to dinner.

George picked her up at precisely 5:30. Had he been in the British Army, she wondered? After a few pleasantries they rode the first few miles in silence. She couldn't help but notice how handsome he looked. He had a button down short sleeved light blue shirt tucked into form fitting blue jeans. On his belt near his right hip was his ever present multipurpose Leatherman Tool, just like her father's, in a well worn leather sheath. She tried to suppress how hot he looked. After a few more miles of silence Marsha asked, "So where are we going? My whole world is charts. I have no idea what the land mass is like around here."

"Neither do I," laughed George. "I've been to my motel, to the marina to the local grocery store, the liquor store and the hardware store. But I noticed on the way to the hardware store there was a restaurant. Let's hope it's open."

"Yeah, otherwise we're having left over chicken and cole slaw aboard the *Boldly Go*."

"You know, I need to tell you something… technically, I'm still married."

"What? Stop the car!"

"Hold on, hold on… my marriage is on the rocks. Sylvia and I are in the process of divorce, but it's ridiculously complicated. I'm British, she's Bahamian, we have a child, and her objective is to bankrupt me. Whatever feelings I had for her are long gone. Now she just represents some evil force I have to deal with without doing psychological damage to my son."

"And I thought my divorce was tragic… You know what? Let's turn around and go back to my boat. I really can make us a meal with the left overs. Why travel an hour if there's a good chance the restaurant is closed?"

"Are you sure?"

"Yes I'm sure."

A short while later they re-entered the marina parking lot. They walked quietly back to her boat and went into the galley. George sat at the dinette while she heated up the chicken in the microwave, made a salad and sautéed some zucchini and squash. Voila! Dinner served.

"Not bad for an impromptu meal," said George. "Okay, so let's have it. What's your tale of woe with your divorce?"

Marsha hesitated for a moment. How does one condense 15 years of marriage into five minutes? She started out very matter of factly but then deteriorated into a bucket of tears, as if she was relating her story to her sister or one of her girl friends.

"There, there…" George said.

"There, there?" Marsha said as she came up for air between sobs. "Are you kidding me? There, there?" She started to giggle and then laughed uncontrollably. "Oh that's funny… I'm sorry, I don't mean to make fun of you... but do men really say there, there?"

"Well, I guess they do, I just said it!" Which made them laugh hysterically.

"Okay, this definitely qualifies for a bottle of wine," said Marsha. She grabbed a bottle from the liquor locker and then two wine glasses. She poured two glasses and said, "So are we just two pathetic people in the throws of divorce?"

"Yes," replied George.

"Yes, that's it, just 'yes'?"

George reached over, pulled her to his face and kissed her on the lips. "What I really want to do right now is make love to you. It's been too long for both of us, and I think it would be mutually advantageous just to have a go at it."

"What? Am I a science experiment?"

"Stop it, Marsha, you want it as badly as I do." And with that he lifted up her dress and slipped it over her head, exposing her bare breasts and black panties.

"Now that's much better." He took her hand and led her back to the main stateroom where a queen sized bed awaited them. He kissed her so passionately it sent shivers throughout her body. He edged her to the bed and tenderly laid her down on the bed. He continued with caressing her lips, her neck and then her breasts. Her nipples hardened as he suckled them. Then he took her right hand and along with his, stroked his growing penis. He laid next to her, reached down and removed her panties. He stroked her mound gently bringing out her clitoris. His fingers penetrated her vagina where he felt her juices flowing. Then he entered her, gentle at first, then with a vengeance. He fucked her as hard as he could. She gasped, resisted and then relented. She wanted to be fucked, and she wanted it hard and fast.

Afterwards, they were a ball of emotion. They held each other until they fell asleep. It was a good sleep.

Chapter 8

Marsha looked over at George in the morning. He looked so peaceful. She didn't want to wake him, but she had to pee so badly she had to get up. The slight movement of course wakened him. He just smiled.

"You're beautiful. Thank you for last night. I needed that. I hope you're okay with that."

"Actually I am. Obviously I needed it, too."

Silence. Nice silence. Marsha returned from the head and announced she was making coffee.

A short while later George sat at the dinette.

Marsha handed him a cup of coffee. "What do you like in it?"

"Nothing, I like it black."

They laughed simultaneously but for different reasons. Marsha for the expected reference to black men's penises and George to the fact that Sylvia was black.

"Sylvia is black and, therefore, my son William is mulatto. It's difficult for him sometimes. He goes back and forth between two worlds. Something Sylvia and I will never fully understand."

"Okay, you trump me there. Both my girls look like me, so no race issues there. I'm so much a WASP that I would never be able to relate to William's world."

"But you see, at least you would try to understand it. That's where Sylvia falls down. She just doesn't see William's world as being different from hers. Just one of the many differences that has torn us apart, not to mention that she's a crazy lady and still in love with her former lover, Victor."

"Just curious, is Victor black or white?"

"Black, very black. She should never have left him for me. I did her wrong and I regret it. I thought I had something to prove and so did she. Basically, she fucked my brains out and convinced me I was her true love. But in reality, all she wanted to do was piss off Victor. It worked. They broke up, she moved in, we married and produced William... I love that little boy. He's ten now."

"All of a sudden my divorce became incredibly simple. My husband just got tired of me and the girls. Apparently, George likes the pursuit, not the conquest."

Silence for awhile while they searched their individual brains for the millionth time. What the hell went wrong?

Marsha broke the silence. "Want some toast or eggs or something?"

"Nothing for now... thanks."

More silence. This was getting awkward.

Then George broke the silence. "I have an idea."

"Okay, shoot."

"You have a week or so, I have a week, you have a boat and we need something to do. What would you say about having an affair? A Georgian affair?"

"A Georgian affair?"

"Yes, a bit weird that your ex's name is George and so is mine and we're in Georgian Bay. Let's title it and go with it… Marsha, you're a beautiful woman. You deserve someone gallant, someone to love you and your children, someone to grow old with. That's not me. I'm still married and trying to get divorced. It'll be years. I have a life in the Bahamas, and you have a life in the States. Let's just have an affair for a week, and then we'll go our separate ways. Think about it. A week of love making without commitment. But at least we're not misleading each other. We know we each have to go back to our own lives."

Marsha was stunned. She didn't know how to react at first. The Protestant in her initially objected, but then the true core depth of her didn't. She wanted to be ravished and adored. But in just under two weeks her teenagers would be on board with her cousin, cousin-in-law and their two kids. She would be jolted back to reality and George would need to disappear. Could she just have an affair without any strings attached? Yes, yes she could.

"Okay… but I don't even know you really. What if you're a serial killer and want to hack me up into tiny pieces?"

"And how do I know you're not a serial killer?" he laughed. "Here," he continued, "here's how you know you can trust me."

He pulled out his wallet and showed her a school picture of his son. William had kinky black hair, light brown skin and dark eyes. His forehead, brows and eyes were all George. The nose and mouth must be his mother's.

"That's my William, the center of my universe."

"What is your custody arrangement?"

"He lives with his mother but I have him most weekends and quite often I need to pick him up from school when his mother is running late."

"Well, that's convenient for her. Is she seeing anyone?"

"Oh yeah, she went right back to Victor in the house she used to live in. If Victor wasn't her lover, we'd probably be friends. He's actually a nice guy."

"Well, okay, now that we've established we're not serial killers, let's look at the weather, look at the charts and hit the stores to provision up for the week." Marsha said in her almost too organized manner.

"Yes sir!" George responded. He stood up and saluted her.

"Stop it, you goof.... hey, there is one more thing... calling you George, well... it's tough sometimes. Do you have a middle name or a nickname?

"No nickname, my full name is George Anderson Wainwright. The second by the way... and there's a third too."

"Oh yes, you mentioned you had another son."

"Yes, I have a 30-year-old son in Germany. He's all tatted up and on his own. I rarely see him and when I do it's pretty awkward. I've forgotten most of my German and he only speaks broken English."

"Wait, how old are you?"

"Fifty. When I was stationed in Germany, I was an idiot, getting drunk every weekend and trying to score with any woman I could... yeah... I see what you're thinking and you're right. I was despicable. I didn't even know I had a son until a few years later. Don't know why his mother named him after me; maybe because the resemblance was remarkable. I couldn't deny paternity. His mother had already gotten pregnant again and was living with someone else. Maybe she named him after me to keep track of who the fathers of her children were. But in any event, George the third considers his real father to be her eventual husband Hans Schmitt. We left it at that. She never asked for child support but I dutifully sent her a hefty allowance for him every month until he turned 18."

Marsha wasn't sure how to process all that, but eventually let out a deep breath… "So any other skeletons in the closet?"

"Can't say I've been a stellar citizen, but once I got into engine maintenance and repair, especially marine engines, work became steadier and I was able to settle down… or so I thought. The upshot of all of this is I'm not someone you want to wind up with."

"Well, at least we're walking into this with open eyes. No expectations then. At the end of the week we go back to our normal lives… whatever normal is."

His name popped into her brain again. "So, George, can I call you Anderson or Andy?"

"God no on Andy, but I guess Anderson will be OK. If I don't answer, however, it'll be because I'll be thinking you're talking to my father's ghost."

"He went by Anderson, not George?"

"That's right."

"Well, thanks. I know it's weird for me to change your name, but what would you do if my name was Sylvia?"

"Good point. But it's still weird."

"I have a better idea. I'll call you George Anderson so that by the time I get to the 'son' part, the sting of George will have worn off."

He looked at her quizzically, wondering if she was really serious.

"Okay, okay, zany I know, I do have my quirks."

"Why not just call me George Anderson Wainwright and I'll think it's my dead mother still yelling at me?"

CHAPTER 9

THEY LOOKED AT THE WEATHER; cold nights ahead with temps dipping into the 40s. Wasn't this summer? Highs in the sixties and low seventies during the day. One day of 80 degrees. A bit of rain coming for Wednesday but otherwise no obvious cold fronts on the way. The winds ranged from light and variable to 15 to 20 knots, nothing horrendous. They poured over the charts and the guidebooks. The plan was to get as far as they could toward Killarney by Wednesday and then turn around, going to different anchorages on their way back. His return flight out of Toronto was on Monday but not until the afternoon. She'd still have a week to herself but that was better than being lonely for 2 weeks. Besides… somewhere in the back of her brain she was creating the movie ending in which he doesn't leave on Monday but instead, stays with her for the rest of her life…

"Marsha?"

"Yes, sorry, George Anderson. Lost in thought. Let's hit the grocery store and the liquor store."

George Anderson picked up things he liked for breakfast and snacks while Marsha was a whirlwind of gathering all the items she would need for six days worth of meals, plus cleaning products and various sundries. He marveled at her efficiency. Next they hit the liquor store for wine, beer, one bottle of rum and one of vodka. Then they stopped at his motel so he could gather his belongings and check out. Back at the marina they unloaded the bags, boxes, his duffle and his tool boxes. He had mentioned to her he felt naked without his tools and never traveled without them. After she stowed the food, they headed over to the marina office. She needed to pay the bill, and he wanted to pick up some oil for her just in case.

Gerry was at the counter. Marsha went ahead and made reservations for another week at the dock when they returned on Saturday.

"Hey, George, thanks again for taking on Lenny. He seemed to have learned quite a bit from you."

"No worries. He seemed to know his way around the tools, knew every name and function, actually. But he had a weird affect about him. You said he had been in trouble?"

"Yes, I used to teach a small engine repair course at the local high school, and he was in one of my classes. Glad to hear he at least retained something I taught him. He had a shitty background, no known father, taken away from his drug addict mother as a kid and then placed in a series of foster homes. I was really hoping he'd do something with his mechanical skills, but he dropped out of high school. He's been in and out of jail for petty theft."

"Petty theft? Hmmm. Wish I'd known that. I caught him once in the Burton's stateroom. He was just standing there, nothing in his hands, so I don't think he stole anything. I just yelled at him for wandering and made it known he was only allowed in the engine room. I do hope he didn't steal anything."

"Yeah, me too. Sorry, I should have said to keep an eye on him. I'll call the Burtons and give them a heads up."

They concluded their business and returned to the boat. On the way back Marsha noticed some milkweed and picked a few leaves.

She anticipated his question, "For my caterpillars, the eggs just hatched. I'll explain underway."

She impressed him with her improving skills at backing the boat out of the slip. She had set a course and first up was an anchorage about three hours away. They should be there by 5:00.

Navigating through the narrow rocky passages was tricky even with a chart plotter. She was glad to have George Anderson on board to confirm her route. They eventually headed down Henvey Inlet in First Nation Reservation Territory. A few boats along the way were actually tied to rock walls. Marsha had never seen that before.

They decided to anchor in a cove called the Flower Pots. On the chart plotter she noticed an AIS symbol. AIS stood for Automatic Identification System. If you paid for the service, you could send and/or receive data about your boat. Marsha loved it. Other boaters could "see" her on their chart plotters, and she in turn knew what type of vessel was coming her way and at what speed. She moved the cursor to the symbol which was a green triangle and clicked on its center.

"Hey look at this, George! It's *Happy Hearts*!"

"What happened to George Anderson?"

"I guess I'm over it."

"Good."

"Let's hail them and invite them over."

"Here? My guess is that they'll want us there."

"Absolutely, but in cocktail protocol you take turns hosting cocktail hour. It's my turn to have them over here. They'll no doubt insist we come to them, and so we will."

"Seems like a lot of rigamarole, but you're the captain."

Marsha hailed them on the VHF and as predicted, they insisted she and George join them on their back deck. This time she packed a bottle of wine, a few beers, some sliced apples and cheese. While she was putting the items together she heard him off in the state room.

"What are you looking for?"

"I thought I'd bring over a few tools. It's actually a great opportunity to check up on some of the work I did. Hmmm.... that's odd."

"What's odd?"

"One of my quirks is that I always put my tools away. Every single one of them has a place. Saves me hours of time looking for them. But one of my smaller screwdrivers is missing...."

"Are you suspecting Lenny?"

"Hate to say it, but yes. He was overly interested in my tools. I was complimented at first, but then just his odd way about him made me suspicious of his actions. Hopefully, Gerry did give them a call and nothing is missing on their boat."

George unlocked a few drawers of his custom made stackable tool box. Each drawer contained graduated sets of tools such as socket wrenches and screwdrivers, while other drawers contained spare parts such as screws, washers, nuts and bolts. The lid of the tool box was a thick slab of wood that doubled as a cutting board. It was held in place by one small screw per corner. Marsha was rather impressed with his organization, not unlike the fastidious surgeons who had their surgical tools laid out in perfect sequences of size. George pulled out a few tools he anticipated needing and placed them in a small canvas ditty bag.

"Doesn't Dennis have any tools?" Marsha asked.

"He does… but not everything I may need."

The Burtons, gracious as ever, didn't ask why George was on board. They waited for that topic to come around. Ginny was excited for Marsha that she was able to leave the dock and not be alone.

"Yes," Marsha explained. "After George finished up with your boat, he offered to do a sea trial with me to make sure the exhaust elbows fit properly and were containing the exhaust. So then we thought, what the heck? Good way for me to do some reconnaissance of the area anchorages and great way for George to see the area before returning to the Bahamas. Sort of a win-win."

"Lovely, just lovely," commented Ginny.

"Say, Dennis, I brought some of my tools with me. If it's all right, I thought I'd check a few things in your engine room. I'd like to make sure the transmission fluid is up to snuff, and there's always a thing or two to tighten up."

"My my, George, you're a dream come true. Be my guest. Do you want my help?"

"No no, enjoy your drink. I'll only be ten minutes or so."

There was no lack of conversation with the Burtons, so it didn't seem odd that George had actually been in the engine room for over twenty minutes.

Finally, he emerged. Marsha thought he looked a little pale but he then asked rather cheerfully: "Mind if I use the sink to wash my hands? The fluid level is fine but there were a few things I tightened up."

"Just use the head off our state room, it's closest."

"Thanks!" He returned with a beer from the bag they brought over. As the night went on, George sheepishly brought up the topic of Lenny. By this time the amount of alcohol the Burtons had consumed was showing its effects: slightly slurred speech and repeated stories.

"So, um… I learned from Gerry that Lenny has a bit of a history of petty theft. Had I known that, I wouldn't have had him on your boat. My apologies. You might want to just double check your belongings, especially in your stateroom to make sure nothing is missing. I caught him staring into your room… sorry… but he was empty handed and seemed to have been there only a few moments. After that, he was always in my eyesight."

"Oh my!" exclaimed Ginny. "So far I haven't noticed any-thing missing, but I'll be sure to take a closer look."

Dennis came back more sternly. "Were you planning on telling us that information?"

"Actually, I left it with Gerry to give you a call to give you a heads up. I gather you haven't heard from him?"

"There's no cell service here. Once we're back in range, I hope I see a message from him."

Fortunately, the conversation returned to more pleasant topics, and soon it was obvious the evening should come to a conclusion. The subtleties of hosts conveying "it's time for you to go now" were readily picked up by George and Marsha.

"I'm so happy we ran into you! Will you be staying here awhile?"

"Yes," replied Ginny. "I think we'll stay here for a few more days before we move on. And you?"

"We're trying to get in as many anchorages as possible, and if we can, weather permitting, we'd actually like to get to Killarney by Wednesday. We'll check out different anchorages for the return trip."

"That sounds lovely, dear... seems like we'll see you again."

"That would be great!"

Hugs and hand shakes were exchanged and they were soon back on *Boldly Go*. "Jesus it's cold tonight" Marsha exclaimed as they dinghied back to the boat. "Guess we'll need the heater on. Gosh I love them," Marsha continued, "it's as if they're my long lost grandparents. Do you want me to make some dinner?"

"Actually, I'm not hungry for food.... just you."

CHAPTER 10

IT HAD BEEN ANOTHER WONDERFUL night in the bedroom. Marsha couldn't believe how different sex was with George than it had been with ex-George. Current George seemed very concerned with her having orgasms. It was almost his mission to make that happen. Marsha actually couldn't remember the last time she had had an orgasm with ex-George. She had just been thankful that they had had sex. She didn't know what she didn't know, and that was that her supposedly good sex with ex-George could have been so much better.

George was buried under the covers. As predicted the night time temperatures did dip to the low forties. The heater required the generator to be on if they weren't plugged in to short power. Not wanting to leave the generator running all night, extra covers were needed. They didn't mind, made for an extra cozy night.

"So where to today, Captain?"

"I'd really like to go to the French River. So much history there. And look, we have to take the Bad River to get there! Then there are the Devil's Door Rapids." As they headed toward the French River, George was on the helm and she read aloud from the guidebooks about the rapids. Entering the anchorage area later in the day, they picked a spot some-what away from the other boaters.

"What an interesting mix of boats," Marsha commented. "Hey look, there's *C'est La Vie*." *C'est La Vie*, a Beneteau 423, was the boat home of Terri and her husband Henry. "They are such fun folks. We'll have to swing by later."

"For someone who claims not to know anybody up here, you sure do have a lot of friends!" George teased.

George and Marsha geared up the dinghy for their trek up the rapids. It would be challenging since they could see a one foot drop in the final rapid leading into the anchorage area. But lots of small dinghies passed through giving them confidence they could, too. They took their time to pass by the other anchored boats. On one sailboat there was an older man hoisting a younger man up the mast. It brought back fond memories for Marsha. When she and her siblings were kids, their parents would actually hoist them up the mast just for fun. The view was great and the ride up and down was a bit of a thrill.

George and Marsha edged over to the sailboat. It was an older boat and not too surprisingly for the age of the boat, it didn't have roller furling for the jib. A couple of bagged jibs littered the foredeck.

"Hi! Looks like you have some mast head work to do today."

"Yes," answered the older gentleman. "I'm hoping it's just a simple job of swapping out the light bulb in the mast head light."

The man in the bosun's chair looked down and said "Me too, don't want to spend all day up here." The man caught

Marsha's eye and for an instant there was a connection. What was that? Marsha asked herself. He was so handsome with his curly long blonde hair framing a handsome face on a rather muscular body. He looked like a perfect match for her. Why am I thinking about other men? Isn't George good enough? Oh God she thought.... is this what ex-George thought all along? Being with one woman who was "good enough" yet intrigued with the next good looking gal?

Marsha snapped back to the present when George asked the older gentleman if he needed any help.

"I think I got it, but thanks."

"Well, good luck with that, but don't hesitate to call over if you run into other problems," George offered.

As they approached the inlet to the rapids a few other dinghies were milling about. A lady in a sailing dinghy called over to them.

"Hey, Marsha, it's Terri!"

"Terri, hey, great to see you!"

She and George motored to them, and Henry slackened his sail to stay put.

"So are you going to try to go up those rapids?" Henry asked.

"We're going to give it a go... oh, this is George Wainwright. George, this is Terri and Henry."

They proceeded with the customary pleasantries and agreed to get together later for cocktails. Henry pulled in the main sheet, and they sailed out of the small anchorage area.

Just as they were about to gun the motor to go up the rapids they heard screams of terror and lots of yelling. Both of them turned their heads to the source of the shouts. It didn't take long to scan the harbor to see a crumpled man on the foredeck of the old sailboat.

George instinctively headed immediately back to the sailboat. Marsha cried out, "George go right to *Boldly Go* first, I'll grab my medical kit." He drove as fast as he could. Today was not the day to be mindful of his wake. Marsha jumped onto the swim platform, ran into her stateroom head and grabbed her medical kit from the lower cupboard. She practically jumped back into the dinghy, and they sped over to the sailboat. By this time two other couples in their dinghies were at the side of the boat with three people on the foredeck.

Marsha, having seen horrible traumas in her career, didn't wince at the scene in front of her. The younger man had obviously fallen from the top of the mast onto the foredeck. Miraculously, the majority of his body landed on the jib bags. His right shoulder was adjacent to a bent stanchion which sent shivers up her spine. Had he landed 3 inches over, that stanchion would have speared his lungs and he would be dead. She could see that he was breathing, which was a good thing, but his left arm and leg were shattered, spewing blood everywhere. The older gentleman was frozen in a state of shock.

Marsha took over. "George, go below and find whatever towels you can. Blue Hat Man, put your hands on his arm here to put pressure on the main wound. Red Hat Man, call for help. Grampa! What is his name?

The older man, still dazed, hesitated a second and then blurted out "George, George Peterson, my son!"

Oh for the love of God, Marsha said to herself, is every fucking good looking guy on the planet named George?

She put that thought aside and looked directly in George's eyes. From his perspective, she looked like an angel of mercy. "George, if you can hear me, squeeze my hand." He did so immediately; he wanted to talk but only screams of agony came out of him. She looked down at his leg. Shit! Was that a bone sticking out? Shit. A compound fracture was not good, not here, not anywhere. She needed to act fast. She dug in her medical bag and pulled out a syringe. "George, I'm going to give you something to ease the pain, then I'm going to put pressure on your leg. Don't move."

Marsha was a clean, honest person, not a drug addict, but whenever there were left over pain medications from a surgical case, she would quietly slip the syringe into her scrub pants pocket. One never knew when an emergency situation would arise, and one thing she always wanted to be prepared for was pain management. She carefully administered a bolus of ketamine. That should help.

George returned with several towels. With the help of the man with the red hat, Mike, and Ralph, with the blue hat, they gently tried to stop hurt George's bleeding. She slipped a rolled up towel under his head, careful not to move him in case there was a spinal injury as well.

"George, can you wiggle your right toes?" Marsha asked. "Oh thank God, you can… that's good." A woman was tending to the father and a second woman came up from the cabin. She stated, "We've contacted the Coast Guard, they're sending help but it could be an hour or so!"

"That's too long!" Marsha screamed, wishing she hadn't said that so loudly. Calm down, she said to herself. Don't panic the others.

210

The woman continued. "I told him he would need to be airlifted, so they're sending a helicopter."

"Well that's good," Marsha said, much more calmly. She noticed hurt George could move his right arm and leg, so she was fairly confident he didn't have a spinal cord injury. Hurt George's screaming subsided; the ketamine was working its magic. "Okay George," she said not caring if he could hear her or not, "I'm going to remove the bosun's chair from you." The frayed jib halyard just above the harness told the whole story. The old halyard had parted, the old school jib bags saved him from breaking his neck and back, and divine providence saved him from being impaled by the stanchion. She took a little credit for pain relief.

His father was wailing by now. "It's my fault, it's my fault… I should have put him up on two halyards… Oh God… Oh God…" Marsha told George Anderson to rifle through her medical kit and search for Valium. Dad definitely needed a sedative. She didn't dare lift up her hand from the leg wound. She had to maintain some pressure.

It was probably the longest hour she and everyone else involved ever endured. Finally, the welcome sound of a helicopter was heard. A simultaneous shout of relief came from all involved.

The paramedic team was amazing, almost like a SWAT team. Marsha had announced to the approaching team that she was an anesthetist and that the first thing she thought he needed was a morphine drip. They were in agreement. She and the others stepped away to allow the team full access to George. Getting him off the foredeck and into a gurney was no easy feat. One of the medics approached Marsha since it was obvious she had the best handle on George's traumatic situation. He needed to know all she knew for George's subsequent care and management. Marsha listed his known injuries, her best guess as to what else was injured, and what had been done for him, leaving out the administration of the ketamine.

"How did you get his pain under control?" the medic astutely asked.

"I… uh… I happened to have a sedative in my first aid kit. I just grabbed it, something that began with a K or something like that. Guess it did the trick…" They locked eyes. In a one minute stare down, an entire silent conversation transpired between them. It was as illegal as hell to pilfer medications, especially controlled substances out of the hospital, an offense that could lead to her not only losing her license, but could land her in jail. And then to add to all that, it was as illegal as hell to smuggle controlled substances into Canada, another jail-able, license loosing crime. Even the Good Samaritan Laws wouldn't help her. But he knew and she knew she had saved the man's life. And they both knew that the half life of Ketamine was very short; there would be no evidence that it had ever been administered. The Medic stared back and without saying a word he acknowledged the good she had done and let it go. A teleological suspension of the ethical. Doing something bad to do something good.

"Thank you, ma'am, he's lucky you were nearby."

Mike and Ralph and their wives stayed with David, George's father. One of the wives cleaned up the foredeck as best she could. No doubt the remnants of the blood stains would never fully wash out. When Ralph saw how much blood had spattered on him he bent his head over the side and threw up. His wife gently attended to him, both happy he was able to hold it in until after George was lifted off the boat.

Marsha was a bloody mess, too. She went down below and rifled through hurt George's belongings in the foreword cabin. She pulled out a long-sleeved shirt, stripped off her blood soaked tee-shirt and shorts, and put on his blue pin-striped shirt. She threw her clothes into a trash bucket. Madness. But no one said a word when she emerged from the cabin.

David looked up at her, tears streaming down his face. "I can't thank you enough.... you're Marsha?"

"Yes, Marsha, Marsha McKenzie. I hope you don't mind I took one of your son's shirts... I just had to get out of those clothes..."

"Marsha, you can have anything you want, I'll never be able to repay you.... you do think he'll survive, don't you?"

"Yes, yes I do." And she did.

CHAPTER 11

"DAMN YOU LOOK SEXY!" George said to Marsha when they got back to *Boldly Go.*

"What? Jesus Christ! How can you think about sex right now?"

"Did I say anything about having sex? I'm just describing how beautiful you are."

"Yeah, but that translates to you wanting to have sex."

"Well, yeah…"

"I need to take a shower. And then I need a stiff drink… and don't say it… I know what you're thinking."

George chuckled and shook his head. Actually, he needed a drink too. He had never been involved with a medical emergency. He was volitionally absent from the birth of his younger son knowing that he wouldn't be able to handle that scene. Give him a dirty engine block any day; blood just wasn't in his purview.

Marsha went into her stateroom and took off hurt George's shirt. She had no idea what made her change clothes on the sailboat. She could have waited to change on her own boat. Something compelled her to take it. And to continue the madness, she had no intention of returning it. She folded it up and placed it in the bottom drawer of her built in dresser. She took a long shower, a Hollywood shower, which meant she let the water run. A navy shower, the prescribed shower on a boat with a limited water tank, meant turning the water on only long enough to rinse off the soap or shampoo.

She came up on deck, her hair only towel dry. She never bothered with blow dryers on a boat. First of all she'd have to start the generator to run the dryer and secondly, just sitting up topsides in the wind would dry her hair in no time. Didn't matter that her hair would be a mess. She had long ago resigned herself to having what her sister and she described as boat hair. George handed her a vodka tonic which had an extra shot in it. He had made one for himself as well.

"Marsha, I have to say, that was outstanding what you did. It was like a performance."

"You know, before I had kids I worked full time at St. James Hospital. It's a Level I Trauma Center, so when I was on call, I dealt with emergencies like that on a weekly basis. But the difference was, the victim being brought into the ER was minutes away from the operating room, not hours away. And not on a boat… timing, yeah, timing, makes a big difference. A compound fracture is a very big deal, but I'm hopeful George will pull through."

"Another George?"

"Another George."

Off in the distance they heard "Marsha? It's Terri, okay to come aboard?"

Henry and Terri were just off their stern rowing toward them. "Yes, certainly," Marsha replied.

Henry and Terri boarded the boat and were soon seated on the stern deck.

"What can I get you? Marsha asked.

"Don't be ridiculous, we brought our own libations. Marsha dear, what a job you did today. You saved that man! The whole harbor is abuzz at what happened. Do you think he'll survive?"

"I do, I do. The medic said it would be about an hour to Toronto, so I'm pretty confident they'll get his pain under control and start fixing all his fractures. Fortunately, I don't think there was any brain injury, and I'm confident he didn't have a spinal injury."

"What a relief!"

Henry then took over. "So now there's the matter of getting his father to Toronto as soon as possible. The other boaters in the harbor are discussing a plan to get him to Toronto and his boat put up at the nearest marina."

"And where would that be?" George asked.

"Probably all the way back to Britt in the Byng Inlet," Marsha interjected.

"I have a rental car there that I have to drive back to Toronto by Sunday. Certainly I could leave earlier," George offered.

Marsha was stunned. "Leave early? Shit!" And then to herself: you little shit, how selfish of you?

Henry unknowingly came to her rescue. "Thank you, George, but see that Sea Ray over there? It can travel at 20 to 30 mph. He can head down Lake Huron and get David to Midland in just a few hours. From there, he can be transported to Toronto. Basically we need to get his boat to a marina, and maybe that can be Midland, too. One of the boaters here has a visiting couple on board who is willing to take on the task.

"So basically, you have this all worked out?" Marsha questioned.

"Yes, we do." said Terri. "Ralph and his wife are staying on board with David. He's distraught as you can imagine. They don't want him to be alone. We just wanted to thank you, Marsha, on David's behalf. I hear you were amazing."

Now Marsha was embarrassed. "Thank you, Terri, but it really is what I'm trained to do... but I have to admit... it scared the shit out of me!"

With that they all laughed. George supplied them with more drinks and the rest of the evening drifted off to tales of adventure and gratitude for where they were.

CHAPTER 12

TERRI MUST HAVE INTUITIVELY READ "it's time for you to leave now," in Marsha's glazed eyes. She and Henry thanked them for the evening and rowed off in their dinghy back to *C'est la Vie*. George led Marsha down to the stateroom and undressed her. She was so tired she just flopped back on the bed and willingly opened her legs to him. He made love to her softly and the two of them fell asleep.

In the morning, Marsha awakened with a start. Did that all really happen? She walked out to the stern deck. The Sea Ray was no longer in the bay and she assumed the owners were making a mad dash to Midland with David on board. David's boat was still at anchor. It was a beautiful morning, and she wondered what her next move would be. Right on cue, George was at her side.

"Here you are! So, what's next, captain?"

"Well, I feel pretty odd about this, but I guess David is headed to Toronto and his boat will get to a marina, so... we're free to move about the cabin."

George laughed. "Guess we are. So again, where to next, captain?"

"Well, looking at the charts, next up is Collins Inlet with

plenty of anchorages. Once we get through the skinny passages we'll just anchor in the first available anchorage."

"Sounds good to me." responded George.

While George was at the helm later that morning, Marsha pondered the plight of hurt George. By now he'd still be in la la land, floating around in a sea of morphine blocking the pain. He'd probably had his arm and leg stabilized by intensive orthopedic surgeries. Hopefully, there were no internal injuries to deal with. Thank God for those bags of jibs. Then there would be months of physical and occupational therapies to retrain his leg and arm. If he was lucky, he would eventually be able to walk again. She was optimistic that his arm would have a full recovery; less so for his leg. But thank goodness for braces, canes and walkers. Again, she was confident that he would not need a wheelchair.

Then current George, or George Anderson, snapped her back to reality. "This is a pretty narrow, shallow channel coming up. I'm thinking one of us should check the depth with the dinghy."

"I'm fine with that," Marsha said. "Let me do it." George put the engines into neutral so Marsha could pull in the dinghy and get into it. Once she had the motor down and turned on, she released the line and yelled out to George, "I'm good!" She put the dinghy in forward and went ahead of *Boldly Go*. She and George were wearing what she called "marriage savers," headsets so that they could communicate to one another without yelling. "Good here, five feet deep." Marsha marked a channel sounding out the depths and then finally they were back into water 10 feet and deeper. She returned the dinghy to the *Boldly Go*. George again put the boat into neutral so Marsha could land the dinghy and climb aboard the mother ship.

"Good grief, can we get through a day without a little bit of drama?" asked Marsha.

"Actually, I was hoping for a lot of drama," teased George.

The scenery along the northern passage of Collins Inlet was breathtaking. There hadn't been much bird life in the previous anchorages, so they were thrilled when an eagle flew over the boat.

"Finally!" Marsha remarked, "I never get tired of seeing eagles. Don't know why, but that reminds me, I need more milkweed leaves. I hope there's some in the next place we anchor."

George found it irritating and charming at the same time that Marsha fed teeny tiny caterpillars. He simply said, "Hope so, too."

They passed by two potential anchorages but decided to keep on going to a third possibility in the hopes there would be fewer boats further along. After another hour they settled on an anchorage in the lee of Keyhole Island. There was a fairly large, but shallow bay behind the island, good for wind protection and a place to use the paddle board.

After ensuring the anchor was holding well enough, George suggested they take a tour of the state room.

"What? Take a tour?" Marsha exclaimed. The impish look on George's face explained everything and then she flushed. She let George lead her into the state room, undress her, and languish in love making for the next hour.

George seemed to have dozed off, so Marsha released herself from his arm around her shoulder. She stepped quietly into the shower. Today was a navy shower, just a quick rinse off and then into her bathing suit and on to the paddle board. George was awake when she emerged from the shower.

"Hey, good looking, why don't you come back over here?"

"Really, George... wow... I guess I'm good for now." And then with a bit of hesitation: "Don't I satisfy you?"

"Of course you do and then some. You need to understand that a man's desire is continuous. It's not like once or twice is sufficient. If I didn't have to earn a living, I'd be making love 24/7."

He detected a hurt look on her face. "Are you mad at me for wanting to make love to you all the time?"

"No, of course not... I'm just wondering why I didn't satisfy my ex."

"Well, here's the difference between me and him. If you were my wife, I'd never leave your side, there would never be a reason to stray."

"So why did he stray... I just don't get it... and why are you leaving your wife?"

George sighed. "Okay, first question, I don't know why your husband had to have other women. Some men like the chase; I guess it builds their ego. I was no saint at first either, just looking for pure sex, no commitment. Then along came Sylvia. I was mesmerized by her exotic looks and all the attention she gave me. I really thought I had found true love. We were equally awful to Victor. But soon I learned that Sylvia's agenda was to procreate a lighter skinned child and to extract every last cent from me so she could go back to her life with Victor. So, I didn't leave her. She left me, to answer your second question."

"Really? She wanted a lighter skinned child? What's that all about?"

"Sylvia is very dark skinned, darker than anyone in her family. I don't get the genetics there. But believe it or not, in her culture dark blacks are actually shunned by lighter skinned blacks. Having a 'bright' child improved her status among her family and peers. Bright meaning fair skinned, not necessarily intelligent. Fortunately, William is light skinned and smart."

"Well again, I'm so naive to other cultures...."

"I guess we can take a rain check on another tour of the state room. Looks like you want to get out on the paddle board. Need some help?"

The paddle board could be launched by just one person but it was definitely easier with two people. Marsha had a water proof bag for her cell phone, the portable VHF and two sandwich baggies for collecting milkweed leaves and blueberries. Terri had told her to be on the lookout for blueberry patches since the berries should be ripe by now. Terri also reminded her about the protected rattlesnake in the Georgian Bay area, the Massasauga rattlesnakes. Apparently, they were rarely seen, non-aggressive but would definitely bite if stepped upon. She'd be sure to watch her step.

"If I need any help I can call you on 16 and you can rescue me in the dinghy."

"Okay, just don't get eaten by a bear. I'd miss you!"

"Stop it!" Marsha laughed as she paddled away.

Instead of resuming his nap, George took the opportunity to check his tool box. The missing small screw driver was really bothering him, especially since it was the driver he needed to undo the screws holding the wooden lid in

222

place. He had specially made the lid to have a false depth to it. Marsha had a paucity of tools on board and none of her screwdrivers were the size he needed. He nearly ransacked the Burton's engine room looking for his missing one, figuring either he or Lenny had misplaced it. When he couldn't find it, he rifled through Dennis's meager toolbox. He found what he needed and slid the driver into his bag. He figured he would run into *Happy Hearts* on the return trip, if they even had moved at all, and he could easily return it then.

His tool box had felt a little lighter to him and he needed to make sure the 50 gold coins he had placed in the concealed compartment were still there. Over the years he had been accumulating one ounce gold coins, mainly Canadian Maple Leafs and Krugerrands, whenever the price dipped down and he could afford to buy more. He kept them in his tool box, not trusting any other place to store them. Now that Sylvia was divorcing him and demanding she was entitled to half, if not all, of his worth, it was more important than ever that she not find them. The request for him to fly north from the Burtons couldn't have come at a better time. He didn't care it was illegal to take that much money out of the country. He made an appointment at a bank in Toronto to open a safety deposit box there come Monday. He felt confident there would be no way Sylvia could get her hands on them, especially since she didn't even know they existed. Currently the 50 coins were worth $66,500. Not a bad nest egg for future investing.

He had to undo all four screws in order to lift up the inner lid. To his horror, the coins were gone.

"FUCK!" he yelled and then yelled the obscenity twenty times more. How could this have happened? When was his tool box out of his sight long enough for this slow process of undoing the screws, emptying out the compartment and then re-screwing the lid back in place? He replayed every moment of his time on *Happy Hearts* and tried to zero in on the times when Lenny was on board.

"Shit! The run to the hardware store!" he said out loud. They were in the middle of the oil change, and he needed one more quart. It was coming up on lunch time, so he volunteered to run up to the store, get more oil and pick up some lunch on the way back. He was probably gone 45 minutes. Plenty of time for Lenny to unscrew the lid, scoop up the two bags the coins were contained in, replace the lid and take the coins out to his bike. His bike had a make shift saddle bag attached to it. Apparently, Lenny had lost his driver's license and used the bike as his means of transportation. If Lenny had had a car, George would have sent him out on the errand.

The situation seemed hopeless by now. That incident happened almost five days ago. Gold coins could easily be turned into cash, and he had no real proof of ownership. But what would make Lenny even think to undo the lid? Giving the whole incident further thought, when he returned from the errand, that's when he caught Lenny in the Burton's stateroom, looking guilty about something but empty handed. His excuse of using their head was a weak one.

He didn't know what to do, but he knew he wouldn't be able to rest until he confronted Lenny. They would have to return to the Britt Marina in the Byng Inlet. Too late to turn around now, however; it would be too treacherous to steer among the rocky shoals without lighted navigational buoys. But could he really just sit around tonight? Would he tell

Marsha what was going on?

He looked across the bay and with the binoculars could see that Marsha had landed the paddle board on a long flat rock ledge and was up on a huge boulder talking on her cell phone. He looked at his phone and saw "no service." Somehow, there was service on shore. He could call Gerry and simply state there were more missing items from his tool box and was concerned that Lenny had taken them to pawn them off. Was Lenny showing any odd behaviors, or did he suddenly have new possessions? It was a long shot.

He hopped into the dinghy in search of a cell signal. He was pretty much at Marsha's landing spot when she concluded her call and yelled over, "Miss me?"

"Of course! But I have to confess it's been awhile since I checked in with William, and I could see you obviously had a cell signal."

"Yeah, I was surprised. I had taken my phone out to take some pictures of the boat in the bay and saw I had four bars. I just talked to my girls. They're doing fine and are actually missing me!"

"That's great, Marsha. So if you don't mind I'll give it a go too."

"Not at all. There's a blueberry patch over there. I'd like to fill up this bag."

George landed the dinghy and stepped onto the rock ledge. When Marsha was out of ear shot, he called Gerry. The line was busy. Damn! He then called William, good chance to call him in any event.

"Hey, William, how's it going?"

"Great, Dad! You should see my new bike! It's so cool!"

"A new bike? I didn't miss your birthday did I?"

"No, Dad, you know when my birthday is. Mom's gone on some sort of shopping spree. She got me a new bike and Victor a new car!"

"What? How can she afford that?"

"I don't know… she said something about running into a gold mine… or something like that. When she saw me listening to her talk to Victor, she shooed me away. But you gotta see it, Dad…"

William went on talking, but George's mind went elsewhere. Could it be Sylvia who took the coins? She never paid any attention to his tools, and, just like with Lenny, even if she had, what would have compelled her to unscrew the lid? His head was about to explode when he heard William repeat "Dad? Dad? Are you listening?"

"Sorry, son, the connection must be bad. Say is your mother around?"

"No, she went out with Victor to get a pizza."

William was at that awkward age of ten when parents struggled with whether or not a ten-year-old should be left alone when in reality most ten year olds were fully capable of being by themselves for a few hours. George snapped back to the conversation.

"Are you okay being by yourself?"

"Are you kidding? Of course I am!" William sounded insulted. George sarcastically wanted to say, "Of course you are, you're ten, you know everything." Instead, he lied. "Hey William, the connection is getting bad. Just wanted to check in. Love you, son!"

"Me, too." replied William and they ended the call.

This is crazy, George said to himself. There's no way Sylvia could have known about those coins. He tried calling Gerry again. His daughter answered the phone. Sorry, Gerry was out on the docks helping a new customer and no, she hadn't seen Lenny for days. But she'd have Gerry call him back when he could get to the phone.

George was standing on the rock ledge next to the dinghy in a state of disbelief. Suddenly he heard a distinctive rustling behind him. No, not rustling, rattling! He turned slowly and much to his surprise he saw a rattlesnake coiled up on the bare rock shaking its tail in a warning maneuver. Jesus! He froze. Next he heard Marsha walking toward him. He silently but frantically motioned to her to stop. Then he signaled her to not talk and pointed down near his feet. She got the message and froze.

Marsha searched through her brain to remember what she was supposed to do if she saw a Massasauga rattlesnake. What did Terri tell her? Then it came to her. Do nothing. Freeze, they usually just slither away if not further threatened. So she remained frozen, as did George. Finally, after a few minutes the snake stopped rattling and slowly slithered into the bushes. They both waited another few minutes before moving or talking.

George was first to talk. "I think you're safe to move forward now, Marsha."

"So do I, let's get out of here. If we're lucky that snake won't have friends… or bear friends for that matter."

Marsha paddled back while George went ahead in the dinghy. I hope snakes can't swim, she thought to herself. Gives me the creeps that I could have just as easily stepped on one of those snakes. Ugh!

When Marsha got back on board, she gave George a hug and then said, "I think I'd like to take you up on that tour of the state room now. I need to do something with all this adrenaline."

"Me, too," said George, "Me, too."

What started out as high energy fondling quickly deteriorated into their brains being elsewhere. Marsha ran through every possible scenario of how they would have managed had one of them been bitten by the snake. She knew they would have had to get an antivenom into their systems within two hours or else the toxins would reach the internal organs, possibly doing irreversible damage. And even if they could get to a hospital in two hours, Killarney being about 3 hours away from them, there was no guarantee the hospital would have the antivenom. And on and on she went with all the machinations. George's brain was consumed with what to do next to recover his coins. Finally, the two of them just looked at each other with blank stares.

"Where did you go?" Marsha softly asked.

"Where did I go? Where were you?" George countered.

They sat up, taking in each other's naked body, marveling how good it felt to be so comfortable with one another.

"Sorry, George, sometimes my medical brain gets the better of me. I was playing out the what if scenario with the possible snake bite."

George just nodded, still struggling with whether or not to bring her into his drama.

"George... so really, where were you?"

"I... I have an unfortunate thing going on, not sure I

want to burden you with my problems."

"Well, if nothing else, I'm a good listener."

"Before I tell you, let me show you something first. I'm a bit curious about your reaction."

They threw on some clothes, and she followed him to the galley. His tool box was so big and heavy that the only place it could be stowed was under the dinette, which they rarely used. He had put it on a piece of cardboard so he could slide it in and out without marring her flooring.

With a little effort, he pulled it out. "There. What do you see?"

"Your.... tool... box?" she slowly questioned as if the answer was too obvious or simple.

"Yes, of course... but is there anything interesting about it?"

"Well, I admire it greatly. I love the tower of drawers with each drawer containing an organized series of tools. And the top is clever being a cutting board too."

"Does the top look like anything other than a thick slab of wood?"

"Not really, I'm just assuming you would need a thick slab for cutting or pounding on it. But wait, is it too thick? Oh now I get it, it has a secret compartment?"

"That obvious, huh?"

"No, not really, you basically led me to that conclusion. I don't think it would have occurred to me that there was anything but a thick slab of wood."

"All right, but now that you know, how would you open it?"

Marsha examined the lid more closely and felt along the edges. "Looks like I'd start by undoing these screws in the corners."

"Yes, that's all it is, undo the screws and lift up the inner slab." George then proceeded to tell her about the missing coins. She didn't interrupt, but her facial expressions were very telling.

"So that's where I'm at…" he concluded. "Was it Lenny? Was it Sylvia? And what's my recourse in any event?"

"I guess on one level you can be thankful no one is dead or dying."

"Right, there is that… but it sets me back quite a bit, just when I thought I was digging myself out of a hole. And either one of them are despicable. Lenny would surely use the coins for drug money and I don't see Sylvia putting the money towards William's education."

Marsha nearly interrupted him. "George, can I look inside the compartment?"

"I guess… sure, let me undo the screws."

George removed the lid and inside was an empty compartment about an inch deep and basically 12 by 12 inches in width. The inside edges and bottom were lined in glued down blue felt. Marsha noticed a few black smears here and there, like swipes of fingerprints.

"Fingerprints! Look, George, is there enough of a print in these smears to be identifiable?"

"Well, I'm no detective, but it would be worth having a detective look at them."

"Oh, but wait, could those prints be yours? When you packed the coins in there, is it likely your fingertips were coated with grease?"

"Not a chance. I always handled the coins with washed hands, sometimes I even thought about wearing white gloves as most coin handlers do. For some coins there's the face value and the numismatic value. I was always mindful of keeping the coins as clean as possible."

"Well, I'm no detective either, but two things favor Lenny over Sylvia. First, if she had taken the coins before you left, you wouldn't have just recently noticed a change in the weight of the tool box. Secondly, Lenny would be the more likely of the two to have grease on his fingers. Perhaps we should get over to Killarney first thing tomorrow morning and report the theft."

"I'm thinking we should head back to Britt and report the theft there, much closer to the scene of the crime.... but it still nags at me that Sylvia has suddenly purchased an expensive bike and who knows how much the car cost. Then there's that reference to a gold mine."

"Yes, there is that... but I still think we should start with the obvious first. Let's head to Britt first thing tomorrow morning. I'll get to Killarney another day."

George replaced the lid and carefully slid the tool box under the dinette using only the edges of the cardboard to do so. It occurred to him that the sides of the box could have fingerprints on it too.

Marsha started to do some prep for dinner, and George continued to be a ball of nervous energy.

"George... you need to do something... why don't you dinghy over to shore and try calling Gerry again. Maybe he's been trying to call you..."

"Yes, good idea. And don't worry, I won't get out of the dinghy."

CHAPTER 13

GEORGE WAS ABOUT TEN FEET away from the rock ledge when he picked up cell tower reception. There were two missed calls. One from Gerry's marina and one from a number he didn't recognize. He listened to Gerry's message first:

"Hey, George, sorry I was a bit tied up on the docks. Lenny stopped by the day after you left with Marsha. He returned a small screw driver, said he was sorry, it got mixed up with his tools and didn't realize it until after you left. I assured him I'd get it to you. But haven't seen him since. I'll see you Saturday?"

Lenny had the tool? Lenny returned it? Either he's stupid as shit or he's not the culprit. I'm going to lose my mind over this, George ruminated.

The second message was from the man who hired him to change the oil in his boat. "You fucking asshole! My engines won't start. What the hell did you do to my boat? Call me back as soon as possible!! I'm out of my mind with this and I'm seriously thinking about having you arrested for fraud and tampering with my engines!"

"Jesus Christ!" George said out loud. To himself he pondered what the hell could have gone wrong with a simple oil change. It was odd in the first place that he was hired to do such a simple, albeit messy, job. Most boat owners prided themselves with the ability to do their own routine maintenance. There was no reason that Ernie, the boat owner, couldn't have done the job himself. Would have saved himself two hundred dollars. George calmed himself down by stating the obvious, at least obvious to George. Ernie's boat was old and had a host of problems. He was just looking for someone to blame, and George was the nearest target. It wasn't the first time George had been blamed for old boat problems and it wouldn't be the last. He'd deal with Ernie later.

He then thought about calling Sylvia, catching her off guard. As he rehearsed possible questions in his mind, he heard some stomping not far off. He looked up the embankment only to see a mother black bear and her cub. He didn't panic. No need. He was in a boat with a motor. He snapped a photo of the bears with his cell phone and headed back to the boat.

About halfway back his phone beeped. A voice mail message. He turned the dinghy around and headed back to shore until two bars showed up. "Okay you asshole, now my boat is sinking and you're to blame. I'm having you arrested for negligence."

CHAPTER 14

MARSHA WAS PLACING DINNER PLATES on the back deck's table when George stepped up from the swim platform. He had tied the dinghy so it would drift off the stern end. Hopefully, they wouldn't hear the incessant "boat slap" during the night if he let it out far enough.

"Marsha, I had a very disturbing phone call from Ernie, the guy who owned that Jefferson 46 in the Byng Inlet. He claims his engines won't start and now his boat is sinking. He's trying to blame that on me."

"What? Wait… you did an oil change and you sabotaged his engines and then did something to make the boat sink? He's a wacko or looking for insurance money."

"Yes, of course, he obviously has a boatload of problems—pardon the pun—with his boat and needs someone to blame them on. That would be me. Shit! Marsha, I know you wanted to check out some other anchorages, but I think we should just go the outside route and head straight back to the marina. I'm so sorry, but I won't be good company until all these issues are resolved."

"That's fine George, I really understand." Marsha really did understand. She was disappointed, but he was right. If

234

his mind was elsewhere, a new anchorage would be lost on both of them.

George then perked up a bit. "Hey, stupid Ernie doesn't have to ruin our evening. In fact, don't we have a bottle of red wine? Might be just what we need to view the sunset. Looks like it's going to be a good one."

His sporadic sentimentality surprised Marsha but endeared him to her at the same time. Why didn't Sylvia see that in him? And for that matter, why didn't ex-George see the sentimentality in her? Shit head. She let it go. After two glasses of red wine, current George became all she needed in life.

CHAPTER 15

G EORGE WAS AWAKE WELL BEFORE Marsha. He dinghied
to shore and attempted to text a message to Ernie. It
went through. He picked some blueberries while waiting for
a response. Might as well do something while I'm waiting, he
thought to himself. After 20 minutes he gave up.

Marsha read his face correctly upon his return. She
laughed to herself, are we becoming an old married couple
already? We've only been together about a week and already
I can read him.

"No go, I take it."

"That's right. But the upside is that I picked about two
cups of blueberries while waiting. Didn't get bit by a snake
nor eaten by a bear."

"Bears and snakes and blueberries, oh my!" Marsha laughed
out loud.

"Silly girl. Come here."

He swept her up in his arms and they returned to the
stateroom. A wonderful round of love making reinforced to
Marsha that sex with ex-George for the two years leading up
to his ending the relationship was really quite robotic. Her
mind wandered to ex-George's routine. He typically left the

house at 5:45 A.M. and sex became something one would put on a check list: Get up—pee—fuck—shave—shower—get dressed—drink coffee—grab toast—drive—work.

"Marsha, where did you go?"

"Sorry, George... but at least you'll be happy to know I've really enjoyed sex with you. So relaxed... so unconditional.... so not routine."

"Interesting... I couldn't get Sylvia to let sex linger. Well at first, yes... but then, it was all business. A means to an end. And then after William was born, that was pretty much the end of our sex life. At least, her sex life with me. I'm sure she and Victor enjoyed a good romp for years, and still enjoy."

"I'm so sorry, George... and I'm sorry for me, too. Damn! All right, enough of the mutual pity party. Let's get on with the day."

"Do you want more coffee?"

"Actually, yes. But I think I'll drink it in bed. Maybe I could find a way to use it to make my mouth hot for you," Marsha said seductively.

"Really? I love that plan."

When they finally re-emerged from the stateroom, it was nearly 10:00. Marsha mixed some of the blueberries into her yogurt and George followed suit.

"Don't remember the last time I had fresh blueberries," George commented. "Most of my fruit comes in by container ships."

"Can't they grow fresh vegetables and fruit in the Abacos? It's hot all year round."

"Well, that would require quite a line-up of things. First, good soil, second a willing labor force, third, some ingenuity.

Any one of those is rare from what I've observed anyway."

"I find that so hard to believe. Why wouldn't you want to do anything you could to have fresh produce?"

"Marsha… turn off your American brain. The soil is rotten for the most part and it would take a lot of incentive to get a work force in place. They like the status quo and that's that."

"Yes, boss…" Marsha said sarcastically.

"Okay, we'll solve world problems later. In the meantime, let's head back to Britt."

The chart plotter on Marsha's boat had left a "track" making it easy for them to retrace their steps. No need to get back into the dinghy to sound out the channels. Then Marsha plotted a course directly back to Byng Inlet.

"Hey look at this, George, my phone is actually picking up a cell signal."

The words no sooner came off her lips when both phones received "dings." Marsha had received some text messages from her kids, and George had another voice mail from Ernie.

This voice mail was even more disturbing: "You fucking asshole. Why don't you return my calls? I'm calling the Canadian Coast Guard to track you down."

George tried to call back but just about as quickly as the cell signal appeared, it disappeared. He hoped that Ernie's phone would at least pick up the missed call attempt from him.

After ruminating about the situation to himself he blurted out "What the hell? This is crazy. This guy is a nut case."

"So reminiscent of a law suit brought against me early in my career. It's a long story."

"Talk away, I think we have six hours before we get back to Britt."

"Well, we had this guy who became what we called a frequent flyer into the O. R. He had an ulcer that wouldn't heal and he needed repeat debridements…"

"Debridements?"

"Cleaning out of the dead cells so as to prevent infection. He was an ex-alcoholic, or so he said. My suspicion was that he never stopped drinking which just fueled his underlying diabetes, making healing difficult. Anyway I probably put him to sleep four or five times, as just about everyone else did in the department. Eventually, he healed enough and was discharged. He returned to his home in Utica, a small town about two hours away from the hospital. About a year later he filed suit against the hospital for pain and suffering from a surgical sponge being left in the stomach. At the top of the list of specific people being named in the lawsuit was me! I couldn't believe it! The job of anesthesia is to keep a person breathing. In a nutshell, we keep air going in and out, and blood going round and round. Nowhere in my bag of tools are surgical sponges, and at no time would I be shoving a sponge down someone's throat. The very idea to any sane person is ludicrous. And to top it all off, at the end of that particular day's surgical notes, was a note from the gastroenterologist stating that an endoscopic sweep of the stomach was clear. In other words there was never a surgical sponge in the stomach, at least, not on that day."

"How did he crop up with that story?"

"Apparently he had some belly pain and saw a local gastroenterologist. He was scoped and the doctor found a sponge which was removed and thrown away. There was no solid evidence that it was actually a surgical sponge—which by the way just means there's a metal strip in the sponge, which can be seen under Xray. Certainly, if he really did have a surgical sponge in his gut in the months he was at our hospital, one of the eight billion X-rays would have revealed its presence."

"So how did a sponge wind up there?"

"I think he intentionally swallowed it in a premeditated attempt to extract money from some very deep pockets. He probably ran out of booze money."

"Well, it seems pretty straight forward that you were innocent."

"You'd think, but he was that annoying little mosquito that just wouldn't go away… so eventually, as in seven years later, the hospital paid him $50,000 to settle out of court. Makes me sick to think of what that money could have been used for instead, never mind the collective headaches and angst he caused so many people."

"Seven years? That's bloody nonsense! Okay, so maybe this thing with Ernie isn't so bad after all. Do you think…… Oh shit!" George interrupted himself. "Something's wrong with the engines, we're overheating!"

Without further explanation George raced down to the helm station in the main salon where the on/off controls were located. He yelled up to Marsha, "I'm turning the engines off!"

Marsha looked at the depth sounder. 50 feet below them and no nearby rocks to drift toward since they had decided to take the outside route back to Britt. They could drift for awhile before needing to make some sort of plan.

The engine noise stopped abruptly, and she could hear George opening the engine hatches. Steam billowed out and was visible from the fly bridge.

"Are we on fire?" Marsha screamed, starting to abandon her usual calm self in a crisis situation and go immediately to panic mode.

"No, that's steam," he yelled up. "Looks like it was the starboard engine that overheated. I'm going to turn the port one back on." Like a trooper, the port engine fired right up, and Marsha resumed driving the boat albeit at a much slower speed. Her pulse rate also calmed down, and she sent a mental note to the Engine Gods, thanking them for not having both engines overheat at the same time, and for not breaking down whilst going through a narrow rock lined passage with current forcing them onto a reef.

George returned to the fly bridge. Sweat lined his brow.

"God, I hate your engine room. It's too hot to do anything now. We'll have to wait until the engines cool down to take a closer look. At the very least we'll have to put in a new impeller. "

"My father made me buy some key spare parts, mainly fuel and oil filters, but also spare impellers."

"What a good dad. You're very lucky."

"Yes, no matter what shit happens to me in life, I can honestly say knowing I have two wonderful parents has saved me over and over again. How about you?"

"Didn't know my real dad. My step father was okay, did the best he could, but my mother wasn't an easy person to live with, which is probably what drove my real father away in the first place. My mother passed away a few years ago from lung cancer. She was the poster child for why you shouldn't smoke."

"I'm so sorry. Any siblings?"

"Just a much younger half-sister by my mother and stepfather. He had two older sons when they got married, so technically I have 2 step brothers, but honestly I think I've only seen them 3 times since the wedding. They stayed with their mum and visits to see my step father were few and far between. Since my mother died I've lost track of the whole lot altogether. And who knows if my real father procreated again or not. I could have a flock of half siblings out there somewhere."

"A flock of siblings?" Marsha mused with emphasis on the word "flock."

"Maybe a herd? A gaggle? I don't know."

"Could be a clutch or a pod. The English language has so many words meaning 'group of.' You can actually google 'collective nouns' and you'll come up with quite a list of weird words. My favorites are 'a murder of crows,' 'a clowder of cats,' and 'a charm of goldfinches.' If I ever write a book, I'm going to title it "A Murder of Crows." The title will have a double meaning since the first scene will be the protagonist looking at a murdered crow. Of course, I have no idea where the story goes from there."

"Well, no doubt with that imagination of yours you'll come up with something clever."

"Hope so, but once I'm back with the girls and with work, there's little to no time to think about anything except daily survival."

"You can say that again."

For the next few hours Marsha and George discussed best case and worst case scenarios. Concerning her engine, if it was just a matter of replacing the impeller, she'd be good to go after about an hour's worth of labor. Marsha silently thanked the Engine Gods again that the problem was the starboard engine not the port engine. To get to the starboard impeller was fairly easy, only the water intake hose had to be removed to get to the face plate of the impeller housing. On the port side it meant slithering in between the engine and the engine room bulkhead. No easy feat for anyone taller than five feet or weighing over a hundred pounds. Going back to worst case scenario, if the heat exchanger was cracked, it would be a show stopper since it would then have to be hauled out and replaced. It was more money than Marsha could imagine, and she shuttered at the thought of having to sell the boat for salvage. There was nothing more to say about crazy Ernie until they confronted him in Britt. And then the matter of the gold coins… Marsha gently suggested that perhaps William had been snooping in the tool box and inadvertently discovered the coins.

"No way," George asserted. "You can take William right out of the equation." Marsha quickly dropped the idea, George's tone told her that any further discussion on William's involvement was a no go zone. As soon as they were back in cell phone range, George preemptively called Ernie.

George left a message: "Ernie, not sure how an oil change could have damaged your engines or make your boat sink, but I'll be in Britt in just a few hours. You can meet me at the marina and we'll sort this out."

Next he called Gerry. His daughter answered and explained Gerry was helping out another boater, but she'd have him call back as soon as possible.

It wasn't too long before Gerry called back. Turns out he was with Ernie trying to restart his engines.

"George, this guy is very difficult. He wants your head chopped off and basically for you to buy him a new boat. My best guess is that he or someone put water into the fuel tank. There was definitely water in the fuel separator which I drained, and then I replaced the fuel filters, but again, more water showed up in the fuel separator. Unfortunately, I'm afraid the fuel tank will need to be emptied. As for the sinking accusation, don't know what to make of that. The bilge pump was going off frequently, but I couldn't find any obvious leaks and the boat doesn't seem low in the water at all."

"Well, I'm sorry for his troubles, but I just don't see how an oil change would create any of his problems."

"Oh, I told him that numerous times, but it fell on deaf ears. And I have to say, he's been acting very oddly. He's been varnishing his bright work endlessly and is constantly sniffing at his rag he uses for solvent between coats of varnish."

"Gerry, would you mind being witness to any conversation I have with Ernie? Sorry to put you in the middle, but I feel like I need a third party just to discuss his accusations."

"Actually, he's already called the Coast Guard and they told him to call the police since workmanship issues really aren't in their jurisdiction. I think it'll be good to have an officer witness your encounter, since you're obviously not guilty. Oh, and not to worry, Ernie has a list of wrongs that Lenny committed, too."

"Lenny? What did he do?"

"Ernie hired him to clean, wax and polish his boat. He didn't pay him because he thought the work was awful and that Lenny had marred the fiberglass instead of cleaning it. They had quite an argument, and I haven't seen Lenny since."

"Hmmm.... interesting.... well, all right then, see you in a few hours."

George relayed the gist of the conversation to Marsha.

"You don't suppose Lenny got so pissed off at Ernie about not being paid that he deliberately put water into the fuel tank?"

"I don't know about that.... couldn't be done during the day since it would be too easily witnessed. At night? Maybe if Ernie was off the boat it could be done under cover of darkness. But that's a pretty serious accusation."

"It is... and so is thinking that Lenny took your coins."

"Guess we need to find Lenny."

Chapter 16

Marsha brought *Boldly Go* back to the same slip she had been in without too much difficulty. Being down an engine made the final turn into the slip challenging, but the bow and stern thrusters did their magic. She was happy for George's coaching. Fortunately, since he wasn't her father, brother or husband, he didn't make her nervous when she manipulated the gears. George handled the lines and soon they were hooked up to electricity and water. The pump out dock was occupied when they came in, so she would have to tend to that chore at a later time. Ernie's boat was only two docks away.

Ernie was standing on the port side of his boat looking very angry.

"Oh hi, Ernie! Nice to see you. George will be over in just a bit." Marsha said as saccharinely sweet as possible. Kill him with kindness was her motive.

George muttered under his breath "Marsha, I really wanted a policeman to be present. Now you'll have to stall him."

"No problem, I'm good at that." She stepped below and put on one of her low cut, sexier tops. Then she changed into her skinny jeans. George put in a non-emergency call to the local police. Britt was a small community with little crime, so basically one officer was chief, cook and bottle washer. As the answering machine promised, the sole officer did call him back fairly promptly. Meanwhile, Marsha sauntered over to Ernie's boat *Seaquest*.

When George explained the situation to Officer Bill Malone, Bill essentially laughed at him. "That's all nonsense and it's really not a police matter. If he's unhappy with your work then he can file a lawsuit or an insurance claim. I assume you carry insurance as a mechanic?"

"Actually, I do, but I've never used it, never had to"

"Well, it sounds like it's time to put all those premiums to work."

"Look, I realize this is nonsense, but Ernie seems like the type of guy who could get pretty physical if he doesn't get the answers he wants."

"I suppose I could justify coming down to the marina to check on the police patrol boat down there. See you in a few."

George looked through his wallet for his worker's insurance card. Some boat yards demanded that outside workers carry their own insurance. He hated paying the premiums, especially since no one had ever made a claim against him. Guess there's a first time for everything, George thought to himself. Then he thought through his plan to actually talk to Ernie. He decided to be as matter-of-fact as possible and not lose his temper. Easier said than done. He would simply apologize to Ernie, saying he was sorry Ernie was unhappy with his work and then just give him his insurance information. Ernie could then file a claim and the insurance company would take it from there. Ernie, you Asshole! And this day has just gone to shit, he thought to himself. He and Marsha should have just stayed in bed and not answered any calls. He still needed to help Marsha with her overheated engine, never mind figure out what happened to all his money.

Marsha had walked over to Ernie's boat ahead of George and thought she heard Ernie talking to someone. She assumed he was having a telephone conversation since there was no one else on the boat. She waited patiently for him to finish before asking permission to step aboard. Then she noticed he didn't have a phone in his hand. That's odd, she said to herself and then looked more inquisitively at him. He seemed to be talking to his engine room. She eventually discerned snippets of his conversation:

"You bastard, I told you not to act up...."

Then he noticed Marsha standing on the dock. "What the hell do you want?"

"Um sorry, Ernie... I uh just told you a few minutes ago that George would be over to talk to you about the oil change problem? I didn't mean to interrupt your conversation..."

"Yeah, yeah, yeah, that engine thinks he knows every goddamn thing..."

At this point alarm bells started to sound off in Marsha's brain. This is not normal behavior... he's being very irrational... I think he was actually talking to his engine! She perused her brain. What causes someone to suddenly be irrational? Her brain search was interrupted with George's arrival.

"What a beautiful boat you have!" George said cheerfully. The insincerity was painfully evident to Marsha, but seemed to momentarily charm Ernie. "The bright work alone is amazing. Did you do all that yourself?"

"Every last bit of it," he said proudly. But then his demeanor abruptly changed to anger. "You no good asshole, you certainly took your time. My boat was working just fine until you put your grubby hands on it. And don't step on my boat, keep your distance, that's far enough! Ever since you changed the oil, my boat hasn't been the same."

Ernie reached for a rag tucked into his shirt's breast pocket and sniffed it, then stuffed it back in.

"Jesus Christ!" Marsha blurted out loud. "You're sniffing! You're high! No wonder you're irrational!" Both Ernie and George turned to her with stunned looks.

Marsha couldn't help herself. She figured it out: "Ernie, what are you sniffing?" Turpentine? Acetone?"

"None of your goddamn business!" Ernie exclaimed.

"Really? It is my business!"

Without further hesitation she whipped out her cellphone and called 911.

By now several other boaters were listening and watching. Also, Officer Malone, who had arrived at the marina and had sauntered down to his police boat, noticed the commotion.

"What's going on?" Bill Malone questioned as he advanced toward Ernie, Marsha and George.

Marsha was in the middle of giving information to the 911 operator. "He's probably 60 years old, conscious but acting irrational. He's sniffing a rag full of some sort of solvent that's affecting his behavior. I believe he needs immediate medical attention. We're at the Britt Marina in the Byng Inlet..."

Ernie lunged at her in an attempt to grab her phone away from her. Bill intervened with George about a half a step behind him.

DIANE E. GRABO: *WAITING ON A PART*

"Let's calm down here, buddy," Bill said to Ernie. "It's all good, let's just get you to the hospital and sort this out."

It took a bit of doing for Bill and George to keep Ernie from alternately lunging at Marsha and trying to reach for the rag. George eventually wrestled the rag from Ernie, and Marsha stepped away. Mercifully, the ambulance arrived in another ten minutes. Ernie escalated and lobbed several threats at the ambulance attendants, Marsha, George, Bill, and everyone else in listening range. Officer Malone helped the attendants get him into the ambulance and then followed the ambulance in his police car.

George turned to Marsha. "What was that all about?"

"Well, certain solvents, if inhaled or sniffed frequently enough, could render someone irrational. If the inhalant is fat insoluble then it's in and out of your system in a very short period of time. Sort of like nitrous oxide, or laughing gas, in whipped cream canisters."

"You mean Whippets?" asked George.

"Exactly, not that I would know first hand… but the effect only lasts a few seconds. Again, in and out of your system. But if it's fat soluble, it can literally stick around for long periods of time, like some glues. And if overdone, some solvents can be lethal. I suspect Ernie has somehow gotten a hold of one of those dry cleaning or film development solvents that can be pretty toxic to one's organ systems. Now that I think about it, I doubt we're talking turpentine or acetone. Those wouldn't really lead to such irrational behavior."

"So what will they do for him in the hospital?"

"If a toxin comes in through the lungs, then it has to go out through the lungs. They'll have to flush it out of his system, basically put him on 100% oxygen. Psychiatry will get involved to check out his mental status and take it from there. So, I don't think you need to worry about his claim against you. Hopefully, he'll come around to his normal self in just a few days."

Gerry, who had been attending to another boater, came down to the dock. Marsha and George filled him in.

"I thought it was odd that he kept sniffing at something in his shirt pocket. Didn't realize it was soaked with some sort of solvent. You know, he was a normal guy until his wife passed away last year. He had just sold his dry cleaning business and was all set to retire with his wife when, just like that, she dropped dead from a heart attack. He seemed to be grieving as one would expect, but then he just started acting so squirrelly."

"Did you say he ran a dry cleaning business?" Marsha asked.

"Yes, had the business for decades before he sold it to his much younger brother and sister-in-law in town. They still run it."

"Well, it seems Ernie took some of the solvents with him. That stuff can be pretty toxic. And it can most definitely make you irrational if you sniff it. Pretty much explains his behavior," Marsha concluded.

Marsha and George were able to wrap up their conversation with Gerry without him knowing how badly they just wanted to get back to *Boldly Go*. They were physically and mentally exhausted. Marsha put together a meal of leftovers, and after dinner they promptly retired to the state room.

"I can't believe how tired I am, especially since I'm used to doing 24 hour calls. Guess I'm out of practice." She started to peel off her clothes.

"Hey, that's my job!" George exclaimed. He gently helped her remove her panties and doffed his clothes as well. They slid under the covers and Marsha seemed to be falling asleep.

"Oh no you don't, lassie. We're not quite done with the evening."

George gently cupped her breasts as he nibbled on her ear lobes. She moaned softly, her loins starting to awaken, wafting between dreaming and arousal. George started to caress and suckle her nipples. Now fully awake Marsha lifted up her chest and said to George, "Oh no, laddie, it's my turn to pleasure you."

Marsha rolled George over on his back. She enveloped his mouth, kissed his lips and sucked his tongue. She slowly descended down his muscular chest, softly licking his nipples, then following the line of his hair leading to his navel, circling briefly until she realized how his cock had grown to meet her lips.

She moved her body so that she engulfed his throbbing penis by her warm mouth. She used her tongue to lick his shaft as she moved up and down to tantalize him. Then she wrapped her hand around him and continued to stroke him, keeping her lips on the tip of his cock. She stroked and pumped until she felt his body tense, on the verge of cumming.

She slid her chest upwards along his chest until she placed her hot, wet pussy onto his mouth. He hungrily lapped at her as electric shocks shot through her body. Sensing she too was on the verge of cumming, she slid down to his hips, grabbed his cock and guided it into her. She thrust down upon him, until the base of his cock was pumping against her mound. She began to grind and ride him. Her back arched as he lifted her off the bed with his back thrusting upward. They both came and collapsed in ecstasy.

Chapter 17

The next morning Marsha found herself intertwined in George's arms. She loved the entanglement and tried to enjoy it as long as she could. Unfortunately, once again her bladder ruled, and she had to get up to pee.

God damn it! Couldn't I have a larger bladder? Marsha questioned. She reluctantly got up and headed to the forward head so as to not awaken George with the sound of a flushing toilet in their aft cabin. She flicked on the coffee maker before entering the forward head. One benefit of this annoying morning necessity would be making herself a cup of coffee before returning to the stateroom. Somewhere in their almost week together they had established a nice routine of her greeting him with coffee. He took a sip and she took a sip. Only her sip was followed by a hot coffee blow job. Made the morning love making a bit more of a thrill.

Once up and about George was all business. "Well, let's take a look at that starboard engine now that she's had a chance to cool down. They rolled up the rug in the main salon, lifted up the four floor boards and George entered the engine room.

"By the way, have I mentioned to you how much I hate your engine room?"

254

"Oh, about a million times," Marsha answered.

"All right then." He looked over the engine as Marsha looked upon him trying to glean as much knowledge as she could. She had an amusing idea of becoming a marine mechanic as her main vocation. If that could ever be achieved, she'd ditch her day job, live full time on her boat and fix engines for a living. At least there wouldn't be any dreaded paper work or new Medicare/Medicaid rules to deal with.

"Marsha, I think it's just a bad impeller. All the hoses are intact and I'm not seeing anything obviously wrong with the water pump. And to ease your mind, no cracks in the crank case."

George had an impeller extractor in his tool box, and she had an extra impeller. Together they undid the hoses over the impeller casing, undid the impeller cover and extracted the defective impeller. That was the easy part. Getting the new impeller in place required a bit of doing. But after a few attempts, it was in place. The cover was returned as well as the hoses. George had dripped some dish soap into the impeller housing before closing it up. When he then turned on the engine, Marsha was instructed to look for exiting water from the exhaust pipes which would be highlighted with soap bubbles.

"Yes!" Marsha gladly shouted to George when she saw soapy water exit the boat. "Oh wow, is that it? Am I good to go?"

"Yes you are. But you should order more impellers, they obviously don't last forever and often fail at inconvenient times."

"So what's next George?"

"Next?"

"Yes, do we venture out again or do we track down your missing coins?" Inwardly, Marsha had counted the days to George's planned departure. Four. Four days and this wonderful affair would come to an abrupt end... and again, she just didn't see a Hollywood ending coming along.

"As much as I want to continue our adventures, I have to admit I can't rest until the coins are found."

"I get that, but where do we start?"

"Lenny. We need to find Lenny."

Chapter 18

George and Marsha gathered up their toiletries and towels to head up to the shore showers. The extra layer of engine grime necessitated a full "Hollywood" shower instead of their usual spartan Navy showers.

As they were about to exit there was a knock on the side of the boat followed by "Hello? George? It's Bill Malone."

George popped his head out the sliding companion way door. "Oh hello, Bill, come aboard."

"Thanks, just wanted to follow-up on last night's commotion. Ernie turned out to be quite a handful, but his brother was contacted and took charge. Actually, it was the sister-in-law who was the most helpful. Seems she has some sort of counseling degree and knew how to talk him down."

Marsha piped in, "Well that's good. I hope he gets the help he needs."

"Yeah, he certainly was on quite a rant. He eventually yelled out about his boat being taken over by gold which was counteracting the effectiveness of his zincs, or some such nonsense as that..."

George quickly interrupted: "Gold? Did you say gold?"

Bill looked a bit startled, but calmly answered, "Yes, something about gold coins."

George and Marsha exchanged glances. Marsha was about to say something but George's look to her clearly conveyed "don't say a word." Out loud he replied to Bill, "Strange fellow…" and left it at that.

"Thanks for letting us know his condition," Marsha quickly interjected.

As Bill started to walk away, George called out, "Hey, Bill, sorry to keep you, any idea where I might find Lenny? I owe him his final day's pay." Stupid to lie but he did it anyway.

"If you mean that ne'er-do-well kid who's always getting into trouble, you'll likely find him at Jack's Bar."

"Jack's Bar? Where's that?"

"About a 15 minute drive from here. You can just GPS it."

"All right, thanks."

After saying goodbye to Bill, George turned to Marsha and said, "Let's get on with the day. After we shower, I want to drive up to Jack's Bar."

"Sure, I could use some time to clean up the boat."

George banked on the bar being open by noon. It's five o'clock somewhere, he mused to himself. The bar wasn't hard to find and already several cars were parked outside. No sign of a bicycle, however.

George walked into the dimly lit bar and glanced around for the bartender. A gruff looking individual appeared from the kitchen area and looked straight at him.

"What can I get cha?" His tone was friendlier than expected.

"A Molson's will do.... say... I'm looking to find a kid I owe money to, I heard he comes here sometimes.... know anybody named Lenny?"

"Oh yeah... you might as well hand that money over to me... he owes me for so many beers it's ridiculous," the bartender replied half kidding, half serious. "But now that you mention it, I haven't seen him in days... probably too embarrassed to return here."

"Do you know where he lives?"

"That's funny too, somebody's couch or garage.... so many people have tried to help him, but he just keeps screwing up and burning bridges.... so sorry, no... no idea where he lives or where he might be."

"I was afraid of that... Can I give you my business card in the off chance he comes around? I'm staying at the Britt Marina."

"Sure, no problem... can I get you anything else?"

"No, one beer should do, thanks."

George finished his beer in silence as the bartender tended to the other customers. He left cash on the bar and left.

Driving back to the marina he decided to pick up some more groceries. As he pulled into the local food mart, he noticed a bike on its side to the right of the parking lot. Could it be Lenny's?

Closer inspection revealed yes; the make shift saddle bags were a dead giveaway. But the bike looked like it had been left there for days, given that new grass blades were poking through the spokes.

George walked into the food mart and immediately asked

the check-out clerk if she knew anything about the abandoned bike.

"Yeah, I noticed that too when I came into work today. No idea why it's there. Would you like me to call my manager? He's here a lot."

"Yes, please." George picked up a few snacks while he waited for her to call her boss. She signaled for him to take her phone.

"Here, this is Martin, you can talk to him yourself."

"Hey, Martin, my name is George Wainwright and I'm looking for a kid named Lenny. I owe him some wages... I see his bike is here... know where I might find him?"

"Try the local jail or hospital. That kid is nothing but trouble. I caught him trying to shoplift some candy the other day. He threw out the candy bars as he ran out the door so technically he didn't take anything. Don't know where he went, but it is odd that he left his bike. Must be he ran into someone who gave him a ride. I'm going to throw that bike in the dumpster."

"Well, maybe if he got his pay he wouldn't have to steal," George proposed. "Mind giving him a day or two to reclaim his bike and if so, let him know I have his wages to give him? I'm staying in the Britt Marina."

"Okay, sure... what the hell...."

After George paid for his groceries, he placed them in his car and then walked over to the bike. He lifted the bike up and leaned it against the back side of the store. Out of sight of any customers he rifled through the saddlebags. A handful of dirty clothes and one crumpled boat card. The boat's logo was unmistakable "*Happy Hearts.*"

"Well, I'll be damned" George said out loud. He stuffed the card in his pocket and returned to *Boldly Go*.

As he approached the boat, George noticed Marsha visiting with another woman on the stern deck.

"Hey George, this is Maria, Ernie's sister-in-law."

"Nice to meet you Maria. How's Ernie doing?"

"Better. But full recovery will take some time. Apparently, sniffing solvents is quite an addiction to get over. I came down to pick up a few clothes for him from his boat and just to check on things in general."

"Mind if I tag along? I could check his bilge for you and just make sure everything is ship shape."

Both Maria and Marsha laughed. Maria explained, "Marsha already volunteered you to do the dirty work. I hate that stuff."

After a few more pleasantries the three of them boarded Ernie's boat. It had a similar layout to Marsha's boat, complete with four floor boards needing to be lifted up. Marsha helped with maneuvering the floor boards while Maria went into Ernie's stateroom to gather up some clothes and toiletries. George checked the oil in both engines and the generator. Then he lifted up the engine room floor boards overtly to check on any lingering water in the bilges, but covertly stalling for time to nose around for any evidence of gold coins. Nothing. Nothing except a sick smelling slick of engine oil, coolant, standing water and molded wood framing. Good thing Maria didn't come down here, he said to himself. She'd be throwing up by now. The mold on the wood did have a yellow sheen to it oddly enough. Was this the "gold" Ernie ranted about? For a moment George thought about volunteering to clean up the mess, but his more practical side simply said 'not my circus, not my monkey,' a phrase he used often.

Marsha must have been reading his mind. "Wow, that's disgusting! Can we just leave that mess?"

"Uh, yes, yes we can. This job is too big, I think it's only the tip of the iceberg. Let's just run the bilge pump and at least get some of the slime out."

Marsha flicked on the bilge pump switch on the nearby electrical panel, feeling a bit guilty about dumping such foul water into the bay. By then Maria had packed up Ernie's belongings and looked down into the engine room.

"What a mess. I'll tell my husband, and he and Ernie will have to work it out. So the boat's not sinking is it?"

"No, not sinking, just stinking," George replied. They laughed but more in resignation than in humor.

"Okay, well thanks, George. Appreciate you getting your hands dirty."

"No problem, Maria, glad to help."

Maria left the marina, and George and Marsha returned to *Boldly Go*. Marsha picked up the small bag of groceries George had left on the stern deck and emptied the contents in the galley.

"I see you're having a junk food crisis. Jesus, George, popcorn, beef jerky, pork rinds…. what the hell are pork rinds? Is that edible?"

"Hey," George kidded back, "a man can only eat so many blueberries!"

"Well, at least you didn't buy any butter tarts."

"Butter tarts? Sounds good, what are they?"

"It's a Looper thing… only found in Canada, way too sweet for me. So, did you find out anything at the bar?"

"Yes and no. Seems Lenny owes the bartender for a bunch of beers and then oddly enough I found his bike at the food mart. The manager caught him trying to steal some candy a few days ago. He ran out of the store but left his bike."

"He left his only means of transportation? That is odd!"

"Yeah, very odd. His saddle bags had dirty clothes stuffed in them and then this:"

He showed her the boat card.

"Well, he was working on *Happy Hearts* so I guess that's not so odd."

"Let's just call Dennis and Ginny, see where they're at. It could be under the guise that we just wanted to see them again before we all go off in different directions."

Marsha dutifully called, but the call went right into voice mail. She left a message stating they were near the Henvey Inlet and wondered if they were still in the Flower Pots anchorage. She left her number and George's.

"They're probably in one of those pockets of no cell service," Marsha offered.

"No doubt…. I'm thinking the coins have to be on *Happy Hearts*. When I came back from that errand and caught Lenny in the stateroom he looked awfully guilty, but again since he was empty handed, I let it go. Suppose he found the bags of coins, was about to take them to his bike and I interrupted that plan with my return? He could have had just enough time to stash the bags somewhere in the Burton's stateroom."

"Well, I guess…. seems like a long shot."

"If he had off loaded the coins, he wouldn't be trying to steal candy."

"True... so let's go find *Happy Hearts*. But first I'm taking your car to get some real groceries."

On her return she went to the office to pay for the dockage and to tell Gerry they'd be back in just a few days. Gerry asked about Ernie, and Marsha gave him the latest details. As she was leaving, Gerry called out, "Oh by the way, I heard through the grapevine that Lenny went out fishing and camping with a friend of his. Maybe that's why no one has seen him for a while."

"Hmmmm...... that's interesting, thanks, Gerry!"

Marsha couldn't wait to tell George the news. More fuel for the fire and reason to get off the dock.

"Fishing boats can travel pretty fast. And maybe a friend of his saw him in the food mart's parking lot and picked him up." George was thinking out loud and continued on with more possibilities. "Or maybe Lenny saw a friend and talked him into taking him out in pursuit of *Happy Heart* to get the coins..."

"Well, let's head out and see what we see..."

CHAPTER 19

MARSHA WAS ABLE TO BACK OUT of the slip consider-ably more easily than entering the slip. Two working engines and, of course, the thrusters made all the difference. She hadn't erased any of her course lines, so it was also a less nerve wracking trip threading through the small boat channel to the Henvey Inlet. She was picking up some AIS signals but not from *Happy Hearts*. The rock cliffs that had earlier in the week been occupied by other boaters were now vacant. There was no sign of the Burtons in the Flower Pot anchorage, so they turned around and tied to shore along one of the rock cliffs. It was getting to be too late in the evening to do any more exploring.

"This is so unique! I've never done this before!" Marsha exclaimed.

"Well, careful what you wish for. The mosquitos could be overwhelming this close to shore. Let's see how it goes. We may want to anchor in the bay where there's more of a breeze."

Between the screens and bug spray, the onslaught of mos-quitos was kept to a minimum and they enjoyed dinner on the back deck. Star gazing was attempted, but the clouds rolled in and obscured any further viewing. Love making was wonderful, but there was no round two. Marsha fell asleep, but George struggled with insomnia.

He eventually did drift off only to be awakened a few hours later by the sound of a passing boat going much faster than it should in the narrow channel. George sprang up and ran to the side of the boat tied to the rocks. Marsha was 30 seconds behind him. It was all they could do to keep the boat from scraping against the rocks given the massive wake left by the passing boat. Fortunately, the well placed fenders did their job and scrapes were minimal.

Marsha and George simultaneously lobbed expletives at the passing boat but to no avail. Their voices were no match for the roaring outboard motor.

"What assholes!" Marsha repeated, and now shaking due to the chilly air she hadn't noticed before.

"Do you suppose that was Lenny?"

"Hmmm… maybe. Certainly had to be a local in any event. For me it would be boating suicide to attempt to navigate these channels at night."

They went below and George turned on their navigation system. "You know, Marsha, this inlet goes well past the Flower Pots. If that was Lenny, maybe he found the Burtons further to the east. Let's check it out at first light."

It took awhile to turn off their brains, but they both fell asleep. George had set his alarm for 6 A.M., which startled both of them when it went off.

"That went by fast… I'll make some coffee…"

Marsha was glad they took the time to make love. Who knew how the day was going to turn out, and their affair had a time limit that was approaching all too fast.

The depth of the narrow channel was surprisingly deep and, once through a relatively shallow stretch of nine foot depths, the water level sunk again to depths of 20 and 30 feet. "So pretty here! But George this channel is coming to an end. You'd think by now if the Burtons were anchored we'd pick up their AIS signal."

"What makes you so sure they have their signal on? Many people turn their AIS off once solidly at anchor."

And then, around the very last navigable bend, was *Happy Hearts*. No AIS signal on the chart.

George carefully maneuvered *Boldly Go* to the starboard side of the boat since there was a bit more swing room. He had tried to hail them on the VHF, but there was no response. It was 8:00 in the morning and most Loopers were early risers, so he didn't think he would be waking them up if he simply yelled over to them. No response. They decided to anchor and then dinghy over.

The anchor set pretty immediately, and it wasn't long before they were in the dinghy. George yelled over again. No response. Finally, with a hand hold along their starboard side, he started to call out again.

"Hush! I hear something," Marsha spoke up.

And then, so did George. Snoring. They heard snoring. Embarrassed, they dinghied back to their own boat.

"Well, let's have breakfast and wait until they wake up," Marsha suggested.

"Isn't everyone up by 8:00?" George replied in a half embarrassed, half angry tone.

"There's that British Army thing coming out. They're retired, no need for them to get up early," Marsha said soothingly.

At about 9:00 Marsha and George began to see signs of life. Then just a few minutes later, Ginny yelled over: "Marsha, George, what a surprise… when did you get here?"

"Just this morning. Hey, as soon as you're settled with breakfast, would you mind if we came over? We have something to tell you."

"You're getting married?" Ginny gleefully asked.

Marsha blushed and it took her a few seconds to respond. "Uh no, nothing like that…."

Ginny quickly detected the embarrassed tone and interjected with "Come over anytime. We're all set with breakfast."

They gave it five minutes and then headed over. Dennis greeted them on the swim platform and took their line.

Once settled in the main salon George explained the situation about his coins, and then asked if anything was missing the first time he informed them that Lenny had been in their stateroom.

"Nothing was amiss," Dennis responded.

"So since you moved your boat over to this end of the Inlet, have you been off the boat at all?"

"We usually go out in our dinghy for an hour or so in the evening to fish a bit. Every once in a while we actually catch something for dinner."

"Any unusual behavior by any other boaters?"

"Not really," said Dennis.

"Wait, Dennis, remember we thought it was odd that those two young boys were camping out across the way and seemed to be fishing a bit too close to our boat?"

"I guess, but this is a narrow channel and we're right in the middle of it."

"I'm highly suspicious that Lenny and a friend have been just waiting for you two to be off your boat long enough to retrieve my coins. Do you mind looking around again to see if now there's something missing?"

"All right, Ginny...." Dennis stood up and politely waited for Ginny to stand up and proceed into their stateroom.

After a few minutes, but what seemed like hours to George, Ginny called out: "My new boating shoes, box and all are missing!"

She and Dennis emerged. Ginny's face was reddened. "I had bought a new pair of boating shoes last time we were at a West Marine and they're gone, as I said, box and all!"

Dennis interjected, "My closet seems untouched and, of course, we keep all of our valuable jewelry in the safe. I checked the safe and everything is there. But what about your costume jewelry, Ginny?"

"I'll go back and look... oh dear... this is awful."

"So now what?" Dennis asked George pointedly.

The wheels in George's brain had already been turning. How best to handle this? His was formulating a response when Ginny announced none of her costume jewelry was missing. Seems Lenny must have stashed the coins in her shoe box and was just waiting for the perfect moment to retrieve them. His mind wandered just a bit, wondering what would have happened had Ginny decided to wear her new shoes only to discover the coins...

"George?" Dennis probed again.

"Sorry, sir. I think our best bet is to report the theft to the Coast Guard and they can advise us which authorities to report to. I'm thinking we won't get a good signal until we're out of the Inlet however. As soon as I get a cell signal, I'll also call Officer Malone in Britt."

"Oh dear, this is dreadful. I can't believe they boarded our boat. It just didn't seem necessary to lock up way out here," Ginny said nearly in tears. "Dennis dear, get me a gin and tonic. I need something to calm me down. Would either of you like anything?"

Marsha politely declined. George wanted a beer, but thought the better of it and also declined. Dennis joined his wife in having a cocktail at 9:30 in the morning.

Dennis announced, "I think it's best we return to Britt as well. We're a bit low in booze and groceries, and we were going to put into a marina anyway."

George was relieved. The ensuing investigation would be so much simpler if Dennis and Ginny were readily available. "All right then. Marsha, we should be on our way."

They traveled nearly eight miles before getting a decent cell signal. George opted not to call the Coast Guard until he had more information. He had no description of the fishing boat, so it would be useless to involve the Coast Guard at this point. First he called Bill Malone who was still at his desk.

"That's one crazy story, George. Now I get the interest in Lenny. There's only a handful of marinas in the area so I'll get the word out. Sooner or later those kids will need gas. But, George, you do understand that Lenny will likely deep six the shoes and the box. Then it's just a 'he said—she said' situation. How do I really know that those coins are yours?"

Of course that conclusion had already swept through George's brain. He had taken the situation one step further and imagined that Lenny would no doubt hide the coins under some rock before coming into port. No evidence whatsoever to pin the crime on Lenny. Out loud he stated, "I'll find the paper trail that leads to me."

He checked on Marsha who was on the helm. It was a relatively calm day so she was having no issues at all. At least the weather was cooperating.

He slumped on to the main salon's sofa trying to collect his thoughts when a picture of Sylvia flashed on his phone. "Sylvia?" he blurted out loud.

"Sylvia? Can you hear me okay?"

"Yes, now shut up and listen. I heard William telling you I ran into some money. Well, yes I did, but it's not your money. It's mine. All mine and I can do whatever I want with it. Understand?"

"What are you talking about?"

"Don't give me that! I know he told you he got a new bike and that Victor got a new car. But that's none of your damn business, so just stay out of it."

"Sylvia, I was never 'in it' so how can I be 'out of it?' Jesus Christ, Sylvia, you call me up with stupid accusations. Of course I'm curious as to how you came up with that money, but did I call you and harass you? Just a reminder, you called me, so just calm down and don't bother me."

"Don't you get all angry on me. You're going to hear about it anyway when you get back. I won a lottery. Got lucky this time."

"Get out, you won a lottery? Now suppose I won that money, you'd claim I'd owe half of it to you. How come it doesn't work in my direction?"

"Because it doesn't. So don't harass me, that's why I called. You're not getting nothing, Sugar Lips." And then she hung up.

"Sugar Lips?" George questioned out loud. That's what she called him when they first met. It was so endearing then, but now she had somehow found a way to pronounce the name in such a way that it was like finger nails on a chalk board. He shook his head and wondered how the hell they got to this point.

Marsha called out to him, "Is everything OK? Sounds like you were yelling at someone."

George came up to the fly bridge. The wind on his face felt good. "That was Sylvia. Seems she really did win the lottery. She just wanted to make it perfectly clear that I wasn't entitled to any of her winnings."

"What if you had won the lottery?"

"Great minds think alike. I asked her that same question. It's tough trying to divorce a lawyer, she knows all the ins and outs."

"She's a lawyer? You didn't mention that before. Interesting."

"Didn't I? Thought I had."

"Doesn't matter." But in her mind, it did matter. That's not a small detail to skip over, she ruminated. Part of her wanted to admonish him for not acknowledging Sylvia's achievement; becoming a lawyer was no easy feat. The other half of her just wanted to let it go. What was that phrase George used to dismiss other people's problems? Not my monkey? Something like that. She took in a deep breath and zoned into the running of the boat.

Returning to her slip at the Britt Marina was now routine, she needed no guidance. George had also called Gerry to give him a heads up, so he was on the dock ready to take the lines.

"So sorry about all this with Lenny... I really thought I was doing everyone a favor," offered Gerry, trying to redeem himself.

"Of course, Gerry, you were doing the right thing. This is all on Lenny. Please don't think any of this was your fault." George stated. "Let's just hope he doesn't go pirate on us and bury the treasure."

That made Gerry laugh. "Wouldn't that be ironic?"

CHAPTER 20

NOW THAT THEY WERE BACK at the dock and in cell phone range both phones were dinging with text, voice mail and email alerts. "Good grief," Marsha exclaimed, "I need a secretary!" Marsha excused herself from the back deck to go below and respond to all the calls.

George had a voice mail from William and one from a Canadian number he didn't recognize. William's message was a repeat of earlier ones reminding George not to forget to get him new electronics. The unknown number was from Martin at the food mart. Apparently, Lenny or someone, had removed Lenny's bike. Martin noticed it was gone when he opened the store this morning. That message put George on high alert mode. No doubt Lenny was already back and trying to find a way to cash in on the coins. George had to find him, but how? He'd at least update Bill Malone.

While he was calling Bill, Marsha learned her cousins needed a list of what clothes and supplies to bring, her parents were fine and missed her, the girls were busy with babysitting Joey, and her friend Terri complimented her on the letter written about her rescue efforts on the Looper's Forum. "Oh gosh!" she said aloud. She had promised herself to catch up on the daily forum, but now more so than ever. Her curiosity was peaked. Once George came into her life, her morning routine of reading through the postings on the forum took a back seat.

She was about to go on line and pull up the forum emails when her phone rang.

"Marsha? This is Ginny."

"Ginny, yes, are you just about at the Inlet?"

"No, honey, we're still at anchor. Silly me, I found my shoes! I forgot that I had taken them out of the box and put them on a shelf with my other shoes. I must have discarded the box before we left Britt. So, really nothing is missing and nothing is amiss. Actually, I'm so relieved, I would hate to think our boat was boarded."

"Well, I'm glad Ginny. Yes, that must make you feel much better." Marsha tried to hide her disbelief as much as possible. This news would not be good news for George.

"So anyway, Marsha dear, we would really prefer to stay here one more night and then head to Killarney tomorrow. Dennis looked at the weather and it's quite favorable to just go straight across to Killarney. We love that town and we've already booked a slip there for a week. I'm sorry if we are disappointing you, but there's no theft, at least nothing of ours, to report."

"No, of course not, I totally understand, and George will too. Thank you so much for calling and safe travels across the top of Lake Huron!"

Marsha hoped she was convincing because she was in fact very disappointed. Basically, now there was nothing to pin on Lenny.

George had finished his call to Bill and had also left a message for William. As he walked into the main salon, he saw the drawn look on Marsha's face.

"Is everything okay back home?"

"Oh yes, everything's fine there, and Terri left a nice message about a thank you letter to us on the forum. That's not what I'm worried about... Ginny called. She found her shoes, so, no theft, no need to come in to Britt... I... uh...

George interrupted her. "Doesn't matter. Lenny still could have stashed the bags somewhere else in the stateroom and just retrieved them and nothing else. He'd only need to be on the boat for two minutes, and there would be no need to disrupt any of their belongings." George had already thought through any number of clever hiding places on their boat. "But you're right, without the Burton's reporting a theft, now I really have nothing. Damn!"

After a few moments George continued, "Well I got a call from the food mart manager, seems Lenny recovered his bicycle early this morning. At least we know he's around. Maybe I'll head back to Jack's Bar..."

He looked up at Marsha. Her disappointment was easy to read. "I'm sorry, Marsha, I know this state of affairs isn't the affair you had in mind..."

"I guess I'm feeling very selfish, you're right. I had us in some secluded harbor making love all day before you leave on Sunday. Basically we only have about 48 hours and then you're gone..."

"Yeah... hmmmm.... I'm at a loss for what to say, but I know I'm no good to you, to me, no one, until this gets resolved. Give me the rest of today. Okay? We can anchor out tomorrow. I don't have to head back to Toronto until late afternoon on Sunday."

"Fine, do that... good luck finding Lenny." She didn't even attempt to hide her disappointment in her voice. George pulled her to him and gave her a very passionate kiss. "Well, that helped," she brightened up.

Marsha decided to busy herself with reading all the emails on the forum. It was like doing homework. She actually kept notes on some of the advice offered whether it be about engine parts, boat electronics, places to visit or marinas to stay in. It took a while to sort through seven days of postings, but at last she landed on the one Terri had told her about: "LOOPERS TO THE RESCUE." It was a letter written to AGLCA which was then posted on the forum by the director of the association. The director introduced the letter as follows:

> "I received this letter from a David Peterson and was once again made very proud of our organization. Through the quick actions of fellow Loopers, a man who sustained severe injuries, was stabilized and then airlifted to Toronto. Here is his account..."

The letter went into great detail about the rescue of his son, George Peterson. Marsha was singled out as the main rescuer, which Marsha thought was a bit over the top. She was glad to read that George's recovery was going well and that he welcomed visitors, especially those directly involved with his rescue. The name of the hospital in Toronto was mentioned and then an idea shot through her head. George and I could go visit him on Sunday! George already had a hotel room booked, she could stay on, visit hurt George a few more times and go sightseeing in Toronto. It might be just the distraction she'd need after saying goodbye to current George. She'd figure out how to get back to Britt later.

While she was lost in planning thoughts, there was a light tap on the side of her boat. She looked over and saw Maria carrying a bucket and cleaning supplies.

"Hi, Marsha, I noticed you were back. I've mustered up some guts and I'm going to tackle cleaning Ernie's boat."

"Really? Wow! Sister-in-Law of the Year!"

"Well, I feel badly for Ernie. He was really just a nice normal guy. But after Louisa died… well, he just hasn't been right since. And this boat is his home, and since I don't really want him living with us, it behooves me to keep up the maintenance on his boat. Also, I bet there's some pretty nasty food items to dispose of."

"You know, Maria, I wouldn't mind helping you out. How about I tackle the galley?"

"Oh, Marsha, just keeping me company will be good enough, I could use encouragement to get through some of the nastier stuff. Thanks!"

"I'll be over in just a few minutes. I have some more emails to catch up on."

"Okay, great. See you in a few."

Marsha read through a few more emails and closed the lap top lid. Enough of that for now. She changed into her engine room clothes in anticipation of getting who knows what smeared on her. She found Maria in the galley throwing out most of the contents of the refrigerator.

"Maria, I'll pull up the floor boards and see what I can do down in the engine room."

"Are you sure? It's really rank down there as you know."

"I'm sure… and believe me, I'm not a glutton for punishment. I'll stop shy of getting too grossed out."

While Marsha sopped up some of the scum, George was sitting in Jack's Bar nursing a beer. He was pondering his next move when two rowdy young men pushed open the door. Lenny! He couldn't believe it.

Lenny looked at George quizzically and then smiled. "Hey, George, how are you?"

What? George said to himself. He's happy to see me? What's going on?

Lenny blurted out "I was hoping to run into you! Eddy here (pointing to the bar tender) told me you had some back wages for me. I thought we were all caught up, but hey, now I can pay for some beer!"

George was completely caught off guard. He was prepared to strangle him until he confessed to the theft. He wasn't prepared to exchange pleasantries, much less pay him money he didn't owe him.

After an awkward pause George replied "Yeah about that, would you mind coming with me to my car? I have your cash there. By the way, where have you been?"

"Oh, me and my buddy, this here is Bruce…

George and Bruce shook hands while Lenny continued, "Well, I kinda ran out of food, so me and Bruce went fishing for a few days. Got us a nice haul."

"Oh yeah? Where was that? I'd love to get out to do so some fishing," George lied.

"Do you know where the Henvey Inlet is? You go way in to the end. It's Reservation territory, but the folks there don't mind us camping there as long as we don't leave any garbage. Oh, and by the way, we saw those rich folks there, the ones on that boat we worked on. But I didn't bother them none."

This is insane, thought George. Why was he being so cheerful and self incriminating?

Lenny and Bruce followed George out to his car. George pretended to rummage around in his glove compartment for the cash. "Damn! Sorry, Lenny, I must have left the cash in my duffle bag back at the marina. Can you get yourself to the marina later today?"

"Yeah sure... but um... um... never mind...."

George read his mind. Every ounce of him wanted to slap his stupid smirk off his face but instead he handed him a twenty from his wallet. "Get yourself and Bruce a couple of beers. I'll pay you the rest back at the marina."

George got in his car. As soon as Lenny was back inside the bar, he put a call in to Bill Malone. Hopefully Bill would meet him at the marina, and they'd figure out a way to arrest him. It was looking bleak.

George thought it was odd that Marsha wasn't on the boat. It wasn't until he grabbed a beer out of the refrigerator that he noticed a note from her. "I went over to *Seaquest* to give Maria a hand. Come join us if you'd care to get dirty." George chuckled at the possible hidden message there. Nah, no way...

Marsha regretted being in the engine room after only ten minutes of cleaning. I don't even do this on my own boat. What am I doing here? she questioned herself. She reached over to a roll of paper towels on a shelf loaded with re-purposed coffee cans full of nuts, bolts, washers and small spare parts. She was trying to dislodge the paper towels from its holder when she accidentally knocked over two of the cans. "Fuck!" she yelled as she helplessly watched dozens of tiny metal objects spill over on to the engine room floor boards and over into the bilge. And then the cascade of grey metal objects was followed by a stream of gold coins. "Holy Fuck!" The coins!

Maria heard her exclaims and yelled over "Are you okay?"

"Yeah yeah." She popped her head up so Maria wouldn't be tempted to look down into the engine room. "I just spilled a canister of nuts and bolts. Will it be okay if I just throw them out? Seems there's plenty to spare."

"Of course, no problem, Ernie is a bit excessive when it comes to saving any and all extra parts. He definitely won't miss them."

"Great, I did bring a wad of garbage bags with me. I'll just add them to the collection of crap I've already started."

Marsha had to think fast. Okay, slow down… load up the garbage bags with the yucky paper towels, the nuts and bolts and whatnot and then all the coins. She'd volunteer to dispose of them. That way she could get the coins off the boat without Maria noticing.

She counted 20 coins. Where were the rest? Probably in the bottom of the other cans… She picked them up individually and carefully emptied out the top items. More gold! 10 more make 30. Okay, he's put 10 in each can. Sure enough, the pattern continued. Just then she heard George saying hello. From the side companion way door he could easily see

Marsha bent over in the engine room. She quickly stood up, said hello, and simultaneously produced a myriad of hand gestures that made no sense.

"What?" he asked, but she quickly gave him a very clear "shut up" signal. Dumbfounded, he turned toward the galley and greeted Maria.

"Oh hi, George! Marsha's being a doll and helping me out. Say would you mind getting a cart? I think we have way too much garbage to hand carry up to the dumpster."

As George was saying "sure," Marsha quickly interjected: "Actually, I need some air. George, could you take these bags? I spilled two canisters of nuts and bolts and thingamajigs so they're a bit heavy. I don't mind getting the cart."

She motioned to George to follow her out. "Hey, Maria, we'll be right back."

Marsha could hardly contain herself. When they were out of ear shot of Maria she whispered "I found them!"

"Found them? The coins?"

"Hush, yes, the coins, all fifty!"

"No shit, where?"

"In the coffee cans, in the bottom of the cans. The coins were hidden by junk parts, nuts, bolts, washers, you name it. Now they're mixed in with all this garbage. Take these bags to the boat, I'll get the cart, I have to pee anyway and I want to use the shore facilities. Then meet me back on *Seaquest*. I think after just a few more minutes of cleaning up, we can give our excuses and be done. Then we can clean up the coins."

George kissed her. He would have given her a bear hug if they each weren't holding on to bags of precious cargo. That could wait.

Once on *Boldly Go*, George just had to look in the bags. Mixed in with all the garbage were the coins. What a sight! Now he really did reach for a beer. "Aah! Yes!" Now he could get his life back together.

He slugged the full can of beer down in less than a minute. Felt and tasted great. Reluctantly he then headed over to *Seaquest*. "Permission to come aboard, Maria?"

"Of course! I think I'm about done in the galley. I'm going to attack the heads next."

"I'll finish up in the engine room."

Marsha returned after a few minutes and joined George in the engine room. They half-heartedly wiped up as much slime as they could and also retrieved more of the spilled contents of the cans from the bilge. "That should do it, for now anyway," George announced. He and Marsha replaced the floor boards.

"Hey Maria, I think we're done for now, how about you?"

"I'm getting there. You guys go along, but you're definitely coming over for dinner tonight, I owe you!"

"Happy to help Maria, happy to help," George responded in an almost singing voice. Marsha and Maria exchanged phone numbers and addresses and agreed upon driving to Maria's house at 6:00.

Marsha wanted to shower first, but her excitement over the coins won out. Besides, sorting through the garbage would be a dirty task. They emptied the bags out on to the dinette. George looked at the piles of garbage and coins as if he were an eight-year-old on Christmas morning where all the presents under the tree had gift tags with his name on them. Armed with a roll of paper towels, they carefully wiped the grime off the coins, stacked them in ten piles of five coins each, then carefully transferred them to George's hidden compartment in his tool chest.

"There! Back where they belong!" George exclaimed.

"This calls for a celebration! I have a bottle of Prosecco. Should I open it?"

"Let's celebrate in the stateroom."

"But I'm filthy!"

"Even better."

They quickly regathered the garbage from the table and stuffed the mess back into plastic garbage bags. Marsha let George lead her into the stateroom where he undressed her. He wiped off the major stains from their arms and legs with a moistened paper towel knowing she'd be hesitant to lie on her sheets with any grime on them. He caressed her breasts and nibbled his way down to her now pulsating mound. He pleasured her until she came. He loved that. Her cumming made his cock even harder. He thrust into her and didn't even try to hold back. He knew there'd be a round two.

As anticipated, round two was even more pleasurable. Lingering in their post coital bliss they were rudely jarred by George's cell phone ringing. It was Bill.

"Hey, Bill, yeah, thanks for calling me back… I uh… well I guess I was wrong…"

George explained the recent events of Ginny finding her shoes, the Burtons having nothing stolen from them, therefore nothing to report, and then running into Lenny.

George concluded with, "I honestly don't think Lenny took my coins… I think it just has to be that Sylvia, my ex, soon to be ex, has them."

"Well, George, let's hope so because the more I thought about your situation, the more you put me into a bind. If you really did have that amount of money on you, I'm afraid I'd have to report you to customs and immigration."

"Hmmmm…. well, there is that. Guess things have turned out for the best. In any event, thanks for all of your help."

After he hung up Marsha sat up. Mixed emotions swirled around in her head. "Man, George, you can weave fact and fiction pretty tightly. Do I need to be worried?"

"Worried? About what?"

"About everything you've told me. Do you really find me beautiful and wonderful in bed?"

"Okay, I'm bloody good at lying. Many times it's been a matter of survival for me… but I've never lied to you. You are beautiful and wonderful in bed. Absolutely. No question. And that's why I don't deserve you."

Marsha looked up at George with eyes that beckoned him back to bed. He leaned forward to embrace her when they were again rudely interrupted. This time they heard Lenny calling out to George as he tapped on the side of the boat.

"Shit! I forgot about Lenny coming here," George said as he quickly donned his shorts and tee shirt.

George stepped out of the boat and on to the dock. "Hey, thanks for coming down. Anyway, I don't think I fully paid you for all the work you did with me so here's another fifty."

"Oh that's great man, thanks. And if you need any more help, I'm available."

"Well, I'm headed back to the Bahamas so no more engine work here for me, but I'll tell Gerry you're available. Gerry always has a project going as you know."

They shook hands and just like that, Lenny walked away and was out of George's life. For the past four days Lenny had occupied way too much of his brain. Now maybe the insomnia would subside. George felt as if a ton of weight had been lifted off his shoulders.

He could hear that Marsha was now in the shower. A look at the time confirmed they needed to get ready to go to Maria's for dinner. Not that he wanted to go, but he'd be a good sport.

On the way to Maria's they pondered how Ernie had gotten into his tool box. "When I went over to his boat I had dragged my tool chest over to his dock since I was all done with the Burtons. It started to rain so we lifted it into his boat. I really didn't pay attention to what Ernie was doing while I was down in his engine room. The job took me two hours so he certainly had plenty of time to go through the tool boxes. But what compelled him to undo the top? And how did I not hear that distinctive clank of coins when he took out the bags? And why would he steal from me anyway?"

"Temptation overrides rationality many times, I don't think that's so hard to figure out, but I do wonder about the rest of it."

"Well, I know one thing, I'm certainly not going to ask Ernie why, when or how."

"That's for sure!" Marsha chuckled.

They pulled into Maria's driveway. She and her husband were on their front porch awaiting their arrival. Drinks were served, a delicious meal was enjoyed, lively conversation ensued and no one even mentioned Ernie.

Well done, George thought to himself as they drove back. Now for dessert…

CHAPTER 21

SATURDAY PROVED TO BE a beautiful July day. Marsha brought up the idea of going to Toronto with him and visiting George Peterson. No convincing was needed. George embraced the idea. She worked it out with Gerry to have him check on her boat on Tuesday, and she'd be back Wednesday or Thursday. Her family was arriving on Saturday, and she only needed one day to do laundry, tidy up the boat and re-provision. Fortunately, her caterpillars that she had gathered for the girls were in the chrysalis stage and wouldn't be emerging until next Sunday or Monday. The timing was perfect for the girls to watch them emerge and fly away. That amazing circle of life never failed to awe them.

"So let's go out the Inlet to the nearest sheltered cove. I'd like to be loud tonight if you know what I mean."

"Oh yeah, I certainly do, tight quarters here in the marina."

Their last 24 hours on the boat together was as wonderful as they had imagined. They checked their cell phones at noon and agreed to turn them off until they headed back the next morning. It was only about a 3 hour drive to Toronto, so they'd have plenty of time to return any calls on the drive down. After lunch when the anchor was down and securely holding, they spent the better part of the afternoon in the stateroom. After a light dinner they watched the sunset with a bottle of red wine. Something about red wine made Marsha even more amorous, much to the delight of George. And then he slept. A good, long sleep.

They awoke at day break. Marsha started up the generator, a necessary evil when not plugged in at the dock, so as to turn on the coffee maker. I love this routine, she said to herself. Hopefully, there will be a coffee maker in the hotel room.

She packed up a small duffle while George drove the boat back to the slip. He never had "gear adrift," so all his belongings were neatly tucked into his bag. She also packed up a cooler bag with sandwiches, snacks and beverages. They hoped to leave by eleven and would eat lunch in the car. It was only a three hour drive to Toronto, so they would visit George Peterson at the hospital before checking into the hotel. Then they could just bunk in for the rest of the day and night. Room service! What a luxury that would be. George's appointment at the bank was at 9 A.M. He figured on an hour at the bank, plenty of time to return the rental car and be at the airport by 1 P.M. for his 3 P.M. flight to the Bahamas. Marsha didn't even want to think about saying goodbye to George. She simply pushed it out of her mind.

Navigating to the Sunnyside Hospital and Trauma Center was annoying given the traffic and construction detours, but finally around 3 P.M., they parked the car and headed in. Marsha had emailed David Peterson, and on the way down she saw he had responded to her announcement that they would be visiting George. He was thrilled and said he normally got to George's room by 10 and typically stayed until after dinner, so any arrival time was fine with him. He was elated.

Marsha had thought about returning hurt George's shirt but then thought the better of it. Too embarrassing. It was just a shirt.

When current George saw a patient being transferred down the hallway with IVs attached, he suddenly paled. "Marsha, will George have lots of tubes in him?"

"Well, not lots, but some I'm sure. You look like you've seen a ghost, are you okay?"

"Actually no. I thought I was over my aversion to hospitals, but I'm not. I'm afraid I'm going to have to sit this visit out. I'll wait for you downstairs in the main lobby... sorry."

"That's fine, maybe I could send his father down to visit with you there. Yeah, that's a good idea. His father could probably use a break anyway, pardon the pun."

"Yeah," George chuckled. "Right, see you later."

Marsha was so used to the hospital scene she forgot how much hospitals bothered the majority of the population. She entered room 304 and was immediately welcomed by David and George calling out "Marsha" simultaneously. She wasn't expecting such an emotional outburst and found herself crying as she hugged David and then tenderly hugging George's head and right shoulder. His left arm was engulfed in a full upper body cast, and his left leg was in traction. Both David and George had tears in their eyes as well.

George spoke first, "Marsha, I can't believe it, you're here! My angel of mercy."

"Yes, I'm here. We have your father to thank for that. He basically put out a request for visitors. So good of you, David, to let us know how you, George, were recovering and where you were."

David looked a little embarrassed, so Marsha continued to derail him from unnecessary worry. "Say, my friend George, yes, another George, is down in the main lobby. He's a great mechanic but hospitals aren't his thing. He'd love to see you if you wouldn't mind."

"No, of course not, and when I head back, do you want me to get you anything, coffee? soda?"

Marsha silently laughed at the coffee suggestion. "No, David, I'm fine."

After David left, Marsha quizzed George about the particulars of his helicopter ride, subsequent surgeries and rehabilitation plan. He didn't remember much of anything about the helicopter ride nor the first few days after his surgeries. But now, about four days later, the rehab specialists were starting to formulate a long range plan for him. Basically the broken bones would have to heal first, a good three months was estimated. Then he'd be transferred to a post-acute rehab center near Rochester, New York, where he lived.

"You're not Canadian?"

"No, my Dad and I were just sailing in Lake Huron. We always wanted to explore Georgian Bay. Fortunately, we did get to quite a few anchorages before the accident. But the boat normally lives in the Rochester Yacht Club. My father moved in with me after my mother died."

"Sorry about your mother.... I live near Albany, New York, but my family sailed up on the St. Lawrence. When I decided to do the Loop, I went over to the dark side. My brother still has the family sailboat on Lake Michigan."

George laughed. It was well known that many sailors had a distain for power boaters. Fortunately, a trawler was an acceptable alternative. Nonetheless, Marsha always felt as though she had to apologize to sailors when they saw she owned a power boat. She secretly shared their opinion.

"So what do you normally do in Rochester?"

"I'm a freelance writer. I've had just enough publications earn me enough money to keep me afloat. Pardon the pun." They both laughed a bit too nervously. Why did she feel like she was interviewing him to be her next boyfriend?

George continued, "I did pretty well with my book, *The Limo*. But maybe you've heard of the play, *A Charm of Goldfinches?* That's been my most successful writing to date."

"No, but that's so weird. I have a thing about collective nouns. I've given serious thought to writing a book called *A Murder of Crows* or *A Clowder of Cats*." And strangely, *A Charm of Goldfinches* was also on my list.

"That is weird..."

After an awkward pause, George continued. "Now that I'll be laid up for a while, I'm going to finally finish up a book I started back when I was waiting on a part in the Bahamas. It's called *Bahama Gem*."

"Really? Sounds interesting. What's it about?"

Just as George was about to answer, a nurse came in to check on his vitals and foley bag. Marsha stepped out, knowing how embarrassing it must be for George to have a catheter in his penis.

She met David in the hall, a sign that it was probably time to go. Poor current George down in the hospital lobby, he must be getting pretty antsy by now.

When the nurse exited, David and Marsha returned to the room.

"Well, this has been just great, but I should be going now. I'll be in Toronto for the next few days. I could visit again if that's okay."

Both David and George answered with enthusiastic affirmatives and thanked her profusely for all she did and for visiting. She kissed each man on the cheek and left.

Back in the car Marsha filled George in on the details of his recovery in as many layman's terms as possible. "That poor guy, he's going to be laid up for months. I'll probably visit him again tomorrow after you......" she couldn't finish the sentence. She didn't want him to leave and felt herself filling up with emotion. "Oh, George, this just can't be the end." He put his hand on hers and gently squeezed her fingers.

Once in the hotel room, Marsha uncorked one of the bottles of red wine she had brought. She placed the opened bottle near the coffee maker. Check. Coffee would come in handy in the morning. She decided that there was no need to hold anything back. She planned to make sweet, sweet love to him as long as they had the stamina. They never even called for room service.

Monday morning's 7:00 alarm went off too abruptly. Marsha reached over for George and he wasn't there. What? Was he in the bathroom? She called out. No answer. She got up and went into the bathroom. Not there either. What? Maybe he went down for breakfast? But why not just call for room service? Then she noticed the note on the coffee maker.

Dear Marsha,

I woke up around 5 and couldn't get back to sleep. You looked so beautiful there sleeping so peacefully, I just couldn't wake you up. Our lovemaking last night exceeded my wildest expectations. You've made me so happy. You've made me feel like a genuine man again. I can't thank you enough. And I just can't bear to say goodbye to you. I don't want to remember you with tears in your eyes. I want to remember you just how you are right now. There will always be a place for you in my heart. But you need someone other than me to grow old with, so I'm letting you go. I know I'll regret this, but I know this is the right thing to do. Forgive me for not saying goodbye directly, but I truly feel it's better this way.

Love, George

Marsha screamed out loud "NO! He can't be gone, NO!" She collapsed into a ball of tears and let herself cry for almost an hour. She got up, looked at herself in the mirror. She looked like a train wreck. Can't have that, she said to herself. She took a long, long shower and washed her tears and emotions away. Deep in her heart she knew he was right. It would have been too emotional to say goodbye. And no doubt she still would have cried for an hour.

"So it's done," she said out loud as she got herself dressed. She put on a little make-up, fussed with her hair and actually used a hair dryer. She slipped on her tight jeans and low cut tee shirt and headed to Sunnyside Hospital and Trauma Center.

"My Georgian Affair is over," she said to no one in particular as she awaited her cab. "Or is it?"

Epilogue
Four years later...

THREE TRAWLERS CIRCLED THE Statue of Liberty. The captains and crew on each boat had traveled together since meeting up in the Atlantic Intracoastal Waterway in South Carolina. Yesterday, the winds were howling. By collective decision, they had stayed put at the marina behind the Statue to await calmer waters and for more crew members to arrive. They worked out a plan for picture taking since all three boats would be crossing their wake today. Each one would in turn take pictures of one of the other boats with the crews on the foredeck hovering around a gold Looper's burgee. Damien and Janice aboard *Mama Sea,* were first to be photographed. Then Brad, Lynn, their daughters and their Portuguese Water Dog, Ruby, aboard *Footloose*, had the honors of taking *Boldly Go*'s picture. Up at the helm, an older gentleman maneuvered *Boldly Go*. On the foredeck lining the starboard side with the Statue in the background, was Marsha, her parents, her daughters, and Lindsay's boyfriend Jay. Behind Marsha was a tall, handsome man with curly, long blonde hair, wearing a blue pinstriped shirt.

Waiting on a Part

DIANE E. GAMBO

DISCLAIMER

This is a work of fiction. All characters have been fabricated with a few exceptions mentioned in acknowledgements. Otherwise, any resemblance to actual persons is completely coincidental. The Red Fox Motel and Diner was completely fabricated. The other locations mentioned in the novella are real locations but utilized in a fictional manner.

ACKNOWLEDGEMENTS

Thank you to my cousin Jeannie who allowed me to use her name, approximate location, her dog's name, and for allowing me to fictionalize her character in the novella. She also proofread the initial manuscript. Thank you to the "Vanderbilt 4" for allowing me to use their names: Camille, Mike, Charlie and Marty, and for allowing me to fictionalize their reunion after 50 years. Thanks to Diana for allowing me to use her name and her very real stores in Altamont, NY: Remedies and La Bella Fleur. Thanks to Tom and Trish for allowing me to mention them as our sailing buddies. And as always, thank you to my husband Bob for standing by while I get lost in my writing.

BACKGROUND COVER PHOTO: Altamont Gazebo, by Diane E. Grabo (taken in Altamont, NY)
COVER DESIGN: S. M. Savoy

Written in 2019

To K. D. and R. R.
I wish you well wherever you are.

Post Script

About a week after completing this story, Hurricane Dorian devastated the Abaco Islands in the Bahamas. Sadly, many of the Bahamian places mentioned in this novella and in my previous novellas were destroyed. Someday I hope to write a novella based on the recovery of the Abacos.

PROLOGUE

THE INSTRUCTIONS TO THE agent, code name Red, were to pick up the envelope containing a one-page letter at the Rotterdam Square Mall on a bench located opposite Kay Jewelers and adjacent to the Food Court. A middle aged man wearing a grey suit would be reading a copy of the local Sunday newspaper. Upon standing up to leave the mall the newspaper would be left behind with the envelope tucked inside the sports section. As per usual, the alteration codes were to be applied and once the contents were committed to memory, the letter was to be incinerated.

Red shook his head in disbelief. Such an archaic means of transferring information. The person paying him to do the current job, code name Blue, was a veteran of the Korean War and had such a distrust of technology and the internet that no information was to be typed into any form of computer or cell phone and transmitted through cyberspace. Messages were to be hand written on flash paper and then destroyed. Shades of *Mission Impossible*.

Red made a mental note not to accept any further jobs from Blue. And if there was a merciful God, maybe Blue, who had to be in his 90s, would just pass away in the night sparing him the awkwardness of refusing a future assignment.

Chapter 1

T<small>HE DAY BEGAN AS</small> most did. A slap to the alarm clock to turn off the buzzer. A lull. Then Gloria reaching over to touch Ben's dreamy face framed with curly, silver gray hair. The soft caressing led to sweet, satisfying love making, a ritual that was rarely skipped over in the past four decades. Another lull. Then groans of "yes, we do have to get up." Then the rapid decent, sometimes chaotic decent, into the daily grind of tending to children and getting to work. Grandchildren had replaced children as the years slipped by. The only deviation in today's awakening was that the alarm was set an hour earlier to get Ben to the airport on time.

Gloria got up first, showered, and started to throw some clothes on.

Ben yawned and greeted her in a still sleepy voice. He looked at his wife through the lens of a 17-year-old. Her thick, wavy red hair, fell gently below her shoulders. Her unruly bangs were always a bit too long which smacked of rebellion and enhanced her sexiness. He eyed the curves of her nice medium build on her 5'6" tall frame. In his mind she maintained a perfect hour glass figure. In hers, she was pear shaped. Just one more cupful might have been nice, she often said. He disagreed, he loved her just the way she was.

"Turn around, Ree."

Gloria loved that nickname. She always thought that "Gloria" was just too much of a name. Early on in dating, Ben had shortened Gloria to Ria, and then settled in on Ree. Much better.

"Why?" asked Ree.

"Because I want to see all of you."

"Really? Nothing has changed since yesterday except possibly a few new wrinkles."

"You don't have wrinkles."

"Okay, flattery will get you everywhere, especially job security in the husband department. I love how you see me, just wish that's what I saw when I look in the mirror."

"Never underestimate your looks, you're just as beautiful now, maybe even more so, than you were as a teenager."

"Well, I'm just going to go with that, thanks. Now get out of bed, we have to leave in 45 minutes."

Ree turned on the coffee machine while Ben showered. She had established a morning routine a few years back of sneaking in snippets of exercise whenever she could. The coffee-making-exercise routine consisted of doing as many squats as she could while the machine heated up, then a one minute plank while the coffee was being dispensed. Somewhere on the internet she had read a study that a marker of intact cognitive skills was being able to count to 60 in 60 seconds, give or take 5 seconds. With her phone on the floor she turned the timer app to one minute, closed her eyes and counted silently to 60 while holding the plank. Most days she was dead on or just a few seconds off. Occasionally she was ten seconds off which scared her. Having two parents with dementia, one living, one deceased, and now a brother with newly diagnosed dementia, she was convinced she was next in line. Her two sisters shared the concern.

Ree took her coffee and peeked in on their sleeping grandchildren, Jenna and Jake. Ree had gotten permission from her daughter Kate to let the kids sleep in while she ran Ben to the airport. Jenna at age 14 had been left in charge of Jake, age 10, several times for short periods. Getting permission had been key. Ree long ago learned she had committed several grandmother crimes in what she allowed the kids to do and not do. There was a very amiable relationship with Kate but their child rearing philosophies differed greatly in many areas. On both parts the eye-rolling wars were alive and well. But to keep peace in the family, Ree learned to suck it up and adopt her cousin's favorite saying: "Shut up and wear beige." More often than not, Ree acquiesced to Kate's rules.

What a relief not to have to wake them up, Ree thought to herself. Waking up sleeping children had always been an anathema to her. Getting them dressed for winter at 5:30 in the morning, getting them into the car, driving to the airport, only to turn around and have them get back into bed to complete their ten hours of sleep seemed ridiculous. Glad Kate agreed.

After a light breakfast, Ben rechecked his brief case to make sure he had all his important documents for his trip and his medications. His bag of tools containing all the gizmos and gadgets he needed had been packed yesterday and was already in the trunk. Ben, a biomedical engineer, was the go-to, behind the scenes guy for a volunteer medical mission based out of the local hospital. This year he was part of a mission to Los Alcarrizos, Dominican Republic. Normally, Ree would be accompanying him. Her occupational therapy skills were quite an asset when splints were needed for the various children in need of hand surgery for burns or deformities. But she had committed to keeping the grandchildren, while Kate and Cullen vacationed in Costa Rica, well before learning the dates of the current mission. Ben grabbed his carry-on suitcase of personal belongings, and they departed for the airport. Even though they had a heated attached garage, the cold arctic air still found a way to blast their senses when the garage door opened. Living in the northeast for all of their lives never fully prepared them for below zero temperatures.

Ree had looked at the weather app before she backed out of the garage.

"Good grief! It's not even going to hit zero today! I can't bear an all-day indoor day with the kids."

"Have to say, sweetheart, I'm not all that unhappy about being in the tropics all week. Maybe after I retire we should think about moving south. I hate this weather."

"Yeah, Florida is looking better and better. You know we really could afford to move in to that development my sister lives in."

"Well, our financial planner would be happy with that. No state income taxes in Florida."

"And maybe we could buy a boat and get a place with a dock."

"Love your enthusiasm... one of the many things I love about you."

"Thanks, sweetie. Well, here we are. I'm so going to miss you. A week of solo grand-parenting is going to be a little challenging."

"Sorry, dear. Next Sunday will be here before you know it."

"I suppose... love you, text me when you get to your hotel."

"I will, love you too, bye."

Ben kissed her and exited the front seat. He grabbed his belongings from the back seat, then hefted the heavy bag of tools out of the trunk. Ree could just make out a few choice words as he muttered expletives under his breath about the cold air.

Even though the patrolling officers were quick to wave along cars dropping off passengers, Ree lingered until Ben was fully inside the terminal door. One never knew how any day would turn out, and if this was the last time she saw Ben, she wanted a good final look. Ben was in good shape. At six feet, 200 pounds with broad muscular shoulders, he was definitely a looker and in good health. But already a few of their friends, who were supposedly in good shape, had died unexpectedly, never mind the ever present fear of plane crashes or the volatile nature of third world nations. An officer gave her the "move along" signal. Okay, okay, I'm being ridiculous, she said to herself, and put the car in drive.

Weaving through the other parked cars and buses in the drop off lane she noticed an inordinate number of limos. Most were black, one was white and one had a vanity license plate stating "MUSICMAN." The others had nondescript commercial plates. She wondered what was going on, maybe a wedding with a band? Once free of the airport drop-off lanes, the limos disappeared from her thinking, and she pondered her tactics for the rest of the day.

As predicted, the kids were still asleep. So was their rescued greyhound. Cookie was the only dog they had ever had that was devoid of personality. Ben and Ree often wondered if Cookie would even notice if one day they both dropped dead.

Phew! Warmth and sleeping kids! Ree declared to herself. Now for my second cup of coffee.

CHAPTER 2

So, KIDS, IT'S FREEZING again outside so I'm sorry, no skating or skiing today. Maybe we could go to the mall?"

Ree knew full well that an afternoon in the mall was number one on their list of things to do; she just hated supporting that habit.

"Yes! The video arcade! Let's go!" said an excited Jake.

"Sure," responded Jenna as unenthusiastically as possible.

Ree wasn't fooled. Jenna's new persona was one of complete ennui. She made a point of looking bored and disinterested in anything and everything. Last year Jenna went through a Goth phase which really made Ree laugh. Her own set of twins, Kate and Kirstin, had gone through many phases, including Goth. What goes around, comes around, she mused. Jake, unaware of his grandmother's trip down memory lane, snapped her out of her thoughts.

"Can Billy come, too?"

"What?… oh yes, sorry, my mind was elsewhere…. sure, I'll give his mom a call. And Jenna, want to give one of your friends a call?"

Jenna and Jake had spent several school vacation weeks with her and Ben over the years. Since they lived in a fairly social neighborhood, the kids had made friends with some of the local kids in the area.

"I don't know… anybody who's anybody went to Disney World this week…. except us of course."

"Okay, Eeyore. Give it a rest. I'm sure you'll see some of your friends there. We could pick out a movie or go to the new Aquatarium or just hang out in the food court near the video arcade."

"Whatever," sighed Jenna.

Ree wondered if it was possible to pack any more emotion into a one word response that was stated without any emotion at all. The ultimate irony of speech, saying so much without saying anything at all. Ree wanted to launch into her "You selfish bitch" lecture. In her head she screamed: Are you kidding me? Have you forgotten you have been to Disney World, more than once? Your parents turn themselves inside out to please you and make your life as easy as possible and you reward them with your "I couldn't care less" attitude? Nothing is ever good enough for you, no wonder you're so miserable, you don't appreciate anything. And don't you dare be mad at your parents for taking a well-needed vacation. Both your parents work two to three jobs, and they just need a break every now and then.

She almost yelled "grrrr" out loud but contained herself. She had learned to take a deep breath and to try to put a positive spin on things. At least her twins, who were both mothers now, understood why she and Ben always took a one-week vacation without them when they were growing up. And someday Jenna would understand, too. Just takes time, just takes patience, she reminded herself.

"Okay, kids, I have to let Cookie out to do her business. Let's leave in about 20 minutes."

A short while later Jenna reappeared wearing a tank top and ultra short cut off blue jeans. Her face was highlighted with overly done blue eye shadow and Raggedy Anne red cheeks.

Ree burst out laughing. "Oh let me get a picture of you to send to your parents. I'm pretty sure that's not a sanctioned outfit."

"What's wrong with what I'm wearing?"

"Well, for starters, it's ten below zero..."

"But it's not ten below in the mall!" protested Jenna. "it's always too hot in there."

"Perhaps if the pockets weren't longer than the shorts I might let it slide, or if your bra straps weren't showing... but the make-up is ridiculous. You look like a prostitute on the prowl."

"Gramma! How do you know what a prostitute is?"

A million snarky responses zoomed through Ree's mind. Deep breath again.

"This conversation is over. When you wipe off your face and put a more weather appropriate outfit on, I'll be happy to take you to the mall. In the meantime, Jake and I will be leaving shortly.

"Oh fine!" Jenna said stubbornly as she stomped off to the guest bedroom and dramatically maneuvered around Jake's iPad on the stairway.

Ree rolled her eyes and started piling on her winter garb. The area behind the house was fenced in but there was no way Cookie would just go out and do her business without considerable coaxing and a human being to escort her.

"Come on, Cookie, just get up, you know you need to go out."

Cookie looked up with disbelieving eyes. A tug at her collar finally got her to move. Then she had to go through her ritual of which paw to put first. Right paw forward, hesitation, right paw back. Left paw forward, hesitation, left paw back. Pathetic whimper. Repeat.

"Come on, Cookie! You're not diving off the Acapulco cliffs, just move forward!" Ree tried not to lose her patience. After all, it was her idea to rescue Cookie. When they agreed to adopt Cookie at age seven, Ree thought the dog would live just another few years, following the expected rule of the bigger the dog, the shorter the life span. Now at age 15, Cookie was apparently trying to compete with Methuselah. She also knew that animals saw things differently than humans, rendering even the most innocuous shadow a formidable foe.

Cookie looked up again, this time with her please-don't-yell-at-me eyes.

"Alright, Cookie, you win. I'll get the rugs." Ree went over to the coat closet and pulled out two rolled up eight-foot-long rug runners. She laid them out in a line from Cookie's dog bed to the back door. This trick often worked in the past when Cookie became immobile. "Here, let's put this across the cauldron of boiling water or whatever it is that you see in your pea-sized brain."

Cookie gingerly moved forward. Ree opened the back door, gasped at the influx of cold air and gently patted Cookie on the rear to encourage her to step out.

"Let's get this over with, Cookie," Ree demanded as she herself reluctantly stepped out into the frigid air. Cookie inspected one corner of the yard, then another, then another.

"Oh come on, what could possibly make one spot more enticing than another? Just do your business before we both freeze to death!"

Finally, Cookie relieved herself and hurried back to the doorway. What a weird world it must be for dogs, Ree pondered. It's not just about sight and sounds, apparently shadows, smells and Saturn all need to line up in some intricate cosmic force to find the perfect spot to poop and pee.

Jake opened the door for them. "Can we go now?"

"Let me call Billy's mother first, and then let's see if Jenna will grace us with her appearance. Oh, and Jake, please don't leave your things on the stairs. Someone is going to trip on them and fall."

Billy's mother was thrilled to have him picked up and taken care of for the next few hours. Like thousands and thousands of mothers across the nation, any gratis child-free hour was valued like gold. It was a win-win guilt free situation. The child got to have fun while the mom accomplished a dozen or so chores that otherwise would have been left undone.

"Jenna, we're leaving, see you in a few hours."

Jenna stomped out of the bedroom wearing a tight tee shirt and full length blue jeans. Only a trace of the blue eye shadow remained. The rouge circles had been scrubbed off. She reluctantly grabbed her coat and hat.

"I'm leaving my coat and hat in the car when we get to the mall," Jenna declared.

"Good enough," responded Ree.

They picked up Billy, and he engaged immediately in non-stop chatter with Jake about the video games they would be playing. Ree and Jenna sat silently as Jenna fussed around for a radio station to her liking. In their minds unbeknownst to each other, they were thinking about how stupid the new mall rules were. Ree was especially annoyed. When she was growing up, she and her sisters roamed their small town shops freely with little to no parental supervision. It was quite likely that her parents didn't know where she was 90% of the time. When Kate and Kirstin were growing up, the fear of kidnapping had definitely increased, but they were still allowed to be dropped off at the mall as teens and picked up hours later. Now, any child under the age of 16 had to be accompanied by an adult and be in eye sight range at all times. No more dropping off kids to be left on their own or even going to a different store while the kids hung out in the arcades or food court areas. Ree had brought a book with her, prepared to read on and off for hours while keeping half an eye on the kids. Jenna was silently plotting how to ditch her grandmother and make-out with Donny, a kid in the neighborhood who was her stand-in boyfriend anytime she was visiting her grandparents.

Ree softened up a bit and dropped the kids off at the entry way. That way Jenna would only have to freeze for a few seconds. Ree was willing to risk being spoken to in case anyone noticed the kids were adult-less for the five minutes it would take her to park the car and walk back to the mall. As she exited the car, a black Dodge Durango pulled in next to her which she only noticed because she was also driving a Durango. She didn't look at the driver; she was fixated on getting into the mall as quickly as possible. The driver, on the other hand, did notice her face. He found her surprisingly pretty.

Jake and Billy had already piled their coats up on a table in the Food Court area and had run into the nearby video arcade. Armed with quarters they started their first round of games. Jenna was talking with a small group of teenagers, which included Donny. Ree smiled. Ah, young love. Nothing like it. Ree moved all the coats off the table and onto two chairs. Maybe Jenna had a good idea leaving her coat in the car. Ree started to read her book and then noticed a newspaper left behind on a bench across from the jewelry store. Great, she thought to herself, hopefully there's a puzzle or two left undone.

As she reached for the newspaper a medium height man with slicked back black hair and a pockmarked face appeared out of nowhere, and brushed against her.

"Oh, I'm sorry. Is this your newspaper? I was just hoping to grab out the puzzle section," said a startled Ree.

He recognized her as the lady he saw in the parking lot. "Tell you what," he said with an edge of annoyance, "I was hoping for the Sports section."

He picked up the newspaper, leafed through it, seemed to lock onto an item with his eyes for a moment, took out the Sports section and handed the rest to her.

"There you go, have a nice day."

"Thanks… I uh…" she started to reply but he had already walked off and clearly was not interested in engaging in any further conversation. She was puzzled by this unusual encounter. Whatever, she mused to herself.

She gathered up the now sprawled out newspaper and all the advertisement supplements including several brightly colored envelopes, no doubt from charities seeking donations. A few envelopes had spilled out onto the floor, and she recovered them as well. She fished out the Arts and Leisure section and placed the rest in a recycle bin. She tucked the slim section under her arm, not noticing one small envelope stuck to the underside of the section. She bought a cup of decaf coffee, loaded it up with milk and sat down. She unfolded the Arts and Leisure section and a small plain white envelope fell out onto the floor. Humph, I missed one, she said to herself. She picked it up off the floor. Even though she was pretty sure it was just another charity letter, curiosity got the better of her and she pulled out the inserted letter. Her eyes widened as she read a rather cryptic hand written string of numbers. The only thing she could make sense of was that some of the number sequences could be coordinates. This should be fun to try to figure out, she said to herself. She left the envelope on the table but tucked the letter in her purse. I'll have to figure this out when I get home.

Out in the parking lot in the black Durango, Red leafed through the Sports section. His face turned ashen when the envelope was not found.

"That's impossible!" he said out loud. He was sure he had seen the envelope, in the crease of the Sports section, just as planned. He was careful, always careful. Did it fall out? If so, where? He'd have to retrace his steps. Red slowly back tracked to the mall. He was so intent upon finding the envelope he didn't even notice the frigid temperature. Fortunately there wasn't much wind so if it had fallen in the parking lot it should be within feet of his traveled route. Nothing. He retraced his steps back to the bench. The remnants of the newspaper were nowhere to be found. He gazed around and saw the parking lot-puzzle seeking lady at one of the tables in the Food Court. Was he that distracted by her looks that he just didn't take the whole newspaper when she offered it up in the first place? What an idiot he had been. She was already engaged in one of the puzzles. How to retrieve the paper from her? After a brief hesitation, he reached into his pocket and brought out a wedding band. Funny that a simple band of gold could transform how a person was perceived. Slipping it on discreetly, he headed to the woman.

"I'm sorry to bother you, Ma'am, turns out my wife wanted me to keep the advertisement supplements. Do you still have the rest of the newspaper?"

Ree was only slightly startled by his reappearance and request.

"I… uh… discarded it, except this section of course. It's over there in that recycle bin. I'm so sorry… I…"

He interrupted her, "No, no, it's my bad, shouldn't have left it on the bench in the first place. Thanks."

It was fortunate that in spite of the mall's efforts to be eco friendly, very few people actually recycled papers. The mess of advertisements and individual sections were the only occupants of the bin. He gathered up the whole mess, careful to inspect the bin for any other papers and rushed out. Back in his rental he combed through every page and advertisement. Nothing! Now what? He'd have to use the wife card again.

This time the woman was surrounded by two young boys and a very cute teenaged girl. The girl seemed to be pleading with the woman, and the woman in turn seemed to be annoyed. He pretended to use his phone but in fact was taking a picture of the table. He enlarged the picture and searched the contents. There! There it was! He could see a corner of an envelope tucked under the puzzle section. He'd just have to wait her out. Sooner or later she would very likely gather up the papers and put them in the bin before leaving. But how long would that be?

The woman stood up and approached two other women at a nearby table. It appeared pleasantries were exchanged, and the two women seemed to be nodding in agreement with whatever question it was the puzzle lady had posed. Puzzle lady then returned to the table. She ripped out one page of the newspaper section, folded it, tucked it in her book and placed the ensemble into her purse. As predicted, she gathered up the remaining pages and envelope and headed to the recycle bin. Then she returned to the table, gathered up coats and hats, called out to the boys and the trio headed toward the cinema section. The teenager had already regrouped with other kids.

When the trio was out of sight Red walked over to the recycle bin and snatched up the envelope. Empty! Damn it! He searched through the remaining papers, still nothing. Did Puzzle lady keep the letter? If so, why? And where? He hurried as fast as he could without attracting attention toward the cinema section. Puzzle lady was in line at the movie ticket kiosk. He watched as she and the boys entered the first featured movie. He asked the attendant at the kiosk how long that particular movie lasted and headed back to the rental. He noted puzzle lady's license plate before entering his car. There he made a few phone calls. Armed with her license plate number, it wasn't long before he learned all the information he needed.

Her house was only 20 minutes away from the mall. It was too cold for people to be out and about, so he felt fairly secure casing the front of her home in broad daylight. A thin layer of snow surrounded the house which negated his ability to walk all the way around for fear of leaving footprints. As with most houses in suburbia she probably entered and exited through the attached garage. The front door was likely rarely used. There were no signs of a private home alarm system. Breaking in during the night to retrieve the letter shouldn't be too difficult, he convinced himself. He knocked on the front door to see if any dogs barked. Nothing. Good. He'd return later.

CHAPTER 3

THE DISNEY MOVIE WASN'T as bad as Ree thought it would be, in fact, some parts were pretty entertaining and bordered on adult humor. She often thought the writers for Disney put in subtle adult themes for the benefit of millions of mothers and fathers having to watch the movies with their kids. If only the main character's mom or dad didn't get killed off in the first five minutes, she'd give all the movies A+ ratings.

Mercifully, the boys wanted to return to her house to play more video games. She had made arrangements for Jenna to be looked after by Donny's mother and aunt who were already planning on staying at the mall for hours. Although Jenna tried not to show her feelings, she was thrilled to be going home later in the day with Donny and his cousin Meredith.

As the two boys in the back seat engaged in imaginary gun fights with all the accompanying sound effects, Ree concentrated on how to approach the kids with what would likely be their last visit with their great grandmother. Meme had been placed in the same nursing home Ree recently retired from as a career Occupational Therapist. Ree gladly retired after the nursing home had been taken over once again by a national rehabilitation company. Too many stupid new rules.

The health care field was always undergoing changes, but at age 63 she decided she had had enough. She also felt the need to make her mother's journey into the next world her full time job. Fortunately, they were doing well enough without her income and Ben would be retiring within the next two years anyway.

Jenna had solid memories of Meme and her great grandfather Poppa being sharp, fun-loving individuals, but Jake and his cousin Moira only had vague memories. Poppa passed away a year ago, and it was looking like Meme would be following suit any day now. Meme slept through most of her days, and if she exceeded an intake of 100 calories a day, that was a good day. She no longer recognized Ree or her siblings. Grandchildren and great grandchildren were non-existent in her ever diminishing memory bank. The only thing that penetrated the fog was Ben's voice. To the great consternation of Ree, her mother would look up and say, "Hello Ben," when Ben greeted her on one of his rare visits. Well, once again, in dementia world, one plus one does not equal two, Ree concluded.

Ree thought ahead to tomorrow and the rest of the week. She planned to take the kids to the nursing home tomorrow morning. She would take a picture of them with their great grandmother who hopefully would remain awake long enough to smile. She'd ask them to give Meme an extra hug and kiss before leaving. As gently as she could she would inform them that it was unlikely Meme would still be alive when they returned in April. Then, as a diversion, especially for Jenna who really grieved after Poppa died, she planned to take them for an overnight or two to her cousin Jeannie's home, the Farm. The weather was supposed to be better in the next few days and hopefully they could all go cross country skiing on the hills behind Jeannie's house.

Ree offered to have Billy spend the night. They stopped at his house briefly to pick up overnight clothes and to visit with his parents. Nice couple, Ree thought to herself. They promised to reciprocate later in the week. Jenna had been invited to spend the night with Meredith. If it had been summer Ree would have hesitated. The temptation to sneak out and rendezvous with Donny was just too great. But with temps below zero, she was pretty sure Jenna would stay put.

After dinner Jake and Billy changed into their Tae Kwon Do uniforms and rough housed in the den practicing all kinds of kicks, jabs, flips and chops. Ree decided to retreat to her bedroom so as not to listen to the cacophony of their sound effects. She had hung her purse up in the mud room adjacent to the garage when they first came into the house, but had retrieved the letter, her book and the puzzle page.

The numbers seemed to convey a date: 0304, a time 1230, and coordinates: 26 29 N 77 00 W. The rest of the numbers were a long string of letters and numbers, probably 25 digits long. Those stumped her. Maybe a car or boat VIN? Going back to the coordinates her eyes widened. Wait a minute, 26-77? I know where that is, she exclaimed to herself. She shot up and ran downstairs to look at an old souvenir chart. Years ago, she and Ben and two other couples chartered a catamaran for three years in a row. They called themselves the 26-77 club. The numbers represented the latitude and longitude of the Abaco Islands in the Bahamas. They had tee shirts made up and had made the numbers even more significant by declaring to themselves that, since most of them started chartering at 26, they would keep chartering until they were 77. We were so naive! After three years all three couples had started families, and their lives moved on to other priorities. Ben and Ree were still friends with one couple, Tom and Trish, but the third couple, Brad and Dorine, sadly divorced and over time they moved on to other locations. Their relationship narrowed down to annual Christmas cards and then nothing at all. I should at least friend Dorine on Facebook and rekindle that relationship, Ree digressed. She set the letter down. She didn't know quite what to do with it, but for sure she wanted to show it to Ben. The paper was very odd, very thin and fragile. She reached into her desk drawer and pulled out a sheet protector. At one point in her career she was known as the sheet protector queen. She didn't mind the loving mockery from her colleagues, and eventually she noticed sheet protectors had crept into their professional lives as well. She put the letter in a protector and placed it in Ben's sock and underwear drawer, that way he'd be sure to see it.

After settling the boys into bed, Ree took a glass of red wine up to her bedroom and leisurely sipped it while reading a few chapters of her book. She fell asleep after an hour. She never heard the click of the front door opening, never saw the small beam of light darting throughout her house, never saw a man dressed all in black enter her bedroom. The man started to slowly and carefully look through her dresser drawers when he heard a faint whimpering. Was that a dog? There was no hint of a dog when he first entered, but now the whimpering was getting louder. The woman stirred.

"Cookie? Cookie? Are you alright?" Ree called out.

Cookie answered with a louder whimper. The woman stirred again. It looked as if she was going to get out of bed.

"Damn, all right, I'll come down," she stated in an agitated voice.

Damn was right! Damn that mother hearing! Red exclaimed to himself. A memory of his ex-wife flashed through his brain. She could sleep through violent thunderstorms, blaring sirens and blasting stereos, but the least little cry from their then infant son would wake her up in an instant. He slid out the doorway, went down the stairs, walked right past the whimpering dog and was out the front door in a matter of seconds.

Ree got up, reluctantly put on her robe, and slowly descended down the stairway.

"What is it Cookie? You never cry at night. Go back to bed."

She knelt down on the floor, curled herself along the spine of Cookie's back, and petted her face and chest until she heard gentle snoring.

"Oh, Cookie, what goes on in that mind of yours? I'd love to be a neuron in your brain and follow it around for a day..."

After nearly falling asleep on the floor herself, she got up and returned to bed.

CHAPTER 4

Monday morning proved to be bright, sunny and in the single digits. Later in the day the temps would climb to the 20s and by Tuesday, low 30s were predicted. Also, a few inches of snow were in the forecast for the afternoon. New snow on the trails would make the cross country skiing even better. Perfect! Billy had been returned to his parents, and Jenna had been retrieved. She seemed happier. Maybe she was slowly moving out of her morose phase.

"Come on, kids. Let's get the car packed up. Meme is most awake before lunch, so I want to time our visit to catch her at her best. Then we'll scoop up Cookie and head to the Farm."

"So, Gramma, when was the Farm actually a farm?" asked Jake.

"Funny you should ask that because that is the same question I asked my grandmother. Probably a century, maybe two, but that's what we've always called the property. Yeah, interesting how a title can last."

Ree was happy her cousin had taken over the property. No one else in the extended family seemed interested in living there in the foothills of the Catskills, nor in keeping up with the expenses, but no one wanted it out of the family either. The battle between practicality and nostalgia tugged at everyone's heart strings and purse strings.

Jeannie and her late husband saved the day by buying out the siblings' and cousins' portions of the inheritance. Another win-win.

Pulling into the nursing home parking lot she and the kids couldn't help but notice the large limo with "MUSICMAN" plates parked near the entry way.

"Wow!" exclaimed Jake. "Do you think there's someone famous here?"

"I don't know, but I do know that's the same limo I saw yesterday. Weird! I'm sure Melvina will have the scoop."

Melvina was the head nurse on Meme's wing. Besides being an expert geriatric nurse, she also had a pulse on all the goings on in the home.

"In fact," Ree joked, "I bet she's got a bulletin all written up by now."

The thought of possibly seeing a celebrity intrigued Jenna, and there was genuine enthusiasm in her voice when she commented, "Well, whoever it is, I hope I can get his autograph."

The receptionist Betty who was always pleasant no matter the circumstances, greeted them warmly.

"Hey, Ree! Oh my, Jake, you're so tall now! And Jenna, you've turned into a lovely lady! Ree you must be so proud of your grandkids!"

"I am, Betty, I am."

"So what's with the limo?" asked Jake.

"Well, I'm not at liberty to say, but suffice it to say a well-known musical artist is placing his mother in the home today."

"Wow, cool!"

"How long will he be here?" blurted out Jenna.

"My guess is the full day. You know how long it takes to get through all the paper work." Betty looked up at Ree who nodded in agreement. "And then I imagine he'll want to spend the afternoon getting her settled in."

"What wing is the mother on?" Jenna asked.

"I really can't say, but my guess is you'll find out soon enough."

That was code for: she's on your great grandmother's wing. HIPAA rules prevented Betty from saying anything about any resident without permission, so Ree hushed the kids from asking any further questions.

"Come on kids, let's not bother Betty anymore."

"Oh it's no bother... but you know the rules." Again Ree nodded in acknowledgement.

Upon exiting the elevator on the third floor, Ree could see Melvina escorting a lean man, just over six feet tall, pushing a well-coiffed woman in her wheelchair. His straight sandy blonde hair edged over the collar of his leather jacket. She followed the jacket down to his jeans which ended at his cowboy boots. Looking back up she saw them enter the last private room down the hallway.

Melvina turned her head to the ding of the elevator door opening, recognized Ree, gave her a silent head nod and mouthed "Can you believe this?"

Ree nearly froze in her tracks. Could that be Kendall Davis? *The* Kendall Davis who just released his umpteenth hit *Don't Leave Me Now?*

"O-M-G, kids!" Ree said in a staged whisper. "I think that's Kendall Davis!"

"O-M-G? Gramma, really? You just said O-M-G. When did you start speaking in text?" asked Jenna.

Ree laughed. "What? Grandmothers can't be hip?"

"No, you're supposed to be old and frumpy."

"Well, not this gramma. Anyway, do you know any of Kendall Davis's songs?"

"No," stated a very disappointed Jenna. "Please don't tell me he's a country singer, or worse yet, an opera singer."

"Sorry to disappoint, but yes, he's country. But a lot of his songs wind up in the top 100 rock charts. He's one of those cross over guys, if you know what I mean. Actually, I think you'd like some of his songs."

Melvina returned to the nurses station before Jenna could respond. She was all smiles.

Ree asked, "Is that really Ken..."

Melvina interrupted with a giggly, "yup."

Jenna whispered, "Did you get his autograph?"

Ree then questioned Jenna, "So now you want his autograph even though he's country and western?"

"It might be cool to have it," Jenna retorted.

"Well, I'll be getting plenty of signatures, just not sure any of them could ever leave this unit, but we'll see. He's really nice, and so is his mother," interjected Melvina.

"Good to know. I didn't know he lived around here."

"He doesn't. He flew in yesterday from Los Angeles and his driver picked him up. I'm sure you noticed the limo."

"Oh yeah, and I saw it yesterday too when I dropped Ben off at the airport. His driver drove all the way from LA?"

"No, New York City. Apparently he has an apartment there and a ski chalet in the Catskills. I also heard he's giving a concert in New York City next Saturday."

"Oh yeah, I heard about that, at MSG I believe."

"MSG?" questioned Jake. "I thought that was a bad thing."

Jenna rolled her eyes, but Ree and Melvina laughed.

"Madison Square Garden, not monosodium glutamate, you retard," Jenna said with as much disgust as she could.

"Easy, Jenna, and don't call him a retard."

"Yeah, Jenna!" said Jake sticking up for himself.

"Well, kids, let's visit Meme. Do you think she's awake, Melvina?"

"She was a few minutes ago.... but you know that could change."

Meme was snoring when they entered the room. A gentle nudge to her shoulder, along with Ree calling her name, awakened her.

"Yes?" said a sleepy Meme. "Frank, Frank? Is that you?"

Ree squashed her desired response of "good grief, mom, can't you even get my gender straight?" And who the hell is Frank? Her father's name was Damon. Instead, she gently said "It's me, mom, Gloria, and look mom, two of your three great grandchildren, Jenna and Jake, are here too."

Ree raised the back of the bed with the electric controller. She positioned her mid way in the bed and fluffed her side pillows to keep her from leaning over.

Jenna stepped in and held her great grandmother's hand. So caring, thought Ree. Oh Jenna, I just know there's a wonderful, warm person inside you.

"Hey Meme, it's me Jenna. I'm staying with Gramma

Ree, your daughter. We're staying the whole week while my parents are in Costa Rica."

"And I'm here too!" piped in Jake.

Ree breathed a sigh of relief when Meme opened her eyes fully and smiled. She was quick to snap a few pictures with her phone of Meme flanked by Jenna and Jake. With no protest at all, Jenna smiled too. Maybe there is a God after all, Ree said to herself.

As predicted, Meme then fell back asleep. The kids hugged and kissed her as best they could and didn't look back when they left the room. Ree noticed tears in Jenna's eyes as they approached the nursing station.

"Jenna dear, here's something you need to know. I actually heard Meme say she had a good life and she did everything she wanted to do. It'll be okay when she passes, and I'm so happy you were so kind to her all these years. It warmed me to my soul to see how gently you spoke to her, and how you just naturally held her hand. Means a lot to me."

Jenna just looked up and then gave her grandmother a hug. Tears turned into sobs.

"Jenna, Jenna…. it's okay, everything is going to be okay." Jake joined the hug too.

Ree looked up at Melvina as if hoping to be rescued or transported to a private place where Jenna could just cry her eyes out. She then saw Kendall approaching the nursing station. He started to ask a question but then noticed the tearful group hug.

"Did someone just die?" he questioned Melvina in a whisper. Melvina looked surprised. "Sorry… none of my business," he added quickly.

"Oh no sir, it's perfectly fine to be curious. Of course I can't give out any personal information, but we are a big family here and we all care about each other. May I have your permission to introduce you to them and to tell them about your mother being here?"

Melvina pointed to Ree and continued, "She comes in almost every day. Maybe she wouldn't mind visiting with your mother as well."

Melvina was amazed at herself for offering that information without consulting Ree first, and more amazed that he obliged.

Ree looked up, also amazed that Melvina and Kendall were approaching them. She released the kids and turned them in the direction of the duo. Ree had always thought Kendall was good looking and seeing him in person only enhanced that assessment. What really got to her in that moment was his intense deep ocean blue eyes that seemed to undress her. She glanced away, chiding herself for having such thoughts.

Melvina introduced Kendall. He shook their hands with an unexpected amount of caring. Was it Ree's imagination or was his hand shake with her a little longer than necessary and perhaps a bit too sensual? She quickly dismissed the notion.

Ree summarized her mother's situation and then asked about his mother. Jenna and Jake stood in silent awe as to how easily their grandmother could talk to a celebrity.

"My mother has been living in an assisted living facility in Amsterdam, New York, for the past ten years, but unfortunately her memory has faded to the point of needing nursing home care. It was quite a search to find a good facility for her," Kendall offered.

"Oh, I know that drill…. I'm sure you'll find this place an excellent environment and…," looking directly at Melvina, "the staff is just superior. You know, if it's of any comfort to you, I visit my mother almost daily. I'm sure you're on the road a lot, so I'd be happy to visit with your mother too."

Melvina's eyes widened. Was Ree a mind reader? How had the two of them so innocently yet so calculating, set that up?

"Actually, that would be great. Let me give you my card with my contact information."

Jake, who could barely contain himself, blurted out "Can I get your autograph?"

Jenna was embarrassed and grateful at the same time.

"Jake, dear, don't be rude," Ree admonished.

"On no, it's okay, I'm rather used to it," Kendall affirmed.

Melvina offered up the clipboard she always carried with her. "Here, you can use the backside of today's menu."

Jenna piped in with "I just love your new hit *Don't Leave Me Now.*"

As Kendall signed the menu he looked up at Jenna and replied, "Well that means a lot to me, especially from a young, beautiful teen such as yourself. Not many teenagers like country and western."

Ree laughed to herself. She didn't know who was better at acting, Kendall or Jenna. Man, they can both pour it on, she mused.

Melvina interrupted the dialogue with "Hey, great to see you kids today, but I need to get back to work. Mr. Davis can you come with me? I just need to review a few more details with you."

"Certainly, good day, ladies, gentleman."

The trio entered the elevator silently but as soon as the door closed the kids burst out simultaneously with shouts of how cool that was to talk to a real music star.

"I can't believe you got an autograph! Maybe you're not a retard after all."

"Jenna, again, stop that with the retard word. Can't you just be grateful without the snide commentary?"

"Yeah, Jenna!" said Jake.

"Sorry, Gramma, sorry, Jake." And just like that, Jenna reverted to her sullen persona.

Chapter 5

R ED COULDN'T BELIEVE THE CIRCUMSTANCE he was in. What should have been the simplest job ever, get instructions as to where and when to pick up the diamonds, had become a ridiculous situation. He had turned in the black Durango and rented a white one. He drove by Gloria Grayson's residence, the name being part of the information he learned from her license plate. He was so tempted just to call Blue and ask him to resend the information, but he knew that breach would result in Blue sending out Agent Orange, and that would be lethal.

The tire tracks in the light snowfall revealed Gloria had at least been in and out of her driveway once, if not twice, but he was unable to determine if she was now back home. He'd have to wait it out... again. His patience was rewarded about an hour later when the garage door opened and he witnessed a peculiar operation of Gloria and presumably her grandchildren, coaxing a large dog into the hatch back of the car.

Before opening the garage door so as to minimize contact with the frigid air, Gloria and the kids had fully stuffed the roof top carrier with cross country skis, poles, boots and extra bags of bulky cold weather outdoor gear. They stowed their small duffles of personal belongings inside the car. The dog bed had been placed in the rear cargo portion of the car. Then Gloria retrieved the special ramp Ben and their daughter Kirstin had built for Cookie. She loved that memory of Ben and Kirstin designing and building the ramp. Kirstin had initially followed her mother's footsteps of first becoming a Certified Occupational Therapy Assistant and then working on her masters to become a Registered Occupational Therapist. Then a rotation at the Walter Reed National Military Medical Center changed Kirstin's direction. She was simultaneously appalled and fascinated with the need for development of better artificial limbs. She felt committed to bettering the many ruined lives of the returning veterans with head injuries and missing limbs. Her father was thrilled she changed her degree to Biomedical Engineering. Gloria was pleased too. She often thought biomedical engineers were just glorified OTs. The only current problem was that Kirstin lived in Portland, Oregon, so far away. Flying out to see Kirstin, Alan and Moira was arduous, rendering visits few and far between. Thank goodness for Facetime.

"Okay, kids, are you ready? Let's get Cookie into the car."

Gloria pressed the garage door opener, Jake stood guard to the left of the ramp and Jenna led Cookie out on her leash. Gloria was to the right of the ramp. With cajoling and coaxing, Cookie tentatively placed her paws on the ramp. After her usual two steps forward, one step back, she eventually sprung herself onto the dog bed. The ramp was removed, folded and placed to the side of the bed on a previously placed hook which kept the ramp from falling over. With that, Gloria and the kids piled into the car and drove off.

Given the amount of effort it took for them to get the dog into the car, Red assumed this outing would be a lengthy one. He had figured out the frequency of her garage door opener and after waiting out a full 15 minutes, he simply pulled his car into the garage and shut the door. Hopefully, no nosey neighbor would notice the lack of a roof top carrier on the white Durango. The presence of a second car in the garage did not deter him. There was no man in the bed with her last night, so he assumed her partner was away. And since there was no need for her to hide the letter, he figured it would be easy to find it in broad daylight. With gloved hands he carefully searched through the dresser drawers, desk drawers, shelves and book cases. What he didn't know was that at the last minute Gloria had put the letter in her duffle bag. She thought she and her cousin could have fun trying to figure out its meaning. It only fleetingly crossed her mind that she really should have taken it to the police. The current slogan of "if you see something, say something" nagged at her.

Red heard the house phone ring and then the answering machine pick up. A male voice said "Hey, honey, I tried calling you on your cell phone, but it kept going right to voice mail. The mission is going well but I sure do miss you. Call me when you can. Love you." Comforting words to Red; at least he didn't have to worry about a returning husband.

After an hour of searching in which he painstakingly made sure nothing looked out of place, he concluded she must have taken the letter with her. But where did she go? He looked at the large calendar on the side of the refrigerator. Several notations were written on the various dates. Saturday: Jenna and Jake. Sunday: Ben 7 A.M. and then a line from

Sunday to the following Sunday which read Ben 10:30 P.M. On Monday the name "Jeannie" with a question mark was penciled in. Okay great, maybe she went to visit Jeannie or maybe Jeannie would be visiting, whoever the hell Jeannie was. More likely she was visiting Jeannie given the loading of the dog into the car. He easily found her address book in the nearby telephone desk. He searched from A to Z and on the last page, there was Jean and Neil Zaban. He snapped a picture of the address and phone number. She had over an hour lead on him but it didn't matter. He'd have to stake out the address and then move in if she spent the night. If not, he'd be following her back to her home.

When he pulled the car out of the driveway the snow was falling more heavily and there were two new inches of snow on the driveway. Soon enough his tire tracks would be covered up with more snow.

Chapter 6

Ree had Jenna look up the weather again on her phone. She couldn't believe how heavily the snow was falling. When she had looked earlier, only three to six inches of snow were predicted.

"It's saying six to twelve inches, more in the higher elevations," Jenna reported. "And now it's a named storm, Helena."

"What? Really? That wasn't in the forecast last night or even this morning."

"Well, Gramma, look out the window."

"Don't be sarcastic, Jenna, I see what's going on."

Jake was entranced with his video game on his tablet and had no contribution to the conversation whatsoever.

"Jenna, take my phone and call your Aunt Jeannie. I only left her a message this morning that we were coming. I didn't actually talk to her. I want to make sure she's going to be home, and I also want to know what the weather is like down there."

In amazing speed that only a teenager could accomplish, she found Jeannie's number and pressed "call." No answer. She put the phone on speaker and held it near her grandmother.

"Leave her another message, Gramma."

Without hesitation Ree dictated: "Hey, Jeannie, it's one o'clock in the afternoon, and I'm headed to your house with Jake, Jenna and Cookie. We're planning on spending the night but the weather is really getting bad. Call me as soon as you get this message."

"Thanks, Jenna," Ree continued. "Now call her cell number." Ree left an identical message on Jeannie's cell phone voice mail.

"That's weird that she's not at least answering her cell phone. But no worries. I know where she hides a spare key in case we get to her house before she returns."

The snow storm continued to worsen, and there were occasional white outs. Ree could handle snow covered roads, but white outs were her nemesis. She considered turning around. But at that point she was essentially half way between her house and Jeannie's house. She pressed on. As the snowfall intensified, so did her white knuckled grip on the steering wheel. The windshield wipers could barely keep up with the snow piling onto the windshield. Then an ice chunk formed on the driver side wiper blade further restricting her vision.

She was about to swear out loud when her phone rang causing her and Jenna to gasp. Jenna dutifully answered the phone full knowing her grandmother couldn't and shouldn't take her hands off the wheel. She put the phone on speaker.

"Ree? It's Jeannie. Sorry I missed your calls, I was out shoveling. This storm is so bad! I just heard they're closing I-88 and there is to be no unnecessary travel," Jeannie continued.

"Oh I'm not surprised, I was just thinking about turning around, I can hardly see."

"I know it's a disappointment, but I'd be happier knowing you were back in your comfy living room."

"Agreed. There's still time, maybe we can come down later in the week once this snow clears out."

"Great idea, call me as soon as you get home."

"Will do," replied Ree. And then to Jenna and Jake, "Sorry, kids."

Jenna was secretly very happy to be turning back. More potential time with Donny. But out loud she mustered up a sympathetic reply. "That's OK, Gramma, this weather sucks."

Jake chimed in, "No prob, Gramma," and returned to his video game. The world could have collapsed around him and he probably wouldn't have noticed.

Ree glanced up at the GPS map. Only four more miles to the next exit. If she wasn't allowed back on I-88 to head north, she could always take Route 7 back home. Her car was now acting as a snow plow, with no cars immediately ahead of her she was literally pushing six to eight inches of snow in her lane. She was trying to calculate how long it would take her to travel the final four miles at her current rate of 25 miles per hour when a pick-up truck completely filled her rear view mirror. The exasperated driver then passed her, nearly forcing her off the road.

"What a jerk!" cried Ree out loud. She was now almost at a stop since the truck sprayed a heavy blanket of snow against her windshield. Just as she was about to continue with a string of expletives, another vehicle filled up her rearview mirror and within seconds it too tried to pass her.

"Unbelievable!" exclaimed Ree. It was a limo. And then it all happened so fast. She and Jenna simultaneously stating "Musicman!" as the limo pulled back into the lane in front of them, the limo catching an edge in the piled up snow along the shoulder, the limo spinning out of control and Ree needing to dodge the limo by exiting off the highway. She hit the snowbank so hard the car jerked to a stop and all airbags deployed. Everyone screamed. Then silence.

What seemed like hours was only a few seconds before Ree called out; "Jenna, Jake, are you okay?"

"Yes," cried Jake. It took Jenna a few seconds more to respond which also seemed like an eternity.

"I'm okay, but I can't move. The airbag has me pinned."

"Yeah me too. Jake, can you check on Cookie?" She could hear Cookie whimpering.

"She's fine, Gramma, just panting away."

"Okay good… now what? Jenna, can you reach my phone?"

"Yes, got it."

"Go to the maps program and take a screen shot of our location. We're going to need a tow truck, and I'll need to tell the driver where we are."

It took some maneuvering to get her hands to the screen given the position of the deployed airbag, but once she could get to the app she easily clicked a screen shot.

Ree was trying to figure out what to do next when suddenly there was a knock on her window. A startled Ree put her window down. A large man filled up the window area.

"Ma'am, are you all right?"

"I am, we're all okay, but it's hard to move from under the airbags."

"I'll help you out, you really shouldn't stay in the car with deployed airbags."

"But where will we go?"

"There's plenty of room in the limo," the large man replied. The snow was blowing into the car from the opened window rendering them miserable and freezing. Ree acquiesced quickly. What a strange coincidence that she would actually know the owner of the limo.

"Even for a large dog?" asked Ree.

"Dog? Um… of course," he replied with some hesitation.

"Is Mr. Davis in the limo?" asked Jenna.

"Yes, you know him?" the man asked in a quizzical manner.

"It's a long story," interjected Ree.

It took some doing, but Ree and Jenna were able to be extracted from the front seats of the car with the large man's help. They learned that his name was Wilson. They also learned that Kendall Davis was in the process of calling the police and a tow truck to get them out of the snow banks. After spinning out of control, the limo landed in the shoulder as well. However, Wilson glided into the snow bank and, therefore, the airbags didn't deploy. Jake had crawled into the back with Cookie. He handed out their small duffles. It took almost 20 minutes to get Cookie to go down the ramp and for the group to walk to the limo. Wilson carried the special ramp which Ree insisted was absolutely necessary to get Cookie into the limo.

Wilson opened the side door to the limo and Jenna and Jake readily entered. Much to Jenna's delight, two teenaged boys were already seated. Ree and Wilson unfolded the collapsible ramp and with much coaxing, Cookie finally entered the limo as well. Ree entered the limo but when Wilson stepped back to close the door, the snow gave way and he fell. As he attempted to stand up he yelled out in pain. He had twisted his right ankle and could barely place any weight on it. Ree reached over to assist him.

"Wilson, crawl into the limo. I'll go up front," Ree volunteered. As large as the passenger compartment was, with four kids, a large dog, dog bed, a ramp, three duffles and now a tall man sprawled across the back seat, the limo's interior was full. "We should be able to drive out of here, we're really not that stuck into the snowbank."

Wilson didn't protest or complain. He was happy to have someone take over for him.

Ree opened the passenger door of the front seat expecting Kendall to be in the driver's seat. He was actually in the passenger seat, on the phone.

Ken looked up in startled surprise. He quickly concluded his call. "Mrs. Grayson? Oh no, it was you we ran off the road? I'm so sorry! Hey, where's Wilson?"

Ree started to answer, but then Ken interrupted by getting out of the car and letting her in.

"Sorry, you must be freezing... um... do you think you can move over a bit so I can get back in?" The limo, being an older model, actually had a bench seat.

Once they were resettled in the car, Ken asked again, "So what happened to Wilson?"

"Um, he fell when he shut the door and now he can't bear weight on his right foot. He's either twisted it, sprained it or broken it. I'm afraid you'll have to drive."

"Um... that's a problem... I can't. This limo has standard transmission which was Wilson's choice. I've never driven standard transmission, and my contract with my record company forbids me to drive. They're afraid I might injure my hands which would preclude my ability to play guitar."

"You can't be serious."

"I'm dead serious."

"So, let me get this straight. You're going to let me drive your limo, in a blizzard, even though I've never driven a limo before, and my husband complains all the time that my depth perception is worthless? And bonus, Mr. Country and Western, who sings all the time about how tough you are, you can't drive standard transmission? That's craziness!"

"Yup. Oh, and more bad news, the police said there are so many vehicles off the road that it could be hours, maybe days before a tow truck gets to us. Again, I'm so sorry we caused this accident."

"Oh, me too. Well, Mr. Not So Tough Guy, you're in luck. I actually can drive standard transmission."

With that, Ree slid across the front bench seat and situated herself behind the steering wheel. She engaged the gears and did a gentle rock and roll with forward then reverse, repeating several times, careful not to spin the wheels. Eventually, the car crept forward and they were free of the shoulder's snow bank. She entered the slow lane and shifted into second gear, then third. They were traveling too slowly to move into fourth. Fifteen agonizing minutes later, she saw flashing lights directing them off the highway at the next exit.

"Okay, now what?"

"I say we go to the next open motel to get off the road."

"Well, google motels and tell me where to go," said a desperate Ree.

He started a google search but it wasn't necessary, a few miles after exiting I-88 there was a motel with a sign fully illuminating "Vacancy."

"Oh thank God, we can just check in here," said a relieved Ree.

As she made her way through the unplowed driveway, Ken was quick to say, "Just pull up to the office and let me out, I'll get the motel rooms."

Ree offered no protest.

"Well that's just great, Mr. Davis, or may I call you Kendall?"

"Please call me Ken. May I call you Gloria?"

"No, call me Ree, I hate the name Gloria."

CHAPTER 7

KENDALL WAS ABLE TO GET five rooms which was fortunate since each room only contained one bed. The thought of having to share a room, much less a bed, with Wilson was rather distasteful to him. He was able to get cots sent into the rooms for the kids since he assumed no teenagers would sleep with their brothers.

The two teenaged boys, Derrick and Drew, who Ree learned were Ken's grandsons, helped Ken lower Wilson into his bed. He refused any offers of getting him to a hospital to look at his right ankle.

"Just get me some ice to put on it, I'll be fine," he demanded in a gruff voice. Something told Ree this wasn't his first go around with injuries that would be left unattended. In fact, it was all she could do not to call him Victor the Cruncher.

Kendall excused himself to make more phone calls in his room. The boys went back to the limo to get their belongings, and Ree went to get ice. Once she made a make shift ice pack for Wilson, she headed to her room.

Jenna and Jake gathered in Ree's room to help settle Cookie into her dog bed. Jenna started with rapid fire complaints.

"Gramma, this motel is so gross! It doesn't have cable or internet and the furniture is creepy! And look at these towels, they're paper thin and as coarse as sand paper. This sucks! How long do we have to stay here?"

Jenna had a point, but as run down as The Red Fox Motel and Diner was, Ree was grateful it was open with available rooms.

"Well, Jenna, look out the window," Ree said sarcastically, mimicking Jenna's earlier comment to her. "Do you not see the blizzard going on? We'll stay here until the weather clears. Believe me, I'm not happy either…"

A knock on her door interrupted their argument.

Jake opened the door to find a snow covered Kendall. He was soon followed by the boys.

"May we come in?" he asked.

"Of course," Ree and Jenna answered together.

"It's a bit crowded here, what do you say we reconvene in the motel lobby? I think there's a snack bar or restaurant there. I'll let you know what I've learned so far."

"Good idea," agreed Ree. "I'll follow in a just a bit, I need to make a few calls."

Ree let her cousin know she was at the motel and launched briefly into the circumstances that led her there. Jeannie had heard of Kendall Davis and was amazed with the series of coincidences that had taken place.

"Yeah, pretty wild, huh? But the most annoying thing is that I'm only 30 minutes away from home and 30 minutes away from you. This motel is so gross, we can't wait to get out of here."

"Well good luck with that. It'll be all of tomorrow I'm

afraid. Call me when you can leave. You could just come on down, you know, you're all packed."

"Yeah, but all our stuff is in the car. I'll try to get down later in the week. I'll call you again tomorrow."

Ree then tried to call Ben. Once again her call went right through to voice mail. She had been leaving messages as had he. "Oh Ben, this storm is epic. I'm at that sleazy Red Fox motel on Route 7 half way to Jeannie's. It's too long of a story, but we're all okay, just annoyed. I'll try you later. Love, you," she stated.

She left some food and water out for Cookie, gave her a pat and assured her someone would take her out to do her business in about an hour. With that she put her winter garb back on, and headed out the door. The snow was now about a foot deep, so that as she trudged to the diner, snow spilled over the rim of her boots which sent shivers up and down her body.

The motel's restaurant looked sad and shabby. The few tables were of 1950s vintage and the wall paper probably predated World War II. But mercifully there was a fireplace with an actual fire going which gave the place just a modicum of atmosphere. Two tables were occupied with other forlorn motel guests and her group occupied two tables near the front windows. The four kids were already engaged in animated conversation. Jenna must be in her glory, Ree thought to herself. Ken's grandsons looked to be 15 and 16, very strong resemblance to one another, only one was taller than the other by a few inches. Ken stood up when she approached his table.

"Really? You must be from the south," Ree said with perhaps a bit too much enthusiasm.

"Yes I am. Old habits die hard."

"Well thanks. So, what's the news? If there's good and bad news, I guess I'll take the bad news first."

"I'm sorry, but it's all pretty bleak. This storm is actually building, not leveling off. The latest report is that we're in some sort of snow band at this elevation, and we could get four feet of snow."

"What? That's impossible!"

"I wish it were, but we might be here until Wednesday."

"No, that can't be true. Oh, and what about my car? It'll be buried, and it's white and it's only a little bit off the road, the snowplows will hit it!" Ree was revving up to hysteria.

"Hey, hey, calm down, don't holla' 'til you're hurt."

"What? What kind of saying is that? Something your Meemaw told you?"

"Meemaw? I'm originally from the south but not that far south. My grandmother, bless her soul, was called Meme."

That silenced her. Tears formed in her eyes. Ken handed her a napkin from the nearby napkin basket. Even though his fingertips only grazed hers as he handed it to her, she still felt a bit of electricity course through her hand. What was that? Ree questioned herself.

"Thanks… I'm sorry… I'm a bit overwhelmed. And to top it off, my mother is called Meme too.

"So what's your grandmother name?"

Ree looked up at him quizzically. He's probably just asking that to distract me, she thought to herself.

"Um, just Gramma. Nothing fancy. My younger sister wants to be called Meme if she's ever a grandmother and my older sister goes by Deedee."

"My grandsons call me Pops. I was hoping to get them skiing at Hunter Mountain for a few days before returning them to New York City. This is their school break too."

"How old are they?"

"Right now they're both 15, Irish twins, but next week Derrick turns 16."

"That's interesting. My husband is an Irish twin too."

"Your husband…"

"Yes, Ben, he's uh… he's on a mission right now…." Why am I hesitating? Ree again questioned herself.

"Go on, sounds interesting."

She explained his situation and how normally she would go with him, but she had already committed herself to taking care of her grandkids. She also threw in the demographics of her twin daughters and three grandchildren.

"There, now you know my story."

"Not really… but good enough. Shall we order some food? The kids must be starved."

The one waitress, herself now also stranded at the motel, wearily took their orders. Ken and Ree correctly assumed it would be a good long wait before getting their food even though there were only about a dozen guests to feed. They ordered drinks to fill the time. Ken also put in an order for Wilson and told the waitress he would deliver the meal to his room himself.

"So back to my car," Ree said. "It occurs to me that when the snow stops falling and we get plowed out, how do I get back to my car and to wherever it gets towed to?"

"Don't worry, I'll take care of that. I assumed you would want to be driven back to your home."

"So who's driving?"

"I'm making arrangements for another limo to meet us here with an extra driver. One will take you home and the other will return us to the City. I've got an important engagement on Saturday and I really should be in the City by Friday at the latest."

"Ah yes, the engagement…"

She guessed he didn't want it known that he was giving a concert. So far none of the staff, all three of them, and the other motel guests hadn't recognized him. She gathered he wanted to keep it that way.

As if reading her mind, he stated, "Yes, as far as anyone knows, I'm just Mr. Smith traveling with my grandsons."

"And no one has noticed the limo? I think your cover will be blown as soon as someone reads the license plate."

"Yeah, stupid me, I need to get rid of the vanity plates."

"They really are vanity plates, aren't they? Was the attention fun?"

"It was for awhile, but now it's getting old, especially since… well, never mind."

"Oh dear, what happened? Sorry, don't mean to pry…" Then it hit her. She wasn't a tabloid reader but in regular news there were accounts of how Ken had performed a number of benefit concerts for breast cancer over the past few years. "Your wife, Janet? Did she have cancer?"

"Yes, my dearly departed wife Janet died of breast cancer 18 months ago."

"I'm so sorry… that's awful…" To herself, she noted, when you count in months, that says a lot.

"Yes, well it's all about life and death, isn't it? But mainly life… It was a long road, we did our best, she was so brave at the end…"

They were interrupted by the arrival of their second round of drinks and apologies that the food was be just a bit longer. Their waitress, Nancy, seemed even wearier than before.

"Nancy, dear, we're not going anywhere and we have nothing to do, so please don't apologize. We know you're doing the best you can," Ree said kindly.

"Thanks, I'll bring out some chips for the kids to tide them over."

"That would be appreciated."

Ree turned her attention back to Ken, "So tell me about Janet."

"Really? Well, she was wonderful. We were married over 30 years, something unheard of in the music industry. My first marriage barely lasted a year, much more typical. Just long enough to produce a daughter. I had two sons with Janet. One's married, one's not, and I have these two grandsons from my daughter Sara."

"But tell me more about Janet."

He narrated a short story of her upbringing, how they met and their life together, some of their problem areas, more so of their good times and common interests, her hobbies and her many personality quirks.

"Wow, I don't think I've talked that much about Janet out loud since she passed," he concluded. "Everyone thinks I'm so fragile when it comes to talking about her. But actually, I like talking about her. She's not dead to me. She lives in my heart."

"That's so sweet. I think I would have really liked her. Sorry I never met her."

"Well that's sweet too." He then motioned over to Nancy. Before Ree could refuse, he ordered a third round of drinks.

Their conversation turned to the music industry and Ree started to giggle at some of his comments. Jenna was holding court with the three boys and seemed to be really enjoying herself and her situation. The kids paid no attention to them and didn't seem to notice the lack of meals.

Dinner finally arrived. There was a variety of god awful fried foods from the limited menu. No one complained. Ree switched to water during the meal, telling Ken she was a cheap date and that three glasses of red wine were definitely her limit.

At the conclusion of the meal Drew asked if the four kids could watch movies on his computer in his room. Ree and Ken answered "sure" simultaneously which made them laugh. Ree added, "But 11:00 is the end. I expect Jenna and Jake to be back in their room by then." There was minimal protest. It was only seven o'clock, plenty of time to watch one or two movies.

Ken took Wilson's meal and they both headed out. On Ken's way back from Wilson's room to his room, he noticed Ree struggling with her dog. The door to her room was open and the swirling snow was entering her room at an alarming rate.

"Cookie, please, just step forward. Let's get this over with!" Ree pleaded as she shut the door.

"Can I help you? asked Ken.

"Yes, either shoot the dog or me, one of us has to be put out of our misery."

Ken laughed. "Let me try. I mean, let me try to get the dog out, not shoot you."

Ree tugged once more on Cookie's leash. She didn't really expect Cookie to budge, but Ken coaxed her too which caused Cookie to move, which caused Ree to fall backwards not expecting the release of tension on the leash. As she fell backward, she bumped into Ken who lost his footing in the loose snow. The two of them fell into the snow and for a moment neither one could move. Then they both started laughing.

"Hey, while we're down here, we should make snow angels," Ree giggled.

"Snow angels? Are you kidding? I haven't made snow angels in decades."

"Well, now's a good time to catch up."

Ree slid over and began moving her arms and legs up and down to make a snow angel. Ken looked at her, smiled and mimicked her.

"Mine's better than yours," he said in a voice imitating an eight-year-old.

"Oh yeah?" Well, we'll see about that!" Ree was able to stand up without using her arms so as not to mar her snow angel imprint. She turned around and extended her hand to Ken to get him to stand up. It took some doing and he did use his arms. They turned to critique the imprints which were filling up fast with new snow.

"Mine is so superior!" Ree proclaimed. Ken was about to protest, but Cookie started whining. There was a yellow puddle near the doorway and evidence of poop not far beyond. A pathetic Cookie was pawing at her motel room door.

"Oh, thank God," said a relieved Ree. "Let's get her back inside."

Ken helped usher Cookie back into her room. His cell phone rang and after seeing who was calling him, he answered. Ree brushed the snow off of Cookie's back, then her paws.

It was Wilson calling Ken, asking for vodka.

"Sure thing, Wilson, I can do that."

He hung up as Ree was settling Cookie into her dog bed.

"Well, duty calls, Wilson needs some sedatives. Do you have any Ibuprofen per chance? I think that would help, and I'll get more ice too."

"Of course, I always carry Ibuprofen."

Ree reached in her purse and pulled out a few medicine containers. She didn't take any prescription medicines, but she always carried the essentials: Ibuprofen, Benadryl and Pepto Bismol.

"Here, take the bottle of Ibuprofen, you can return the remainder tomorrow. By the way, thanks for dinner… and the drinks… although I definitely over drank."

"I don't think so, you're perfectly fine."

"Well thanks…. I'd better check on the kids… we don't want to be great grandparents just yet…"

"What?… wow… didn't even think about that. Should I come with you?"

"No, tend to Wilson, I'll tend to the kids."

Ken bent over to pet Cookie a few times. Neither one noticed his cell phone had slipped out of his side coat pocket while doing so.

"OK, well, good night," said Ken. "Good night," replied Ree.

Ree tried calling Ben again before checking in on the kids. Voice mail! She was so frustrated but managed to leave a message: "Hey Ben, me again. Just wanted to say goodnight. Love you."

She trudged out the door into 18 inches of snow and knocked on Drew and Derrick's door. "Come in!" shouted a collective group of kids. They were having a blast watching some inane movie on Drew's computer. So innocent, thought Ree. Thank goodness for the presence of Jake, however. She reminded them of their 11 o'clock curfew. They hardly acknowledged her presence when they replied with a weak "yes, Gramma."

Ree returned to her room. She changed into a night shirt, brushed her teeth and gave Cookie a final pat to her head.

"Wait, what's this?" she said to Cookie as she felt something hard in the dog bed. "Is this Ken's phone? I'd better return it."

She slipped her coat on around her night shirt which was devoid of underwear underneath it. Then she placed her bare feet into the snow boots. I can't possibly get that cold walking 25 feet to his room, she convinced herself.

She knocked at his door, thank goodness his lights were still on. A surprised Ken opened the door and readily let her in.

"I found your cell phone and figured you'd need it before morning."

"Wow, didn't even know it was missing. Thank you."

And just like the accident, it all happened so fast. She put her hand forward with the cell phone, he reached for it with his right hand only he didn't just take the cell phone, he grabbed her hand as well and pulled her into him. He was taller than her by a good six inches so he basically swept her off her feet to envelop her in his arms and kiss her. She kissed him back and then he landed her back on her feet.

"Ken! No! I'm a married woman! I was just returning your cell phone!"

"Then why did you kiss me back?"

"Um… I don't know… too much red wine I guess."

"Ree, darling, come here, let me kiss you once more, you're gorgeous."

Darling? she said in shock to herself. Out loud she protested, "Ken, no… stop… I shouldn't… it's not right…." But the electricity between them was too much. For reasons she couldn't account for, she allowed herself to be swept back up in his arms and kissed him passionately.

He slipped off her coat and she shook off her boots. He gently pulled her into his bed. His hands were all over her. She felt like a teenager, wanting to rip his clothes off and wanting him to do the same to her. Then a voice of reason came over her. It was as if Jiminy Cricket annoyingly appeared on her shoulder reminding her about her conscience.

"No, Ken… I can't. I can't cheat on my husband… I'm sorry. Obviously, I find you attractive… and what a thrill that you find me attractive…. but I'm not looking for love. I'm already in love… in fact… Ben could call me any time now."

"I'm sorry too, Ree, I shouldn't have. It's just you're irresistible. Do you know no one has ever talked to me like you did in the limo? And that was incredible how you got us out of that snow bank. Everything about you is amazing. Right down to making snow angels."

"But what about Janet? She still lives in your heart… isn't that a bit much that you're on the prowl?"

"I'm not on the prowl. Yes, Janet is gone. Yes, she lives in my heart, always will. But I can't stop living. I have to move on with my life. She would understand that. So should you. It's all about living life."

Ree sat silent for a few minutes. She rubbed his chest and then cuddled into his arms. "I'm sorry, Ken, I just can't take this any further. I should go."

"Stay for just a little while longer. I just want you in my arms for a few minutes. It's been so long since I've held a woman. Do you mind?"

"Well, if you're just going to hold me and nothing else, I guess that's okay."

He held her. She nestled under his chin and over his chest. Their legs were wrapped around each other. She started to fall asleep. She felt so at peace and dismissed any confusing thoughts. But then her phone in her coat pocket rang. It was the ring tone she assigned to Ben. Like an automaton she disentangled herself from Ken, put the phone on speaker mode so she could talk while she put on her coat and boots, walked out the door and continued to converse until she was in her own bed.

Neither she nor Ken noticed that another car had pulled into the motel's parking lot. Ken breathed a heavy sigh, undressed fully and went to bed. Ree filled Ben in on the events of the day. She did tell him she returned Ken's cell phone but glossed over the details of the delivery method and aftermath. That would have to wait until later.

CHAPTER 8

RED WAS SEETHING. It had been a long frustrating day. After he left the Grayson residence he Google mapped Jeannie's address. At first he was relieved the location was only an hour's drive from the little hamlet of Altamont, New York. Then he Googled nearby motels and hotels. What? Seemed Schenevus, New York wasn't really close to anything, the real boonies. There were plenty of places to stay in Oneonta which was another thirty minutes beyond Schenevus and a few places near Cobleskill, thirty minutes away in the other direction. He opted for the motels near Cobleskill, given they were closer to his current location and the weather was rapidly deteriorating. He tried to take the most direct route, which was I-88, but he was met with a barrier of snow plows and flashing road hazard signs stating the highway was closed. Turn Back! No Unnecessary Travel!

No way was he turning back. He continued south on Route 7. He was then traveling at a very slow pace of 20 mph. There was a long line of cars in front of him and a long line behind him. Three vehicles ahead was a tractor trailer, no doubt turned away from I-88. The trailer lights provided guidance for the following cars since the road had all but disappeared. There was no choice but to stay in the wheel ruts and follow the tamped down tire tracks of the car in front of him. Only a few cars were heading north.

He was nearing the town of Cobleskill when the truck disappeared from view. The wind was howling and the white outs were nearly constant. Then there were flashes of brakes going on and off. The car in front of him slid to the right. He was going so slowly he was able to slide to the left without hitting it. The car behind him also avoided the swerving cars, but all of them became stuck in the unplowed lanes and shoulders. Red had never experienced a snow storm of this magnitude. But he did know he needed to keep his exhaust pipe clear from the snow or else he would be slowly committing suicide.

He got out of the car, no easy feat, pushing against the snow bank. Walking to the rear of the car was even more arduous. He used his gloved hands to clear the snow away from the exhaust pipe. In doing so he noticed a man outside of the car behind him.

The man yelled out, "Are you okay?"

"Yes, and you?"

"So far so good. I have plenty of gas to keep us warm."

"Is your exhaust pipe clear of snow?"

"Good call, I'll check it out, thanks. Looks like it'll be awhile. A buddy of mine is in the car behind the tractor trailer. It jack knifed when an on-coming car ahead of it swerved in front of him."

Red stifled the expletives he wanted to yell out. Out loud he yelled, "Thanks for the information."

Six miserable hours later a parade of snow plows, tow trucks, utility vehicles and patrol cars made their way to the multi-car accident scene. Miraculously, only two of the eight cars and trucks actually crashed into one another. At the low speeds, no one was hurt but three cars had run out of fuel. The two truckers kindly took in the passengers of those cars. Red was just about out of gas himself when a tow truck attendant offered him fuel and a tow. Red paid for the services in cash and gave the worker a hefty tip. Once freed of the snow bank he followed the snow plow in front of him for another five long miles before reaching The Red Fox Motel.

He had called earlier to make a reservation He scowled when he heard the motel attendant say to him over the phone, "Today's your lucky day, I have one room left."

Lucky, my ass, this is the worst day of my life, he said to himself.

The motel room had been left unlocked since the motel attendant had gone to bed. Red had been instructed to come into the office in the morning to square up. He noticed a handful of cars in the parking lot, now all looking like igloos with over a foot of snow fully blanketing them. There was also a limo off to the side which he found mildly interesting.

He entered his room, swigged down several shots of whiskey from his flask and went to bed.

CHAPTER 9

R ED DIDN'T SLEEP WELL. He gave up at 5 A.M., trudged to the restaurant and helped himself to coffee and a few doughnuts that had been left out at a courtesy table. No one else was around. He trudged back, drank the coffee, ate a half a doughnut and dozed back to sleep.

Ken awakened at seven. Upon entering the restaurant, the other four guests were now sitting at the same table. Apparently, the two couples had introduced themselves to one another and were now fast friends. Ken acknowledged their presence but was reluctant to enter into any conversation lest they recognize him. Too late...

"Hey, Pal, care to join us? We may be here for awhile."

"Uh, thanks, but I need to get some coffee to my group, I'll catch up with you later. You're right, looks like we just need to hunker down."

First Ken went to Wilson's room. Wilson was actually sitting up in bed with his right foot propped up on the extra pillows. He announced he was feeling better and that he was able to limp to and from the bathroom without too much pain. He failed to mention that a full liter of vodka was no doubt doing its magic to mask the pain.

"Hey, thanks, Boss. Any news as to when we can get out of here?"

"From what I can get from the weather channel and talking to Frank, the other limo driver in New York City, the roads are passable forty miles to the south and twenty five miles to the north. Seems we're in our own private blizzard. We probably won't be able to leave here until tomorrow. Frank and another driver will head north as soon as they can. Then I insist we get you to a doctor."

"Okay, Boss, whatever you say…"

There was a slight slur to his speech. Ken didn't say anything. He'd probably get drunk, too, if he was in Wilson's situation.

"Well, let me get this coffee to the other guests before it gets cold."

Ken knocked on Ree's door. There was no sound at first, then he heard a faint whisper.

"It's okay, Cookie." Then a louder response, "Coming, just a moment."

Ree opened the door expecting it to be Jenna or Jake, but Ken nicely filled the door frame.

"Oh gosh, let me comb my hair, I must look like a wreck."

"No, just your beautiful self."

"Stop it, Ken."

"Sorry, sorry… but actually I'm not sorry. You are beautiful."

"You must be really horny if you think my frizzy, unkempt hair, my wrinkled skin and my baggy knees are attractive."

"What baggy knees? You don't have baggy knees or wrinkled skin for that matter."

"You must have the same vision my husband has. Come on in, I see you brought me some coffee. Savior!"

He set the coffees and bag of doughnuts on the desk, took off his coat and sat in the one chair of the motel room.

"I guessed you would want cream in your coffee, didn't know about sweetener but I threw a couple packets of sugar in my pocket if you want some."

"You guessed right on the cream, and thanks but no thanks for the sweetener." She took a sip. "Umm... not too bad for motel coffee."

She looked up at Ken, his eyes were undressing her once again. Every ounce of her wanted to jump into bed with him. She chided herself and looked for a diversion. The kids, of course, the kids.

"Have you checked on the kids yet?" she asked Ken.

"Not yet, my grandsons probably won't get up until nine or ten. No use in waking them up earlier. There's really nothing for them to do."

"Oh yeah, I'm definitely from the camp of letting sleeping kids lie. I did peek in on them last night when I finished talking to Ben. I'm happy to report Jenna and Jake were back in their room by 11. Your grandsons were perfect gentlemen."

"Thanks, they are pretty good kids. I don't get to see them too often any more with my road schedule, but when we do get together, I really enjoy their company."

"Do they live in New York City?"

"No, they actually live in Houston."

"So where were they when you were at the nursing home?"

"They were flying in from Houston. Wilson picked them up at the airport. They visited with their great grandmother briefly and we headed down here. After a few days of skiing we were going to continue to New York City for my concert and then they'd fly back to Houston from JFK."

"Well, that could still happen. Surely we'll be able to leave later today or tomorrow."

"I hope so, my agent is going crazy about whether or not to cancel the concert."

"These storms are fickle. You'll be fine, don't cancel."

"Well, thanks for the vote of confidence."

"You know, I need to get Cookie out. If you're done with your coffee, do you think you could borrow a shovel from Nate?"

"Nate?"

"Yeah, I learned the motel attendant's name is Nate. Apparently he's part of an 'N' family. The waitress is Nancy, as you know, and the cook is Nora."

"Makes it easy to remember I guess. But sure, darling, I'll get a shovel. Are you digging out for Cookie?"

There was that 'darling' thing again. She loved it, not sure why. She snapped out of her reverie when she heard him clear his throat.

"Yes, don't want to step in pee and poop every time I go in or out."

"Would you like more coffee while I'm at it?"

"Yes, that would be delightful."

She combed her hair and got herself dressed while he was out. Then she called Melvina to check on their moms. Both were fine, she needn't worry, Melvina assured her. Melvina also erased her guilt for not being available for the next few days to make personal visits. Ree learned that most of the staff had to spend the night but now the nearby roads were becoming passable. That's a relief, maybe there was light at the end of the tunnel. She had told Melvina almost all the details of how she landed at a motel, leaving out Ken's presence. She simply said a kind passerby got them to the motel. No use in starting a rumor mill. She was about to call Jeannie when she heard Ken outside her door. Figuring his hands were full, she opened the door for him.

"Here's the coffee, I'll put the shovel over here, outside the door."

"Thanks. I called Melvina. Our moms are fine. Just so you know, I didn't mention you were here. I'll leave that to you."

"Thanks for that, I was about to call myself."

"You probably should at some point."

She saw him shiver as he took off his coat.

"Here, sit on the bed and put this blanket over you. Let's try to catch the weather report on the TV."

He gladly followed orders. She sat next to him on the bed and fiddled with the remote. Without cable the channel selection was extremely limited.

"Is this the motel that time forgot? Why don't they have cable? Maddening."

"Probably why the rooms are only $60.00 each."

"Well, that is a bargain... I guess... I'll reimburse you for our rooms."

"Don't be silly. It's my fault you're here in the first place. Trust me, you don't owe me a thing."

"Well okay, just don't want to be a kept woman." she teased.

He looked over at her, put his coffee down on the night stand, put his arm around her and pulled her closer to him. She started to resist but he interrupted. "Don't worry, that's as far as I'm going to go. I get it, you're a married woman."

"So how long has it been since you've been with another woman?" Ree surprised herself with her forwardness.

"Well, for the first year after Janet died I was just lost, sex was the furthest thing from my mind. Then, about six months ago when I was visiting my daughter, Sara, I had, well, I had an interesting encounter with a woman named Rachel…"

He hesitated but Ree jumped in with, "Come on, tell me more, your secrets are safe with me, I'm a good listener."

"Okay, Mother Confessor, but it does get a bit weird…. Sara's mother-in-law, Rachel, is also a recent widow. I knew her husband obviously, we shared many family occasions together. Nice man, James, but he passed away from pancreatic cancer about the same time Janet died. It was really tough on Sara and her husband David, both of them losing parents at the same time…"

"But Janet wasn't her mother…" Ree interrupted.

"No, but over the years since Sara spent just about every weekend with us, she developed a nice relationship with Janet. Sara considered Janet her second mom. Anyway, Rachel and I decided to go to a movie and well, one thing led to another and we wound up in a local hotel."

"I hope it had better amenities than this one," Ree interrupted again.

"Didn't really notice."

"Oh, I see, she was that good in bed?"

He looked at her intensely. "What can I say? I'm not apologizing for my gender's needs, but we were both starved for a sexual liaison."

"Well, that's nice. So are you still seeing her?"

"That's the crappy part, yes and no. When my daughter and Rachel's son found out, they exploded. We actually had a falling out over the matter. I'm just now back on talking terms with Sara. I think in their minds I was inappropriate. Plus, Sara couldn't get over the connection between the families. She thought it was incestuous and David agreed."

"What does Rachel think?"

"I don't really know, she's been a little standoffish. Yet at the same time, she seems to be leaving the door open. Right now she's busy with her work and I'm on the road, so things have definitely cooled off. Haven't seen her in months now. She told me I'm 'free to move about the cabin.' Otherwise, I wouldn't be sitting next to you in a bed... But anyway, she's a wonderful woman. I'd like to pursue her, if she's willing, and we can get Sara and David to get over themselves."

"Well, in fairness to them, I suppose it's a bit weird. If you got married to Rachel, then technically Sara and David would be step siblings. But on the other hand, how convenient? You guys share grandchildren. In my mind, that convenience alone would make the liaison worthwhile."

"I suppose..." He looked at her with adoring eyes.

"Stop it, basically you're cheating on Rachel and I'm cheating on Ben. Grrr.... okay, enough of this, let's get Cookie out."

"We're not cheating, I haven't even gotten to second base with you, so it doesn't count."

"Second base? It doesn't count? Really? Are we 17? And besides, yes, we have cheated, or at least I have, I'm actually married and I've already made love to you in my head." Ree couldn't believe she said that last part out loud.

"Well, if making love in your mind counts as cheating, thank you Jimmy Carter, then I guess we've cheated. But I subscribe to Bill Clinton's thinking: 'I have not had sex with that woman,'" Ken replied, mimicking the former president.

"Oh, you bad boy," she teased. And with that she reached over and started to tickle him. He tickled back and before they knew it, they were a tangle of arms and legs, sheets and blankets. "Cut it out, stop, stop…" she squeaked and giggled and didn't mean one word of her protests.

Cookie whimpered and actually stood up.

"Oh, thank you, Miss Chaperone," giggled Ree. "Come on Romeo, let's get going."

Ken reluctantly got up. They put their coats, hats, gloves and boots on and headed out the door. A dark haired man three doors down also exited. He barely acknowledged them as he shuffled through the snow heading to the restaurant.

Hmph, Ree said to herself. That man looks vaguely familiar. She was quickly distracted by Ken starting to shovel a pathway and gave the pockmarked faced man no further thought as she put Cookie on her leash. A leash certainly wasn't necessary to keep Cookie from running away or running into traffic, but it was necessary to coax her into moving forward.

"I wish I had a shovel too. Then I could be more helpful."

"Don't worry, I'm not digging to China. This may be good enough," Ken replied. As fast as he shoveled was about as fast as the snow filled in his efforts. Maybe they would get four feet of snow after all. Looked to be about two and half so far, he thought to himself.

Red entered the restaurant with a brighter look on his face. He only looked at the woman briefly but her shocking red hair and pretty face were unmistakable. Gloria Grayson. Why was she here and why was she with another man? He had seen the family portraits on the wall of her house. Clearly, Mr. Shovel Man was not her husband. Was this trip a set up all along for her to have a little fling? Maybe it was a long standing affair. But where was her car? He was very observant, had to be for his job. Even though the cars were all buried with snow, none of them were the shape of her model Durango with a roof top carrier. It didn't matter where her car was, only if she left the paper in the car. He was pretty sure the paper would be in her belongings. It would be too risky for him to enter her small room with a large dog, and now a large man, at night when she was sleeping. Better to wait until she was out of her room eating a meal. But at least he found her. The wait was worth it after all. Maybe he was lucky.

Ree looked up at Ken which was in the direction of the passing man's room. The car in front of his room was not as buried as the others since it arrived late last night. From what did show, she could make out the model and color. She gasped. Did a snow plow fairy arrive in the night and tow her white Durango to the motel? No, she dismissed the thought, just wishful thinking and yet another coincidence. She thought further, maybe no coincidence at all. Durangos were pretty popular cars and there was no roof top carrier.

"Come on, Cookie, look at the nice area Ken dug out for you."

It took both of them to coax her forward. Finally, after inspecting every square inch of the very small space, she relieved herself. She was quick to turn back to the motel room door. No coaxing was needed to get her back to her dog bed.

"What do you say we get some real breakfast? The kids should be getting up by now."

"Great idea," she replied. "Hey wait, I just want to grab my purse, there's something I want to show you."

She went back in the room, took the letter in the sheet protector out of her duffel bag and carefully placed it into her oversized purse. She was back out in a matter of seconds.

To their surprise, all four kids were already in the dining area. It seemed they picked up their animated conversation from where they left off last night.

"Hi kids, sleep okay?" Ree asked.

"Yeah," said Jake.

"It was weird sharing a room with Jake, but it was okay," responded Jenna. "Do you think we can leave today? There was some reluctance in her voice, as if she was hoping for a no answer instead of a yes.

A memory flashed through Ree's brain. Until she was seven, she and her two sisters shared one bed and her poor brother slept on the living room couch. Even when they moved to a larger house, she still shared a room with her younger sister. Then in the six years of post graduate studies, she always had roommates. She married Ben two weeks after graduating with her Masters. So it occurred to her, she never did and still did not, have a room of her own. It was something she never had and therefore didn't miss. Her trip down memory lane was interrupted by Ken answering Jenna.

"It's not looking good right now for leaving this morning," chimed in Ken. "We'll be tracking the weather. Believe me, you'll be the first to know when we can go."

"I wish we had our skis," Jake bemoaned. "It'd be fun to try to cross country in all this snow."

"So sorry, Jake." Ree then looked up at Ken. "They're in our carrier on our car," she explained.

"That is too bad. We have downhill equipment, but no cross country skis."

"Wait a minute, your contract won't let you drive, but you can ski?"

"Actually no. The kids have downhill skis, I don't."

"That's a weird life, Ken."

"Yes, yes it is."

The kids ordered pancakes and waffles whereas the adults ordered eggs and toast. The man who had brushed by them earlier sat with his back to them at the table closest to the exit. He kept to himself. No one noticed when he slipped out.

CHAPTER 10

RED STARTED TO UNLOCK Ree's door, which would be easy for him. The locks were so antiquated he wondered why they bothered with them at all. But he found the door had been left unlocked which bothered him even more. Damn fool lady. How can she be so cavalier to leave her room unlocked? Ree's motel room seemed even smaller than his with the large dog bed and large dog in it. The dog looked up but then put her head down. Great watch dog, Red said to himself sarcastically. This room was a dream come true for him. So little furniture, so little possessions, he'd be sure to find the paper in a matter of minutes. He carefully rifled through her belongings and then through the bedside stands, the dresser, the desk and the closet. He even looked in the small bathroom. Nothing. He felt through the tousled sheets. Guess they had a good time here, he snickered. Nothing. Now the only places to look would be her car or her handbag. He did notice she had a rather large purse tucked in under her chair when he left the restaurant. He slipped out of her room. No one was outdoors. He entered his room and pondered his options.

Just as Ree, Ken and the kids were finishing breakfast, the other two couples sauntered in. They had decided during their earlier breakfast to return to the restaurant to play Bridge. The man who greeted Ken previously, approached their tables.

"Hi, folks," said a pleasant gentleman, looking to be in his 70s. "How are you holding up?"

"About as good as we can, not sure what we're going to do all day," replied Ree.

"Well, we discovered there are plenty of decks of cards and some old board games on those shelves over by the fireplace. Perhaps they might be of interest to you. We're going to be playing Bridge. By the way, we're Mike and Camille, and this is Charlie and Marty."

"And I'm Ree, this is Ken and the kids are our grandchildren... I mean, the older boys are Ken's... and the younger two are mine..." stammered Ree. She blushed slightly at having given the impression that she and Ken were a couple.

"So Bridge, huh? interjected Ken.

"Yes. So here's a good story for you. We were headed north to our home in Connecticut and Charlie and Marty were heading south to Annapolis when the snow storm forced us to exit here. At dinner last night we discovered we all went to the same college 50 some years ago where we used to play Bridge together! Isn't that an amazing set of circumstances?"

"That is amazing. And you didn't recognize each other?" asked a surprised Ree.

"No" answered Charlie. "A half a century later, white hair and few extra pounds have changed our appearance somewhat."

His wife Marty, who did have white hair but was quite slim, patted Charlie's belly. "Yes, about those extra pounds, dear," Marty added affectionately.

"It wasn't until we got to talking about our backgrounds that we put it all together," added Camille.

Camille then looked at Ken a bit more closely. "Say, aren't you Kendall Davis, the country and western singer? That would explain the limo."

Now Ken blushed. "Yes, um, yes I am."

"How exciting! Would you mind if I took a selfie with you?"

Jenna's ears perked up at hearing the word "selfie." Why didn't I think of that? she asked herself.

"Uh, sure… only it doesn't have to be a selfie, I'm sure one of my grandsons would be happy to take the picture."

Drew and Jenna both volunteered. In the end, pictures were taken of Ken and the foursome, the foursome alone, Jenna and Ken, Jake and Ken, then Ree, Ken, Jenna and Jake, then Jenna with the boys. Nancy and Nora who were sitting near the kitchen doors had had no clue that Ken was a famous singer. No matter, they approached the group and had their pictures taken with Ken as well.

"I guess that about covers it," said Ken.

"Thanks, Ken, can we have your permission to submit our picture of us with you to our alumni newsletter?" asked Camille.

Ken didn't hesitate to say yes. Positive publicity was always a good thing for him, no matter the platform.

"Oh thanks, that'll be great," said Camille. "And one more thing… maybe later you could entertain us with some of your songs?"

Now he did hesitate… "Um… well… sure, what the heck? I do have my acoustic guitar with me."

Jenna couldn't help herself. She blurted out, "Wow, that would be fantastic!"

Ree was once again surprised by Jenna's new persona, or rather the emergence of the persona she knew Jenna had all along.

"Hey, Pops, I'll dig up some stuff to use for percussion," Derrick offered.

"And I can play your harmonica!" added Drew.

"Can I be your back up vocalist?" asked Jenna.

"Me too!" chimed in Camille. "I can hit a few high notes."

Ken chuckled. "Sure, let's make it a group effort."

Jake was quick to step in. "But Jenna, you can't sing!"

Jenna reacted quickly. "Jake, you re-...." She stopped herself seeing Ree's stern glare.

Drew rescued her with, "I'm sure you have a great voice."

In that moment, Donny vanished from her memory and Drew filled her brain.

CHAPTER 11

JAKE EYED THE STACK of dilapidated board games. He pulled out Monopoly and found most of the pieces and stacks of fake money were intact. The board was worn but usable.

"Hey guys! Let's play Monopoly!"

Jenna was all set to object, but when Drew and Derrick gave an enthusiastic response, she readily joined in. They set up the board and started rolling the dice. Ken and Ree, and the two older couples quickly slipped out of their focus, as did the rest of the world.

"So, Ken, there's this paper I want to show you," Ree said after watching the kids for a few minutes. She pulled out the sheet protector and slid it across the table. "I've figured out the first numbers are coordinates and then there's a date and time, but after that, I don't know."

Just as she was about to say she knew the location of the coordinates, Ken looked up in surprise and said, "I know those numbers! I actually have a tee shirt from the golf club I belong to in the Bahamas with those coordinates on it. Well, the 26 N 77 W part, that is."

"Yes! That's right, I recognized them too. And I have a tee-shirt with those coordinates on it too!"

"You do?" asked Ken a bit dubiously.

"Why the tone? Can't I know the coordinates of the Abacos?"

"Well, yes of course, it's just that, well, not to sound haughty, but you need to have assets totaling over 12 million dollars to be a member of the club I belong to. The properties start at about four million."

"That's ridiculous, but now I understand your disbelief. Those figures are way out of my league."

"So how did you come by a tee-shirt with those numbers?"

She explained how she and Ben had chartered with two other couples in the Abacos and dubbed themselves the 26-77 club.

"We've chartered there a few times since, but I think it's been over twenty years since we were there last. Never heard of that golf resort."

"It's beautiful, but at the same time, not my scene anymore. I guess I'm getting tired of being part of the 'rich and famous.' I probably only go to my townhouse once or twice a year. I have a home in Nashville, but my go-to place when I just need to get away and get some inspiration, is in my cabin up in Michigan. I love looking over Lake Michigan with its amazing sunsets. I'm pretty anonymous there."

"So, once again, let me get this straight. You have a four or more million dollar home that you only go to once or twice a year? That's insane. Again, I can't even think in seven digit numbers… or is it eight digits?"

"Um…. maybe eight," he said quietly and sheepishly.

"Hmmm, well any time you need someone to check up on your place, give me a call."

He laughed. "Enough of me. Let's look at the other numbers."

He studied it for a while. "I agree with 0304 being a date, which is next week. No doubt 1230 is the time. 338099957, 9 digits…. a social security number? FL4765GH… that could be a boat registered in Florida… AB 19212… another boat but registered in the Abacos?… no, wait." He looked at the contacts in his phone. He scrolled down to his address in the Abacos and noted the address contained PO Box AB 17658. "Almost all residences and businesses have PO Box numbers, that's probably a PO box."

"So someone has to go to that location next week, find whatever or whoever is 338099957, get on a boat and then go to the post office?"

"That's a good guess. Let me feel the paper."

He slid the paper out and noted its fragility. "You know this is flash paper?"

"Flash paper?" quizzed Ree.

"Used mainly by magicians because when you light it, it makes a big flash and then the paper is completely incinerated, no ashes left behind. You know, Ree, I don't want to scare you, but someone may be trying to locate this information. Where did you get it?"

She explained about the newspaper and the man at the mall.

"The weird thing is, that guy? The guy who is staying in the last room? He looked oddly familiar to me. Maybe it's him. Maybe he's going to try to get it back from me…"

Ree was revving up her imagination. Ken quickly stepped in. "Ree, darling, calm down. It's one thing that Mike and Camille, Charlie and Marty ran into each other by such happenstance, but this guy following you here in a blizzard? And how would he have found out your name or where you live? Do you think he followed you home from the mall? And even if he did, how did he follow you here? He arrived hours and hours after we did."

"Well, I don't think I was followed, but you have to admit, it's weird that he looks like the guy in the mall."

"Tell you what. Let's take a picture of it. I actually have a friend who's a retired detective. I'll send it to him for his opinion. But when the snow clears and you're back home, I think you should really hand it over to the local police. In the meantime, so that the boogey man doesn't get you, I'll keep it in my room."

He rolled it up and placed it in his inside coat pocket. "The kids look pretty entertained. I'm going to check on Wilson and then go back to my room to make some calls. Meet you back here for lunch?"

"It's a date, thanks," Ree replied. "I'd best check on Miss Cookie too. And then there's a book I'd love to catch up on."

Ree walked over to the kids and informed them they were going back to their respective rooms but that they'd be back for lunch. The kids were so engrossed in the game there was barely any eye contact, just head nods. Nice to see kids interacting with each other rather than with their cell phones, Ree thought to herself.

Ken walked her to her room and then went on to Wilson's. Wilson was snoozing but awakened easily.

"How's the ankle now?"

"Better, I should be able to drive. Can we leave yet?"

Ken walked over to the window and pulled back the curtain. The snow was piled up to the window sill and the visibility was barely three feet out into the parking lot.

Wilson sighed. "I guess not."

"Yeah, I think we're stuck here for another night. But there's hope the storm front should move out tomorrow. Can I get you anything?"

"Nah, I'm okay for now, thanks."

"Well, I'll stop by before I go to lunch. Maybe with the boys' help you can hobble into the restaurant."

"I'll try. I'm getting a little stir crazy in here."

Ken returned to his room. As soon as he shut his door, Red peered out of his. He had heard a series of doors opening and closing. Okay, next opportunity to look in Gloria's handbag would be lunch time, he said to himself. Hopefully, she'd be leaving it behind this time. He trudged to the restaurant. The kids and the other two couples paid no attention to him. He asked Nora to make him a few sandwiches to take back to his room. After a 15 minute wait, he trudged back to his room. No sign of Ree, her boyfriend or the mystery person. Given there was a limo, maybe the mystery person was the limo driver. But it was still odd to Red that the person never emerged from the room.

Ree didn't bother to coax Cookie out of the room. Under normal circumstances, Cookie only braved the outdoors twice a day. Why torment the dog? She'd be fine until after her evening meal. Ree sat upright on her bed and read her book. She was distracted momentarily by a vague memory of reading something somewhere about an exclusive golf club in the Bahamas. Maybe it'll bubble up from the tar pits, she mused, and went back to her book.

Ken didn't let on as to how worried he really was about the letter. He forwarded the picture of it to his friend along with an explanation. There was no immediate response. His buddy traveled frequently in his retirement so it was possible that wherever he was, cell reception was poor. Ken then went down the rabbit hole of checking his email and getting in touch with the road crew for his upcoming concert. He was relieved to learn the equipment trucks were coming up from Nashville and so far didn't have any weather issues. Most of his band was already in New York City. His keyboard man, Keith, however, was snowed in in Buffalo, having left the other band members to visit his family there. There's still time, Ken reassured himself nervously.

At lunch time Ken gently knocked on Ree's door. "It's open," she called out.

"So I guess you're not too worried about the boogey man?"

She laughed. "You know, I'm just not in the habit of locking up. Guess I should be."

"So, Wilson thinks he can stand up and maybe walk to the restaurant. I'm going to help him but we may need the boys."

"OK, I'll come with you and if he needs them, I don't mind getting them."

"That'd be great."

Shuffling through the snow was now becoming routine. Wilson had left his door unlocked for Ken. He perked up when he saw Ree. "Good morning, Ma'am. How are things with you?"

"As good as can be, given the circumstances."

She and Ken stood on either side of Wilson, He was sit-

385

ting up at the edge of the bed.

He attempted to stand and bear full weight. No go, he yelled out a loud "ouch" followed by colorful expletives. "Oh sorry, Ma'am."

"Don't worry about me, I think I've heard just about every form of expletive." Wilson sat back down, defeated.

"I think you should keep it elevated and iced. I'll go to the kitchen and get some."

"That's a lot of bother, Ma'am."

"I'm really not busy, and it's no bother."

Ree left without further commentary. It actually was a bother. What should have taken five minutes turned into 20 given how arduous it was just to walk through the piling up snow. As she walked past the possible mall guy's door she thought she saw the curtain move. It sent shivers down her spine to think he might be spying on her. Or maybe he's just curious and bored, she rationalized.

Once she had Wilson situated, they took his lunch order and headed to the restaurant. Ken said he'd have one of the boys deliver it.

Red waited another 15 minutes before re-entering her room. This time she had locked it, but it only took him a few extra minutes to break in. The dog barely acknowledged his presence, and he quickly saw her purse on top of her desk. He looked through it thoroughly. Nothing. He rechecked her drawers and duffle bag in case she had relocated it. Nothing. Damn! The paper could only be in her car. He was now at the mercy of the weather gods and snow plows. He went back to his room unnoticed. Any foot prints would be quickly covered by the constant fall of snow.

CHAPTER 12

THE FUN OF MONOPOLY was starting to wane, and the kids were happy to put it away for lunch. Nancy informed the guests that their food supplies were dwindling since their food delivery service was unable to get through to them. She stated lunch would be limited to hot dogs, hamburgers and a few cold cut sandwiches. There was tomato soup and also chicken noodle soup. For dinner, they were down to veal cutlets, chicken, a bit of salad, potatoes, canned vegetables and a few desserts. She also apologized for the lack of maid services. She did offer whatever fresh towels were left if needed.

"Don't worry," Camille said in a very motherly fashion. "This will all be over soon and it'll just be a distant memory by next week."

"I hope so," Nancy said in an unconvincing tone.

No one complained about how awful the food was. Ree was tempted to volunteer to cook dinner with whatever was left. She loved cooking and creating meals from a hodge-podge of left overs.

After lunch Camille came over to Ken. "So, Mr. Davis, how about some entertainment this afternoon?"

"Sure, why not? I need to get a meal to my driver and then I'll get my guitar. Derrick or Drew help me out, OK?" Derrick delivered Wilson's meal and Drew went with Ken to get his guitar and a bag of small musical instruments. Ken was thankful he had the boys pull out the guitar from the trunk when they first arrived. Had they waited it would have taken hours to shovel it out. Hardly any part of the limo was now visible. Ken always carried his acoustic guitar with him, almost like Linus and his blanket. His thoughts drifted back to Janet and how he played to Janet every night in her final months, even when she was supposedly in a coma. He was convinced she could hear him. There was just a slight change in the cadence of her breathing when he played to her. Oh, Janet, you left this earth too soon…

Drew noticed his grandfather looking sullen. "What's wrong, Pops?"

"Hmmm, sorry, just thinking about your grandmother. I miss her."

"So do I, Pops, we all do."

Ken hugged his grandson and fought back a tear. He took a deep breath. "Okay, you got that bag of instruments?"

"Yes, sir!" Drew responded, glad to move on from that sentimental encounter.

Drew dipped into his room on the way back to pick up his computer. It might be handy he thought to himself, to look up some lyrics.

Derrick, an aspiring percussionist, was in the kitchen asking Nora if he could borrow some of the larger kettles, pot lids and a few wooden spoons. He was determined to create a make shift drum set. On several family occasions when he had access to his own drum set, his grandfather encouraged him to play along. Drew was also an aspiring musician and had learned to play the harmonica fairly well. Both boys had visions of being in their grandfather's band some day.

Nate was in the kitchen too. There was little need for him to man the office since no new guests would be arriving and the current guests wouldn't be leaving any time soon. It turned out that he was married to Nora, and Nancy was their niece. They had Nancy bunk in with them on their couch since she was unable to drive home. Nate was softly humming "Hotel California," while washing some of the dishes which made Derrick laugh.

"Hey that's a good one, Nate. Maybe that should be the first song we have Pops play. Kind of ironic!" Derrick sang out the verse of "*You can check out any time you want, but you can never leave.*"

Nora piped in, "That's terrible! I've always hated the words to that song."

"Oh come on, Nora, it's such a great song," protested Derrick. "Do you know all the words?"

"Sadly, yes." She proceeded to belt out the remainder of the song in a surprisingly good voice.

"Wow, guess you can sing! You'll have to help Jenna and Camille with the back up vocals."

"I guess I could join you guys for a bit. Not too much prep needed for dinner tonight."

Derrick didn't know if that was a good thing or not, but he was happy to have her join them.

"How 'bout you, Nate? Do you sing or play an instrument?"

"I used to fool around with the bass for awhile. I was even in a band for a bit. But that was long ago. It's just collecting dust in the back room."

"Here?" quizzed Derrick.

"Yeah, we sort of live here."

"Well, go get it, man, this could be awesome!"

Drew entered the kitchen. "Was that you singing, Nora?" he asked.

"Fraid so. You're really stuck with me now, chief, cook, and back up singer!"

"Well, let's get it on!" Drew replied.

CHAPTER 13

DERRICK HELPED NATE DIG OUT his bass. The back room was filled to the brim with miscellaneous, long forgotten items. In their digging they came across a set of crutches that Nate said they could use for Wilson. Then they collected the pots, pans, lids and spoons and tromped through Nora and Nate's living quarters to join the rest of the motley crew in the dining room.

Ken was tuning his guitar and looked up in surprise when he saw the bass. "A bass! Wow! Our band is growing."

Ree had dubbed Mike, Camille, Marty and Charlie the Vanderbilt Four, after their collective alma mater. She and the Four were assembling a play list of songs they knew and wanted to sing. Jenna and Drew scrolled through his computer to find song lyrics they wanted to sing. Nancy and Nora added a few of their favorites. It would be quite a mix.

Nate started to tune his guitar. A few strings were in need of replacement but he'd have to make do with what he had.

Derrick and Jake tried to create a drum set. The kettles had too much of a tinny sound so they emptied out the wood bucket containing kindling wood. The sound wasn't great, but better than the tinny sound. Jake beat on the pot lids with the wooden spoons. Not bad, Derrick agreed.

With little encouragement, Ken first played his latest hit solo. Ree was smitten. She felt like one of the teenagers on the Ed Sullivan Show when the Beatles first appeared in America. To calm herself down she touched her cell phone and her husband's smiling face appeared. I love Ben, I love Ben, she repeated to herself.

After a bit of heated but amicable discussion the group settled on what song they'd start out with. "*Hotel California*" won out. Ken was amazed at how well Nate followed his lead and didn't try to take over with the bass part. Nora's voice was outstanding, and he briefly contemplated lifting Nate and Nora out of their hell hole of a motel and have them join his band.

They went through four more songs by the Eagles, then moved on to the Band. Charlie had switched from his morning beers to his afternoon martinis. Mike readily joined him. The wives continued with red and white wine. After Charlie's second martini he insisted on taking the lead vocal in "The Weight." It took several hilarious tries to get the harmonies and the words correct. By the fifth try the group sounded fairly decent.

"Wait, wait, wait!" exclaimed Derrick. "I want to video this."

He set his phone up on a chair, hit the timer button for 10 seconds and they blasted out the lyrics. Ken couldn't remember when he had had such fun recording a song. Knowing it wouldn't go public, or so he thought, took the pressure off being so precise.

They cruised through a dozen Beatles songs, a few songs by Elton John and then a string of one hit wonders. Camille did an amazing rendition of Melanie's "I've Got A Brand

New Pair of Roller-skates." After that, the grandkids insisted on singing some of the more popular songs from the current pop charts. Then Nora swayed them back to the 70s. She actually sounded like Linda Ronstadt, so they let her take the lead for several of her songs. Ree, Jenna, Marty and Nancy were quite content to be back up singers. It was nice to see Nancy smiling. Jake, Drew and Derrick filled in with make shift percussion and harmonica. Charlie and Mike intermittently tapped their feet or joined the choruses.

It was nearly 5 o'clock when Ken said he needed a break. Mike suggested one more song. "After all Ken, it is 5 o'clock somewhere!" They all laughed and ended with that song.

Nora announced that they would be serving a family style dinner at 6:30. Ree did volunteer to help out in the kitchen, and Nora readily accepted the offer. Ken grabbed a few beers and some snacks to bring back to Wilson.

"Hey, Ken, would you mind knocking on Room 9's door? I'd like the guest to know that we'll be serving a group dinner at 6:30," Nora asked.

"Sure, no problem."

Ken picked up his guitar and the bag of foods and drinks. Derrick followed with the bag of musical instruments. They shuffled to Room 9. Ken knocked on the door. A gruff sounding "Who's there?" belted out.

"Um, just one of the motel guests. The cook wanted you to know she's serving dinner at 6:30, family style."

"Okay," was all he said. Ken and Derrick shrugged their shoulders and moved on.

Meanwhile, Jenna and Drew were plotting how to be alone in either her room or Drew's room. "Maybe Derrick wouldn't mind playing cards with Jake for awhile," Jenna offered.

"I think we'll have to bribe the both of them to make that happen."

"Okay, I'll work on Jake, you work on Derrick."

As they were about to leave the dining area, Ree shouted out to Jenna. "Hey, Jenna, I'm going to be in the kitchen for awhile. Would you be a dear and feed Cookie? Then you'll have to take her out."

"Um... sure, Gramma. Is it okay if the boys help me?"

"That's fine," said Ree with a bit of amazement in her voice. Not getting an argument from Jenna was refreshing. Little did Ree know that Jenna and Drew had no intention of including Derrick or Jake in tending to Cookie. Jake had gone back to his room to play video games and Derrick was catching up with his friends on his cell phone in his room.

Ken sat with Wilson to keep him company for awhile.

"Hey, Wilson, would you mind if I left my guitar here?"

Wilson said of course he could, but thought the request was strange. Unbeknown to Wilson, Ken had transferred the letter in the sheet protector to his guitar case. Since Wilson wouldn't be leaving his room, he figured that was the safest place for it.

The Vanderbilt Four were content to remain in the dining room and play more Bridge. Fortunately, Mike and Camille had purchased a few bottles of Sauvignon Blanc for their trip home, so they were in good shape for the evening's cocktails. Marty had a bottle of red wine and Charlie sipped on some Scotch. At no point did they run out of conversation. Fifty years was a long time to catch up on.

CHAPTER 14

RED WAS FUMING. No way could he sit and eat with the other guests. For sure Gloria would recognize him. He had eaten his sandwiches hours ago and was actually quite hungry. Plus, he was nearly out of whiskey. Could he really risk heading to the kitchen to have more sandwiches made up? Why couldn't this motel have phones in the room or room service? Then he chided himself for being so stupid. He could just call the manager on his cell phone and have the sandwiches brought to him.

Nate was surprised to hear his cell phone ring. He had consumed several beers by then and just assumed he was off duty until the weather cleared. "Dammit!"

He was relieved that it was only the weird guy in Room 9 requesting a few sandwiches, two beers and a bottle of whiskey to be brought to his room.

"I don't have a full bottle of whiskey, but I'll send what we do have." There was only a groan and the man hung up.

"Weirdo," commented Nate. "Good thing we had a beer delivery before this stupid blizzard started."

"Who was that?" Ree asked as she looked through the refrigerator to find something, anything, to spice up their upcoming dreadful meal.

"Oh that weird guy in Room 9. He sure does keep to himself."

"Yeah," agreed Ree, "He's an odd one. Quite frankly, he gives me the creeps."

Red thought through his next moves. Having all the guests in the dining room at the same time was a god send. He could search all the rooms related to Gloria, five in all. By now he had noticed Shovel Man had his own room. Room 8 would be tricky however, since so far, that guest never left.

Derrick remembered that he and Nate had found crutches for Wilson. He returned to the dining room, picked up the crutches and joined his grandfather in Wilson's room.

"Hey thanks, Derrick. Wilson, do you want to try standing up?"

"Sure."

With the help of Ken and Derrick, he stood up and was able to advance a few steps. "This should work!"

"But I don't think you should go outdoors just yet, the snow's too deep and unstable. I'm afraid you'd fall again."

"Couldn't agree more, Boss."

"We'll be sure to send you your meal, and um… more refreshments?"

"Yes please, thanks!"

They visited a few minutes longer, and then Ken and Derrick returned to their respective rooms to catch up on phone calls. After about an hour Ken decided to get himself a beer. Nate had told him earlier to help himself for the rest of his stay. He noticed Ree in the kitchen with her hair swept up into a mess on top of her head and she was wearing a too large apron with a very tacky print of pots, pans, kettles, cans, and other kitchen items. No doubt the apron was borrowed from Nora. He almost started to hum one of his songs that was popular for those who like to do the Texas Two Step. It seemed to fit her rhythm as she flitted from one cooking task to another. He grabbed a beer from the fridge just outside the kitchen. He lingered for a bit and then returned to his room without her seeing him.

Ree had convinced Nora not to fry the chicken. Instead, she concocted a chicken-potato-green bean casserole. First, she baked the chicken and potatoes with plenty of rosemary and onions. While the chicken and potatoes were baking, she had to sauté the beans to get rid of the notorious metallic taste of canned vegetables. Once cooked, she cut up the chicken into cubes. She had already cut up the potatoes into small pieces. She used cream of broccoli soup to hold the chicken, beans and potatoes together. There was a bag of croutons that she crushed up to blend with butter to use as a topping garnish. She placed the concoction in a large casserole dish and returned it to the oven for a final warm up and crisping of the crouton topping.

Meanwhile, Nora tended to the veal cutlets and the salad. The lettuce looked very sad but she hid it with plenty of carrots, peppers and celery.

Nancy arranged the dining room so that three tables were brought together to seat the group in one location.

Red peered out a small slit between the curtains to keep tabs on the guests. He found it somewhat amusing to watch the young girl and boy struggle with the large dog. As soon as the dog did her business, they were quick to return to the

Ree's room. Around 6:30, Shovel Man, the older teen, the young boy and the teen couple left their rooms within minutes of each other. Where was Gloria?

About ten minutes later, Nate shuffled to Room 9, and knocked on the door. Red opened it as minimally as possible.

"You're in luck with dinner tonight," Nate said as he handed Red his meal along with two beers and the half full bottle of whiskey.

"Turns out we have a guest chef who made up this casserole."

Red barely muttered a thank you and swept up the dinner delivery. He correctly assumed it must have been Gloria who made the meal, that would account why she hadn't left her room. Apparently she never left the restaurant.

"You're welcome too, asshole," Nate said under his breath as he headed to Wilson's room.

Wilson hobbled to the door on crutches and gladly accepted the meal. "You guys are just terrific, and thanks for the crutches too."

"You can keep them, Wilson. Hopefully I'll never need them again."

"Thanks again!"

Red waited another ten minutes before systematically going through the five rooms. Both teenager rooms were a mess of unmade beds, cots and belongings scattered everywhere. There was hardly any floor space to move around in. It just added to his growing list of why he hated children. Ree and Shovel Man's rooms on the other hand couldn't have been neater. Beds were made, belongings were neatly placed in their bags or drawers. The large dog again only looked up at Red briefly. What a waste of space, Red commented to himself about the dog. He was unable to inspect the assumed driver's room since the person hadn't left the room. He'd save that for the middle of the night. If the paper wasn't in that last room, he'd have to wait to inspect Gloria's car. He ate his meal and started in with the whiskey. He actually gave Gloria a silent compliment. The casserole was pretty tasty.

Back in the dining room, the group of 13 were involved in a lively discussion as to what to name their new band. *Motel California* got some mention as a reference to *Hotel California*. *The Blizzard 13, Blizzard Babies, Snowbound,* and *Motel Rats* were possibilities among several others. Derrick replayed their earlier recording of *The Weight.* Everyone agreed it wasn't too bad. Dinner managed to stretch over a two hour period since Nora had forgotten to defrost the frozen pies and they needed extra time to be warmed up. No one seemed to mind.

After dinner was concluded, the Vanderbilt Four started to pack up their beverages and head to their respective rooms. Ree asked if she could bum a glass of Mike's Sauvignon Blanc since she found the house white to be pretty much undrinkable.

"You don't have to bum anything, Ree. Thanks for whipping up that casserole, it was delicious. This bottle looks like you could get a drink or two out of it, just take it."

"Thanks, appreciate it."

Charlie then offered the rest of his Scotch to Ken. "My lovely advisor has informed me I'm done with Scotch for the night."

Ken laughed and thanked him too.

The kids headed to Drew and Derrick's room to watch

more movies on their computer. Ree again gave them an 11 o'clock curfew.

Ken left ahead of Ree so as to deliver dessert to Wilson along with more beverages. On his return, he again saw Ree struggling with Cookie.

"This could be habit forming," he teased.

"More like a dreadful routine. What was I thinking when I adopted this dog?"

"I don't know, but here she is."

"Hey, do you want to have a short nightcap?"

"Absolutely. I came prepared," Ken answered as he lifted up a small bag which had an obvious bottle in it.

Ree looked up at the sky as they entered her room. "Hey, look! The snowflakes are bigger."

"And?" asked a puzzled Ken.

"When the snowflakes get really big, it usually means the snow is coming to an end. And, it's not so windy either."

"I didn't know you were a meteorologist too," teased Ken. "But I think you're right, the latest weather news is that this storm should be ending by tomorrow morning."

"Well, that would get my vote."

Ree brushed her coat off and hung it up. She did the same for Ken's coat. Then she looked at the two plastic cups on the dresser.

"Darn! I forgot to snatch up some real glasses from the bar."

"Never fear." In the bag holding his Scotch were two glass glasses.

"Oh thank God. I don't know when I got to be such a snob, but I can't stand drinking out of plastic."

"Then I guess I'm a snob too."

"Doesn't that go along with owning a four million dollar home you rarely use?"

"Oh... low blow, Ree."

"You know I'm only kidding."

He just smiled and poured their drinks.

"By the way, I finally remembered why that golf club you belong to sounded so familiar. You said you can only get there by boat and the boat is out of a local marina?"

"That's right, actually there are a bunch of boats at the marina that are dedicated to their clientele."

"Well, I read a book, fiction, about a golf resort on some small island in the Abacos. I belong to a book club at our local library and one time this woman who lives in Altamont, brought in copies of her boyfriend's novella called *"Bahama Gem."* It was just a caper about mixed identity, but it revolved around going back and forth from Marsh Harbour to the resort. Don't know if her boyfriend ever got it published or not."

"Well I'm sure there's lots of fodder at that resort for several books."

"I'll bet. Anyway, this one was pretty amusing. I still have it if you'd like me to send it to you. You might find it a good read."

"Might be fun, sure."

"So what's on your docket once we get plowed out?"

"Well, my agent wants me back in New York City as early as possible on Friday. We've got to get in a few rehearsals and there are always endless details to work out. I'm arranging to have the boys get in one day of skiing on Thursday. My limo drivers are currently headed to Binghamton. They'll stay there for the night and as soon as they are allowed on I-88, they'll fetch us... provided we've been dug out... But I've been thinking about some other details, and bear with me... this may sound a bit complicated..."

"Apparently I love complicated."

He laughed. "So, your car will have to be towed to your dealership since it's not drivable with deployed air bags. I assume your husband has a car available to you?"

"Yes of course... why? Is that a long process to deal with air bags?"

"I'm guessing it'll be a few days before you get your car back. I know you can drive your husband's car in the meantime, but I'm concerned about how you're going to get yourself to the dealership to retrieve your car. You said your husband won't be back until Sunday?"

"Yes that's right."

"Well, my driver, who will be taking you and the kids back to Altamont, can stay in a motel and be at your beck and call until your car is ready and then..."

Ree interrupted, "Oh, Ken, that's very generous of you, but I do have friends and there's always Uber. It's really not necessary to have your driver stay around."

"Well, I have another proposal..."

"Marriage? I thought we were through with that." Ree joked.

He smiled and blushed a bit. "No, let me continue... I'd really like you, Jenna and Jake to come to my concert on Saturday... my driver could drive you down and back..."

"Wow... I don't know what to say... Jenna would be thrilled... I mean, so would I, and Jake too, of course... but how would that really work out? Where would we stay?"

"Finding a hotel for you is not a problem, it's what my staff does."

"But I need to drive the kids back to their home on Sunday and then pick up Ben..."

"No problem, where do the kids live and what time does Ben get in?"

"The kids live in Pittsfield, Massachusetts, that's about an hour and a half away from me. Their parents fly into Boston on Sunday and they should be home by 5. We had planned to have dinner together, get in a visit, and then I'll go back to the airport in Albany in time to pick Ben up at 10:30. Long day, but geographically it makes sense."

"Geographically?"

"Yeah, that's left over from my days doing home care as an Occupational Therapist. I'd get handed a list of six or seven patients to see scattered over two counties and would have to create a route that made the most sense geographically."

"Got it... well, I think my driver can accomplish all that."

"Get out, that's crazy."

"Think about it... you could enjoy some wine at dinner on Sunday and not have to worry about driving."

That actually did seem appealing. But then Ree protested, "No, Ken, that's really too much, I...."

"Yes you can, and besides there's one more reason... I haven't told this to the boys, but I'm going to work them into one of my songs at the concert. Derrick will play percussion and Drew will play the harmonica."

"Really?"

"Yes, I've been thinking about it a lot. I was really impressed by their talent at our little song fest. And between you and me... if they screw up, the sound mixers can just fade them out."

"Jenna would be beside herself, to say nothing of your grandsons. By the way, have you noticed the little romance brewing between Drew and Jenna?"

"Yes, I have, but it's a doomed affair..." he said, looking straight at Ree.

"Yeah... about that..." Ree said softly. After a short pause she continued, "Let me sleep on the concert proposal."

"Fair enough."

Ken poured them each the remains of the bottles that were given to them. They sipped their drinks and sat in silence for a few minutes.

Ree broke the silence. "You know, this has really been an incredible day. Our impromptu band was such a surprise. And, believe it or not, I really enjoyed cooking that meal. It was a day of firsts..."

"Have to admit..." Ken interrupted. "I watched you in the kitchen for a few minutes when I went to get myself a beer... a few lyrics for a new song came into my mind..."

"What? First of all... Stalker! And secondly, how can you possibly write a song about someone in the kitchen?"

"Easy, it's how you moved around in the kitchen. You just took over and you just looked so god damned sexy with your hair swept up and wearing that ridiculous apron..."

"Oh man, again, you must be really horny if that vision does it for you."

"It's more than that Ree... I know you feel it too."

Ree took a deep breath. Jiminy Cricket was once again sitting on her shoulder. *I should just give him a farewell kiss on his cheek and send him out the door,* she thought to herself.

As if reading her thoughts Ken said in a too seductive voice, "I know I should go... let me just kiss you goodnight, darling."

She melted. He didn't wait for her answer. He ran his fingers through her hair and pulled her into his chest. He tilted her head back and passionately kissed her.

Ree allowed the kiss to linger and then gently pushed herself away. "Yes, about that doomed affair..." she whispered. "You should go now."

Ree's cell phone rang which jarred them out of their reverie. She knew Ken recognized the ring tone.

"Your husband has good timing, Ree... I'll see you in the morning."

"Goodnight, Ken," she said as she reached for her phone.

CHAPTER 15

RED HEARD FOOTSTEPS GOING by his room. With lights off he looked through the narrow slit between the drawn curtains. So Shovel Man, you got booted out so early? Red set his alarm for two in the morning. He knew the chances of the paper being in the fifth room were pretty remote, but he couldn't leave any possibility unattended.

Ken noticed that Wilson's lights were still on. He needed one more drink to settle down, so he knocked on Wilson's door.

"Huh? That you, Boss?"

"Yeah, Wilson, mind if I come in?"

"Sure, door's not locked."

Ken hesitated for a moment. Hmph… it's not snowing. Guess Ree was right.

"So, Wilson, here's some good news," Ken said as he took off his coat. "It's not snowing anymore."

"Thank God! Here, want a night cap?" Wilson asked as he reached for his bottle of vodka.

"Thought you'd never ask."

Just as Ken was filling Wilson in on his plans for tomorrow, they heard the unmistakable sounds of a truck being started, doors opening and closing and then the scraping of shovels.

Ken peered out.

Nate was digging out his pick-up which had a plow attached to it. Ken was tempted to give him a hand but then thought better of it. The last thing he needed headed into a concert was sore arms and back muscles.

Wilson read his mind. "Relax, Boss, have another shot."

"Actually, Wilson, I think I'm going to grab my guitar and head back to my room. I've got a new song swirling around in my brain."

"Sure, Boss. Leave the door unlocked, saves me from having to hobble to the door in case you return."

"Yeah, can't imagine they'll be any break-ins here…'night, Wilson."

It was nearly 11 P.M. Ree's lights were still on. No doubt she was still talking to Ben. Ken headed to Derrick and Drew's room to be the heavy enforcing Ree's curfew. To his surprise, Jenna and Jake were exiting from the boys' room and went to their room. Wonders never cease, he said to himself. "Night, kids," he called out. They seemed surprised and bid him a good night too. He then turned and entered his room. He laid down his guitar case and opened it. When he picked up the guitar he didn't notice that the sheet protector containing Ree's letter became unstuck from the back side of the guitar and slid out. It glided downward and lodged between the wall and the desk back. And there it remained, nicely nestled in years of dust since the cleaning ladies rarely, if ever, moved furniture when they vacuumed. He sat down on the edge of his bed and picked away at his guitar. At his side was his iPad. He had an app to record his musings. Slowly, and then with more feeling, he started to create a song. "And there she was in that old worn down diner among pots and pans, kettles and cans..."

Nate was on a mission to clear the parking lot as much as possible. He heard the temperatures were going to rise in the morning meaning the snow would get heavier and heavier. Best to clear it now while the snow was light and easy to move around. Nora armed him with a thermos of coffee. It was likely he'd be up most of the night.

By two in the morning, Nate had most of the immediate parking lot plowed out. Then he started on the road way connecting the motel to Route 7, basically his life line. Had he been more astute, he might have noticed the lights were still on in Ken's room and in Ree's room. He might also have noted the weirdo in Room 9 making his way to Room 8.

Red turned the knob to Room 8, the last room he needed to inspect. The knob turned easily, it was unlocked. What was it with these people? Can they really be this trusting? As he entered the room, his slim flashlight reinforced his preconceived notions. The man had minimal belongings and there was next to nothing to inspect. The man was snoring at first entry but as Red approached the dresser to give the room a thorough search, Wilson awakened. His former years as a body guard trained him to sleep with half an eye open.

"Hey, Boss, is that you? Door's still unlocked...." said a sleepy Wilson.

Red slid out as fast as he could. The door didn't quite shut allowing a cold current of air to rush into the room. Wilson shivered, got up, hobbled to the door with the crutches and locked it shut. In his sleepy mind he figured the wind had blown the door open. Since he was already up, he visited the bathroom and went back to bed.

Ken turned off his lights shortly after two. He was pretty pleased with what he had written so far. Ree was on the phone for almost an hour with Ben, filling him in on the latest details and asking his opinion about going to Ken's concert. Earlier she had sent him the picture of her with Ken and the grandkids. She was initially surprised by his comments.

"You know, Ree, that guy just wants to get in your pants." said Ben.

"What? No he doesn't... well, maybe he does. Honestly, honey, I really didn't think I was coming on to him when I returned his cell phone... but I have to admit, I did kiss him back. I should have slapped him in the face."

"Seems like it was a harmless kiss. I would have kissed you too."

"You do kiss me. That's the point. I feel like I cheated on you."

"Did he get to second base?"

"What? Second base? Did you really say that? Is that standard vocabulary among lusting men?"

"Don't be so naive, Ree. All men have only one agenda."

"Well, he didn't get to second base. I did kiss him goodnight again tonight, but then I shooed him away."

"Good girl. Leave it at that. But I do think you and the kids should go to his concert. Seems like that's a once in a life time event."

"You do?"

"Yes, and me being picked up at the airport by a limo? Sounds like a hoot."

"Oh, honey… thank you for not being mad or hating me."

"I could never be mad at you, just keep telling me the truth, that's all I ask."

A twinge of guilt swept through her. Yes, she had told Ben the details of her encounters with Ken… but was it a lie to omit telling him about the electricity between her and Ken? She shuttered a bit and returned to their conversation. They eventually concluded with their usual love you and miss you. Ree got a second wind and couldn't fall asleep. The alternating sounds of the snow plow plowing and the backing-up beeps kept her awake as well. She read for awhile but found herself going back to her twinge of guilt. She finally put her book down, turned off the lights and imagined herself confessing her sins to Father Patrick Michael O'Shaughnessy for having feelings for another man and almost having had an affair with him. Then to add to the self-flagellation, she composed a letter in her head to *Dear Abby*, eventually signing off as "Almost, in Altamont."

Red stewed in his room. The paper had to be in Ree's car. He was running out of time.

CHAPTER 16

REE SLEPT THROUGH TILL EIGHT. Cookie was wide awake and looking at the door. "Oh sorry, Cookie, give me just a minute to throw some clothes on."

Ree couldn't believe her eyes when she opened the door. The sun was out! The sky seemed impossibly blue. The cars were still snow capped but the sidewalk was cleared and the parking lot was plowed. Surrounding the motel property was a sparkling winter wonderland of snow capped trees. Cookie was able to relieve herself without too much of a fuss. The temperature had come up a bit, felt like the thirties. Ree sampled a handful of snow and made a perfect snowball.

"Cookie, this snow is perfect for making a snowman!" Ree exclaimed. She heard Ken's door open.

"Hey, what's all the noise?" he asked in a joking manner.

She threw the snowball at him which grazed his shoulder.

He bent down, gathered up some snow and winged her in the arm with his snowball.

"Hey, cut that out, you actually have good aim! We should get the kids up, this snow is perfect for building a snowman or better yet, a snow fort!" Ree continued.

"Uh, Ree... some of us have jobs to get to?"

"Oh, don't be such a stick in the mud. How often is there an endless supply of perfect snow for building things?"

Derrick opened his door and peeked out. "What's going on?"

"Seems Mrs. Grayson here wants to build a snowman." Ken said.

"Did I wake up in the middle of *Frozen?*" he asked kiddingly.

"That's funny," Ree admitted. "But seriously, I'm getting Jenna and Jake up. It's too beautiful to waste this moment."

Derrick receded into his room to get dressed.

"Ree, I need coffee before I can do anything. Care to join me?"

"Oh, all right," she answered reluctantly. "Let me put Cookie back in the room first."

The Vanderbilt Four were already eating breakfast when Ree and Ken entered the dining room.

"Good morning!" Mike said enthusiastically.

"Good morning, beautiful morning isn't it?" Ree replied.

"Sure is," Marty answered.

Charlie continued. "Looks like we'll be leaving as soon as we're done with breakfast. Have to say, I've never had so much fun being snowed in before. Ken, that was a real treat to sing with you."

"You're so welcome, I think everyone did a great job. You've got a great voice, Charlie, you too, Camille."

They continued with pleasantries and then excused themselves to get coffee and order breakfast.

Ken and Ree sat at a table closer to the window. Nancy, looking much happier, took their orders. Once she was out of earshot Ken asked, "So did you think about going to the concert?"

"Yes, I did. Happy to report I got the seal of approval from Ben. And I think he's quite thrilled about being picked up in a limo."

"Well that's great. Oh, the drivers should be here in about an hour, I just got off the phone with them. They said the roads weren't too bad. By the way, I noticed your lights were still on when I went to bed at two. That must have been one long phone call."

"Well, we did talk for about an hour, but then the sound of the snow plow kept me up, so I probably read for another hour or so." She paused and then continued, "Ken, I told Ben everything…"

Ken interrupted, "Everything? Really? What was his reaction? Is he going to send a hitman out?"

"No, no, nothing like that… You have to remember, besides being husband and wife, we're also best friends. We have no secrets. There's no way I couldn't have told him. I definitely don't have a poker face."

"So he doesn't want to shoot me? That's good."

"He did comment that you probably just wanted to get in my pants."

"What? He said that?"

"Oh yeah, and then he asked if you got to second base. That must be a universal man code."

"I can't believe this. I'm not sure if roles were reversed I could be as accepting. You guys must have a rock solid marriage."

"I'm sure you did too, Ken."

They paused their conversation since the four kids entered the room. Ree was happy for the distraction. She really didn't know what to say next.

The kids settled in to the same table they had the day before. Funny, Ree thought to herself, if we had assigned that table to them, they would have objected.

Ree looked up at Ken, "So, when are you going to tell the kids about the concert?"

"How about we enjoy our breakfast, and them too. Then we can tell them."

"Sounds good. Oh, I almost forgot, I should probably retrieve that letter from you."

"I forgot too. It's in my guitar case, I'll get it out when we're packing up." It then nagged at Ken that he really didn't remember seeing the letter when he lifted up his guitar. His recollection was that he had slipped it behind the guitar and therefore, it should have been resting in the base of the case. Hmmm.... well it was late and dark. He guessed he just wasn't paying enough attention.

The Vanderbilt Four came by to say their goodbyes at about the same time Nancy arrived with their breakfasts.

"Hopefully, if our paths cross again, it'll be somewhere warm!" Camille said.

"That's for sure, well, safe travels!" Ree said.

After they finished up with hugs and promises to stay in touch, Ree turned to Ken to resume their conversation.

"You know, Ken, it's only Wednesday. I really think that once your driver gets us back to Altamont, he could just turn around and head back to New York. The kids and I could take a train down to the city on Saturday and then your driver could get us back on Sunday. I hate to have a driver just sit around for three or four days."

"Hmm, I suppose... but only if you're sure you can recover your car without too much of a hassle."

"It'll be fine."

They finished their meals and reviewed some of the details of the Saturday night concert. He told her his secretary would be in touch as to what hotel they would be staying in. Once settled in to their rooms, he'd have a limo drive them to and from the concert.

"I'll feel ridiculously special. I guess it'll be my 15 minutes of fame.... okay, show time..."

Ree approached the kids and started, "Jenna, Jake, I'm afraid I have some bad news... we're going to have to go back to my house, not to Aunt Jeannie's."

Jenna tried to act disappointed, but on the inside she was relieved not to be forced into endless rounds of Scrabble. Jake, on the other hand, was disappointed.

"Man, the skiing would have been great!" Jake protested.

"Well, Jake, there's plenty of snow around, we can still get out on skis over at the fairgrounds." The fairgrounds in Altamont lay dormant in the winter, and the owners allowed people to cross country ski there.

Ken quickly took over, "But I have some good news for you. I've made arrangements for your grandmother and you two to attend my concert Saturday night."

Jenna nearly burst out of her skin, "What? Really? I can't believe it!"

Jake was smiling, as were Drew and Derrick.

"And, boys, I have a surprise for you too. I'm going to work you into my song "*Rodeo Blues.*" Derrick on the drums and Drew on the harmonica."

The boys high fived each other and then hugged their grandfather. They were beaming with excitement and pride. Jenna gave them a hug too, and then Jake had to join in.

"Oh my god, what am I going to wear?" questioned Jenna.

"I'm sure we can find something for you," laughed Ree.

The group then heard a large vehicle pull up to the office. Ken looked out and acknowledged it was the limo he had sent for.

The next hour was a blur. Everyone went back to their rooms to pack up. It was then a group effort to clear the limo from its snow mound. Jake was the first to fling a snowball. It landed on Jenna's back. She flung one in return but missed him and hit Drew instead. He grazed her and then belted Derrick. It wasn't long before all mayhem broke out. Ken got into the mix, but Ree stepped back. She just enjoyed watching them all have such fun. She quietly started making a snow man. By the time they noticed her efforts, she was trying to roll the head up on top of the middle part. Ken came to her rescue and lifted it up and placed it securely.

"Thanks. Now we need a hat, a scarf, some eyes, nose and mouth…"

Jenna ran into the kitchen and Nora helped her find suitable substitutes for the original list. Then picture taking ensued. Four happy kids bookended by Ken and Ree showing off the snowman with the limo in the background. Their snowbound adventure permanently immortalized on their phones.

"Okay, boys, time to give me a hand with Wilson."

Ken and the boys helped Wilson into the MusicMan limo. Then they helped Ree with the dog ramp and coaxed Cookie up and into the other limo. Drew found the whole procedure comical and took a video of Cookie doing what he called the Texas Dog Step. He then announced he would add in some music to his video and send it to Jenna when his new project was completed.

The drivers, Frank and Tony, had been patiently waiting inside the restaurant sipping on coffee. Nora gave them some to-go cups so they could drink more coffee en route. When they saw the obvious signs of the passengers saying goodbye to one another, they thanked Nora and headed out.

Jenna had tears in her eyes as she hugged the boys good-bye. She lingered a bit with Drew. Ree gave Ken a hug and again, he held her perhaps a second or two longer than necessary. She hesitated, too, took a deep breath and then stepped back. Fighting tears herself, she simply said, "See you Saturday, thanks!"

Nate, Nora and Nancy stepped outside to bid them farewell and made them promise they'd come back someday.

Red stood in his room waiting for them to leave so he could go to the office, pay his bill and leave. He didn't dare show his face to Gloria before then. Since there were two limos he assumed Gloria would be heading back north. He also assumed she had abandoned her car in the snow storm. More waiting.

Chapter 17

Jake was a bubble of excitement. "Wow, this is so cool! I love this limo!"

Jenna was quiet but then spoke up. "Do you think we'll have good seats on Saturday?"

"Oh, I'm sure. Usually there are saved seats for special guests and family. This is amazing how this all worked out. Just hope my car isn't too badly beat up."

Her phone rang. It was the ring tone she had assigned to Ken. Jenna looked up in surprise. Her grandmother knew how to change ring tones?

"Hi, Ken, miss us already?" she joked.

"More than you know," he answered quietly. "Say, I just heard from the tow truck company. They've found your car. Apparently, that screen shot of your location was very helpful. I told them the name of your dealership and they'll tow it there. I've also called the dealership and told them to contact my car insurance company to deal with any charges."

"Wow, Ken. Thanks for all that."

"It's the least I can do… And I wanted to tell you I won't be able to see you before the concert, but I definitely want you three to come back stage after the concert is over."

"Oh my god, the kids will be thrilled. Looks like I'm moving into 30 minutes of fame."

"I'm not so special, Ree, just a country boy who likes to sing and play guitar."

There was a lot more she wanted to say but she knew the kids were listening. She signed off with, "Well, thanks again. We're all looking forward to Saturday."

"Good news, kids, my car is being towed as we speak... oh gosh, it just occurred to me, our driveway isn't plowed out. I need to call my neighbor."

Ree called Bill next door. He told her he would call his nephew who had a plow. Normally, Bill and Ben cleared their own driveways with their snowblowers, but this amount of snow was just overwhelming. Bill said he would at least snow blow a path to her door if his nephew couldn't get there right away. She thanked him and set the phone down.

"Hey, Gram, can we go to the mall later on?" Jenna asked as sweetly as possible.

"The mall, today? Oh gosh, Jenna... maybe... if not today, tomorrow for sure." The mall, thought Ree, probably the last thing I want to do today.... The mall, the letter!"

"Oh no!" Ree exclaimed out loud.

"What? questioned Jenna in a startled voice.

"I completely forgot about the letter!"

"What letter?"

"The letter I found at the mall on Sunday. Gosh that seems like a long time ago now. While you kids were with your friends, I snatched up an abandoned newspaper so I could do the puzzles. I found this weird letter in the Arts and

Leisure section. I gave it to Ken to look at to see if he could make sense of it."

"So, what's the big deal? Can't he just take a picture of it and text it to you?"

"Actually, he did take a picture of it. I'll just call him later. No sense bothering him now," Ree resigned. Hmmm, she said to herself. Great excuse to call him when I have some privacy. Then she thought the better of it. Damn that Jiminy Cricket.

"You know what, Jenna? You're right, I can just text him."

She texted: "Hey, Ken, forgot about the letter. Can you just text me the picture you took? I'll retrieve the actual letter when we see you this weekend. Thanks, Ree."

Even though the highway was plowed fairly well, there were still areas of snow covered pavement, forcing Tony to drive well under the actual speed limit. They looked with interest at the numerous cars off the road still awaiting towing. Ree hoped her car was well on its way to the dealership.

A short while later Ree's phone beeped. It was a text from Ken: "Sorry, Ree, totally forgot. It's in my guitar case which is in the trunk. But I can text you the picture of the letter in the meantime. Still haven't heard back from my detective friend. Hope your trip is going well. We're making good headway now. It was slow going for a while. Ken." A few moments later he texted over the picture of the letter.

"Can I see?" asked Jenna.

"Um, sure, I guess so."

Jenna looked at all the numbers and number-letter combinations. Making no sense of it whatsoever, she shook her head and said, "That's weird, Gramma. Is this like a spy thing?"

"Something like that. I'm going to turn it over to the police. You know that slogan? If you see something, say something?"

"Oh yeah, that's plastered all over my school."

The remainder of the trip back to Ree's house was uneventful and took just under an hour. Before long, the limo parked at the end of her driveway. As promised by Bill, there was a pathway to her front door. Tony helped with the dog ramp. With the collective encouragement from the humans, Cookie stepped down and gingerly picked her way through the snowy path to the front door. Tony then carried in the ramp and the dog bed. Ree offered to have Tony come inside, use the facilities and have more coffee, but he declined. He was anxious to get back to the city. Ree asked if he would be their return driver on Sunday, and he said he didn't know.

"Well, okay then. Thanks for the lift. I hope you have an easy trip back."

"Thanks, Ma'am."

Red had waited only a few minutes after the limos departed before checking out himself. It took a good half hour to clear the snow off of his car. He headed north. He would do a drive by of Ree's home to confirm that was her destination and then check into his hotel. After that, he would turn in the white Durango for a darker colored vehicle.

Ken and the boys arrived at his chalet a few hours after their departure from the motel. He planned to have Frank drop the boys off at Hunter Mountain the next day while he worked on his new song, among others. On Friday, they would leave early to get to the city. Ken brought his guitar up to his room, opened the case and lifted out the guitar. No letter! What the hell? Where could it have gone?

He called the motel. "Hey, Nate, it's Ken... yeah, the drive was fine, thanks.... say I think I left something in my motel room... um.... do you think you or Nancy could take a look and see if you find a one page letter? It was in a sheet protector. Thanks. Yes, of course, we'll be sure to stop by again some day... okay, call me back one way or the other... hello to Nora.... thanks again."

Ken suppressed his growing paranoia that the weird guy in Room 9 had entered either Wilson's room or his room and taken the letter. As he was pondering the situation, his phone rang. It was his detective friend Doug.

After they caught up with one another for a few minutes, Doug told him his opinion of the letter. "You got the gist of the message correct. Clearly there is a location and a date. And you were correct the location is in the Abacos in the Bahamas. I think the nine digit number is an AIS number..."

"What's an AIS number?" interrupted Ken.

"It stands for Automatic Identification System, basically it's a tracking system for boats. A boat sends out a signal that can be read on chart plotters by other boaters that have receiving units. You can choose to just have a receiver, or you can transmit and receive. It's really great for traveling through fog or tight passages with limited visibility. So putting this altogether looks like a pick up point for two boats and then a drop off point at a post office. But I have to say, if this is some sort of illegal drug or commodities transaction, it's way too revealing. This is a message a friend might send to another to get together for an afternoon of fishing. If you're an illegal boat or doing something illegal, you're not going to be announcing the location of your boat complete with a registration number. Where did you get this information again?" Ken explained Ree's story. He then continued with the re-location of the letter and now its disappearance, coupled with the presence of the man in Room 9. "The message may just be a simple note to a friend, but why did it disappear?"

"Got me there, Ken. But I have a few fishing friends who frequently run their boats over from Florida to the Abacos. Guess there's good fishing outside the barrier islands. I'll touch base with them and see if one of them will be in the vicinity. Worst that could happen is that it turns out to be lousy fishing at that spot."

"Hey thanks, Doug. Appreciate your time. Send my best to Mary."

"Will do, and break a leg, hear you've got another concert coming up. When are you going to retire, man?"

"Hopefully never."

"Well, to each his own… good talking to you."

Ken was now more stumped than ever. He was half tempted to fly down himself after the concert. It had been a good long time since he used his townhouse. Might be good in any event to check on the place. His mind wandered over to Ree who wanted to do just that. And that thought brought him back to working on his new song.

What Ken, Ree and Doug didn't know was that the numbers and letters didn't add up to what they now assumed. The AIS number and Florida registration numbers marked the identification of an undercover Coast Guard boat posing as an amateur fishing boat Red needed to avoid. It was likely the boat wouldn't be emitting the AIS number, but it would have the registration number on the hull. The pick-up point coordinates and date were off by the numbers embedded in the post office number. Add two numbers forward and one number back was always the key.

Chapter 18

Jenna combed out her long brunette hair after showering. She had refused to wash her hair in the motel shower. She approached her grandmother with a new round of pleas for why they had to go to the mall this afternoon.

Ree listened with only half an ear. She looked at Jenna, who was lanky like her dad but had her mom's eyes. Jenna could be so challenging at times, she thought. Ree was quick to remind herself that Jenna was just a normal teenager coming into her own.

"Gramma, really, not only do I need a new dress, I need new shoes too. I can't be taller than Drew!"

"Aha! The real reason for the shopping spree!" Ree teased. Even though Jenna was only slightly taller than girls her age at 5'4', she towered over most boys in her grade. Ree knew that likely Jenna was already at her adult height and would soon be considered short compared to future six foot tall boyfriends. Drew was taller than Jenna, but only by an inch. Give him a few years...

"Gramma, please!" Jenna begged.

"Okay, okay, maybe we can drop Jake off at Billy's."

"Ditch Jake? Oh, thanks, Gramma, you're the best!"

At least for the next few hours I am, Ree thought to herself. Billy's mom was happy to have Jake over. Two days of indoor captivity because of the weather was becoming unbearable. She needed a break from Billy, and Jake's presence would do just that.

Ree promised Jake they would get out cross country skiing tomorrow. They could go to the fairgrounds as she earlier had suggested, or maybe they could make their way up to the trails in Thatcher Park. She liked that idea better, the view across the valley would be spectacular.

The instant Bill's nephew finished plowing the driveway, an anxious Jenna, Ree and Jake left for the afternoon.

"Hey, kids, I just need to make a quick stop at Remedies. You guys can just stay in the car, I'll only be a few minutes."

"Fine, Gram," Jenna offered no complaint. She was too thrilled with herself for talking her grandmother into not only going to a mall, but also going to the bigger, better Crossgates Mall where the clothes and shoe selection were far superior.

The proprietor, Diana, greeted Ree warmly. Ree thought the name of this wine and spirits shop was very clever since the building had once been a pharmacy. Adding to its charm was that it was coupled with a flower shop, La Bella Fleur.

"You know what, Diana? No matter what, your customers always leave here happy, either with a bottle of something or a bouquet of flowers or both! Smart marketing!"

"Thanks, Ree, Can I get your usual bottles of Vouvray?"

"Yes, you can, and I'll need some red wine too, for Ben when he returns on Sunday. What do you suggest?"

"How about this?" She showed Ree a bottle that was in

the 12 dollar range. Diana knew her customers well, and Ree only bought wines in the 10 to 15 dollar range.

"That's fine, thanks." Ree said when she saw the price.

"Say, did you have much business during the snow storm?"

"Oh you'd be surprised how many people trudged through the snow… I did shut the flower store down since deliveries were slow, but this side was booming."

"That's great, well, see you around."

Ree took no notice of the dark Suburban parked across from the store. Red saw her husband's car parked as he was headed to her house and pulled over to the opposite parking lane. He waited til she pulled out of her parking space before continuing to her address. He wanted to make sure she wasn't just out on a short errand and would herself be headed back to her home. Red cursed her neighbors. He couldn't believe how many people were outside shoveling walkways and snowplowing driveways. He kept moving. He'd have to come back at night.

It took two hours of traipsing through a dozen or so stores before the perfect, or in Ree's mind, least offensive, outfit could be found. What a trick it was these days not to come off as a slut and yet still look appealing, Ree thought to herself. She also thought the outfit quest was a total waste of time since any old jeans and a tee shirt would have been fine. Not many people dressed up for concerts anymore. But Jenna had visions of being photographed with Ken and then Drew after the show and was sure the pictures would go viral. She had to look her best.

On the way home Ree told Jenna she wanted to check in on Meme and Ken's mother. Jenna didn't object.

"That's fine, Gram. Hey, would it be okay if I invited Meredith over for the night?"

"Sure, chances are Jake will wind up at Billy's tonight anyway."

Melvina was surprised to see Ree and Jenna. "Where's Mr. Jake?" she asked after greeting them.

"Oh, he's at his friend Billy's. They've become great pals."

"So, I understand you guys had quite a snow bound adventure. Mr. Davis told me he wound up at the same motel. That's quite the turn of events!"

"Yeah, he's such a nice man, no pretenses. Really, you'd never know he was so famous. He even let us put together an impromptu band and sing with him. It was hilarious."

"But the best news, Melvina," Jenna chimed in, "is that we get to go to his concert on Saturday!"

"Get out! Wow! You must be so excited. Send me pictures!"

"Will do!"

Meme barely awakened during their visit. Both Ree and Jenna fought back tears. Melvina had told them she was barely eating or drinking. Meme had advance directives clearly stating no artificial nutrition or hydration. It was only a matter of time before her body parts would be shutting down. Oh, I hope she goes quietly into the night, Ree wished to herself.

Ken's mother, on the other hand, was awake and actually quite chatty. Ree mentioned she knew Kendall, but Mrs. Davis had no idea who Ken was. She thought Ree and Jenna were her daughters. Jenna was taken aback at how much gibberish Mrs. Davis produced. Ree just let her rattle on and simply affirmed what little she could understand.

Back in the car, Jenna asked, "What was all that, Gram?"

"Hmmm, how to explain an entire semester of dementia in just a few words? Well, basically the memory and language components of the inner brain break down and eventually the outer parts start to wear down too. You may think it's cruel that we're not putting a feeding tube into Meme, but actually it's the opposite. Meme is no longer detecting hunger, and if we were to force feed her, her body wouldn't know what to do with the food anyway. Mrs. Davis is obviously not at that stage yet, but eventually she will be. Right now she's processing things in a very bizarre manner and nothing adds up or makes much sense. But there's no point in correcting her, that would only serve to anger her. In her mind she has things right. I hate dementia, such a horrible process. If you want to do something for the world, Jenna, you should go into some form of neurological research to figure out how to resolve the dilemma of dementia."

"I don't know about that, Gram. Sounds too sad to me..."

Ree let it go. What was she thinking putting such a heavy spin on Jenna's question?

Ree's phone rang, and Jenna dutifully put it on speaker phone. It was the dealership announcing Ree's car would be ready to be picked up on Friday. There were only a few scratches in the front fender for which they could use touch up paint. Otherwise they only had to repack the airbags and return them to their compartments.

"Well, that's good news," Ree said to Jenna. "Do you want to call Meredith? I need to get a few things at the grocery store, but then we could pick her up."

In the end, it worked out that Jenna spent the evening with Meredith since Meredith already had planned to go to the mall to watch a movie with a few other friends. Once again, Meredith's mother and aunt had resigned themselves to an evening at the mall. It was no problem for them to pick up and return Jenna. Billy wound up at Ree's. Billy's mother, Kim, was hoping to go out that evening to catch up with one of her girlfriends. Kim offered to have Jake spend Thursday night with them in return. The two women made arrangements for Kim to drive Ree to the dealership on Friday when she came to retrieve Billy.

Ree bribed Jake and Billy with freshly baked chocolate chip cookies if they would shovel out an area for Cookie behind the back door. It was another circus event to get Cookie to go out, but she did. By midnight Jake and Billy were sound asleep in a makeshift fort they had created in the den. Jenna had been returned and went to bed around 11:30. Ree had her usual night cap of white wine while talking to Ben on the phone. She then read a few chapters of her book before drifting off to sleep.

Red pulled the dark Suburban into her driveway on Ben's side. He didn't use the garage door opener since the rattling sound would likely wake up Ree. He easily unlocked the front door and let himself in. Cookie was in her dog bed. He decided to give her a few pats on the head so she wouldn't whimper. He was surprised that she snarled at him. He pulled back and headed to the kitchen where there was a door leading to the garage. He needed to know if her car had been retrieved. No! More waiting. He slipped out and drove away.

Chapter 19

Red pondered where the car could be. He decided to start with the obvious and check the local Dodge dealership to see if it had been towed there. On Thursday afternoon he posed as a potential car buyer, specifically in the market for Durangos. He entered into light conversation with the delighted salesman about how the car would hold up in the snow. Without the salesman being aware of Red's true agenda, he revealed that he actually had a Durango in the shop right now that had been handling the snow covered roads quite well until the driver was forced off the highway into a snowbank in the recent snow storm. It had sustained only minimal damage. He was happy to report that the airbags deployed as they should have and there were no injuries. Red tried to weasel himself into the garage to take a look at this "amazingly safe" vehicle, but the salesman said as apologetically as possible, that customers were not allowed into the garage, especially since it wasn't his car.

"No problem. Let me have your card and I'll get back to you."

The salesman gladly complied, but he knew, having been in the business for several years now, that he'd never see this customer again.

Breaking into a car dealership's garage was too challenging. There were night watchmen, several locked gates and an elaborate security system. Cameras were aimed in all different directions. Red learned the car would be ready for pick up on Friday anyway. Better to wait it out.

Ken spent Thursday working on his new song. He was determined to sing it as a solo encore. His agent didn't usually go for these last minute changes but Ken would insist, that is, if he could work out a few more lyrics. He was only interrupted for a few minutes by a volley of texts with Ree. She informed him she had visited his mother and she was fine. Ree left out the part that his mother had no idea who Kendall was. He texted back how grateful he was for her visit. She then informed him she and the kids would be getting into NYC at four. She had heard from his secretary and knew where the hotel was. She'd take a cab since it was a short distance. No need for a limo. He then replied that a limo would pick them up at 6:15 to take them to MSG. The driver would have their passes for the VIP seating area. VIP? Ree texted back some emojis. Ken didn't exactly know how to respond to that, so he simply signed off with, "See you after the show." He loved how even through something as banal as text messages, she could convey such teenaged enthusiasm. Oh, Ree, he thought to himself. In another space and time, universe or galaxy, if there wasn't a Ben, if there wasn't a Rachel, maybe, just maybe, there would have been Ken and Ree…

As promised, Ree took Jenna and Jake cross country skiing up at Thatcher Park. Fortunately, the trails had been groomed by previous skiers and they were able to glide along fairly well. They stopped several times to look at the valley below them. Even Jenna was impressed with the vista from atop the escarpment.

Ree dropped Jake off at Billy's on the way back to her house. It was a quiet night for Ree and Jenna. They watched a movie together and then had a late night snack in the kitchen.

"Gram," said Jenna, "After we go to the concert and meet with Ken and Drew and Derrick... do you think I'll ever see Drew again?"

"Oh, Jenna, I so want to say you will, but in reality, I don't think so... I'm sorry... he lives in Houston, and that's just so far away."

"I really like him."

"I know, I saw that."

"You did?"

"You're like me, you can't hide your feelings."

"Gram?"

"I guess I just miss your grandfather."

"But you see him everyday... well except this week."

"Love never dies, it just keeps getting stronger. Even old folks like me still need love."

"Gram, I love you."

"Thanks, sweetheart. I love you too... it's late, we should get to bed."

Cookie only gave Ree a slight fuss about being put out one last time. Ree grabbed a glass of wine and headed up to her bedroom. She called Ben and gave him the latest update. Soon she found herself giggling. Ben, her love, her life.

CHAPTER 20

FRIDAY WAS ARRANGEMENT DAY. That's how Ree categorized her day. Ree loved to-do lists and loved placing things into categories. It neatened up an otherwise chaotic world.

First off was getting someone to take care of Cookie Saturday afternoon and evening and then Sunday all day. Next up, train tickets. Oh crap! she said to herself. We can't traipse all the kids' ski equipment on a train… OK, Ben and I will drive to Pittsfield next weekend with all their gear. It'll be a great excuse to spend the weekend with the Montgomery Four. Ree had dubbed her collective family as the "MAGnificent 9": Four Montgomerys: Kate, Cullen, Jenna, Jake, the Adamskis Three: Kirsten, Alan and Moira, and the Graysons Two: Ree and Ben. Next up, getting someone to drive them to the train station. She pondered all this while Jenna slept in.

Red noticed a new car pull into Ree's driveway. Two young boys exited the car and then Ree entered the car. They drove off in the direction of the Dodge dealership. So she has friends, Red said to himself as he followed them at a distance. The girlfriend had left just after dropping off Ree. The wait at the dealership wasn't too long. Soon he saw the white Durango heading back to Ree's residence. Good. He'd return after midnight.

He actually waited until one in the morning. When he pulled into the driveway, he was quite dismayed to see another car parked in the driveway. What the hell? Ree had an overnight guest? What he didn't know was that Jeannie was bored and in need of company. She drove herself and her dog, Sadie, to Ree's in the afternoon and they began a marathon of Scrabble. Jenna joined them for one game and then mercifully, Ree said she could invite Meredith over for the night. Jake also talked Ree into letting Billy spend the night. A full house.

Red had left the front door unlocked from his last visit. He banked on Ree not noticing the door was unlocked, and he was right. He slipped in and went immediately to the garage. A careful inspection did not find the letter. He was not surprised. No doubt she had moved it back into the house. He started with desk drawers, the den and then the kitchen. Nothing. Then he moved up to the upstairs bedrooms. Had to be in her room....

He heard a slight whimper and then a bark. No! Not another dog!

Sadie continued to bark which woke up Jeannie who was sleeping in the bedroom next to Ree and Ben's room. Normally, Jake slept there but he was downstairs in the den in yet another fort he and Billy constructed.

Red was already in Ree's room and couldn't just slip out without the visiting woman and her dog noticing. Between Sadie's barking and Cookie's whimpering, Ree awakened as well.

"Cookie? Cookie?" Ree called out.

Red had had it. He took out his gun and placed it directly on Ree's head. She gasped.

DIANE E. GRABO: *WAITING ON A PART*

"Don't say a word. Just give me the goddamned letter. You know what I'm talking about."

Ree's mouth and throat went completely dry. She couldn't utter a word or swallow.

"Tell me where the letter is, now!" Red insisted.

Ree managed to say in a whisper, "I don't have it… I gave it to a friend."

"Not good enough. I need that information right now!"

"I… uh… have a picture of it on my phone. I can show you that."

"What? On your phone?"

"Yes… if you let me reach for my phone, I'll show it to you… so it was you at the Red Fox Motel… I thought so."

"Stop talking and just get the picture up on your phone." Red demanded.

Jeannie called out, "Ree? Ree? Are you OK? I thought I heard a man talking."

Red gave Ree a silent signal to convey she'd better say everything was OK.

"Oh, it's nothing, Jeannie, couldn't sleep so I was watching an old movie. Sorry I woke you up. I'll turn off the TV."

Excellent, Red said in his mind, if I didn't want to kill her, I'd actually like this woman.

Jeannie returned to her bed, but Sadie was restless.

"Hey, Sadie," Jeannie said gently. "Settle down, girl." Since she was awake she got up to go to the bathroom, an all too frequent event in Jeannie's nightly routine.

Red looked at the information on Ree's phone. He took a picture of the picture with his phone. So against the rules of his Boss. He didn't care.

"Now delete that!"

"No problem. Now get out of here."

"Sorry, Ma'am. You've seen my face now."

"What? What do you mean?"

"You know what I mean."

His gun had a silencer on it. He had already decided to shoot her in the head, slip out the front door before the house guests could respond and then he would quickly drive away. Bad enough he had to kill her, he didn't want to have to kill the others as well.

What Red didn't see was that when Ree picked up her phone to show him the picture, she had first hit the 911 button on her phone. She figured she was a dead person in any event, but at least she could try to save her family from being murdered. Unlike her mother, she would not go silently into the night. She yelled out "Jeannie! Kids! Help!"

Jeannie grabbed the toilet plunger and ran into Ree's room. She saw a man hovering over Ree in her bed, but didn't see he had a gun. She ran forward and jabbed him with the plunger which knocked him away from the bed. The gun discharged which woke up the kids. Red recovered quickly, struck out at the women and tried to re-aim his gun. Jake and Billy ran up the stairs armed with toy light sabers. They tackled Red as well not knowing the gravity of the situation with Red holding a gun out of their sight. Jenna and Meredith joined the commotion but then froze in fear when they saw the intruder and his gun. Jeannie yelled out, "Jenna, call 911!" Jenna came back to life and slipped out of the room to get her phone. Jake and Billy did their best to employ Tai Kwon Do chops to Red's back. Sadie kept barking at Red who had now twisted around and again held the gun to Ree's head.

"Shut up all of you! Now get off me or she's dead."

The group quickly obliged. Red scanned the room. There should be one more teenager. Where was she?

He pulled Ree upright and the two of them edged to the bedroom door.

"Nobody moves!" Red demanded as the two exited the bedroom.

Sirens! They all heard sirens. Red suppressed his panic. He had enough bullets in the chamber to kill all six but where was the sixth? Would he have enough time to find her before the police entered the house? Best to switch to a hostage situation.

Jenna opened the front door as soon as she heard the sirens. She was on the phone talking to the 911 operator and couldn't believe the response time. The operator gave her concrete directions.

"We've already received a call for this location. The police are on the way. Get out of the house!"

Although she was only wearing flannel pajamas and socks, Jenna readily complied.

"Stay on the phone, whisper what's happening if you can."

Jenna repressed her sobbing. "I see the patrol car!"

"Good, now, stay put. Put one hand up over your head and don't move. Let the officer come to you."

Meanwhile Red guided Ree down the stairs. He saw the open front door. His plan now was to keep holding the gun to Gloria's head and face the officers when they arrived. He'd demand they let him pass through to his car with her in tow or else he'd kill her.

Red was so intent on focusing on the front door he didn't see Jake's video game player on the next step. His right foot slipped out from under him as he glided over the half hidden player. He momentarily lost his grip on Gloria, but it was all she needed to wiggle a foot away.

Jenna beckoned the officers with silent hand signals, pointing inside the door with her hand shaped into a triggered gun.

The first officer rushed in with his gun ready, yelling, "Stop! Police!"

Red twisted around as he attempted to re-grab Gloria. In the process he aimed the gun at the officer. The officer didn't hesitate. He shot Red in his leg so as not to shoot Ree in the process.

By three in the morning, pictures of the crime scene had been taken, the blood stains had been cleaned up, statements were completed and the last officer left the house. Earlier, Red had been hand-cuffed to an ambulance gurney and was transported to the hospital with a police escort. It had taken quite awhile to settle down the traumatized sextet. Finally, the kids returned to their beds. Jeannie and Ree sat down at the breakfast nook and poured themselves a glass of wine.

"So, cuz. What was that all about?" Jeannie asked.

CHAPTER 21

REE WOKE UP AT NINE. She reached over to Ben's side of the bed. "Oh, right… you're not there… wait, did what happened last night… I mean this morning… really happen?" she asked out loud, as if Ben could somehow hear her two thousand miles away.

Ree shuddered to think how close she and Jeannie and the kids had come to being shot to death. But like Scarlett O'Hara, she decided to think about that later.

Jeannie was already up and had coffee ready.

"You're a godsend." said Ree.

"Hey, it's the least I could do. So what's next?"

"Coffee first."

Ree decided that the show, literally, must go on. Their train was set to leave at one in the afternoon. Jeannie would drive them to the station in Ben's Suburban and then return to the house whereupon she, Sadie and Cookie would return to her home in her own car. She had no interest in staying in Ree's house alone. Ree would recover Cookie some time on Monday. After being fortified with two cups of coffee, she left a cryptic message for Ben. She didn't want to worry him more than necessary. She assured him she and the kids were all right and that she was going to go to the concert as planned. Next she called Ken. She knew she would get his voice mail too, and left him a message stating she'd give full details later but in the meantime, she needed the letter to turn into the police as evidence. Ree and Jenna fussed with their outfits after long showers and, finally, the foursome left the house to head to the train station.

Ree and the kids delighted in the scenery along the Hudson, still a winter wonderland. Getting a cab to the hotel wasn't too difficult, and soon they were in their suite. Ken's staff had arranged for them to have two bedrooms joined by a common living area. It was magnificent. At precisely 6:15, they descended to the lobby to await their limo. Jenna was a ball of excitement at being escorted to the VIP section. Ree tried to conceal her identical excitement but at Jenna's urging, "Gramma, just enjoy it," Ree let herself smile as she'd never smiled before. Jake was beside himself.

The concert was amazing, and Ree saw tears from Jenna's eyes when Drew and Derrick were introduced. The boys did well and as far as Ree could tell, the mixers didn't have to fade them away.

The crowd cheered and clapped insistently at the conclusion of the concert to bring Ken back for an encore. It wasn't long before he reappeared. He played a well known crowd pleaser which got everyone on their feet. Then after much clapping the band members were introduced once again, one by one as they exited until only Ken remained. He waited for the crowd noise to settle down as he pulled a stool closer to the mic and picked up his retuned guitar from a nearby rack. He adjusted the microphone and spoke out to the fans.

"So, how 'bout that Helena? One heck of a storm, huh?"
The crowd went wild with comments and then settled
down.

"So, I had a little time to write this song while I was
snowed in. Got holed up in a worn down motel, and I saw
a special lady there. She inspired this song... it's called 'Pots
And Pans, Kettles and Cans.' Bear with me, it's still a work
in progress."

Ree couldn't believe it. Could it really be her in that ridiculous apron she was wearing that he was referring to? If that
was the case, Nora should have the apron framed. And thank
god Jenna and Jake didn't see her wearing the apron. It was
all Ree could do to suppress a mountain of emotions. And
then Ken sang:

Wasn't looking for love when he went into the motel diner,
Just needed something to eat and a place to rest his head.
And there in the kitchen was a woman,
Reaching for pots and pans, kettles and cans.

Her blaze red hair was a mess atop her head,
Her apron hung loose and was worn and torn,
She moved to a silent Texas Two Step rhythm
Among pots and pans, kettles and cans.

She handed him his dinner and grazed his hand,
He felt the electricity course through to his heart,
He stood up and just pulled her into his arms,
Witnessed only by pots and pans, kettles and cans.

He held her so tightly and went to kiss her,
She looked at him with the most adoring eyes,
But then she pushed away, saying she needed to get back
To the pots and pans, kettles and cans.

And that's when he saw her big strong man,
Who put his arms around her and gave her a kiss,
He whispered something in her ear and they hustled to cook
Amid pots and pans, kettles and cans.

Wasn't looking for love on that snowy day,
But for one brief moment he found and lost
The woman he didn't know he was looking for
Among pots and pans, kettles and cans.

The audience again rose to their feet in applause. A very confused Jenna tried to connect the dots. Ken couldn't possibly have thought Nora was a special lady. Certainly she was nice enough, but Jenna thought of her as rather dull, plain and plump. And she certainly didn't have red hair.... oh, no, ... couldn't be...

"Gramma?" Jenna said out loud in a most accusatory tone.

Ree shrugged her shoulders and shook her head as if to say, "I don't know, I don't know what he's talking about..."

But she did know. And she resumed her clapping.

EPILOGUE

Ken's new song was an immediate hit and won him yet another Grammy. Nora did have the apron framed. It wasn't long before word got out that Ken had stayed at the Red Fox Motel and Diner, and had the staff and customers singing in an impromptu band. Nate and Nora's business boomed as a result, and they were finally able to renovate and expand the restaurant and motel rooms. The pictures of Ken, Nora and Nancy and the other guests hung proudly in the entry way. In the renovation process the letter that had slipped behind the desk in Room 7 was finally found and returned to the police.

Ken and Ree texted one another on a nearly weekly basis so Ree could report to him about his mother. Ree's mother died in April while Ken was on tour. He sent flowers and condolences but didn't attend the services. Then, only two weeks later, his mother died suddenly from a stroke. Honoring her wishes, no services were held. Once his mother had departed, the need for texting came to an end.

Just as well, Ree thought to herself for the millionth time months later, as she gazed at the picture of her, Ken, Jake and Jenna on her cell phone. So many times she was set to delete the whole series of pictures. What's the use? The pictures had already gone viral and the ensuing media circus had become quite overwhelming. Her picture actually appeared in a tabloid with the caption of "Ken's Special Lady?" Fortunately, Ken's staff was able to squelch any further pictures and articles from being printed. And then at about the same time, two other celebrities had a well publicized affair. Ken's special lady faded away from the attention of the ever fickle fans. Ree exited out of her pictures and looked at the weather app on her phone. Another snowy day ahead. She donned her winter garb and walked to the post office as she normally did around 10:30 in the morning. It was generally an exercise in futility since most days the box was either empty or filled with junk mail. But this day there was a large envelope post marked from Nashville.

Inside was an itinerary, a few pages of instructions and a post-it note from Ken.

"Hey Ree, I need someone to check on my place.
Thanks, Ken"

The following February school break, the MAGnificent-9 were taxied to the Harbour Side Marina, in Marsh Harbour. There, Ken had made arrangements for them to be ferried to his town house in the golfing resort.

As the group assembled around their suitcases Ree noticed two couples sitting at a round table adjacent to the marina pool. The foursome were playing cards. Could it be? Ree asked herself. In subsequent, sporadic contact with the two Vanderbilt Four couples, she learned both of them had sailboats. They had planned to sail their boats to the Bahamas. They had probably mentioned where exactly they would be going, but she hadn't retained that information. Now it all came together.

"Ree! I don't believe it!" exclaimed Marty.

It was a wonderful reunion for the Vanderbilt Four, Ree, Jenna and Jake. Ree quickly introduced Ben and the rest of the family members.

"I'd hoped we'd meet up again in a warmer climate!" exclaimed Camille.

The vacation was better than Ree could have imagined. The only flaws were in Jenna not so covertly pining away for a surprise visit from Drew, and in Ree hoping but not hoping Ken would appear. As it turned out, Ree never saw Ken again. Shortly after the vacation Ken sold the townhouse. He reduced his touring schedule so as to spend more time in Houston. There he pursued Rachel and eventually wooed her to his cabin in Michigan. On a beautifully warm autumn evening with the sun setting over Lake Michigan and the harvest moon rising, he and Rachel were married in a small, private ceremony.

Ben and Ree were smitten once again with the turquoise waters of the Sea of Abaco. After Ben retired they bought a 42-foot catamaran so as to spend the rest of their winters sailing around 26 N 77 W.

Made in the USA
Coppell, TX
07 October 2021